JEAN DAVIDSON

C000253367

MY NAME IS REBECCA

Sam Burnside

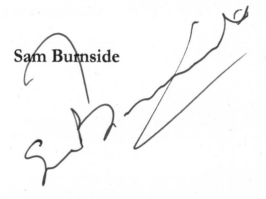

HOBART BOOKS

HOBART BOOKS

MY NAME IS REBECCA

ISBN 978-1-914322-06-8

First Published in 2022
by
Hobart Books, Oxfordshire, England
hobartbooks.com

Printed and bound in Great Britain by Clays Ltd, Elcograf S.p.A.

MY NAME IS REBECCA

A Novel

By Sam Burnside

Novel, a small tale – generally of love
Samuel Johnson, *Dictionary (1755)*

For **Stella**

Prologue

(September 1983)

I cannot forget. That memory is always present: it is like a red-hot coal, resting among the blackened cinders of the past. It is a day in September. The year is 1983. I am walking along a Belfast street with my sister, Ruth. It was she who had wanted to come to the city centre, to visit a shop she had heard about; she wanted to look for a new dress and I was the one who was in a hurry, as usual. She fell behind – wilfully, I considered for I was in a temper – so I refused to delay for her, dashing on ahead. Nevertheless, at some point I faltered in my intention; I stopped and turned around. I still do not know why I did this, just at that moment. Instinct... foresight, perhaps... something outside time, certainly.

It is always with me, that image, frozen, unchanging and unchangeable: as I turned, the view before me was as one in a painted scene, partially glimpsed hanging in a stairway or in an old photograph exposed, and carelessly glanced over in passing, in a half-open drawer – a moment caught then lost, leaving behind only a fleeting remembrance. As I turned, I became aware of a handful of people immediately behind me, positioned between my sister and me. Then there was a movement, like the wind's sudden brush across a field of corn, followed by a sudden hiatus in the crowd, leaving a gap

11

with Ruth alone at its empty heart. She has stopped to peer, in that short-sighted way she has – had – at something, some displayed goods on sale in a shop window, and I remember catching a glimpse of something white and thinking it was probably a wedding dress... but, of course, I was in such a panic...

She looked so vulnerable, alone in that empty space, and I could only think to say impatiently, 'Can't you hurry, please!' Then I become aware of people in the far background, behind her, they were mingling about, some had stopped, frozen, a few were caught in the process of turning away. Ruth alone remained peering in at the shop window, oblivious to all that was around her.

No, that's not it. That's not right. Time, that is what I mean. Time seemed to become somehow slower, to somehow... shiver. People moved, slowly, without hurry, or were still; but quietly, something moved them, caused them to shift their ground, in odd, old-fashioned, sluggish ways.

As I turned and took in the scene, time, or something like time, did indeed appear to stop. I became aware of an all-pervading, profound and powerful silence – it was like a great weight, pressing down. Then, the day emitted a sigh. A sigh: a comma breaking apart a sentence, a slow-falling pause. Then a great sound imploded upon the scene and an unknown force shifted me physically, lifted me off my feet and hurled me backwards. Noise wrapped around me. I saw Ruth rise up in the air. She was taken from me. She hung there; it seemed for ever and ever and ever, like a puppet presented against a backdrop of make-believe smoke and red pantomime fire. Then her body descended... or rather, that's too firm, too purposeful... no, it floated... towards the earth, from which it came.

And in its descent, her clothes were taken, plucked from her body. I think 'plucked' because I remembered, when thinking about it later in the night, when I fought against and then for sleep, of how, when I was a child, I saw once or twice a chicken's feathers being plucked and cast aside: a hand rising and falling, casting billows of white and brown feathers. And this was the same, this careless separation of body and the body's covering.

The fabric remained, or at least the threads remained, hanging there, in mid-air, stationary for a time, before floating earthwards, light as eiderdown, easy as dandelion fluff, soft and silent as feathers... As they fell they scattered, pieces of unnatural plumage, light and yielding as snowflakes, they descended, descended so condescendingly, so waywardly towards the earth.

And through it all, the bright shards of shattered, burst glass flew upon the day, upon my sight, spreading, hard and shining in the sunlight. As they fell, they glittered and sparkled, like diamonds. Through the curtain of dust they cast their sparkle.

And then it was over: this economy of destruction and all was changed and the world inside my head was overflowing with far-off voices and sirens and blue lights and white tiles and more and many and brighter, blinding lights...

And that is how my sister Ruth's life here, on earth, ended.

It is of her translucent spirit rising up through a melee of feathers and flowers and diamonds, a bright centre, rising up, unstoppably, irretrievably, through a storm of dust and fire, rising up in that terrible silence. It is how her body met its end, even now, for if truth be told, when I dream, as I do often, I dream the same dream: it is of her body being pushed and pulled and then falling to earth.

Book One

Autumn, 2005

(Thursday, Friday, Saturday, Sunday, Monday)

Shall the thing formed say to him who formed it, Why hast thou made me thus?

Hath not the potter power over the clay, of the one lump to make one vessel unto honour, and another onto dishonour?

Romans 10.20-21

Thursday

Overhead, the familiar grey sky hangs, inert, cradled behind jumbled strands of telephone and electric wires. Underfoot, their filigreed outlines lie, their softly meshed, delicately figured pattern redeeming the hard pavement's concrete surface.

All about her the city lies. Sometimes she appreciates the blending of old and new things; although, in some way, she was fond of the old uniformity, she rather enjoys the anonymity to be found moving among the new shopping centres and office blocks and apartment blocks, yet she dislikes the necessary outcome of that same anonymity, this bland undercutting of her own, inbuilt, sense of belonging, her sense of who she, Rebecca, was or had been or might be. Her sense of being rooted in a place known and once loved.

Increasingly, she finds this modern town a hard place; looking out at it again, she perceives it is all surface, all façade, shiny but firm and hard and impervious to the assault of her enquiring gaze, a gaze nurtured in a softer, more intimate time.

Today, she moves like a ghost of a memory through this cold terrain.

She keeps her eyes directed to the ground: it is as if she travels through a tunnel.

I am a ghost, she thinks, I am a memory; I exist in an empty tunnel.

And then – and as always it happens suddenly and without warning – out of the corner of her eye, sliding past in the periphery of her vision, the hard, polished veneer having melted away, having peeled or curled away, she involuntarily catches a glimpse of a figure sliding silently and unheedingly past. And then, as quickly as it came, the moment is gone, the fissure closes, the figure is no more.

As she makes her way through the crowds, the world inside her head is without noise and, oddly, in her consciousness, she is aware of this. She is aware also of the expansiveness of the sea that carries her and of the meagreness of her own body as it is carried out, soon to be overwhelmed by the heavy ocean.

She is fatalistic; she is without fear; the figure disappears. She observes the scene, and her own reaction to it, in a wholly disinterested way, but she is aware that her sense of peace is blooming. For the moment she longs to be swept up, to be cradled finally in the waves' arms.

It is mid-afternoon and the sky above the city is blue; it provides a perfect backdrop to an army of scurrying regiments and battalions and companies of fluffy white clouds. It is one of those blustery days that are to be found in the agitated, jittery, uncertain periods that occur intermittently between late summer and early autumn. The wind is rising, coming in directly off the Lough, causing the sudden, erratic skittering of pieces of old newspaper and scraps of detritus. These dart on the wind and dance through the air.

There is a sub-text to the day whose meaning is there to be read easily and instinctively by men of a certain age. Such men can be heard speaking of the promise of rain to come, raising their noses and sniffing. Boys, or even young men, might simply smell a hint of heat in the air but these older men contain within themselves an ancient, instinctive sense of impending disaster. They sense fretfulness in the tiny, fleeting oscillations of sunshine and cloud-shadow. The air is full of many turmoils of wind from the east that gives some few a feeling of elevation, but whose sharpness leaves the majority with uneasy feelings of approaching dislocation.

Rebecca pays no heed to the day or to the people who surround her. In turn, she is another anonymous figure to those who pass her by as she progresses swiftly through the thronged streets towards her home. That means skirting the city centre, then crossing the Lagan before navigating a maze of little streets. Soon, she finds herself traversing Donegall Place without knowing how she got here. Instinctively, she turns eastwards into Castle Lane, the wind in her face, a dark cloudbank now assembling overhead. She pushes forward, against the press of people. As she approaches the Post Office, and just as she puts one foot forward to step off the pavement, she feels a hand, heavy and commanding, on her shoulder. She is halted in mid-step, pulled back onto her heels, just as a large, yellow Roads Services tanker turns into Bridge Street, passing within inches of her body. The driver swerves abruptly, while sounding his horn, but she ignores him; she is hardly aware of the vehicle's existence, let alone of its driver's mood. She looks over her shoulder, murmuring an instinctive 'thank you' before continuing on her way; she is fuelled by an impulsive need to find the river bridge.

18

She proceeds; she is lost to the world, totally. She is only vaguely conscious of her surroundings. Her universe has been scooped out of her introspection; the inner voice that contemplates her life brings all into focus:

Then she is on the High Street and suddenly she is passing the Albert Clock. A forest of white feathered quills dance across her path. As she advances, she realises they are jets of water; the thin streams struggle valiantly against the combined forces of gravity and wind and the intentions of four or five small boys who are beating the gleaming jets. They are attempting to slap hand-sized plashes of water over one another. As she passes, an icy-cold splash strikes her legs and abruptly reawakens her to the outside world.

She looks about. The street is busy: an old lady is being pushed along in a wheelchair; despite the sharpness of the day, three men are sitting at separate tables outside McHugh's public house staring into glasses of Guinness; a thin, poor-looking woman wearing a shawl and carrying a baby, makes her way towards Rebecca. Her head bends forward, and her eyes are directed downwards. She stops and holds out a magazine. Without thought Rebecca's hand goes to her pocket and she hands over all her spare change.

She is aware of this only indistinctly, seeing the scene as a whole, unaware of the detail; she does not hear the boys' yells or the sound of water falling onto the concrete slabs; she is unaware of the water's slow, silvery, snaking passage through the air, she is unaware of how its changing form is highlighted against the grey slabs of grimy concrete. She barely sees the drinking men; nor has she really been conscious of the traffic on the roads she has traversed in this, her own turbulent odyssey through the city. She is hardly conscious of the presence of the woman with the child, only their plight registers and calls for a response. She is half-conscious of the woman in the wheelchair, but mechanically, noting how young she is and wondering, in her trained professional way, what her story might be.

She does not stop. Yet, she walks more slowly now, for she finds she is breathless; she leaves the Custom House Square behind: she crosses Donegall Quay, passing the huge blue and white fish that stands here, elevated, between the roadway and the river. It looks out without interest to where the water runs past. When she has come this way in the past it has always struck her that there is something high-minded, noble, yet stoic about this fish, left high and dry yet within jumping distance of the water, glued to its concrete foundation. It is so big, so rounded, so… actual. The fish has always intrigued her: its being reminds her of Robert and always leaves her wondering if it might be a piece of ceramic. She has never asked. Today, she hardly notices its presence. Exhausted by the intensity of her emotions, she sits down on the first of the riverside seats she comes across.

A movement catches her attention: it is a seagull circling, floating languorously, and high above and between the earth and heaven.

That was then. Now, day follows day. And now, on this day, she passes by once more, as in a dream. A huge ceramic salmon appears, it seems to swim – incongruously - as if floating heavily above the concrete - there suddenly between her and the Lagan. It is, she knows, suddenly, briefly – bitterly, taking in and then rejecting inside her head the very idea - it is supposed to represent in its many scales the regeneration of the place. Regeneration!

The ground beneath her feet ebbs and flows. She looks up. There, high above white seabirds float, circling on unseen currents of air, lazily. And then she releases her passion. Quite suddenly she accepts how things are.

Yet, she walks more slowly now, ducking and weaving through unfamiliar lanes, streets. She finds she is breathless; days in time seem to collide, they appear to mingle. The world swims. She is disorientated.

A passing dog jumps up towards her, rising up against the strain of its lead. Its owner apologises and she returns, nodding in acknowledgement, smiling. She is back. She leaves the Custom House Square behind: she crosses Donegall Quay, passing closer to the huge blue and white fish that stands here, elevated, between the roadway and the river. It looks out without interest to where the water moves slowly. It sees neither the water nor the white bird in the sky.

And yet, the thought strikes her, when she has come this way in the past it has always seemed to her that there is something high-minded, something noble, yes something somehow nobly stoic about this fish, left high and dry yet within jumping distance of the water, glued to its concrete foundation. It is so big, so rounded, so...actual. The fish has always intrigued her for its being somehow reminds her of Robert and of his work and always leaves her wondering if it is really only a mere piece of ceramic, a thing with a heart of clay. A body without a heart. She has never mentioned this to Robert. The sky and the seabird and the fish and the passing traffic swirl about her head. Exhausted by the intensity of her rising emotions, she sits down on the first of the riverside seats she comes across.

Just as she sinks onto the seat, and quite without warning, it begins to rain heavily. She is without coat or hat or umbrella and within seconds is soaked. She jumps to her feet, rainwater running down her back and legs and seeping into her shoes. She looks up. The air is thick with a floating greyness, the sky is half-hidden by the rain, and she can see a black cloud approaching fast from the direction of the open Lough. She looks around for shelter, then runs, head covered by her hands, towards the narrow pedestrian bridge that rises up and over the river. She takes what shelter she can underneath its narrow walkway.

She stands under the bridge, watching the rain slant down, watching it drip off the metal struts and fall to the pavement, then, within minutes, and just as suddenly as it had started, the rain stops and the wind – it has arrived without her noticing it and its being there has somehow shocks her – dies down.

The air is fresh and as her attention is drawn to that she sees too that the light has attained a tremendous clarity. Luminosity pervades the scene before her; she grows conscious of the rhythm of her own breathing, of the coldness of the wet on her legs, of her own acute awareness of every sharpened detail in the cityscape. The pavement slabs are grey, black pitted, their edges broken.

There is something else that tries to impinge its presence on her, but she cannot be sure what it is. Is it something to do with her surroundings? Then a droplet of water falls off the bridge and plops into a puddle at her feet. The noise of its fall breaks the silence. That is it: silence is the quality of which she has been aware, a quality to the day she could not name.

Now she moves a little. The traffic passes unnoticed on the road behind. Men on a boat sail past. She hardly marks what has happened, not even the impression that anything has happened. Her mind refuses to recognise the incident that sent her running through the city streets, to this place, here beside water.

The river is so still, now. Empty and still.

For a brief moment the city remains without sound. It is a little pool of perfect peace and she floats at its centre. And then, another droplet falls, heavily and fatally, into another pool of water at her feet. Another follows it. She counts the seconds between each sound; sometimes it is six, sometimes seven.

She looks across the river. Out of the silence she follows the flight of the white gulls; she sees the two yellow cranes in the shipyard and notices a small patch of blue in the cloud-filled sky. Something stirs in her memory.

Isn't it odd, she thinks, when I see Ruth, I have never, ever heard her speak! It's strange! I have never thought of that before! Yet, there is a sound I always hear when Ruth is present...

She cannot recall what the sound is, or what it is like: it is too far removed... it feels as if a heavy, dark curtain keeps it apart from her.

It has grown colder, but she is hardly aware of bodily discomfort. She exists only within her mind and her mind is all borderless space – she is both inside and outside this vast emptiness that has no light, and therefore no point of reference. Her thoughts come and go, wandering. For a moment she is aware of this. She thinks 'it is as if I exist in the black reality of a cavernous vault, a wondrously expansive vacancy that is without bottom, or sides, or covering. It is so huge it can accommodate and lose all that my mind might imagine...'

23

The thought departs. A form of numbness pervades her being mirroring the coldness of her body. The world has nothing but silence to offer, then she is saved by the music made by each individual flattened, unreverberating note created by water striking water, as it exists, momentarily, but real only in relation to the one that went before, and the one coming after.

Slowly, the rhythm returns her to comprehension. The rain has stopped. She feels the cold creeping across her skin. Awareness seeps into life in her consciousness.

Words run through her mind. 'I stand here: not pondering, not thinking, and not mediating, not considering.' She pauses, reflectively considering the words she has uttered inside her head. 'Perhaps these are the wrong words to use, the wrong verbs; perhaps it is not about doing anything, maybe it's just that I have become conscious of the silence, overwhelmed by the silence. And that is fine. It's fine to be overwhelmed, sometimes. I have to allow myself that. Yet, I must be aware. And I have to think before I can become aware. This is how my mind works, these days. Meanwhile I shall – *cogitate* is a good word – I shall cogitate about thinking. It is as if my mental function has been locked within a strange form of refrigeration. But now, here I am thinking about thinking about this... I could speculate like this for ever and ever, all the time becoming more and more aware of the layers of thought that co-exist within my head.'

Inside her coat she shrugs, the wet lapels rise and fall. Under the grey material's sodden surface she is aware of the dampness and of her skin's involuntary shivering. She looks around. She moves closer to the wall and peers down, over the parapet and into the water. The Lagan moves sluggishly, idly almost. It seems to her to have no purpose and this she recognises. She sees three rafts of debris floating; how

24

patient they seem, caught between currents, imprisoned in the places where the concrete pylons artificially and violently split the river's being – they make her think of a caesarean opening of the water: they are, she considers, dirty, watery cesspits that have spawned a sprawling litter of plastic bottles, a jumble of bits and pieces of blackened scraps of wood, encircled with ancient twigs, curled and plaited like hair.

She wonders at her mind's selection of this word 'caesarean', it must come from some textbook, read long ago. Why am I associating Julius Caesar's birth system with such a dingy utility? Such a demanding governor of his people. Isn't it strange, she considers, how so many disparate things turn out to be related, in so many ways? She remembers James talking about Julius Caesar once and quoting from him to make some point or other. 'If you must break the law, do so to seize power – otherwise observe it.' A scattering of seagulls sit out there on the water; a couple of men stand on a boat, engaged in desultory conversation.

Power: of course, that is a man talking. And what of birth and death, they are so close, one to the other.

She raises her eyes: beyond all of this, there in the Harland and Wolf shipyard, the yellow cranes stand, solid. To her left she sees the Royal Mail building; away to her right stand the Hilton Hotel and BT Towers and the Waterfront Hall.

Home. This is where she lives, a watery waste set in a trap of rising buildings, where so much death has taken place.

Death. A feeling of claustrophobia settles about her, like a dark cloud; she experiences the approach of a panic attack; she waits, and the feeling passes. She breathes more freely;

her gaze returns to the familiar yellow crane. She is calmer now.

This is familiar; this is home, this is where I live, this is where I belong.

Her attention is caught by and drawn back to the weir itself. It is a shallow trough, formed by seven or eight uniform sections, each one a place where water descends from one level to another. In their long, running form and in this twinning of light and shade they remind her of women's hair. The streaming silver strands are highlighted against under shades of a darker colour. It strikes her that there is something primeval, something pagan about it. The thought, in the half-realised form of a vague memory, comes to her of women, in ancient times, swimming upstream, sisters perhaps, their faces beneath the water, their long hair streaming behind them. Perhaps, she thinks, they are mermaids, the half-spawn of that great blue fish, their mother. They are mermaid sisters…eyes, mouths, submerged, changing from this world to another, striving to move forward yet never advancing, always remaining static, struggling against the water's powerful push.

Once more, she experiences a sense of suffocation. It is as if a clamp has been placed on her chest; her throat constricts. The question forms itself in her mind, what has this country done to me, to us? Then it passes. As she turns away, she finds her teeth have begun to chatter, it has grown colder and colder. It is that, together with her own wet condition, that finally drives her from this spot that lies at the heart of her world, and as she shakes herself and begins to climb the steps leading up to the footbridge it is as if she is born once more into the life of the city.

At the top of the steps, she stops short and looks back.

Born once more…

Yes, it is like a womb…

It is the fate…

From here so many generations of individuals were conceived and born. becoming doctors, nurses, scientists, adventurers, scientists, inventors; thieves, rebels, liars – she can hear the submerged murmur of their voices, can sense their energy, rising up out of the river that drew so many ancestors to its sides. Such a great melee of imagination and creativity fills the air: quite suddenly, she feels pride.

As she resumes her journey towards home, she deliberates on what has happened during the past short time; for some reason, her thoughts turn on the sounds of water. It is as if the sounds and the silences are jealous of each other, yet they could not exist without each other. Silence without sound would be wholly nothingness; sound, without silence, would be meaningless noise. Balance, acceptance, multiplicity, being useful – these are what count. Her revulsion has turned to pride, to love. This is where I belong; this is where I have my roots. This is where my few friends are, yet, she thinks, why do I so often feel such loneliness? Roots but no shoots. She continues to ruminate on everything except the encounter that sent her here.

***

As she opens her door the telephone is ringing but she ignores it. 'It will be either James or Robert,' she thinks, 'and just now I am in no state to talk to either of them'. The ringing stops. She takes off her coat, then her wet clothes, and goes into the bathroom where she puts on a robe and runs a bath.

27

Soon, she lies, submerged in the warmth of the bath water. She should have answered the telephone, she worries. The trouble is, I am most wholly myself when I am alone and just now, I want to be myself. When I am with others, I freeze up, I feel constricted – I feel like a snail withdrawn inside its shell: so tight, so firm, so little space. I fill my constraining shell; there is no room for anyone else to get inside. I am so well protected; proofed, she thinks wryly, against even the sneakiest of a Houdini attempt. She resolves that as soon as she has had her bath, she will call both James and Robert. It is second nature to her. They have always been there, ever since early childhood. When they were children, they had even been regarded by neighbours as cousins, even though that is not the case, for they are not related in any way. Or – at least as Robert sometimes says, jokingly – it is not the case as far as anyone knows. Once, they were four: the two sisters Rebecca and Ruth Porter, and the two boys James Ferguson and Robert Orr. Today, as she enters her apartment, the two men are out there, somewhere in the city or on its outskirts, going about their individual bits of business. On this day, at this moment, they are oblivious to each other's existence. Nevertheless, she feels their presence.

They were born into suburbia and lived in a long, sweeping crescent of houses that faced onto a narrow road. Situated between town and country their middle-class homes, if not immediately adjacent, were close to each other. Each house had a large back garden that narrowed off to a point where it came to the boundary with a field. James still lives here, single and on his own, in his parents' house.

The four children started at the local primary school on the same day forty-odd years ago and immediately the two boys became friends. Gradually, the two girls, who were twins, got to know them, and joined them in creating what gradually became this enduring friendship. They began by walking home together from school, and then gradually they started to get together after school, meeting always at the point where their gardens touched the open fields that lay behind their homes.

It was here that the boys built their own little house, a rough shelter constructed from old bits of wood and two sheets of rusted corrugated metal, all held together by bits of wire and string and rope. The two girls brought various things discreetly purloined from their mother's kitchen cupboards – cups, two plates, a knife and a spoon, an old tin box to store them in. They grew into it, and into each other. It was to this place, hidden in thick undergrowth, that Ruth came on her own to read whatever book she had on the go at the time. It was here that Robert smoked his first cigarette, taken from his father's coat pocket and shared with Ruth. He never mentions it but remembers it still: it was the day he got his eleven plus results; it was the day they all got their eleven plus results. He was the only one to fail.

The undergrowth developed and grew into a copse of trees; on one side the land was wet and boggy, especially where it ran down to the stream. When they were older, fourteen or fifteen, James would borrow his father's shotgun and shoot pigeons at dusk, as they came in to roost. On each occasion, at the sound of that first shot, the girls' mother would blow long, urgent blasts on her whistle, a pre-arranged signal for them immediately to return home.

When they meet now, which they do most weekends, and the conversation becomes companionable and maudlin, they are moved to hunt for warm, shared memories of those days. Then they talk about the field and the small copse it ran down to, and then, in turn, they mention the woods beyond and then the river – in reality, a small stream. They talk about the sunnier weather that seemed more common then, or

29

about other children who went to the school, or they occasionally recall some saying of the School Master.

They rarely, if ever, speak of Ruth; her name is rarely mentioned. Yet Ruth's presence remains real, as the ground upon which they tread, or the seats upon which they sit.

***

As they grew, they became easy in each other's company. They were more than acquaintances, they remained close, and they grew together and grew in knowledge of one another. They became friends. Yet each one of them viewed their friendship in a separate way. To James, it was, if he had thought about it – which he didn't, basing his life's philosophy on a series of clear and simple givens – a matter of pragmatic benefit, primarily so to himself. He was, he would have said, supremely indifferent to any sentimentality that might lurk around their acquaintance. Yet he, of them all, could have told you how many years, months… indeed, he could probably have said how many weeks they had known each other, for he overtly valued their being together as a solid cement, as the basis for a set of good social relationships.

On the other hand, Robert believed, with a deep but wholly unexpressed passion, in the value and worth of enduring friendship. He was, to James's mind, wholly adolescent in this regard. He was, he would have asserted, being ignorant of his own, natural behaviour, if asked, totally sentimental about it 'and what's wrong with a bit o' sentiment?'. He took delight in baiting any unwary interrogator. He had developed and now often deployed the half-dead Ulster-Scots dialect as an effective cloaking strategy, a method of shielding himself from unwanted scrutiny.

Robert was a friend to many people, but although he was naturally compassionate, generous and benevolent, for him real, true friendship was something beyond the ordinary. It was something that was to be recognised and nurtured when it mysteriously appeared. This sense of value was one he had shared with Ruth, firstly in their early teens when they had been especially close and had talked for hours together, discussing the things teenagers discuss. Most people move on from the innocence that exists at that stage of life, but Robert had not: he stuck tenaciously to the values discovered, developed and shared with Ruth before her sudden death.

Rebecca's perspective was slightly different. In some ways, she was at the heart of this friendship. If asked, the others would have said that she was its heart, for she was the overt reason why they had come together again, after a brief period when they had met only occasionally as a group. To her it meant continuity, a family of sorts – the only family she now had. With James and Robert, she had a special place of rest, security, a space where absolute trust could be requested. It offered her the opportunity to believe in something outside the self. But of them all, she was the most distant: in some ways she remained more, and more absolutely, remote than any of the others.

Now and again, she became aware of this quality of coolness on her own part and put it down to the fact that she instinctively adopted the role of a woman as opposed to their roles as men. Perhaps, she argued, in these moments of self-awareness, this lent a certain distance to her position in the group – and, deep down, she knew, the other two regarded her with something like awe, always subscribing to her good sense, to her superior sensibility. So they followed her, and she encouraged them; she was enabled and allowed to play the combined if faintly ambivalent roles of mother and leader. In addition, she encouraged each of them to assume the part of father, brother and trusted friend, thus giving each a recognisable role while remaining untouched by conventional status herself.

And, yes, with this went a certain tenderness, a certain caring, as well as the certain remoteness, a certain withholding: she was always the first to accommodate the others' wishes, always the first to bend this way or that in order to grease the cogs of social discord. Nevertheless, she dictated the level and depth and degree of intimacy.

Love? She often thinks of love. Love – physical love – left abruptly in September 1983, on the day Ruth departed, never to return. Love? The other sort? That too had gone, apparently.

***

And what of home? Rebecca Porter lives alone in a bright, uncluttered apartment that looks out over central Belfast. From her large balcony she can see the river, and beyond that the city streets. The apartment has been decorated in grey and greyish-white tones – this was its colour when she bought it, three years ago, and she is content to leave it as it is.

Her given names are Mary Rebecca Anne – an adherence to the tradition of calling grandchildren after their maternal and paternal grandparents. So, her sister was named Margaret Ruth. Their mother was a nurse, and their father was a doctor, a GP who had one of the last single-handed practices in the North, situated on the edge of the city and attracting a mixture of suburban and rural patients. He worked long hours, took solitary walks out into the country every evening, bird-watched on holidays, invariably in

Scotland, and read lots, mainly historical fiction. He accompanied his wife and daughters every Sunday to the local Presbyterian Church; he did not smoke or drink. He died, quite suddenly, one evening early in 1984. He had gone for his customary walk. Rebecca remembers it well: the loud, abrupt knock at the door, a neighbour speaking to her mother; 'your husband ill, on the roadside'. Their rushing out; his body lying on the ditch, crumpled, white, and silent. He was dead, a heart attack. It had happened as quickly as that. He was just 62 years old. Not more than six months after his daughter's death.

Afterwards, she remained at home, living with her mother. In her memory, the following years remain hazy. The heavy silence in the house, the insistent tick of the hall clock, the gloom that seemed to hang in the air, the painful, mute meals taken together. It was never spoken of, but she knew her mother blamed her for both deaths: her mother blamed her for taking her sister into town that fateful day and she knew beyond doubt that her mother held her responsible for her father's dying of a broken heart. Deep down, she blamed herself, but nothing was ever said, in private or in public.

Rebecca is still not sure exactly how one incident is contingent on another, in life, only that it is so. In life, she believes, everything is connected.

***

She is standing here, now looking at the photograph of her father and mother on the mantelshelf: it is a wedding photograph, distant in its black-and-whiteness. Another century; another world. They stand stiffly side by side; her mother is wearing a trim two-piece costume, her father is neat in a black suit, white shirt and dark tie; he carries gloves, clenched in one fisted hand. They do not look happy, she thinks, not inside. Her mother, although standing by her father's side, seems to be almost not there, or not wishing to be seen to be there.

Her abiding memory of her mother is not of those final few difficult months – more difficult than she would have envisioned, too fewer than she could have wished – rather, it is of her mother standing by the upstairs bedroom window, half hidden by the curtains, watching out to where the four of them played. That memory always returns to her nowadays, that image of the white face, blurred, immobile and mute against the darkness of the room. 'Like a lily at dusk,' Robert had said once, catching her gaze and looking up to the window, seeing her mother's face there. She wondered: had he been aware that Lily was my mother's name? Robert, she thought, Robert was like that, even as a child, always coming up with the right word. What a thing for a child to say, or to consider. He was more poetical, had, still has, more apparent emotions, than James has; but without James, she thought, I never would have got through that period. He never once mentioned my bad moods, never criticised me though he was, and still is, critical of everybody else. Turning away from the photograph, she smiles, the dark, reflective mood suddenly broken.

Miles away across the city, at the moment when Rebecca turns away from the white wall, as she turns to face into the emptiness that is her apartment, James, who was an only child and who has never been a stranger to solitariness, is sitting at his desk. He is in his office, at the heart of the family business, and he too is alone. For twenty years now he has been sole owner of the firm started by his father, and for the past ten years he has lived on his own in what was the family home. His mother and father have moved away to live in retirement, on the north coast, close to the sea. He sees them

34

regularly but is not close to them. His only other known relative, an elderly uncle, died a few years previously.

He has been left with the family home; he knows it is too big for one, but although he has never said this in so many words, he loves it. He loves its shape and feel, the spaciousness of the entrance hall and the steep stairs with light from the stained-glass window gleaming dimly off the old mahogany, the reception rooms, the big square kitchen and the old scullery. He loves the dressed stones of the outhouse at the rear and the gardens that cosset the house and provide him with privacy. He always responds to the smells in the air here, thinking them somehow different, perhaps unique to his senses, in their freshness and softness. He hardly admits it to himself, and certainly not to others, but he likes their delicacy. He loves, above all, the constantly changing views out over Belfast Lough. As the years pass, he finds his attachment to the place strengthens. He has, he considers, over the years of quiet intimacy, of steady investment of time and money, made it his own. He has grown into it. He gives the fabric of the house continuous attention; he employs a housekeeper and a gardener and a handyman – they all are part-time; still, every key in every lock turns with a smooth click; every piece of brass and every tile glitters. He derives much pleasure from the care he lavishes on his house. He loves to see its results; he loves to see things shine in the sunlight.

James deals in buttons. Everyone will tell you so, for he is well known in the small universe he inhabits. His factory turns out thousands, perhaps millions of buttons each year. He is the top button seller in Ireland. Everyone knows this to be the case. Occasionally, when he is introduced to new people as a button manufacturer, they are invariably surprised. This irritates him, as no-one thinks that buttons have to be made – 'they don't just appear,' he sometimes says. His father, and now he, has supplied a great many of the local shirt manufacturers, as well as those further afield. Their firm supplies buttons, cardboard stiffeners and plastic clips.

What James is reluctant to explain to the world at large – he feels it would take away some of the allure he believes button making suggests – is that he does not make the things he supplies, not even the buttons, rather he imports them and then dyes them. His workforce does not consist of dozens of people, but nowadays comprises a lady who looks after bookkeeping and administration, a man who looks after the dying, a storeman who looks after everything else and a young lad who runs messages and looks after whatever might crop up. This includes washing and polishing James's car. Apart from the lad, the others have been with the firm for many years, a fact evidenced by their referring to him still as 'Young Mr. James.'

If the truth be told, the button-making business is nowadays little more than a hobby. Much of James's fortune came to him from his one and only relation, now deceased, his Uncle Fleming Fulton, an unmarried and unusually thrifty shopkeeper. Much of James's time is taken up with managing his investments and with Territorial Army business. He is also a long-standing member of the Freemasons. He has grown into being a man's man; to those who think they know him he appears content with his life.

Luckily – although he would argue it had little to do with luck but more to do with diligence, even though he has come into a number of inheritances – his father gave him the business while his uncle left him a useful sum of money, and these endowments have been supplemented by various little bequests – he is comfortably off. He foresaw the demise of the shirt-making industry long before it came about and decided his prime purpose was to ensure he remained a wealthy man. For James is wealthy, but not ostentatiously so; he is not ashamed of his money, nor is he mean – merely careful. He indulges occasionally in enjoying feelings of pride, considering he has worked hard to develop and stabilise the business. And, although numbers of directly created jobs may be relatively few, his business has maintained its standing as an integral part of the local economy, sustaining the shirt-making business for nearly a century.

However, he had been raised to be judiciously modest, to be circumspect about what he has and who he is, and never mentions any of this. James will not be seen driving a new black Mercedes, as many of his contemporaries might be - rather, he drives a six-year-old Jaguar, bought four years ago and that will last him for another year, at least.

Physically, he is a big man, well over six feet, and moves with the traditional tall man's slight stoop, a characteristic that first appeared when he was still a teenager. At work or while attending meetings, he favours double-breasted suits and stout brogue shoes; at weekends he wears one of his many tweed jackets or a blazer, with what he still refers to as slacks.

All of his employees have been with the firm for many years so when he 'walks the factory floor', as he puts it, daily, he chats to each one in turn. He listens to his handful of workers, and he listens to the machine that is his workplace. He likes to think that he hears any little sound or noise that is out of the ordinary, with machine or man. He knows their first names and their family histories and keeps abreast with the difficulties of their lives. In the past, it has not been unknown for an envelope to be passed, without comment or condition, to a man or woman who is experiencing some particular difficulty.

That is how he spends his life. That and, increasingly, going by himself on occasional trips to visit other European countries; by this stage, he has been to so many major cities, he claims he has grown to love the architecture, the art galleries and museums, the music, the sense of life continuing to ooze out of centuries of human endeavour. In truth, by this stage the buildings he has seen have merged into one another, and the museums and art galleries, whose catalogues and brochures he collects, are rather jumbled in his mind. He loves, above all, the sense of anonymity he experiences on these trips; there, he is one man, lost among millions; there, he can forget about leadership. For, while he has worked to develop what is an innate ability to be sociable and finds it easy to talk and to listen to others, his personal life and his life at the factory are lives overflowing with people, mapped and intersected by numerous relationships and by many responsibilities.

If interrogated about his responsibilities (he often interrogates himself, especially as he brushes his hair in the morning, applying the brush to his still-dark hair and the little comb to his thin moustache), he would admit to regarding himself primarily as a leader. He believes a leader must stand a little apart. Sometimes he must take tough decisions; he must be able to command and control. He must understand and respect the authority of the law and he must respect the order that law brings. James takes leadership very seriously.

James considers himself to be the most democratic of men, for he is indeed a gentle giant, and underneath he is extremely soft and often emotional. But still, he is fond of saying that 'the factory is not a democracy; the army is not a democracy.' Somehow, he lives with the always-present

38

awareness that he has never been elected. Still, he considers himself a leader. Above all, he lives with the knowledge he has many acquaintances but only a few close friends.

James has never been to a gym in his life but keeps himself remarkably fit. He does not smoke and drinks hardly at all. He has taken out numerous insurance policies over the years and for these, because they are for significant sums, he must have regular health checks. 'A futile gesture,' Robert calls it when he and Rebecca discuss it, as they do on occasion, for James always tells them of these regular visits to the doctor. 'There are no pockets in a shroud, and who is he going to leave it all to?'

'I don't know, I think it just makes him feel more secure,' she replies.

In pursuit of a healthy lifestyle, James breakfasts every morning on a dish of yoghurt and prunes, followed by a pot of Earl Grey tea and two slices of toast (without butter and never marmalade). He prepares this himself and eats it off a tray in the breakfast room. He resolutely persists in this practice – even though the kitchen, with its always burning Aga, is comfortable – not only because he has such a room and believes it should be used, but because it faces east and the early sun streams through its double windows. He finds additional benefit from this arrangement since it offers him an excellent view of the garden and the lawns running down to the wall together with sight of the wonderful world that is coming to life out there beyond his boundary and out over Belfast Lough. It provides him with his first connection of the day to the wider reality.

Sometimes, if it is a particularly fine morning, he dawdles a little, and on these occasions, he invariably finds himself to be in a reflective mood. At times like this he allows himself the indulgence of following whatever wandering thought might come along. So, sometimes when he is sitting at the breakfast table, teacup by his hand, looking out at the sun burnishing the cropped grass of his lawn or dancing off the leaves of his pruned trees, his feet laced into his heavy shoes that are firmly set on the oak floor, sometimes on these occasions, he daydreams a little. 'What if,' he allows himself to ask on these occasions, 'What if there were the four of us here now, as we were once?' He makes a little drama in his mind's eye and in it he creates images of all the things that could have been. The meals together, trips taken by road and by air, holidays shared, lives shared, emerging families of children...

This is by way of being an aspiration and a delight. It is not a theatre of regret; he insists on that. He allows the curtain to fall, carries his tray to the kitchen, tidies away the bits and pieces, and gathers up his coat and keys and case. He commences the journey to work.

**

A few miles away, on the outskirts of the city, this Thursday Robert is alone in his pottery studio. After leaving Art College he worked for two years as an assistant to a well-established potter. His college tutor had introduced him to this man. 'Learning the trade,' he called it. Then he set up his own studio in what had been his grandfather's home. His father's father had been a small farmer and a blacksmith, as had been his father before him. The forge, last seen working in the fifties or perhaps early sixties of the previous century, stood with its few acres and a cottage on a hillside, between Belfast and Ballyclare. It has a pleasing prospect, looking out over the valley towards the blue line of the Antrim hills, away to the east.

One Christmas, Robert's father had taken him out for 'a run in the car' and with no introduction or explanation had driven to the old family farmstead. There, without preamble he said, 'twelve acres and two tumble down buildings. It's yours. I've signed it over to you. That's the size of your inheritance. Your sister and the grandchildren will get our house when I go. I think that's a fair division of what little there is – your sister was very good to your mother when she was alive.' He paused briefly, 'Are you content?'

'Of course! That's very fair,' Robert replied, surprised and moved by his father's offer. Even as he looked at the weedy yard, the cottage and the smithy with its tarred roof, the tree and the pond where horses had once drunk, all of it layered as it was in decay and dilapidation, but also layered in memories and family mythologies, he felt at home. After all, this was where he had spent many days as a child. The forge itself was a mere shell, in its present state offering an imperfect protection against the elements yet, as he looked, he was transforming it in his mind's eye, instinctively identifying where he could strengthen its defences against the looming decades.

From then on it was hard work; a small loan from the bank, an equally small one from his father, a new Bangor Blue slate roof for the forge, paint bought by the gallon and applied liberally.

Nowadays, he sees little of his father, who has retired from his job as a primary school Head and now spends most of his time in Scotland with his daughter and grandchildren. Essentially, Robert is alone: he lives what is a rural existence, though only a few miles from the city, with his sheepdogs, Benson and Blue. As he explains to visitors, he used to smoke – Gallagher Blues and then Benson and Hedges. 'I gave up a few years ago, but I like to keep the language of addiction alive,' he says, patting the dogs.

He has retained the big double doors that once allowed the entry and exit of carthorses, but they are seldom opened fully nowadays. At one end of the forge, he has installed a modern gas-fired oven (with the aid of another loan, like the first almost paid off, painfully so) in which he stacks and cooks his pots. At the other end he has his potter's wheel and a workspace.

In the middle of the space, close to the double doors, he has created a display and sales area where customers can look at his work. Then, close to this and at the heart of the workshop, stands his grandfather's old anvil, adjacent to his potter's wheel. 'Like twin altars,' he sometimes says to visitors, only half-joking.

Robert had moved into the cottage in the month he turned twenty-three, and over the succeeding years restored it, bit by bit. He has kept all the essential features. The half loft remains, the one big bedroom with its two small windows cut into the enormously thick walls is much the same as it had been for well over a century, and the stone-flagged main room with its open fire remains largely the same. The little flat-roofed scullery – it had been added on at the back at some time in the distant past – has been tumbled and rebuilt, turning it into a modern utility space, with white-tiled walls, sink and larder, and a gas cooker and even a dishwasher. Showing it to visitors, and by way of responding to their praise, he says ironically but truthfully, for he is both proud and ashamed of his achievement, 'A little palace!' He often follows this with, 'Just waiting for a princess...'

At the end of the lane, he has erected two home-made signs, one above the other. One says, 'Forge Pottery,' and the other 'Open for Sales'. He never takes the latter sign down, even on Christmas day and if someone were to come on that day, and if Robert was at home, he would open the showroom. Not for the sake of making a sale (welcome as that would be) but because he takes a genuine pleasure in revisiting and sharing with others his delight in what he had made.

It does not matter where he is on the twelve acres, he always seems to know when someone is about to call. Firstly, there will be the abrupt metallic rattle and clang of the old cattlegrid that protects the entrance to the laneway, then the low, sustained crunch of tyres on the deep rough gravel of the laneway and yard. Because the laneway is curved, like the blade of a scythe he always thinks, it takes a few minutes to drive what would have been a short distance, had it been a straight line. So, he is always at the door, waiting.

Initially, only a few tourists called, and they seldom bought anything. Now their numbers are increasing. These, and the people who call in on a more regular basis to buy wedding presents or gifts for birthdays or Christmas, stand in the yard, looking out over the green fields that run to a valley and then eastwards to the blue of the Antrim hills. Looking about, they invariably tell him how much they envy him his idyllic life. They point to the pond with the three flagged steps leading down to its water, the spreading tree with the bench under it, the old forge (it even has climbing roses clinging to the gable wall). They can see the freedom there is for him to do as he pleases, to be his own master in this, the Garden of Eden, this oasis of peace. After more than twenty years, such compliments are now familiar to him and he accepts these litanies graciously yet lazily, as if they were no more than his due. They do not see the greenfly, he sometimes thinks.

They do not see the arduous work, only its fruits. Once a year he takes a load of stuff, the regimented cups and saucers and mugs, the things he least likes making, because of the repetition and boredom that is involved, to craft shops, but his real love lies in building up the unique, the one-off bowl or pot.

Early on, he took delight in experimenting with glazes, but lately finds himself sticking more and more to the known, to the tried and tested. This troubles him. He feels himself growing stale. This leads to a gnawing doubt which he once shared with Rebecca. As usual, he laughs at this emerging trait, describing himself as creatively lazy, inviting laughter. Rebecca fails to find it funny but on the day he confides his feelings to her she is feeling so flat she does not fully engage. The question is left, hanging, and is not returned to again. Like so much in their lives these days.

He has a curious way of encapsulating his life when in conversation, of reducing its (and his) importance, by repeating descriptive and reductive phrases about the small things that have become his life: the cottage and workshop and the little wood of planted trees. It is a habit he learned as a child, listening to the grown-ups: it was their way, now it is his. 'It's a place of fire and water', he says; or 'where the anvil is, can be found the heart' or again, 'I am only a kind of alchemist…' When a little tipsy he is fond of asserting, 'my secret lies in the mixing of clay and water, the memory of shape and form that inhabits my hands. My legacy *is* my hands, my family were farmers and blacksmiths and weavers: I am a potter…'

When he talks like this to Rebecca she replies, 'You are an old romantic.' As indeed he must be for, he loves to lie in the big bed, listening to the wind buffeting the old beech tree, or to stand on the flag-stone step on the night of a full moon, watching its refection where it lies full on the pond's surface with the clouds speeding past. At times like these he fills with pride at what he has and who he is. He is pleased enough with what he has. He thinks in the world's terms it is small enough, yet he is happy enough too, most of the time. He knows somewhere or in some way that he is lonely, but the word never passes his lips, not even in a whisper, nor is the thought processed into the form of a word in his mind.

But all the time, underneath, deep within him, there exists a great smouldering restlessness. On a winter's night when he damps down the fire before going to bed, he feels it. Deep down, he despises the status quo and all the small injustices that have their roots in men's minds. All this, the place and the work, he knows are so much damp slack; they are simply ways he has of damping down and controlling his own anger.

Occasionally, he seeks to escape but these breakouts are rare, and he keeps them distinct and different and at safe distances, one from the other. Occasionally, he gets drunk. Then, he drinks whiskey. First, he drinks it in small, savoured measures, on its own, neat. Then he adds water in tiny amounts. By the end of the evening, he is drinking water with some whiskey added, just to 'open up the flavour,' he says. Actually, he does this because he was told once that the secret of a long life lies in the marriage of genes and lifestyle; he has an inherited fear of alcohol and what it can do to a man's mind and body, and he loves life enough to want it to continue for as long as possible.

On these occasions, he listens to Van Morrison and then, always as the night extends, to John Coltrane,

'Acknowledgement' and 'Resolution' filling his mind and filling the cottage, the moon low in the sky, the wind in the tree, the turf fire glimmering, the telephone lifted out of its cradle, a glass by his hand.

He is, he sometimes considers when he is in such a state, a curious mixture: he thinks of the languages available to him, when he thinks of this at all, as being Ulster English and Ulster Scots: he is extremely aware that the latter is a highly stigmatised language, a tongue few so-called educated people willingly speak in public, yet he feels comfortable in using it. He feels at home speaking and thinking in its rhythms and idioms for these are the words he had grown up hearing when he visited his grandfather at this same forge. He still has the big Burns's *Collected Poems* that his grandfather had used; this remains a kind of touchstone, a link with a wider, older reality. There is, to his ear, a musical element, verging on the lyrical embedded in the vernacular and a softness that must necessarily express some fineness of character in those who speak it. He can switch between the twa as easily as he could change frae yin suit o' clothes tay anither.

Yes, sometimes, now, he feels old beyond his years. 'I think too much,' he thinks. Sometimes, as he sits alone by the fireside, he feels he knows what it might be to be eighty-five or ninety, though he is at least forty years short of that age. Still, the road ahead increasingly is foreshortened; foreshortened and, to his trained eye, quickly narrowing to a point where it ceases to exist. And then, to his mind, everything ceases.

***

There is much on Rebecca's mind as she moves about the apartment. She is drawn towards, and then stops in front of, one of the two photographs that sit on her mantelshelf, a photograph of Ruth Porter, her twin sister – brown-eyed, vivacious, a person whose life was as full of fun as her brown hair was full of bounce. Robert once, in one of his poetic moments, described her hair as 'black as *slaes*…' As she recalls this, she remembers his voice, hearing the lilt in it, as the Ulster Scots words rolled off his tongue, the two long vowels at odds with each other, yet aiding and abetting the poetry of the language, like a man and a woman dancing together. 'Black!' Robert's control of reality was often suspect! She smiles. He gives way to the poetic impulse too easily, she thinks, seeing again Ruth's hair, brown with mahogany highlights. Still, she remembers the laughter and the love in his eyes as he spoke. As she ponders these things, she reaffirms in memory the fact that the photograph had been taken in the summer of 1983, only a few weeks before Ruth's death. Above all, she remembers Ruth; she feels once more the always-growing reality of absence.

She walks about for a bit. The nervous tension remains, and she knows she must do something, she must engage in action if she is to dispel it. She crosses the floor to where a table sits against the wall. She takes a book from its drawer and sits down. She begins to write:

Apart from the mornings, when I have been having these flashbacks again, I have not consciously thought of Ruth for at least a couple of days and then, suddenly this morning there she was ahead of me on the escalator. A girl in a green dress. I recognised immediately the toss of the gleaming hair, the turn of the head. My heart leapt: I called out, 'Ruth! Ruth!' But the girl did not stop; there was a lurch inside my body, my stomach seemed to swim up, filling my chest. I could not breathe; all of this happened in a split second and then I realised that this was not Ruth, I was mistaken.

But then, I knew this already, just as soon as the call was emerging from my mouth. I had probably known it was not Ruth even before the

47

words were formed and I knew, deep down, that the wish was father to the thought.

Immediately afterwards Rebecca had gone into a coffee shop and sat at a table by the window. People hurried past, engrossed in a thousand thoughts. She watched them, allowing the feelings of desolation and emptiness and loss to swell up and then to die down. Soon, she felt better: it was as though she has shouldered off her own feelings, shouldered them onto the backs of all those hurrying, anonymous people. Remembering this, she turns to the page.

I have successfully off-loaded my feelings onto the backs of the guilty and the innocent alike; looking at the people as they flow past, I wonder once again how one could tell who is the guilty, who is the innocent. How could one tell, which one or two or three, from that mass of busy, rushing, purposeful, ordinary-looking people, had fired a shot, had driven a car, had lent a room, had given money, had urged on and encouraged others? Who among them had sung inflammatory songs in pubs? Who among them, by word or by deed, had caused injury or had helped others to give injury?

She grimaces. This is not her way at all, and she does not like to acknowledge the existence of such petty and vindictive thoughts. She does not wish to admit the presence in her heart of such mistrust of her fellow citizens: it is the not knowing who – who behind a smile, shared on the street or in passing in a shop doorway, has a killer's heart? She recalls something Robert (why does she still think of him as Robert at times like this?) had once quoted when talking about his hero, Van Morrison; it was about a song with a line that had a reference to there being a crack through which bad things enter into this world.

She turns and turns her coffee mug but does not drink. Her hand is trembling. She wonders, 'Why today?' The answer comes quickly enough – she really does not have to consider the question – and then she realises there are two answers. Firstly, their birthday is fast approaching. And, secondly, that meeting; looming for so long. Looming, but it was something to which she had given no thought, at all. Or rather, she has not prepared for it. It is something about which she had not wanted to think. Until today, that is.

***

The day fades. For now, the door is shut, the double lock applied. She sits again at her desk; she faces the white wall; she thinks about their birthday and about the meeting. She takes up her pen.

Why? How do we get to the origin of this act that he carried out? What kind of seed was it that gave birth to such a cruel deed? Out of what kind of soil did it grow? Has this question been asked? Really? Of him, of others? I mean, take this man and his life… his mother and his father, his brothers and sisters… what kind of life did he lead? Was he happy, unhappy, loved, or was he dismissed, ignored or mistreated? How would one answer, as opposed to another, explain what he did?

Was he taught to hate at home, or did he learn it at school or on the street from others of similar mind… is 'hate' the right word? Were the beginnings of the act that ended in his planting that bomb to be found in the time when he was a young man, or when he was a young child? Or was it to be found a hundred years ago, or eight hundred years ago? Was there a law to which his action conformed, a law that put him beyond the laws I recognise?

What did he experience when engaged in that vileness? What precisely did he feel? What did he feel when planning that act, when executing it? Was he acting on his own behalf, on behalf of a community, on behalf of a small, insane, ignorant group? What did he hope to achieve by setting down a bomb in a busy street, on a sunny afternoon?

49

Did he feel odium for nameless, faceless Ruth? He had no way of knowing she would be there so presumably not, but did he feel odium for all people, for humans in general? It could have been anyone – caught there – a ceremonial sacrifice.

A 'ceremonial sacrifice' – looking at what I have just written I cannot help but draw the obvious comparison – I will let it stand, however, horrible as it is – Ruth, offered up by an unknown hand, to save others – or as a payment, or as a hostage, or as a bribe... a token...

On one level I can understand the need for us to move on. It's just that Ruth cannot move on. She is where she is. And what capacity do I have to move on without her? ...but even so, I was finally prepared to give it a try... to give it a go; me, the leader, the nurse, the healer...

It was as I approached the door, as I walked down that eternally long, tediously long, light-denying, dull, yellow-painted corridor, that my reservations raised their heads, as I approached the brown-painted, paint-flaked door, as I saw the brown, worn, door handle, it was then that all my expectations disintegrated, became merely shoddy reflections of this world I was now entering... I feel I am clefted between wanting to reach out to another human being and feeling repulsed by the horror of what I believe, of what I know, is there.

I can still see that door handle so clearly. The door handle was brown, round, wooden, worn smooth, polished, by many hands, by many years' wear... the realisation fell on me, the question exploded inside me, had that hand, the hand that left the bomb there, had it physically touched this door handle, the one that my hand was now being asked to reach out towards, to touch, to touch the same surface his hand had touched?

If it hadn't been for Peter Wright I might still be standing there now, my right hand squeezed into a ball, my fingers tightened into,

locked into, a fist. Peter leaning forward and opening the door and
waiting for me to step into the room...

I remember nothing about the room – not the colour of its walls, not
the floor-covering, not what was in it – I remember nothing for I saw
nothing – except for a table, a man sitting there, a chair sitting, empty,
waiting, I knew, for me to sit down. I remember nothing but a narrow,
horribly shared, emptiness, the emptiness in his eyes, the emptiness in
me... and I was pushed back, back onto the absolute hard rock floor
of my past, for comfort, for safety...

She puts down the pen and goes into the bedroom where
she sits down and mechanically begins to brush her brown
hair. A flash of late afternoon sunlight streams in and
highlights her hair's strong mahogany tints as it springs and
bounces under the vigorous brush strokes. She has grown to
like her hair again, recently; she likes the way it has a life of
its own. She looks at herself in the mirror. She looks at her
eyes, and into her eyes, remembering Robert once making
the comment that they 'are brown, like melted chocolate'. It
is a remark she reads as a good description. She does not
think of it as a compliment – though, she thinks it apt
enough, and considers her eyes against her skin, which is
darker than the average: for some reason, it always reminds
her of a Mediterranean – of a Spanish or an Italian or a
French woman's – skin. She thinks then, as she always thinks
nowadays, of Ruth's hair and eyes and skin... For some
reason she does not think 'my hair, my eyes, my skin...' The
sunken, dark tide of her mood is rising up to approach her,
once more; she is aware of its imminent arrival. Suddenly
agitated she rises from her chair; she prepares to meet it.

Friday

Rebecca gets out of bed very early on Friday morning. It has been a fraught night, largely spent tossing and turning, half asleep, half awake, her mind filled with a flow of images that culminated in the nightmare of her again reliving the instant of her sister's death. She had calmed herself by counting and recounting the three pictures on the wall opposite her bed. They are nondescript prints of meaningless landscapes brought from her mother's house following her death. One is of a doorway with roses sprawling around the red frame, one of a mountains with green fields in the foreground, one of a riverbank, yellow flowers strewn across the green grass. She counts them without seeing them: one, two, three; one, two, three. In the past she has found that this repetition calms her.

Her thoughts are like dry leaves, blowing here and there by any passing breeze. Sucked dry, they have seemed to have no volition of their own: like my life, she thinks, the sap has all gone.

She gets up, partly dresses herself, and then stops, a disregarded stocking hanging from one hand. She feels disorientated. She has lost her foundation. She has no roots. She feels she needs to reconnect. Above all, she needs to think, yet, she knows, she will not, cannot, consider the thing that troubles her most. She is aware that she must confront it yet is unable to do so: she will approach it obliquely, if at all, but not now. Now, she feels only the absence of feeling: she is numb. She dithers, unable to take a decision about work, then, abruptly, she picks up the phone and calls the hospital.

'Can I speak to the Clinical Director, please?' She waits impatiently while she is being put through, the piped music sounding far away and remote.

'Susan? It's Rebecca.'

'Good morning. Is anything the matter? You sound a bit... agitated?' Susan's voice expresses concern.

'No. Oh, it's just that I'm not feeling very well. Probably a bug. I don't think I should go in today.'

'That's okay. Take it easy and don't worry. What's the matter? Flu? There's a lot of it going around.'

'Yes, I suppose so. Or it might just be a touch of what people like to call 'flu-like symptoms.' I'm fine, really, it's just that I don't feel 100% and if I take today off and rest up I'm sure I'll be fine by Monday. Sorry if it puts you on the spot: I know it's late to cry off – and I was off yesterday – but I had been going to finish at three today anyway and I'm off this weekend. So, it's really only this morning and a couple of hours after lunch.'

'Don't worry. I'll contact the Clinical Services Manager and we will sort out some cover. Keep warm and stay in bed!'

'Yes, I think I shall. James and Robert had a birthday party planned for tonight. Just the three of us, but I think I'd better call that off, as well. Thanks Susan. Bye.'

'Bye Rebecca. Take care.' And the line goes dead. She holds the handset, listening to the hum.

She puts down the telephone, feeling somehow grateful. She has known Susan for many years and appreciates her brisk sympathy. She hates disrupting work, like this. 'This is the first time I have taken sick leave in… decades…' she thinks. And then, 'And I'm not really sick at all. What's come over you?' she says to herself out loud, standing in the middle of the floor, wondering what to do now.

She goes to the oak desk that sits in the living room, opens the drawer and takes out the familiar blue book: it is her diary. Amazingly, it falls open at once at the page she has been searching for, an entry where the date and place is given simply as 'August: Ulster Hall', no day, no month, no year, but she has no need of these. She remembers it clearly: it was just last year, just about a year ago. Time flies, she thinks, irrelevantly. She recalls the staging that has been set up outside the City Hall: she saw it yesterday, as she was passing on her way to that meeting. Her thoughts fly, like leaves in a storm. She controls her thoughts. She refocuses. She sits at the table and begins to read:

Last night the three of us went to the Ulster Hall to hear a BBC Summer Concert given by the Ulster Orchestra. Something strange and startling happened. It was a Saturday evening, warm and heavy. During the second half of the programme, they performed Stravinsky's Firebird. I felt so relaxed and rather sleepy, for the music in the first half was languid and I had had a glass of wine during the interval. The piece was new to me and so I had made a point of reading the programme notes, though only in the most cursory fashion. So far as I could make out, the plot was this: an old Russian folk tale, a magical garden, golden apples, a beautiful bird with dazzling plumage, a prince out hunting for her, a feather plucked and given, stone figures dancing, an egg containing a soul... the living thing spilled... and then, a young woman (they called her a damsel in the notes) rescued and the dead brought to life...

As I sat there reading the notes I remember thinking, all this imagination, this fancy, stands in direct contrast to the Presbyterian austerity of the Hall, with its series of cream and green grids set into its ceiling, the sparse utility of its unadorned balcony and its extremely hard seats. Yet, the oppressive, chest-pressing heat of the evening air, together with the soporific effect of the wine, carried me off on a musical journey, carried me off, far from my surroundings, accompanied only by the images that emerged out of my half-assimilated reading of the notes.

Out of this languorous enchantment there slowly emerged an image of Ruth smiling at me, and I was aware of myself smiling in response when, suddenly and without warning, a great detonation went off all around me. The crash of the explosion of music disintegrated Ruth's image, abruptly sending it hurtling far away. I was on my feet at once – in an instinctive leap of fear, I suppose. I know it was an exaggerated response but what could I do? When it was done, it was done I was on my feet, my programme and bag on the floor, all around startled people staring.

Robert and James both reached out to me at the same moment, one was sitting on either side: a few of the people around us glared at me; a few smiled, in sympathy, I suppose, thinking me merely startled out of a dream world, as they had been also, by the sudden change in the music's force. I immediately sat down, embarrassed, feeling foolish, strangely out of breath, apologizing.

'Are you okay?' Robert asked, bending to pick up my programme, while James continued to hold me by the elbow.

'Yes. Yes,' I replied, still flustered. 'It was the suddenness that startled me. I was surprised. I was actually thinking, dreaming, of something else. I'm alright now.'

Then Robert said something very odd; I think he must have been referring to the sudden burst of musical noise for he said something about our 'being in a burlesque of violence' and in a strange way his use of that unusual word focused my mind on the violent expansion of vibrations through the atmosphere, on the force of the orchestra and its relationship in my mind to the bomb explosion.

I did not ask him what he meant, nor did I tell them, then or immediately afterwards, that I had reacted so fiercely because the music had burst into my consciousness, taking me instantly to that day when Ruth was killed... for a long, long moment I was back there, again: now, I wonder now if I ever left...

Reading this, she thinks, for a moment – and with an unusual and frightening surge of bitterness – of that dead young girl brought by some miracle back to life, but for one tantalising instant only. She sits, staring into space, her hand rubbing and rubbing the tabletop. Again, she takes up her pen, opens the diary at a fresh page and writes.

To be a human is to be in a – is actually to exist as a – flux of physicality and spirituality, constantly in a state of change and alteration. Is this what growth is, this flux? Or is it decay? I don't know. Ruth, she thinks, does exist but in such an altered state of change that she is beyond touch, beyond reach. She relies on me now for her continued existence; only I can deliver her from the oblivion he cast her into. 'The question is this,' she continues, 'did I have I the right to accept an apology? Or was it an apology? What makes me think it might be? Why did I... no... how could I not tell him what I felt?' She stares at the wall for a long time. Then she writes:

Ruth, at that meeting, I could not in all conscience speak for you. You are the one who was hurt, at your core, hurt, your existence destroyed, and your life thrown into the bondage of death before you had time to do anything with it.

She stops, waits, starts again.

I don't know what to do! I need guidance. Where does my duty lie? Do I redeem him by forgiving him, or do I redeem you by keeping you from oblivion? He has rendered you invalid! You have lost your ability to be, to speak, you have lost your voice, it was taken away from you. What right do I have to speak for you? I certainly feel I have no right to say I understand why your life was taken, or to forgive on your behalf. I have no right to offer absolution, even if I had the power, or to confer words of understanding, or to accept some kind of apology.

She stops for a moment, then adds, in a daze of unknowing and confusion.

I don't regard this as a political statement. It is a moral, ethical statement. What had you to do with politics? And yet that fire burnt you...

She rises from the table; still, she is agitated; still, her mind is whirling. She thinks, or she attempts to think but her attempt is half-hearted. She feels nothing, is aware only of a great blankness; her mind feels as if it, or she, is in some kind of coma. She walks about the apartment. She sits down by the balcony windows. She makes tea. She looks at the clock. To her surprise she finds it is midday. The morning hours have drained away, and she hasn't noticed. Or, she has been asleep. Jumping to her feet, she decides. She goes into her bedroom and dresses, brushes her hair, puts on a little make-up. Then she picks up the phone and makes a call. She calls Robert. She says she is free all day, she would like to see him, and can he take a couple of hours off. Yes, he says: he is on his way. He does not ask why.

By the time Robert arrives it is after two. 'Volvo! Wouldn't start!' is all he says by way of explanation for his lateness, and she knows the ancient car has broken down again. He finds her listening to Beethoven; the air in the apartment feels dampened by the regal nature of the sounds. He looks at the CD cover that lies open on the table.

'John Rutter…' he says, by way of a statement more than a question.

'I find it full of solace,' she says. He feels tempted to ask, 'Solace from what?' but remains silent: he knows the answer already, and anyway she wants to listen in silence; she will tell him – eventually. He prevaricates, pretending to read the CD cover. This has happened before: just after Ruth's death, then a long period of near normality. It was just after the peace process was announced, in 1994. And again, after the prisoners were given their release, and then the Omagh bombs in 1998. Each of these events brought about short bouts of Rebecca's unresponsiveness, her daydreaming and detachment. And now, here it is about to start all over again.

He sighs deep inside and without sound. They sit quietly just inside the balcony doors. They drink coffee. The coffee is cold. The doors are partly open, and the noise of traffic can be heard. Little whiffs of cloud speed across the sky. The sun is trying to shine.

In some ways, at certain times, the world is very productive, she thinks. At other times… They sit at peace for many minutes. The clock ticks: in the distance, in the other room, the music continues to play.

Then as the music finishes, she turns to him, indicating by a nod of her head the source of the music saying, 'Beautifully made. Don't you think that making beautiful things is important?'

'Yes, of course I do.'

'I remember the first time I watched you work. It still – it always – fascinates me. I can remember the very first time I saw you taking a ball of clay: you threw it, or placed it, on the wheel and then it rose up, out of your hands. I watched you and I was seeing the birth of something that was not there before: the ball of wet clay became something else. A new something in the world, something that has form and shape and a real function. That is a great thing to do, a great talent to have... I always envy you that gift. I wish I could be creative. I wish I could make things. I haven't been to the pottery for a while. I must come soon. Do you still enjoy it? Do you still get satisfaction from making things?'

Robert continues to stare out through the open doors. The river's colour is brown; the water seems to barely move. Under his attention, the brown water barely moves. The clock ticks, each tick seems exaggeratedly loud and slow.

He speaks slowly, thoughtfully. 'I don't know. I don' think about it too much. When it's going well, I just give the actual doing of the work my full attention. When I'm making something, I get somehow drawn in, absorbed in it and forget everything else. I cease to exist during the process. Just before and during the act of 'making' as you call it...'

She asks, 'What does that mean?' She has heard this before, but today that does not matter. The act of talking is what matters, that and being answered.

'What you are saying is all very well and good, but you must have some thought about why you do it, or how you do it… If I just 'did' things for my patients, without some kind of evidential base for what I do…'

'My 'evidential base' as you call it is this: when I did approximately the same thing last time a pot appeared!' He is smiling.

'You're laughing at me!' she accuses him, half amused, half annoyed. She finds she is frustrated once again by his always-present obtuseness. She gets annoyed by his hiding behind this assumed dimness. That, or, as is so often the case, a disturbingly black, cryptic, destructive kind of humour. And also, she thinks now, she never really knows when he is being serious or when he is being merely flippant or off-hand. She decides to plough on, to force an answer from him.

'What I am asking is what is your relationship to your material, what will be your relationship to the cold clay? Do you *force* it to assume a form, working against its nature? Do you *seduce, entice, beguile* it into becoming something it is not yet but could be, if only it puts its trust in your vision for what is possible?'

'Some days I think that I am a craftsman potter – that is what it says on the sign at the bottom of the lane, where it meets the road, anyway – other days, I think of myself as a working artist… sometimes, I just don't think…' He says this with a smile. He doesn't know where this conversation is going. He feels it's the kind of topic that might be better explored late at night, on a night when too much drink is being taken and nothing exists beyond the stall of the stone walls.

'I know that. That's all words you are using to divert me!' She says this, smiling in response, in apparent empathy with him, yet he is certain she is deeply serious.

'Yes, you have a degree in ceramics. Yes, you make your living creating pots. What I want to know is, when you make a piece of pottery, must you have *faith* in what you are doing? I mean, a simple faith that it won't collapse, a belief that it will be good... Surely that's not too difficult a question? You must be aware of something else, something beyond the science or art of the thing you are doing?'

'I think you are getting dangerously close to inviting me to say that art is a religious experience,' he replied. 'For people like us that's dangerous... me with my Gospel Hall background, you with your Presbyterianism, James with his good old Church of Ireland – so far as I can see, they are all built on fear, or on hatred, or just blind indifference! Or even on blind faith! Anyway, a shared thing they all have in common is fear of art, or of the artist, fear of the unbridled imagination. That is what informs their view of what religion is. The truth is, they just didn't trust the imagination, in fact they fear it and they fear the places it might lead to. I'm happy to keep it like that: the two don't mix, to my mind. I stick to art. I let them stick to religion!'

She does not reply and they are silent for a time. Then she goes off to put on another CD. She asks him does he want tea. He says yes. She goes to the kitchen. During her absence, he recants his difficult behaviour. It's just, he mutters under his breath, that these questions make me feel uneasy.

When she returns, and says, 'I suppose it must be an act of faith. And I suppose to tell you the truth, I have thought about it in that way. But I prefer to think with my hands! I don't normally go in for a' this high falutin' stuff.' He pauses, and this time she lets him be.

'But it's not exactly a leap of faith,' he continues. 'I know what the result will be. And you know, when it's good, when it really works, it's like revealing some kind of existing principle of the thing that makes it all tick – the universe, I mean... all I can say is, the harmony, the proportions, the balance, they all come together, and the dynamic of reality takes on a life. Life is suddenly present...'

'Yes,' she says, 'I see.' But he can see she has lost her energy for the topic. However, something has been released inside, and he feels compelled to continue.

'Men... I suppose they have been men, mostly... have been making pots for thousands of years. There's nothing new in it. If you make pots, you should know what the result will be. Every action you take has a consequence.'

Rebecca did not appear to hear him. She simply waits until he finishes, then says, 'Look, what I mean is, I *suppose* what I mean is, do you take risks? Is there any risk-taking in your making of art – as opposed to a doctor or nurse trying to make people better, and not succeeding?'

'Oh, yes, well, it depends on what you mean by *risk*,' Robert replies instantly and with renewed energy. 'Or, even by *making*. Still there is risk, sometimes, even after all these years, on a cold, wet, grey Monday morning, I find myself shrinking from making that first throw, and then attempting to make something from that. It's all contingent. It's grey outside and the forge is empty. There is condensation on the windows. The clay is cold. I'm faced with another day, another week, another ball of inert wet clay that has to become a hollow pillar of wet, dynamic clay that will not fall into a heap. At those times, reason, if you were to ask it, says it will collapse. I suppose, it is me versus the clay – now is the time when you have to find the perseverance to keep on going forward.'

'What does keep you going?'

'What my da, and yours, used to call 'thickness', I suppose: a desire not to lose, to never give an inch - if not to win, exactly then not to lose! It's just a case of perverse perseverance!'

'Look,' he continues, 'I'm not really interested in talking about art. I am a doer, not a talker. You are the one who has studied philosophy. You tell me.' He paused. 'Have you had any lunch?'

'No,' she replied.

He got up and left her then and left the room. As he went out through the door she called after him. 'It's about more than philosophy.' She heard the door open and shut. She remained where she was, sitting, looking into space. A little later she heard the front door open and shut. She heard him in the kitchen, rattling about, cupboard doors opening and closing, plates rattling, before he entered the room. He had two mugs of coffee and a plate with sandwiches.

'A peace-making gesture,' he smiled. 'I went to the sandwich shop. Will you have one?' She nodded, but did not reach out, did not even look at the sandwiches.

'Look', he said, 'I know you are genuinely interested but I don't often talk, or even think, about art or craft or whatever you want to call it. I remember when you were doing your Queen's University course you talked to me a couple of times about some guy, a philosopher, who was born near Belfast...' He left the sentence unfinished, hanging in the air.

'Hutcheson,' she responded. 'Francis Hutcheson; he is often referred to as the father of aesthetics. That's why I talked to you about him, I suppose... I don't really remember. It seems so long ago.'

'Well, I remember you describing how Hutcheson linked beauty and virtue: to experience either was to receive pleasure. I think I agree with that. He thought they were independent of the will, and I certainly agree with that, and he thought that by expressing something you were also actually describing whatever you were expressing.' He paused, looking out of the window, searching for the right words.

'Making pots to me is like a form of religious experience, or *observance*. Yes, that's a good, a better, word. When you make a pot, you have to learn to – not suppress exactly – but to leave go of your own will, your own sense of personal individuality, your ego. You have to learn to love the clay *and* the kiln *and* the wheel – to love them better than your own self, I would say. That's where it all comes together, love, expression, beauty, freedom, virtue... it's like seeing your child leave home. At least, that's my theory...'

'Even though you don't have any children!' interrupted Rebecca, bitterly, rudely, she realised, too late, but by now he was too hotly engaged to take heed of her.

'When I say 'love' I mean 'know', I suppose, you have to *know* them, deeply and intimately. It's having *empathy* with the other...'

'But when you say you have to *know them*,' she replied, 'what does that mean?' She felt the need to offer some sort of challenge, so added, 'Don't you simply learn a set of techniques? Isn't it the *techniques* you know, and you simply keep on applying them, day after day? What is there to 'know' in that? I would say it was mechanical, compared to knowing a child, who grows and develops and changes each and every day.'

'No, no. You have it wrong! Take the firing, for example: kilns come in so many varieties – wood-burning, electric, coal, gas – and the fuel used influences the pottery. And not only that, there are other things that cannot be controlled: the weather, the state of the wood, if it's wood I am using, the kiln atmosphere – these all have an impact on how it will turn out. You learn to trust your instincts… you learn to have faith in your instinctive response. You *feel* what it's like, for the clay. For natural glazes I like to use wood-burning anagama which produces ash that settles on the pots, melts and creates a natural ash glaze that has unique results each time it happens.'

'You do make it sound a bit like child-rearing,' she said, smiling now, 'with all that circumstantial impact stuff – all that responding on the hoof that good parents seem able to do…'

'It is a bit like that,' he replied, seriously. 'You can't force or bully. It takes a light touch! As Burns said, 'Prudent, cautious self-control is wisdom's root.' He had been about to say, but stopped himself, 'What do either of us know about children or child-rearing', for he knew it would hurt her. In reality, he was pleased to see that she was following his argument, and equally delighted that she was arguing against him, for normally she just listened to him and agreed or, if she disagreed, did not often say so. This engagement offered him a sense of closeness, of attachment. And so he went on: 'You have to have the ability to accept and follow accidents – to allow accidents to become part of the process, you have to allow accidents to take their place and to accord them their own order of significance in the making. To that extent one does lose control.'

'Yes,' she spoke slowly. 'You're saying that it's a bit like community – we all rely on each other, the way you rely on what you call accident or chance... it's a kind of faith... we rely on, have faith in, each other's help in fixing what goes wrong... maybe that's where wisdom's root is to be found, in having faith in others...'

'We do have to make choices,' she continues. 'We have to discriminate between the good and the bad bits of reality. I remember James saying once that it is all explained perfectly adequately in the story about the struggle between God and Satan.'

'Like Star Wars!' Robert interrupts, grinning. 'Don't tell me that James has based his philosophy of life on Star Wars. Remember, you're the philosopher, here.'

'Come off it! You are just trying to stir up trouble! Anyway, I'm no philosopher; I'm just someone who went on a quest, once... A quest to a night class! I'm a nurse. Got that buster?' She gives him an exaggerated dig on the shoulder, and he laughs.

'Well, did you discover anything on your quest, I mean did you come across any new information about Satan and God and the great cosmic forces of good and evil?'

'What I discovered was – is – very simple: if there is a 'battle' it's a straight fight between free thought and the tyranny of inherited ideas. It's a bit like what we talked about earlier, about beauty and virtue, the intuitive and the will. You seem to apply these ideas in your work...'

She stood up abruptly, looking intently into his face, she said, 'Thank you. For listening. For talking. It was what I needed.'

'Excuse me, a moment,' she said. She left the room and he heard her shut the bathroom door. Idly, he picked up a newspaper that sat on a small table. He was glancing through it when she returned. 'Listen to this,' he said, peering out from behind the newspaper. He reads aloud:

'Robot nurses could be bustling around hospital wards in as little as three years. The mechanised 'angels' – being developed by EU-funded scientists – will perform basic tasks such as mopping up spillages, taking messages and guiding visitors to hospital beds.

They could also be used to distribute medicines and even monitor the temperature of patients remotely with laser thermometers.

Working in teams, the intelligent robots will be able to communicate with each other and coordinate their duties.'

What do you think of that, then? You are to be replaced by a robot! Imagine, 'Robot Nursing Sister Porter, at your service.'

'Chance would be a fine thing,' she responds, but blankly. He sees she has reverted to her earlier, agitated state. He puts down the newspaper.

'That's enough about me and my job. We've rather exhausted that topic already. What remains so important to you about nursing?' Robert asked. 'It's a part of you: it's who you are; I mean you've been doing it for…'

She broke in on him, not allowing him to finish, replying in her best, very matter of fact and firm voice; it was a fine lecturing voice, he thought. 'It's very straightforward.' Robert shifts in his seat, leaning forward towards Rebecca. 'Nursing is totally about ensuring the well-being of others; it's about caring for others; it's caring in equity for those who are in need – whether its physical or emotional need, and irrespective of whether they are young or old, rich or poor…'

Robert wasn't really in the mood to be lectured. In an attempt to divert her he replied, tongue in cheek, 'It's okay your saying that. I know, I have known, many people who have said similar things. But you make it sound a bit…' He pauses, searching for the right word, 'You make it sound a bit, clinical, in what could be a dreaded *do-goody* sort of way.' Then, as if some new thought has struck him, his tone changed. 'Haven't you ever come across some right bastard, someone who has done something really terrible, something inhuman, and haven't you ever had second thoughts about helping him?' He paused, before muttering, darkly, 'or her, for the sake of political correctness.'

And then, since she has not answered, 'I've never, ever heard you talk about that. You know, about having to deal with that sort of situation: and yet, you must, it must have happened many times in the hospital over the years that you were confronted by situations, things, people…'

'No. I can honestly say that that never happened. Perhaps it's because I am in the Medical Ward.' She knows he is thinking of victims of violence, of shootings and punishment beatings, who finish up in hospital. She carries on, 'I am away from lots of acute issues of the kind you might be thinking about, that others might meet more often. Anyway, it just does not cross your mind. A human being lies before you, needing attention – I have never known or heard of a nurse or a doctor or a technician or a porter or an ambulance-man – who refused to care for anyone, not in all the years I have been a nurse.' She smiles at him. She looks tired, he thinks. And then she says, 'It is what being a nurse is, really, it's about people and values: it's why the great and glorious NHS is there!'

'But why? How? I would have thought...'

'I know it sounds rather do-goody, feeble but it's what being a nurse is about; it's the underlying value we, nurses, human beings who are nurses, all hold to and work through, day to day. That's why I have always been proud, am still proud, to be a nurse.'

'Yes,' he countered, 'but can you put it down to being a nurse? I mean, you are, you were, a human being before you were a nurse. It's human instinct to look after people who are connected to you. People you know and trust, and who would help you if the need arose, before people you don't know, if only because you do know them and know how they feel, and you'll feel better by helping someone you know and who knows you.'

Robert replied, 'You say that, but others might not agree. Take James, for example. Have you ever looked at his library? There's a whole shelf devoted to Hobbes! You know, he of *Leviathan* fame – I think that that is the only one he has read, actually! When I went through that period at the University, you remember, I was doing the evening classes and studying philosophy, I remember telling James about Hobbes's views and saying how much I disagreed with them and how we as nurses cared for every patient equally and worked to make them better! We were 'doing' Hobbes (for one whole week!) at the time. Next thing, he's out buying Hobbes, and reading him, and quoting him – all that stuff about the need to put your own self first and the need for strong government…'

'Yes and *agreeing* with that! Or agreeing with what he thinks it means. Sometimes, with James, it's a simple but severe constriction of the imagination he's suffering from.'

'No,' she said, sadly. 'It's not James who suffers from that: it's me: the nurse whose profession is to heal and make people better, the survivor who is only half-alive.' She looks up at him, but he is gazing out across the river. 'I met that man this morning. I ran away. I couldn't face him. I had nothing to say to him. I needed to speak for Ruth – I let her down. I let myself down. I let him down, for he too needs healing.'

'Well,' Robert said, turning to look at her, and speaking with compassion 'I can tell you the NHS has no cure for that, and neither have you: if you had you would be inundated with patients, living in this place!'

***

Later that evening, after a phone call from Robert, after he arrived, after some sporadic small talk, and after they had sat in silence for a while, James spoke out of a heavy silence, 'Do you remember, when we were little, you and Ruth used to dance with your shadows? You would open the kitchen window and turn round the radio, so that it was facing out, and then we would all go into the back yard. There was a whitewashed wall there; if the sun was in the right position it cast shadows onto the white wall. Once, when I was there, I remember your mother came out and danced with you. I always liked that, it was… somewhat bohemian… for her to do that, you know…' His voice trailed off.

'Yes! Isn't it strange: I was thinking of this just the other day? Do you remember how she loved the Bee Gees? And the Beatles! She loved the Beatles most of all – but then, I remember, she would suddenly become shy and stop and just look, stare at us as if we were strangers. And we would dance for her and for ourselves, and the yard would be full of our cries. That was what I call happiness. A real jamboree of joy!'

'I know it does sound strange, but when I was very small, I remember I was really, really, terribly conscious of my shadow.' She glances up and sees that Robert is smiling, looking at the floor. She carries on. 'It seemed to go with me everywhere. Then, as I got older it seemed never to be there. Or, if it was there, I seemed not to be aware of it. I missed it! But then, I suppose, what is a shadow, after all? I mean, compared to mortgages and motor cars and pints of Guinness.' She broke off and gazed into nothingness.

'It was a good past, wasn't it?' She was speaking to James. Robert thought immediately that, despite what she says happened, this was Rebecca at her coolest, her most detached. Looking at her, he thinks he sees something different in the famous melted chocolate of those deep brown eyes – a heat, a fire, a glow that was more than a glow – there was a hard flint-like spark there. 'This really is Rebecca at her most remote yet most intense,' he thinks. 'It was,' he interrupted her, 'it was a good past; indeed, it was…' Despite himself, he hears his voice trailing off before he could reach the end of the sentence.

During this exchange, James watched them. Then, he put his elbows on the table, leaning forward, inserting his body between the other two in such a way as to almost exclude Robert. 'Yes,' he says, staring at her, 'it was a good past – but, Rebecca, the past is the past: you have to learn to leave the past behind you. You owe that to yourself.' He was going to say, 'you owe that to me', but stopped short. He spoke with an unusual intensity. 'You are what is important: I am sorry, but Ruth is dead. You are alive. You have to accept that fact. All this business of seeing, or of thinking you see her, in crowds, on the street, on stairs – it has got to stop. It's not good for you.'

Rebecca looked at him briefly but did not reply. She felt hurt and resentful. He doesn't know, she thought, bitterly, he doesn't know anything; he doesn't know about what happened yesterday, or about tomorrow's birthday party. He doesn't know I have decided to cancel our dinner. He doesn't know I want to have a party for two or he really would have something to get on his high horse about. He doesn't understand what my memory of Ruth is like. He does not understand that I remember her in my very bones, in my very flesh. He doesn't know I remember her absence in my flesh and bones, in my blood and brain.

But she remained silent; she did not intend to say any of this. She breathed deeply, then after a prolonged period of silence and of rising tension she replied, apparently coolly – candidly, James thinks. Remotely, Robert thinks.

'Look,' she said, 'we have known each other ...well, for ever, really and truly. I appreciate very much how both of you devote so much time to me and I truly love our times together. You are what sustains me. There is no noise, no fuss, no tension, no guilt, no striving, no competition, no power struggles...It's so comfortable, somehow, so egalitarian. Only...'

'Only... only, Ruth isn't here: or rather, Ruth is here!' James interrupted her, harshly, for him. 'Every time we sit down together, there is a fourth person present. Ruth or Ruth's ghost!'

Robert joined in, immediately, but more softly. 'Yes, perhaps you are right, Rebecca. Perhaps it is as egalitarian or democratic as you describe it, for we all share in it. But recently to me it's become more and more like a democracy of silence: we hear no evil; we certainly speak no evil. I sometimes think it just another aspect of the old Ulster shibboleth of whatever you say, say nothing thing. In fact, it is like a virus that has infected all of us – I sometimes feel like a nomad roaming over a strange land that doesn't belong to me, my tongue cut off...' Robert's face has grown flushed. He leaned back in his seat now, his eyes closed. James and Rebecca remained silent. He opened his eyes: they both look so strained, so uncomfortable, he thought. Then, suddenly, Robert leapt to his feet and addressed Rebecca: 'Look, I miss Ruth. Every day, I think of her. For a long time I was very, very angry. I still am angry.' He looked at Rebecca. 'Not against the person who killed her – I know you met him – to me he doesn't matter, he didn't even know her, but I am angry against the system of thought that believed that by killing her, and others like her, innocent people, the cause could achieve its goal...'

Tension saturated the room; it crackled like frosted grass.

'But that's all over. We have moved on. Things have changed. We have to move too, we have to change as well...' James, who evidentially was not really interested in what Robert had to say, interrupted: he was concerned with Rebecca, who looked pale and wan, who was sitting, or rather lying slumped in her seat, staring at the table. A feeling of great tenderness swept over him. He did something he had not done for a long time. Spontaneously he put his arm around her shoulder to comfort her. For a fraction of a second, she leaned into his arm, allowing her body weight to rest in the corner of his upper arm and chest. She fitted perfectly; for a moment, James felt a sudden spark of triumph, and as he felt this, he became aware of the treachery of such a feeling. Then she pulled away abruptly.

'I'm sorry,' he said, disturbed, straightening up in his seat.

'No. No.' she said. 'It's me who should be sorry.'

'Nothing is fair,' she added. She pauses, then, within moments, she continues, inconsequentially, 'One of the girls at work asked me to go to New York. To shop, to sightsee. I wouldn't go.'

James looked blank. He waits: the connection will emerge.

'I was – I am – afraid. I am afraid of flying, afraid of terrorist bombs. Just as I am afraid of you touching me. I am afraid of everything that lives, afraid of life itself!' She reaches out to put her hand to his cheek. 'I think… I think I have been living what they call an unexamined life. I have been dream-walking. I have no imagination. There is no creativity in me. I have been living in the past. I have been afraid to live, to really live, to explore the possibilities. And I think I'm dying for want of tenderness. For fear of love.'

James is red-faced and uncomfortable; Robert sits very still, staring at the floor. He is embarrassed for James, she thinks, they are both startled by my outburst.

She says, 'Look, I'm sorry, really sorry. It's late and I'm tired. I need to go to bed.' She pauses, before continuing, 'Something happened yesterday. It has kind of upset me. I'll explain to you about it some other time. What I want to say now is, about tomorrow – would you mind if I pulled out? I just don't feel like celebrating birthdays at the moment. And I want to go to bed.'

***

They have gone. The clock's insistent tick competes with the apartment's emptiness. She is alone. She stands by the open door, looking out across the river. Numerous lights illuminate the sky above the City Hall. She wonders what it is, then remembers. The scaffolding she saw earlier, outside the City Hall. It's the Proms. It is *The Proms in the Park*. It is that time of year, again. The people in different cities are being linked by music, she thinks. She feels suddenly very tired.

Earlier, after they left, she had stood for a while out on the balcony. A faint sound of music drifted across the river. The same waves of music pulsated through the night air as James walked back to where he had parked his car. The sound drew him, and on impulse he took a diversion and soon found himself standing across the street from the City Hall, looking directly at the big screen.

He stood for some time, shadowed in a doorway, listening to the music, then to the voice from London calling out, 'Welcome Cardiff, Welcome Glasgow, Welcome Belfast!' Then with a mighty noise a group of aircraft swooped by. He stood out on the street's edge, the better to see, hand shielding his eyes in order to divert some of the glare that the streetlamps threw out.

'The Red Arrows!' a nearby man explained, seeing James's questioning look. Immediately, James felt a mighty surge of pleasure. He is pleased that he is part of this great, webbed linkage of word and music, of technology and engineering; he rested on this feeling for a few moments, then he walked towards his car. It is late. It has been a long day. He feels the need of home. And, he has much to consider.

Robert, too, is on the road, heading towards his home. He is cocooned in the warmth of a taxi and is as unmindful of the concert as he is unaware of the presence of the Red Arrows. He is thinking about Ruth and Rebecca, about James and about himself. How or why did it all unravel, he wonders? There is no point in asking such a question, he answers, there are no rational answers. And, more importantly, what has happened to Rebecca?

Meanwhile, Rebecca stands alone on her balcony. She is aware of the planes sweeping in low over the City Hall. She is aware too of police sirens wailing across the rooftops; she hears an ambulance siren. Away to the west, red light reflects off the sky. Somewhere, she thinks, a house is on fire. She wonders if anyone has been injured or killed in the fire. She wonders about the cause. She thinks about the possible strain on hospital staff.

She steps inside. She has turned off the internal lights and as she enters she notices how the city lights throw multiple shadows across the walls of her white apartment. The grey-black shadows weave and dance an erratic whirl on the white walls as she stands there, silent, watchful.

Saturday

Long before he got up on Saturday morning, as he lay awake and restless in the hour before daybreak, Robert had half decided to discuss matters with James. But then, an hour later, he had half decided not to mention his concerns to James.

He got up, let the dogs out, took a stroll around the front of the cottage, mulled things over and then, when he started to shiver, for he is still wearing his pyjamas, returned indoors.

He had not slept at all well, worrying about Rebecca, remembering Ruth, concerned by the bits and pieces of the story he has gleaned about Rebecca's still untold, still mysterious meeting, and her subsequent and decided edginess yesterday. He feels edgy himself. He fears she may be about to go over the edge. By eleven thirty he is so concerned about Rebecca that now he has decided firmly that he will talk over the situation with James. He plans to travel by bus: partly because his car is playing up again but also because he has decided he will splurge out today. First, he thinks, he will travel into the city, have a drink and then go to James's house. He makes a quick phone call, locks the cottage door, hides the key under a square stone that always sits beside the doorstep and then sets off towards the lane that leads to the road and eventually to the bus stop.

Taking a shortcut across the grass on his way to the lane Robert feels the usual sense of pride at the state of the old place. When he arrived, it had been throughother and uncared for but now it is neat and tidy. He stops for a moment to look at the pond. Years ago, one of his neighbours had referred to it as 'a glaar hole'. This is not a term that endeared itself to Robert. It reminded him of a place full of mud, stinking and weed-infested. Robert had immediately taken up the challenge of cleaning it out that first summer: 'All done, and by my own fair hand', he told Rebecca, but in fact he had enlisted the help of a neighbour who owned a JCB. This was something she knew well enough (and he knew she knew) but there was enough truth in his boast to allow him the claim. For, 'in all honesty' he had done a lot of it himself and when he finished his hands were calloused from the unusual contact with the wooden handle of the shovel and his back was sore and his muscles were stiff from the filling and carrying of buckets of mud. Because of this work he discovered that the pond was fed by a tiny spring well that bubbled up, slowly but constantly, keeping the water fresh and clear, now that it was properly maintained. He liked to stand and look at it sometimes and, while he could not see the spring bubbling away, just to know it was there, beneath the surface, to have such a life force here on his own bit of land, always gave him a little, flowering, sense of pleasure.

He passed the little wood, 'the Plantation', as he called it. This was where, years since – what was it… fifteen or sixteen years ago? – Rebecca had come one day with bags of clothes. After the funeral Ruth's possessions had been a worry to her. Her constant concern was 'what should I do with them?' He remembered her saying to him that to do anything would seem to be an act of betrayal, an acceptance that Ruth would never again have need for them. 'A final acceptance, an agreement of a kind, that she is dead,' was the way she put it.

He knew, in his heart, that Rebecca was not then ready, or able, to sign off her sister's death. So, for a time, things were left as they were. Their presence provided continuity, and continuity was important for her, he knew, just as it was for James.

At that time, grief-stricken as he himself was, he watched Rebecca carefully. He regarded Ruth's clothes as a kind of measure. For the first year she continued to do nothing about them. For most of the second year she did nothing, but on the eve of the third anniversary she burst into sudden activity and cleared out the wardrobe and drawers. She kept nothing for herself: it had not crossed her mind that she might, and that he understood.

That was when she came here with her bags. She gathered many things – dresses, jeans, underwear, stockings, sports socks used with runners, shoes worn down at the left heel, old jumpers with holes or runs in the sleeves – out here to the country to this spinney, and there she burned them. He had offered to help, but she had refused.

He knew she had kept two good dresses and a very good suit bought, but never worn, for the anticipated interview that would one day come up. She had shown them to James and himself once, saying she could not bear to burn them. Eventually, he thought, she had come to terms even with these and had promised to take them to a charity shop from where someone might find them useful. She took them to the door of the shop, delayed, then brought them home and hung them in the wardrobe where they hung still, as far as he knew, in silence and stillness. She could not bear to think of someone else wearing Ruth's clothes.

'And now, all these years later when we thought it was all coming to an end, the shadow of her death remains, still lies over the three of us – over Rebecca in particular, as this weekend is showing,' he thinks. He makes his way over the grass to the loanen – this is how he always thinks of it, it's what his grandfather called it. It has not changed in years, not since his grandparent's time; still the grassy middle strip; still the hollowed-out tracks made by successive generations of vehicles; still the thick, trimmed hedges of thorn and ash studded with bits of holly; still the two old beech trees at the entrance. Today its verges are thick with black and green and red blackberries. The haws are still small and green. He hears pigeons in the nearby trees, he sees a flock of crows drive past. Magpies chatter in a far-off hedgerow. He feels contentment here. But he is leaving all this behind to go to into the city, something he never, or very seldom, does on a Saturday morning.

It is nearly twelve o'clock when he arrives at his first destination, the junction of his little side road and the main road that runs to Belfast. Immediately, he notices three boys waiting by the bus stop. He sits down on the grassy top of a stone ditch opposite. Two boys are sitting on the stone wall that stands on their side of the road, legs dangling, leaning back, resting on braced arms, hands to the side and behind. The third boy has a football that he bounces, dribbles, occasionally spinning it with one hand with the easy skill of a basketball player. Now and then, he puts his foot on it, stopping play, taking ownership of the action; Robert recognizes this, admiring the control; admiring, too, the poise of natural leadership. The boy stops, his hands thrust now into the back pocket of his jeans, while he speaks to the others. The two on the wall remain unmoving – like figures in a painting, Robert thinks – then the one with the ball moves again, swaying, turning with a little sashay, a little swagger, engaging in a little dance of bravado, a little acknowledgement of his ability.

As he watches them, smiling, there is something he can only describe to himself as beautiful, something to do with in the way the boy handles the ball: the coordination of hand and eye, the interaction of body and ball, the poise of a ballet dancer, the effortless out-turn of skill embedded in perfect and unconscious coordination of hand, eye, foot and brain.

The focus of concentration shifts in a continuous flow; now it is on the boy with the ball and his action, the others still, watching; now their collective attention shifts easily to the ebb and flow of conversation. It is like the undercurrent that one finds in the ocean, he thinks. Yes, I feel like I am on a boat, carried to the shore by the relentless strength of an unseen tide.

All the while, they talk. He can see the intensity that underpins the exchanges. There is something right about the scene that lies under his scrutiny and something pleasing about the way its elements come together to form a little, unimportant tableau, and one held together by this unseen but real and positive current of energy.

'What do they have to talk about?' he wonders, 'they are so young, their lives can't have produced much experience – they are too inexperienced to be able to talk of love, of sex, of money, of success or of failure? What can they know of life and death? What would they make of the reason for my being here, on my way to see James to talk about Rebecca, to help her to try to come to terms with something that happened before they were born?'

They are blind to his presence. They carry on, intensely yet casually. 'No,' he thinks angrily, 'I do them an injustice: the human mind is capable of empathy. I do believe they would understand, if told. They are innocent enough still to believe they understand... they would believe in the fiction of their own belief… and without knowing it is a fiction… But is that right?' he wonders, 'The young have an instinctive response to life, a response that is there before we grow into the learned response…'

He tries to remember what he was like at that age. The four of them had left primary school. The others had gone off to the grammar school, he, alone, had gone to the secondary school. They still met, but with decreasing frequency; by the time 'A' levels began to kick in he hardly ever saw them. He had vague memories of a party, of a disastrous introduction to alcohol, then of the others going off to different third level educational institutions. From that time, they really did go their separate ways – for a bit. For a bit. Then, somehow, they were all together, once more. But they had always been there, really, always there for one another.

With feelings of a sudden pleasure, he recalls the intensity of that kind of youthful engagement, an engagement that, when it found life, when it came into being, somehow stood outside time. He thinks of Ruth, of how they had enjoyed life, uncaring, abandoned; she had been his girl, he had been her boy – it had always been like that, would always be like that; they gave no thought to it and how good it had been. How could these lads stand outside time? Now that she was gone and that time is something that exists only as a memory, it could not be relived. He feels a quick stab of bitterness, but the moment passes. Then, he feels foolish: he realises he has just experienced jealousy, nothing more or less than base jealousy, brought about by three boys and a ball!

He sees time congregate around them, and they, oblivious to the growing swarms of seconds, minutes, hours. He sees old men: he sees old women; he knows he should not and wishes he did not, but there they are, waiting patiently in his mind's eye, waiting for those boys, waiting for him, for Rebecca, for James. Expecting redemption.

He seems to be always thinking this weekend about Ruth. There is something in the air, a rawness that has suddenly emerged. He remembers how, last year, at this time, on her birthday and Rebecca's birthday, they had celebrated quietly but without any strain. Yet yesterday there was such tension in the air, and Rebecca's abrupt cancellation of the birthday dinner was strange indeed.

Then the bus draws up, obscuring the boys from his view. After a few moments it pulls away, taking him and them with it, leaving the bus stop bare and vacant, waiting without any other purpose for whoever might next turn up.

In Belfast, he left the bus station and crossed over Victoria Street to the Crown Bar, which had just opened its doors. Inside, all was gloomy, dark and polished, like the inside of a church, he thought. What little light there was fell off the ceilings and off the many mirrors, it seeped and dripped off the bottles and glasses. Men entered and the noise of conversations quickly grew and mixed with the reflections of light, leaving a cocktail of colour and sound. What should be a pandemonium of sense impressions was strangely quietening, he thought. It creates a virtual web made up of little pockets of noise and light. They occupy the room, filling the otherwise empty spaces that might exist between the numerous customers.

He ordered another pint of Guinness and took it back to an empty little snug near the door; here he sat alone, closely observing his surroundings. The floor in the snug was of black and white tiles, old, small and rectangular tiles that reminded him of something. The windows were made of many pieces of coloured glass through which light struggled, to fall at last, strained and exhausted on the interior. The delicate structure of the windows stands at odds with the heavy, blackened ceiling, their precision contrasting with the crude scrawls and hackings in the mahogany from which the walls and doors are constructed. In the far corner two circular windows had been set into the wall; each one showed evidence of strange, cabbalistic marks. Or were they Masonic symbols? That's it, he thought. He looked down at the floor, remembering his grandfather being in the Masons and vaguely recalling talk about the symbolic significance of black and white, the black and white directly representing day and night, good and evil.

He signalled to the barman for another pint of Guinness. He had brought a newspaper from the counter and now glanced at it but could find nothing of interest. He looked again at the decoration in the snug: it had many glass panels, set into its walls, with two large windows in the end wall. The sunlight streamed through in an unexpected burst. The glass became alive. To his potter's eye the place had become a cornucopia of fruitfulness: dark green apples sat beside strawberry-coloured strawberries, pineapples and grapes tumbled over the edges of cups, a robin stood jauntily on a branch. The few bright reds, together with the browns and sun-washed yellows and rain-faded greens, merged into one another. In the window, two sketched faces, cheeks ballooned, reminding him of the pictures of the wind he looked at in childhood comic books, sit beside two fishes that stand on their heads. Time stands still. He orders another drink, even though he knows he should not.

Later, Robert felt rather tipsy as he entered into Cornmarket. I have spent too long in the Crown, he thinks. Now, he sits down on a bench, enjoying the sense of light-headedness, enjoying the unusual warmth of the autumn sunshine, enjoying the sense of life and bustle. He enjoys his life on the farm, but he also enjoys people and watching people, wondering about them, making up little stories, divining their histories.

The sight of a man wearing an oddly shaped hat caught his attention. To his, admittedly slightly out-of-focus eye, the man appeared as a curiosity – not quite of average height and plumper than most, his rotundity constrained within the silo of a close-fitting, fully buttoned and carefully zip-fastened three-quarter length coat. He might be aged forty or fifty: he might be sixty. He walked with his arms held motionless by his side. The buckled coat-belt followed the extremity of his midriff and being of a slightly different hue, acted, to Robert's potter's eye, as an unfortunate measure designed to guide the onlooking eye as to the extent of his slightly rolling motion.

On his head he wore an old-fashioned and, it had to be admitted, slightly-the-worse-for-wear felt hat, and upon the hat's crown, naturally, or so it appeared, was built a little windmill. The windmill spun when the light wind caught it properly and squarely and in order to make it spin to its ultimate ability the man, as he walked with his rolling gait, moved his head continually in a ducking fashion, in order that the windmill and the wind should met in productive harmony. When the union was successful, the red and white and blue blades raced in a virtual rainbow of colour. He smiles, and his smile seemed to Robert to be truly beatific. His rolling motion, his bobbing head, his persistent smile, each of these appeared as a separate thing that ebbed and flowed about his person, and yet, Robert thought, together they are what make him as he is. He was a happy person; his face still wore that smile. In his happy journey across the city square, he was oblivious to the throng through which he passed, and unaware of the great and serious weight of granite and cement and steel that marshalled his passage through mercantile Belfast.

From the back streets, Robert thinks. Just then, an empty Coke can flew through the air and hit the man on the shoulder. Robert jumped up in time to see a few youngsters run off, a few girls and a few boys, hoots of laughter filling the air suddenly then quickly disappearing. Robert felt a quick flicker of anger; the haters and begrudgers are getting younger, he thinks, but the man did not seem to notice what had happened and kept on in his pitching and rolling journey.

'How strange,' Robert thinks, 'how utterly unknowable are the pleasures that are given birth to and live within each individual head.' He is genuinely bemused by the boys' and girls' behaviour and by their idea of fun, then by the man. Is this man as mad or as eccentric as he appears? 'Who isn't a bit mad?' He asks himself, rhetorically. 'No, of course he is not mad,' he answers his own question; 'he is obviously just what my mother would have called 'simple' – simple-minded and happy, totally unselfconscious and fulfilled, in a state of innocence. Did he have dreams,' Robert wonders, 'did he have a vision for what his life might be, could be? In addition, is it not strange how the stupid, the senseless, the bullies, the cowards, always pick on the odd, the simple, the innocent, and the oblivious? The tin can lies where it fell, numerous well-shod feet stepping over it as they pass by.

Robert starts up. Later, he might, if he remembers, tell Rebecca about what he had seen, what he has thought; he might describe the man in detail. It is the kind of story she would normally find both humorous and touching. It would depend on how he might couch it. Yes, he might talk to her about this, or he might not.

As he walks along his thoughts keep coming back to the man and to Rebecca. He thinks he might tell her there is a truth beyond the various 'truths' put forward by all the self-righteous, the self-promoters, the scared, the blinded and blinkered, the merely vicious and the stupid: all those who operate the blame-game we have become so skilled at, over the years. We should, he thinks, feeling the bitterness swelling up from his stomach, construct a common memorial to our skill at playing the unending blame game.

He is aware he feels tired. He realises he has been tottering on the edge of sleep, dreaming again; he sits down on another bench. 'Too much drink, too early in the day,' he thinks, smiling. He looks at his watch. It is well after two o'clock. Now, he thinks, it really is time to rouse himself and call on James. Robert considers a bus, and then decides to take a taxi out to James's house. Although he has been more times than he could count, as he approaches the house he takes careful note of his surroundings, observing each detail. He commits to memory a record of what he sees; he compares it to what was and notes any changes, although there will be few changes to note, he is sure, apart from the houses. His family home has gone, demolished and replaced by a stand of town houses and apartments. Rebecca's family house still stands, but in the garden someone has built another substantial house. A little down the road, an estate has erupted boils of multi-formed houses. James's house, it seems, is the last remaining one of the five big houses that once stood here; it seems overpowered by modernity.

The taxi drops him off at the entrance. He notes the familiar pillars with the original wrought iron gates, painted shining black. Robert tries the gates, but they are securely locked, stopping his only way through the high stonewall that stretches to left and right, jagged slates set into its top.

He can see a short but powerfully sweeping granite-kerbed driveway that leads to a wide, cobbled, parking area.

Robert presses the button on the intercom and within moments James's voice issues from the little grill.

'Yes?'

'It's me, Robert.'

'Robert? Come in, come in.'

With a smooth, unerringly silent action, the gates swing open, and Robert makes his way through and along the pathway. The front gardens slope sedately and in an unbroken line towards a stand of trees and through the gaps between their trunks, and in contrast to the black of the gates, he can just make out the steely grey waters of Belfast Lough. The grounds are laid out in the form of lawns, edged by mature trees and shrubs. Along one side there is a balanced pattern of six formal flowerbeds. The flowerbeds are empty, brown earth raked, weed-free, and flower-free. To one side a little orchard of apples trees stand; six trees to be precise, for Robert counts them, or rather, counts them implicitly, as he notices they form an octagonal-shaped pattern. It's strange, he thinks, he has never noticed that before.

It is a large, solid, detached house; its thick walls are finished in grey plasterwork with wooden, white painted sash windows; it is stoutly roofed in Bangor blue slates. It is, he thinks, exactly what an estate agent would describe as a 'handsome period house set in spacious grounds' and surrounded by tall, rather elegantly-built, stone walls, though to his taste it is rather heavy and perhaps a bit dull. It is obviously a very well-maintained property. He approaches the entrance. The door is open; the brass knocker gleams and the stone steps glisten with little bits of granite chips, polished by decades of use and years of regular scrubbing.

He mounts the steps and as he enters the open porch, with its twin pillars, he notes above the door the white, oval plaque that gives in ornate, black-painted numerals what he takes to be the year of the house's construction, '1898'. This is new, he thinks.

He peers inside. The hall floor is of black and white slabs, set out in uniform rows, like old-fashioned lozenges. Off to one side there is, given the scale of the hall, what always seems to his eye to be a rather meagre staircase with many uniformly thin but glossy-white spindles and a rather heavy mahogany balustrade. The half landing is visible, but he is barely conscious of it for his attention is caught by the large stained-glass window that lets in waves of coloured light.

He steps inside. It is unusual to find James's door open. He calls out, 'James!' An answering call comes from upstairs. He wanders into what was the drawing room but is now referred to by James as 'the library'. It is a square room and has the original marble fireplace intact, with its cast iron inset; light reflects off the tiled hearth, while the polished French oak floor also picks up the lingering light (the heavy curtains are drawn, even though it is only just past midday) in whose presence everything in the room seems to glow and gleam.

The ceiling is high and defined by a deep, plain cornice. Between the picture rail and a dado rail the two longer walls are hung with orderly rows of framed prints, watercolours and drawings. Off to one side and intruding into the bay stands a partner's desk; its leather top, devoid of papers, glows in sympathy under the light that falls in from outside.

James enters. 'I see you got in – I left the door open while I attended to a small domestic matter.'

So, that explains James's absence, Robert thinks, absentmindedly. 'Nae bother,' he replies, knowing that James hates what he always refers to as 'the vernacular'. He feels in a rebellious, vindictive mood, not helped by the locked gates, something he had forgotten about until now, and James is here – miraculously – as an object, a target for that mood. For a moment they engage in exchanging scraps of gossip. Then, as they leave the library, Robert points to an array of framed pictures hung on one wall. They almost cover it entirely. 'A dinnae think ah've seen these afore.'

'Yes,' replies James, again ignoring the attempt to rile him. 'Hugh Thomson – he is an interesting character. He was born in Coleraine and began his career with an apprenticeship to Marcus Ward & Co. here in Belfast before moving to London in the 1880s.' James is showing off, Robert knows. He allows him to continue, his demeanour that of the lord of the manor, his tone that of a formal lecturer. Perhaps he too feels vindictive or rebellious today, Robert thinks. But he too ignores James's attempt to rile him.

The voice rises slightly. '*The English Illustrated Magazine*, which was owned by Macmillan. Randolph Caldecott, the illustrator of children's books, was already on the staff, and Thomson was influenced by his style. Thomson illustrated a series on the character Sir Roger de Coverley and one on *Coaching Days and Ways*, both later published as books. He was very good at depicting horses.'

'I didn't know you were a horsey man?' said Robert, rather surprised. He is conscious that he is rapidly experiencing deep boredom mixed with growing irritation. So, if that's the case James is winning this little game! he thinks. You never know with James, he's so phlegmatic, or he's so slippery, or he's inscrutable: I never really know what to make of him...

James continues to be oblivious to everything outside his own self. His voice re-emerges into Robert's consciousness: 'I am not, really, and not in the sense I think you mean. I do like to see skilled work and his line is very alive, yet very delicate. I came across Thompson's work in children's books and then again when I read Austen... Jane Austen, you know... I've been collecting him for years, quietly you know, and I kept these at the office until recently. I've been rearranging things a bit lately, so I brought them home.'

Robert nods, listening dutifully, maintaining an attitude of interest, while thinking, 'What pretentious twaddle! And when did you ever collect things 'quietly'? And when did you ever read Jane Austen?' But James, Robert can see, is on a roll – as they say in the movies – and so he stays silent and allows him to carry on. 'His work has imagination and humour, but above all he has what I would classify as charm; his drawings are charming. For me, he helps my imagination bring alive a world that is sadly long lost, except in the works of... say... Dickens.'

They move into the kitchen where James pours Robert a cup of coffee from the gurgling percolator. 'I suppose, what really intrigues me about Thompson, beyond a genuine liking for his work, which is charming and humorous and skilful – in fact, all the things I have spoken about on previous occasions to you – what intrigues me is what I might call his example, his trajectory through life. He was born and educated here, in small town Ulster, and went on to become a force in his own field in London and New York.'

Robert makes a reply, of sorts: 'Well, he's not alone in that, is he? I could name you a good dozen…'

James retorts abruptly. 'Oh, yes, I know the men you mean! Not one of them has a flaw…' Robert feels the beginning of a tremor, a little tingle in the air; he feels irritated enough to interrupt James, in turn: 'What flaw? Or flaws? What about James Galway, or Samuel Ferguson, or the thirteen presidents we gave to the United States…?'

'You know very well who I mean – George Best, Alex Higgins, Van Morrison – Oh yes, men of talent, no doubt, men of genius, perhaps, but each one of them to me marred by a character flaw! You may talk about tragic genius… it seems that character chaos is an intrinsic part of some of our characters – or maybe it's no more than lack of rigour, a want of personal discipline. Anyway, it's a weakness that repeatedly shows itself!'

Robert is stung into replying, rather too hotly, 'Well, there you are. I could ask you what you have ever accomplished, but I won't!'

'Keep to the point, can't you?'

'Look, I don't read much, but when I read something that I agree with, I make a point of remembering it! I noticed you have a copy of this.' He held up a copy of an Ulster Scots grammar. 'Did Rebecca give it to you? She gave me one, as well.'

He goes to a shelf and brings back a green-jacketed book. He opens it and searches for a bit, before reading, 'The inhabitants much resemble the Scots in their habits, customs and dialect. They are rather dogged, obstinate and blunt.' That was written in the 1830s! About the inhabitants of this county, County Antrim! So, you are absolutely correct – we are dogged, obstinate and blunt, and we produce some of the best fiddle-players in Ireland! Some people have trouble in accepting the simple fact of who we are. I'll concede there are bits of mongrel mixed up with bits of genius... creativity, endeavour, tenacity, entrepreneurship – visionary individuals, all of them.'

But James ignores all this, or at least he ignores the fervour with which it is uttered. He carries on calmly. 'No, the age he lived in is what adds interest to Thompson's story. To me it's a story about progress built upon a foundation of integration. A great social movement based on planned development. For example, the rise of mass education in the Victorian era led to a greater demand for reading matter, including popular reading materials, and the demand for reading matter led to more books, and that, coupled with new techniques for printing led to more new publications – essentially the mechanisation of printing.'

'Whatever you are talking about here sounds to me like old-fashioned political statement, or good old-fashioned nostalgia... whatever it is, you are longing for things long gone – forever,' Robert replies. 'To me, the past is the past – at least, I want to make it that way. I want to recognise an enduring quality of character when it's here, now...' The telephone rings, abruptly interrupting him; James, with a dismissive wave of his hand, hurries off to answer it. Robert takes the opportunity to wander about the house. The whole establishment, he realises once again, but then he realises this afresh each time he comes here, is what he regards as a mind-numbing testimony to physical order and domestic efficiency. He pushes open a door and enters a room that has, among a small regiment of easy chairs, two long sofas facing each other. Two identical rows of cushions are displayed, neatly – static, dead, he thinks, unused and untouchable – and he involuntarily compares this room to his own, with its easiness and its throughother mess of habitation.

But this stasis extends beyond the merely domestic, important as that might be to its owner. It is something that runs across the entire face of James's world. His emotional canvas, Robert thinks, is so austere, so lacking in ordinary human chaos... surely, he was not born like this? He must have caught the disease from human contact – his family, perhaps? Yes, his family, and those who formed his cultural background.

Through the open door he can see the hall and its floor. Even the plain black and white tiles, a relatively recent addition and installed only a few years ago, connect their owner to the Masonic order in some obscure way that remains, partly at least, a mystery to Robert.

James gave him a long, sideways glance and seemed about to continue the conversation but then he recalled the image on the upstairs landing. He thinks he knows the significance of the black and white: balance, order, day and night, good and evil. What would happen, he wonders idly, if someone or something were to smash a hole in this surface of such an apparently tranquil world ord? He allows his imagination to freewheel: what maelstrom of hungers, what fearsome appetites might be released? None, he decides, with a grimace: it is a self-healing thing, this kind of order, it is something that would regenerate itself instantly and James would hardly be aware that anything had happened.

He turns away thinking, as he emerges into the hall, that it would be like thrusting your fist into a basin of water then withdrawing it and watching the notional space left filling up, effortlessly.

'Have you finished your coffee?' said James as he reappeared. 'Let's go into the garden. The sun should still be well up over Cave Hill. When it gets low, the hill throws a shadow.' On the way-out James, apparently impetuously, takes Robert's arm and steers him into another of his many rooms. There he points to a round, mahogany table that supports a similarly round glass-topped cabinet.

'I said I'd been reorganising things; I want you to see my other collection.' James points to a row of particularly pretty buttons. 'These are Calico buttons; they belong to the class of clothing buttons known to collectors as 'utilitarian Chinas'. Until the 1840s, China buttons or porcelain,' (here he points to another row) 'were moulded by hand – as you can imagine that made them expensive objects, luxury items in fact. Then, in 1840, if my memory serves me right, an Englishman named Richard Prosser invented a way to mass-produce China buttons. This new method involved using a mould to press dry China clay into various shapes. The buttons were then glazed and fired. The result of Prosser's invention was a cheap and sturdy article…'

'Isn't it odd,' Robert interrupts him, 'How attached one can become, to buttons?' He glances at the other, but James does not seem to notice the sly half pun. Robert carries on: 'Isn't it odd that we both make our living from working on the same sort of material. Clay, glazes and heat! The only difference is the things you make protect their users from immodesty, and I aspire to an opposite effect, when possible!'

James again ignores this. 'Well, you may still work in the old ways, but it has changed, for me. Now buttons are made from a variety of materials – they are mostly manufactured in the Far East – what's not, nowadays? And in Greece and Germany – increasingly, and especially for up-market goods.

I remember my father going off on buying trips, but that has all stopped now. Today I buy them in bulk and add value by dying and polishing them. The polishing hasn't changed though: we put bamboo shoots into a large drum, together with the buttons, and spin the lot around and around.'

James shifted his focus, as if wanting to leave the old methods behind. 'We do a lot of laser work on buttons now, to customise them.'

'Very creative!'

'Well, to tell you the truth, it's a way to help our customers avoid paying tax if, as happens, a company or school logo is cut into the button, they are not subject to taxation!' There is a pause in the conversation and then, 'Americans like things made in Ireland,' James says, in a musing kind of way. Robert does not feel it requires a response. Instead, he points to where two rows of particularly majestic buttons are set out slightly apart from the others.

'Ah, those are Military Dress Uniform buttons. I have a particular interest in collecting those. There are many Irish regiments represented there. We never did supply dress uniform buttons. Though, we did install a small laboratory a number of years ago to help us make buttons for the services.'

'Why did you need a lab?'

'Well, we had to do additional tests for durability, dye tests, boil-washing tests – to ensure that the buttons did not weep off into the cloth behind.'

'Buttons! Weeping! Ruth! Rebecca!' Wild thoughts race through his mind. His head is throbbing, and he feels tired and heavy. Robert turns away to stare out of the window, leaving James to carefully close the lid on his display cabinet.

***

Eventually, and having returned their cups to the kitchen, they make their way out and into the garden. James seems reluctant to leave the house, but they have both become restless and discontented and as they stroll across the lawn Robert suggests they go for a drink. In doing so, he comes to the point of his visit. 'It's about Rebecca. Did you know she called me yesterday? Just before lunchtime. I dropped what I was doing and went over. She seemed to suggest it was urgent. When I arrived, we just talked.'

James stopped, looking closely at Robert. 'Is she alright? What was it about?'

'The truth is, I don't know what it was about. She seemed upset but wouldn't go into detail. And then, on top of all that, she has cancelled our get-together for her – should I say, for her and Ruth's – birthday!'

'It's strange,' James said. 'I do know she had some kind of meeting planned for the other day, on Thursday, I believe. It had something to do with Ruth's death, but again, she didn't go into detail when she mentioned it to me. Look, let's go into town and we'll call on her and try to find out what's up.'

They make their way back to the house where James locks up. Getting into the car, they crunch down the gravel drive and leave, the gates swinging open and then closing behind them.

'I see the great unwashed are closing in on you,' observes Robert as they pass another new housing development.

'There's room for all of us,' James replies, looking at him narrowly.

'Yes. There's room for them, as long as they leave your apples alone!'

***

James drives them both into Belfast. On the way he gives Robert his mobile phone to call Rebecca but there is no reply. When they arrive, they go for a quick snack, since Robert has not eaten all day and is steadily feeling the effects of his early drinking. On the way back to the car a group of men and women standing on a street corner catch their attention. They are singing a hymn, while one of the men plays a guitar. By unspoken consent Robert and James stop for a moment to watch and listen. The singing stops and one of the men steps forward. He carries a small microphone in his hand. The others seem to physically withdraw, with the effect of placing the preacher in the foreground. He is a man of average stature, in his mid to late fifties. He wears nondescript grey pullover, white open-necked shirt and grey trousers. He is coatless, despite the sharp air, and they can see a pile of coats resting on the pavement. He speaks, or rather half-speaks, half-sings, in a mid-transatlantic accent.

'They are here every Saturday,' Robert says 'Yer man there, the Preacher, is a great turn. I listened to him a few times when they have been here.' Despite his small stature the man has a powerful voice, one that grows stronger as it becomes increasingly energised by a kind of evangelical fervour.

'Friends, I want to speak to you about personal experience. I want to plead with you to seek out personal experience, and then to listen to it. No less a man than the Dean of St Paul's Cathedral in London had a personal experience. I want to tell you about his experience. John Donne was a great preacher because he was a great communicator. When he spoke of Hell, he spoke of what he knew. As a young man in his early twenties, he sailed to Spain to fight against the new armada. He watched as the besieged crew of a Spanish ship tried to escape their blazing wreck. He watched them plunge into the burning sea. That memory has never left him. When he spoke of the inferno, what he spoke of was that personal experience – Cadiz, 1596. 'Friends,' Robert hears the words rising in a mixture of exhortation and menace. But are they spoken by the preacher or by Donne? He hears the voice, he sees the figure, in real evangelical mode now, his right hand raised, his brow furrowed, his eye flashing, 'who among you has had an experience such as this!'

Robert merely shakes his head and moves away, followed close by James who soon steps to one side of the pavement to use his mobile phone to call Rebecca again. This time she answers, and he quickly arranges to meet her.

'Let's go,' he urges Robert, who is laughing. 'Where else, but Belfast, would you hear a street preacher give a sermon based on John Donne?'

'Where else, indeed!' James grimaces.

'It's a unique place, sure enough! Where else could they have built the Titanic and be proud of it?!'

'Indeed; anyway, let's get on.'

'Where else could you have so much secular Protestantism, alive and well...and so little protest-ing? Against the things they should protest!'

'Are you sure you have that right? Do you not mean so much pro-test-antism! Is there anything we don't protest about?'

***

They arrive at Rebecca's flat. She greets them warmly, though she appears to be surprised by their unexpected visit. She is dressed in jeans and jumper, and her feet are bare. Robert looks around the room and immediately notices an ashtray on the table; he knows Rebecca does not normally smoke but decides not to say anything. She offers them coffee but they both refuse. Then James spots the ashtray.

'Have you had visitors?' he asks.

'No,' Rebecca replies, but refuses to advance any further information. They sit, while an awkward silence grows. Robert is looking at Rebecca out of the corner of his eye. The cigarette has awakened a long-forgotten memory of their childhood.

'Do you remember your Uncle Fleming Fulton?' he asks suddenly of James. 'Do you remember his shop?'

'Of course I do! Cigarettes and newspapers. The newspapers were the *Newsletter* and the *Belfast Telegraph*, the cigarettes were Woodbines, in packets of five and ten and twenty – 'Woodbines' and 'Park Drive' and 'Players Plain' and 'Gallagher Greens' – isn't it strange how their names are embedded, still, in my memory...'

'Yes', indeed,' says Rebecca. 'Capstan, for example, or Senior Service...Do you remember the colour of the packets? I never smoked – well, I never smoked much – but I do still remember the various colours – and the names, and the shapes of the names.'

Robert smiled. 'I smoked, for a bit, and it's strange how you become attached to the shape and form of something like a cigarette packet – the colour, the shape of typeface, the slogans... You internalise such things, they become a part of who you are... they grow to be like old, deeply dependable friends... it's true what they say, old friends are the best.'

'You're never alone with a Strand...,' says James, smiling.

'Ourselves alone...' Robert replies, instantly.

'Not an inch...' says James

'Brand loyalty!' laughs Robert!

They are silent. Robert thinks how James can be human, sometimes, funny even. He smiles. He recalls, in some detail, James's Uncle Fleming. For as long as any of them can remember, James's father's only relation – everyone called him Uncle Fleming Fulton, though he was really James's father's cousin – lived above his newsagents shop in east Belfast, on one of the major pedestrian arteries that led to the shipyard. In his day, men generally walked to work, or came by public transport, and whatever way they came they had to walk past his shop. Over the years it was a real money-spinner.

Uncle Fleming was short and plump and habitually wore a curious green, beige apron over a striped shirt and grey flannel trousers. He had a great mop of untidy, boyish-looking hair that made him look a lot younger than he really was. There was something about him that was difficult to pin down, something almost girlish. James and his father made a habit of visiting him about once a year and he came very occasionally to the house. It's strange, he thinks, but James's mother never liked him and never went to visit him or his shop.

His premises were on a corner where two streets met; the building had two doors, and he had it organised so that his customers came in one and out the other. His customers were made up almost entirely of shipyard workers and to them he sold the essentials of life – namely, morning and evening newspapers as well as cigarettes, tobacco and matches. The silence is becoming oppressive.

'To get back to Uncle Fleming,' Robert says, 'I went with you to his shop a few times – we must have been at primary school. I remember that shop counter: brown, wooden, scratched, battered, very old... well, very old to us, then. My head barely reached to its top. I remember the little avenue between the counter and what to me seemed like a wall of old newspapers. There was only room for people to approach the counter in single file.'

'Yes. I remember the newspapers clearly! He never did throw anything out. Not even those old papers. When he died we found the house and shop stacked to the ceiling with them. It was like a paper museum. I remember the smell of old paper, and the dust – terrible! The strange thing is, he was so clean and tidy. Personally, I mean. Always the fresh shirt. Shoes polished daily.'

Robert, looking over his shoulder, and winking at Rebecca, asks, 'Didn't I hear somewhere that he sold other things – apart from newspapers and fags?'

'Oh, yes. Well, you know he did provide what could be termed an important social service to the shipyard workers!' James replied. Rebecca, who knows well enough what Uncle Fleming was supposed to have sold, asks in apparent innocence, 'What kind of social service are you talking about?'

There is silence for a few moments. Then, knowing James will not answer, Robert responds, 'It was said that he sold contraceptives, and he was supposed to sell what at that time were referred to as *dirty magazines*! He kept them under that indecently innocent brown, wooden counter. I remember, when I was at Art College, it was well known as the one place to go if you wanted anything of that sort – in east Belfast, at least.'

James listens in silence, his head thrown back, his gaze directed towards the ceiling. Then he says, 'You know, it's all very well laughing at these things and I know what you are trying to do, but people like Uncle Fleming did perform a useful service. In those days, where were you to find things like – well – what you call 'dirty books' or contraceptives?'

'Yes,' replies Robert, 'And his last social service was to die and leave you and your Da a great big pile of filthy lucre!' And laughing, and then slapping the leather armrest, 'I'd say, it takes more than buttons to pay for your life style, old boy!'

James smiles, but stonily so. He rises to his feet and says, 'Look, Rebecca, I must go. I promised to meet one of my friends. Arranged it this morning, after you called off the birthday do. We are planning a reunion for some of the men in the Regiment so we've agreed to meet to discuss it, to make arrangements. I see you are fine. I thought something might be wrong, seeing you cancelled the party…'

'No, I'm, alright. Thanks for coming. I am becoming a terrible nuisance, I know.'

'No. No, not at all. I shall call you, later.'

She goes to the door with him and shows him out and returns to find Robert grinning.

'Isn't it strange how the future always rises out of the past? We can't escape it. He's the very image of his uncle and has all his mannerisms and is every bit as tight with the old dosh!' And then, bitterly she thinks, he carries on. 'He's so narrow. He makes me angry, sometimes! As they say, he knows the value of everything and the worth of nothing.'

**

Time moves on, carried by the tick, tick of the clock. They sit in silence, as they have done so often. The light is falling in from the window. Robert is seated at the little oak living room table. The day has become grey and dark: it is as if evening is creeping closer and the light is not strong, yet it is not yet five o'clock. The air in the room is calm as a millpond; they are neglectful of each other; each is sunk in a malaise. His mind meanders, remembers twilights just like this, a light that is not strong, nevertheless, it creates luminous panes on each brown eye. He and she are together, alone, and he feels contentment; he watches her, marvelling at the wonder of her. The whites of her eyes show a delicate marbling. A latticework of tender little veins cross and criss-cross. Her eyebrow is an arch whose proportions are perfect. He remembers thinking, if only I could make a pot with that perfection of form, of line. I am hungry to see, and by seeing to own everything that she is and to note each perfect piece of this perfect whole and to take this image away.

He returns to the moment. His eyes scan her face repeatedly and then her eyes move and she too is looking up from under her eyebrows; her eyes engage with his eyes and he is aware that these two ponds are impenetrable and unfathomable. These luminous panes are one-way mirrors. He thinks of the uncrossable distances that lie between the galaxies. He thinks of the night sky's cold beauty. He considers its distance. Abruptly, he is aware of the impossibility of knowing even this person, known – half-known – to him for so long, and he feels the terror of absolute aloneness.

And then she smiles, suddenly and warmly and he starts, momentarily enraged at the unfairness of this co-mingling of spirits, at the bestowing of the wrong smile, the very presence of the wrong face. Then, as quickly, he is all guilt, all shame; he considers in his sudden enragement that this smile came too easily, there is something suspicious about such a smile at such a time but, nevertheless, his guilt and shame and rage is also fear – a fear that within her very being there is some great, unknowable other person, buried deep and mute in the body of her being. For a moment this fear presents itself, then vanishes.

'How I love to remember these moments,' he acknowledges, half lying, half truth-telling, half asleep, half awake. 'How I love to keep on living with them, replaying them like old movies.' He is aware that he lies, but still he does it. He knows he does it. He also knows how much he loves to live in the past. He relies on such living. And even now, he is half aware that he never speaks of it to anyone, even to Rebecca. 'Is this normal?' he wonders.

In his head he tries to examine the issue, to answer his own question. He speaks. 'I suppose it's not that I consciously do it – it's more that my memory is – no that I am – like a well… my memories float on the springing water that rises up out of the past.'

'You can't help it,' she says, simply. 'Neither of us can.'

He looks at her, surprised, but she is gone again, absent-mindedly nibbling, grazing, it occurs to him, but with a disturbing gnawing motion, at the base of her right hand, her hand turned away, fingers splayed outwards, like a leaning fence erected there between her eyes and the world. She is unaware of the beat of her pulse against her lips, she is unaware of his gaze, and she is unaware of his concern, just as she is unaware of his existence. She is in another world, entirely. Yet she has spoken. She has answered his question.

He is now all protection, he wants to protect her soul, her spirit, her body, her being. He leans over, he reaches out, he gently secures her hand in his, drawing her hand down to rest in his hand where it lies on the tabletop. She is startled into the present; she looks at him as one might look at a stranger. She looks at her hand under his. Then, like a river trout sliding out of shadow into sunlit water, her spirit is back from an outlying place of outrage, back to the here and now. Her hand withdraws.

'I'm sorry,' is all she can say.

***

Time passes. The incident, small as it was, intrigues her and remains with her. She feels still the touch of his skin on her skin. She glances at him as he sits, staring out of the window. For the first time, the first time for a very long time, she really sees him. Physically, she sees him. He is, she supposes, about five foot nine or ten inches tall. He has that rural, scrawny, yet healthy appearance she imagines shepherds have, though she knows no shepherd, making this a hunch, a guess. He is clean-shaven; he still has a mop of hair that he has always had clipped very short around the sides but leaves more or less untouched on top. It gives him an unusual aspect, that and his habitual old brown cords and jumper; there is something that speaks of frugality about him, something that brings to her mind the word 'Fabians' – although, again, she knows no member of the Fabians – it is something he has, or carries with him, she assumes, that indicates he inhabits a different world.

Looking at him, she allows herself to wonder, what if… What if, all those years ago, on that day of the fight, what if I had been closer to Robert and Ruth had been closer to James? Would things have turned out as they have? Would we be sitting here today, like this – or would…

'Life takes strange turns,' he says, unexpectedly.

She looks up at him, surprised. He is staring at the floor. 'He can read my mind!' she thinks. She blushes, for the first time in many years, but he is not looking at her. The moment passes. She is grateful: everything, she thinks, passes. Another day ebbs away.

***

And then, out of his musings, coldly and objectively, he thinks of something, and thinks of the idea that was conceived deep in his being and that drifted so quickly to the surface, 'that is rather a good image. I mush share it with Rebecca. She will appreciate it…' But of course, he will not share it with Rebecca. No, nor the flow of thought that led to the birth of the image, or of the part she, Rebecca, has played in the process. No, he will not tell her. They do not share much, really, normally, by way of words. They have other ways. These days, increasingly, after the meeting of eyes, they can sit for minutes – he has no idea how many – silent, each passive, thinking perhaps, each, independent of the other, remembering the past, toying with, fingering the future, as if it were a bolt of material that is up for sale, to be haggled over, accepted or rejected. He could not now recall content to fill in the emptiness of those minutes. And as quickly as it came the idea goes, and with it the image.

Suddenly, she stirs beside him. The clock ticks. And then, 'Can I get you some tea?' she asks. Out of a great void, her voice materialises, not loudly, yet he starts, as if awoken from a dream.

'Sorry. I was half-asleep. I think I was dreaming. It's the light, it's so peaceful.' Then, 'Yes! Yes, a cup of tea would be really nice.'

She waits for a moment. He is a little flustered. Off she goes, into the kitchen. He can see her through the doorway, a grey shadow moving through the kitchen's white emptiness. The kettle whistles. She has one of those, what he thinks of as awful, highly polished, silver-seeming things that holds little or no water. Then she appears. She is holding a bottle of wine and two glasses. She is smiling... not smiling, more a grin, a wicked grin, an inviting grin but one that indicates her mood has shifted once more. She holds up two glasses.

'I've changed my mind about the tea. Can I tempt you to a glass of wine? I'm having one.'

'What's this? Tippling in the afternoon, is it? Well late afternoon. What's got into you? Are we celebrating something?'

'No. Well, yes, I suppose. We can celebrate, can't we? We should celebrate. Let's celebrate life, and all the good things we have and just... let's have a glass of wine in the afternoon, just to celebrate the fact that we can.'

They both share the same unspoken thought as she hands him a bottle and the opener. She turns on the radio.

'Lyric FM. I like it – good music, and none of those distracting advertisements every couple of minutes.'

They sit down; they listen to the music; they sip their wine.

'How are things, really?'

'Okay. Well, they're all right; I suppose. Or, they were, for a bit...'

She pauses, takes a tiny sip of wine, then takes a deep breath before going on, 'Once, James asked me, 'How is she there?' Not understanding, thinking perhaps that she was there just in my memory, that her form of existence was only as a memory. Well, to some extent that was, or is, true: she does exist as a memory, or series of memories – as a little girl: once, say, I remember her screaming, skirt billowing, legs out-flung, tipped with white socks and red shoes. I can see her still, all that against a blue sky, our father pushing her on the swing, she terrified as she gained the maximum height and terrified again on the downward rush. But that memory was, or is, of a little girl – and while I can recall, vividly, the blue sky, the red shoes and the white ankle socks, I find, increasingly, that I cannot fill in her features. Shockingly, I have misplaced the image of what Ruth looked like! As that little girl! But memory is not where she is to be found: that is the point, surely – but I did not go into that with James on that occasion. Instead, I said something along the lines of how I used to be walking in the street, or going through a station or busy shopping centre, and I would catch a glimpse of a head and something else – the shape or colour of the hair, or the way the person turned or moved – that would make me believe, instantly, that it was her, and I would think, 'that's Ruth' and find myself stepping out towards her. But it never was, and then I find myself doing that less often. Until the peace process started, and then it began to happen all over again.'

Robert remains silent. He wonders, what can I possibly say? What should I say, to help?

Resting in the silence, she rehearses things in her mind while she turns the glass in her hands, at the same time, in that mixed up, multi-layered way we do when we remember the past and contemplate the future simultaneously, she finds she is making a note to herself that she must not forget to buy batteries for the bathroom radio (it had not worked this morning) and then deciding she would, after all, buy James one of those new digital radios for Christmas, and all the time thinking of Ruth.

'I don't understand.' His voice punches into the silence.

'What don't you understand?'

'Well, you say you are beginning to forget the details of how she looked… but you see her…'

'I know it's difficult: I can't explain it any better. It's like the gap between what I remember of her, and what I remember of her as she exists in me and the absence of her… I don't know… You know, sometimes I catch a glimpse of myself in a mirror as I pass it and I think it's her.'

'But that's normal enough – you were identical twins. It's only natural you should see her face in your face…'

'Yes, I know that. It's to do with her absence, more than with her presence – it's to do with her absence in me… and with guilt… if she is not there it's because I have allowed her to depart… into silence…'

***

They decide to have another glass of wine, then they decide to take it out to the balcony, and then, because it has turned windy and chilly, they decide to share a rug, draping it around their knees. They laugh together: so many decisions, and for people who never take decisions!

'Like two decisive pensioners,' he'd said, laughing, as she spread the cover across their knees, comfortable with this feeling of closeness. They say little, really: they watch and listen to the ebbs and flows of the city getting ready for the night, to the steady passage of the river water, the occasional seagull veering past at eye level. They sip their wine. In their different ways, they remember the past and consider the future.

He has got nowhere in his attempt to find out what is the matter. He wonders should he go full tilt at it or should he leave it, for now? Through the dull, swaying glow of the wine he looks out on a world of flux and motion. Yes, he will leave it, for now. He will divert her. He raises his glass dramatically above his head. He says, 'A very fine wine.' He says, 'You know, I'm just, really, an old-fashioned radical; to me that's always been an intrinsic part of the Dissenter tradition. I like to delve in to the very bottom of life's dunghill, just to see what's there. I like to grub about, in among and through the roots of things. I need to believe in the freedom of the individual to do that, in personal autonomy to explore, in the supremacy of individual independence. We had a chance here, once, of reinventing ourselves as libertarians, while at the same time creating a better world, a richer world, a braver world – but that chance has long gone. There is no place for the likes of me in this world of new right-wing republicanism.'

She considers what he has just said. He waits; he gives her time, and eventually she replies. 'There could be a place, for you I mean. Do you think we do what we will or do we will what we do? It's an important distinction. I feel lost a lot of the time. I seem to have fallen into a crack between the two 'wills'.'

He says, 'I was watching a group of young lads today, at the bus stop. They had the balance just right. Everything they did was 'willed' but in such a relaxed, organic kind of a way. I could sense a moral beauty in their physical actions, in the way they moved and in the way they behaved – interacted is a better word – towards one another. Balance is the answer. You know, Burns was right: friendship is what binds people together, not ideologies, not great systems of organised thought, and not even the profit motive has that power.'

Rebecca frowns. 'I don't really understand. Though, I think I might: I'd have to think about it. I'm afraid I'm a bit dim, today. I think you're a bit quick for me.' She smiles, 'I don't mean 'quick' intellectually, though you are that – I mean you jump too fast, you jump to opinions too easily...'

He replies, 'You may be right: I know it sounds a pathetic, a really condescending, thing to say, but I have always had the sense of you that you are a good person, a better person than me. If you do what you will it's because you believe in it, for its own end. There is no side to you, as they say. You just want to do something good – and no one knows what the good, the right, human, thing is, instinctively. But that's where you get your strength. Not from words or concepts or from philosophies, but from being really rooted in humanity, that kind of internal knowledge that I think human experience is built on and grows from. People matter to you.'

She is quiet. 'Thank you,' she says. That is all she says. He senses that she wants to be on her own. Eventually and reluctantly he says, 'I have to go.' He holds up the wine glass: 'I'm bussing it. If I run I'll make the half-seven: anyway, I have to get home to feed Blue and Benson. Then I think I'll have an early night, maybe... maybe not... I seem to have been drinking all day...'

'Yes. I'm sorry, I've not fed you, at all. I'm being inhospitable, but I feel I want to be on my own this evening. That's why I asked you and James to cancel our dinner. I'm sorry about that. But there's something I have to do. I need to be alone to do it.'

'What is it?' He asked, innocently enough, but watchful of her from under his eyelids.

'Oh, heavy stuff!' she said, lightly. Then, seeing the alarm on his face, 'No, I'm joking. It's very simple, really. I'll tell you some other time. Later.' He goes to the door. He stops, and says abruptly: 'You had a meeting the other day?' She looks at him sharply.

'Yes. Who told you that? I didn't say anything about it... did I?'

'No. I don't think you said anything, overtly! James mentioned it, this morning.' She hesitates, takes his point, then, 'I met with the man who killed Ruth. It was a kind of mediation meeting. He had asked for it and I agreed. When it happened it came as a bit of a shock, that's all. It seemed to creep up on me. I was not ready or prepared for it. I am still thinking about what happened. I'll talk to you about it later, if you don't mind.'

Later, out on the street, he finds he feels confused, half dazed. And it has nothing to do with the wine.

***

She draws the little round table up to the glass doors that lead to the balcony. She covers it with a white cloth. She sets places for two: two plates, two knives, two forks, two glasses and a jug of water. She has put ice cubes and a slice of lemon in the jug. She fetches the little vase that had belonged to her mother and carefully places it in the middle of the table. She goes to the kitchen and takes one bright red bloom from a bunch of flowers that she had bought earlier and puts it into the vase.

She surveys the table and is happy. She fetches two chairs, determining to take for herself the one with its back to the glass door. She can look at the view any time, she thinks. She takes off her apron, then puts it on again and goes to the kitchen to fetch the casserole dish and a serving spoon.

As she eats she makes an occasional remark across the table: about her day at work, about the way the light has gone, and it not yet eight o'clock and still September; and yes, the chill in the evening air. A squall of rain hits the window glass, and she thinks, but does not put it into words, how nice it is to be here, cosy, how lucky they are to be so cosy and complete. The rain and the wind lifted her, have taken her away. 'The clock will change soon,' she says. At one point, she raises her water glass, saying, 'Happy Birthday, Ruth, Happy Birthday, Rebecca.' She speaks awkwardly, feeling the words are called for, yet at somehow at odds with something...

Then, her plate is empty and she lingers only a little while before busying herself, clearing the table, scraping off the uneaten food and placing it in the bin, putting away the chairs, removing the cloth. She folds the cloth neatly. It is made from old linen and falls heavily into its accustomed form. She puts it away in its drawer. A piece of heritage passed on from her mother. She thinks, suddenly, of her mother and Ruth and herself dancing with their shadows. She smiles. She shifts the table and sees that the rain has stopped. She steps onto the balcony. She lifts her face to the wind and for many minutes savours its sharp little caresses. Then she turns into the kitchen, brings a stool to the dresser and, standing on it, reaches up to where a packet of cigarettes lies hidden. It has been there for months, but only two cigarettes have been taken. Now she takes another, and with matches and a heavy rug in one hand and the stool in another, she goes to the balcony. She sits, the rug around her shoulders, and lights the cigarette. 'This balcony is one of my favourite places,' she thinks. It has strong metal railings and to these she has had attached panes of thick, shatterproof glass. These protect her. 'Shadows,' she thinks. 'Ghosts,' she thinks. 'Memories, everything is so real, yet so intangible...' She smokes her cigarette. She says, aloud: 'Losing you was like losing my shadow. I thought of this the other day; it came to me, quite suddenly, unexpectedly... this idea about you being a kind of shadow, my shadow.'

'Ingenious: your very own plate glass partition,' Robert had said, the irony being he was at that time involved in taking down an old partition in the cottage – he is always tinkering with that house, she thinks. He had described it once as being made of: 'ancient wood, plaster-board and lots of dust'. She detected the emphasis on the word glass and recognised his attempt at irony – or was it sarcasm, she wondered – and responded in what she hoped was a similar tone.

'It's just a protection for my knees *and* my plants; the wind can be bitter, here.'

'A pragmatic solution to a pressing problem,' James had said, when told about Robert's objection.

***

She smokes her cigarette, sitting there unseen but seeing what so recently she did not see: the city that has come alive. A bus passes on the other side of the river, taxis and then an ambulance speeds past, and people cross the road, straggling groups of threes and fours, heading towards the brightness of the theatre. Lights fall on the river; one particularly long beam stretches from a distant window, lying at an angle to her sight. Where it lies, the water shivers, like skin, she thinks. Is the river perhaps cold, or afraid, or nervous? It may be any or all of these things, she thinks. She knows it is alive and living.

She feels used up and empty. A terrible tiredness hits her, suddenly. She gets up to go to bed. It is now ten thirty. In bed, she cannot sleep. She lies there, counting and recounting the three pictures that hang on the wall; it is a way she has of calming herself. The phone rings. She decides not to answer it, but its insistent tone drives her to pick up the receiver. It is James.

'Hello. Just calling to say 'Hello',' he says.

'A fine story,' she replies. For some reason she decides to treat his call with flippancy. Then she changes her mind. 'But thanks. Yes, I am fine, before you ask.'

'Are you? Are you?' He goes on, 'You have been acting a bit strange recently...'

She bursts out, 'I want to get away, away from here, away from this city. Even if only for a day. If only for an hour. I feel as if I am being suffocated!' On the other end, she can imagine James looking alarmed but all he asks is, 'Where do you want to go?'

'Anywhere. Somewhere. A place where there is lots of space and lots of air to breath. Let's go on a quest for air and space!'

'To the edge of the world,' he said. She can hear the smile in his voice. 'Yes,' she replied, calmer now, back to her old self, 'the edge of the world sounds good. Lots of emptiness, a lot of space there. And lots of air there, I'm sure – at least, until you step off the edge! Then the air stops.'

He hears the bitterness in her voice. Then, reluctantly, they say goodnight. Later, just as she has climbed into bed, the phone rings.

'Hello,' he says. 'It's me again. I have just thought of the perfect place: the end of the world, or rather, the edge of the world, just as you said.

'And where is that?'

'It's a spot near Killybegs. I was there once and it's just what you described!'

'Killybegs?' She sounds sceptical. 'It's hardly the place for a 'quest' to end!'

'At least, it's near Killybegs. The place has the highest sea cliffs in Europe. Spectacular views. And not too many people, if any, at this time of year.'

'When can we go? She was delighted and her delight infected him. 'Tomorrow. We could go tomorrow?'

'Well, tomorrow, if you are sure…'

'Don't argue or try to get out of it!' she commanded. 'We will go tomorrow, early.'

'Fine. I'll drive,' said James.

'And I'll bring a picnic. Oh, sorry, I don't have much in the house… Nothing elaborate… but I'm sure there'll be enough.'

And I'll call for you and then we will call for Robert. We will be passing his house. I'm sure he'll be able to come.'

He is sure of this because he has just called Robert, but he does not care to share this information.

'Good,' she says. 'Tell him he can help make the journey shorter – he can tell jokes and sing…'

For the moment, he senses, she is purposeful and happy. And so it is settled.

'Goodnight.'

'Goodnight.'

Sunday

Rebecca gets up early. For the second time this week she has slept badly. She puts on her white and cream dressing gown and makes coffee, then goes outside and looks across the city. From her vantage point she can see a couple of cars pass, seemingly moving without sound, on the other side of the river. A few birds fly past, following the run of the water. She watches a man cross the street opposite; he is carrying a translucent plastic bag with a red logo on its side. The bag, she can see, contains papers, Sunday newspapers, she realises. Apart from these sporadic little twitches and turns, the city slumbers. She wonders in passing what shop is open so early? It is Sunday. She remembers again… she starts… she had momentarily forgotten she is going on a trip today. To the edge of the world, or so James has promised! Bits of last night's conversation float up into her consciousness, but she remembers little: what does it mean, the edge of the world, she wonders? Images of huge voids appear, opening up before and beneath her.

She turns away; she is thoughtful. 'Yes, that's one possibility: today I go to the very edge of the world. What will happen? Will I fall off? Will I fall off the edge of the world – if I do, will I just keep on falling, forever?' She stiffens for across the edge of memory something flits, but then is lost, only its dewy evanescence half lingering, causing annoyance.

She looks again at the water and remains gazing for a long time. Her being is overtaken by a kind of torpor, a feeling of encompassing *ennui* settles within her head and invades her body and being. No, she decides, it will be nothing dramatic, just the edge of Ireland, the meeting of land and sea, earth and water, a border she won't, or cannot, cross.

She feels – how does she feel? She feels stale; she senses she has allowed herself to live a life of hesitation, to fail all such crossings, not for a moment only, nor for a month, nor for a year – but for all the years since Ruth's death: she has fallen prey to the overpowering force of this inertia.

These past few days have brought it all to a head. She is aware of that. She experiences panic. Her only way out of this is to keep on remembering. She must focus on keeping all the memories alive and fresh. That flitting image, the one she lost a few moments ago, is still present. With an effort, she shakes off her languor: she crosses the room to the desk, opens the drawer and takes out the blue book. She sits down and takes up her pen.

I remember, she writes, *looking back & seeing Ruth & then I remember a feeling of being suspended, suddenly, in a kind of vortex and without knowing how I got there. The light split – it was as if the sun had shattered, it was as if, all around me, the air was full of shards of splintered glass. I could hear voices, they were human but very distant voices, talking, calling, their tone – it had the clarity of bells, they were so pure but they were also very far away & I could not make out what they were saying & I was just on the edge of something, watching Ruth standing there for so long & then & somehow I knew what was happening but I was helpless to stop it… I was without power to stop it…*

121

She reads what she has written. She sits for a long time staring at it, then leafs back through the pages. She stops at a page; it is dated almost a year before: a year, a whole year of lingering... She reads,

I remember, looking back & seeing Ruth & then I am suddenly lifted up. She sits up. She lives again that feeling of helplessness, that feeling of being suspended, of being in a kind of vortex and not knowing how she got here...

She shivers. She shuts the book and replaces it in the drawer. Then she takes it out again, opens it and writes:

Is writing this stuff - 'cathartic'? Is this reliving that day... healthy...?

She looks at it, then under-scores the word 'cathartic' several times. She leafs back to the page she used earlier, then compares the two pages, briefly. She shakes her head. Her hair falls over her eyes and she impatiently shoves it away. She takes up the pen again and writes,

Is this remembering good? Does writing this twice mean it's twice as cathartic? Does it mean I am mad?

'Or does it mean, simply, that my memory is going?' she wonders. She puts the book back into the darkness of its drawer before going to the mirror; she finds herself wondering idly, is there a difference between remembering and remembrance? She looks at herself in the glass, grimaces and says, 'At least, I still have the semblance of a sense of humour.'

She remembers the coffee and goes in search of the mug she left on the balcony. Its contents are stone-cold. As she lifts the cup, she notices faint coffee smudges commingling with lipstick traces on the edge of the mug where she had drunk from it. They remind her of old rust marks, of iron seen in ditches when she was a child, the slow, immobile stains of iron ore seeping out of ancient riverbeds. They remind her, she realises with a shock, of old bloodstains on hospital bed sheets. A little shivery quiver runs through her body and through her mind; she goes to the kitchen, washes the mug, makes fresh coffee, goes into the bathroom and has a shower; then she dresses. She sits down to wait for James to knock on the door.

'I am becoming morbid,' she thinks.

With a start, she jumps to her feet. 'The picnic!' She looks at her watch. 'All this dreaming and daydreaming – I completely forgot – I promised to bring a picnic. There is still time. I can rustle something up,' she thinks. She goes quickly to the kitchen, leaving the full coffee mug sitting on the table.

She has barely finished packing an incoherent variety of potential picnic ingredients, some bread, crackers, cheese, apples; she has found two tins of tomato soup and she has heated these and put them in a flask. These bits and pieces have been found in various cupboards, the fridge, the larder, and put together hurriedly. She hesitates, a hand half reaching out towards a bottle of wine, wondering if it was appropriate for a Sunday picnic, when the doorbell rings, breaking violently into the silence in the flat, into her concentration. She leaves the bottle where it is and opens the door to find James standing there, a smile on his face, his arms open, his hands apart in a gesture designed to underscore his one-word question.

'Ready?' he asks. His obvious excitement transmits itself to her and she literally grins in response.

'Yes,' she says, 'You bet, I'm ready – ready for anything.' Yet, as she looks at him, as she says these words, as she feels happy to be happy, she is thinking, 'This is not James, the real James: this is a front, a mask of happiness put on to make me feel happy,' and as she thinks this she thinks, 'Why can I never be happy with what is there, in front of me? Why do I have to question everything?' But she does not articulate any of this; she continues to smile while pointing to the two plastic containers and the cold bag that contains their picnic.

'Will you make some coffee and put it in this flask, while I go and get a coat and hat: I won't be a minute. By the way,' as she leaves the room, 'I'm afraid the picnic isn't very exciting. I forgot all about it until a few minutes ago! I've just thrown in bits and pieces.'

'Don't worry,' James replied, but she was gone.

It is forty minutes later, and now with the second passenger on board, James swung the Jaguar onto the motorway and almost immediately Robert said, 'How about a game? I spy with my little eye something beginning with PSM.'

'Patterson's Spade Mill,' the other two chorused in mocked-bored voices. They have been here before and all three look spontaneously to the left, out of the passenger windows. The long, black slate roof of the mill is only partly visible through a screening of trees. They all feel excited; even Rebecca feels elevated by the prospect before them. The morning is beautiful – bright sunshine, blue sky, the leaves on the trees shimmer in a light breeze. The fields and hedges look alive and trim and cared for.

124

As the car speeds along Robert grows pensive. 'You know,' he says, 'when we were passing Cave Hill I was thinking if I had lived in the eighteenth century I would probably have been involved with those real, flesh and blood intellectual entrepreneurs: entrepreneurs of the imagination – people like the McCrackens – Mary Ann and Henry Joy – seeking justice, fighting slavery…

'What about you, James?' Rebecca asked.

'Too much opposed to law and order, for my liking,' he replied, leaning forward over the wheel, peering at the road ahead.

'The law was written in the book of Moses: we all know what it says.'

'It was written in men's hearts, also: we all instinctively know the difference between right and wrong!'

'I'm not going to allow you to drag me into this discussion!' James replied firmly. 'It's too good a day to waste harrowing old ground. Look up there.' He pointed to Donegore Hill.

'Sir Samuel Ferguson is buried there. I went to see his grave once…'

'Yes, with me. I took you! To the fort of the heroes!' Robert interrupts but he is ignored.

'He lies up there, all alone: a great poet who tried to approach our shared history through story and myth – but that's all in the past, now. We are all middle class now…Radio Three, Lyric FM…'

'I listen to Lyric FM!' began Rebecca, in protest, but Robert interrupted her.

'Yes, we are all middle class… our lives are ordered and run by the banks! But perhaps you're right. Perhaps it is too good a day.' Robert lay back in his seat, staring out across the speeding green fields.

'Well,' James said, as they passed a mileage sign, 'Only 62 miles to Derry. We should be there in an hour and a half. However, we'll not stop in the city. Best to keep on going, don't you think?' He was answered by a significant silence. They knew there was no point in agreeing or disagreeing with James on matters such as this. He would do what he wanted to do, in any event.

'Look at him,' thought Robert. 'Brown driving gloves! Bloody affectation! Bloody army commandant! All he wants is a swagger stick!' However, he said nothing. He closed his eyes and settled into the seat, feeling a bit under the weather. Too much whiskey last night, he thought. Too late to bed, not enough sleep…I should have stuck to my plan for an early night. Robert ponders for a moment, and then he drifts off into oblivion.

Meanwhile, James concentrated on the road ahead. Rebecca sat in the back, alone with her thoughts. She had wanted to go to the edge of the world and here she was, on her way… What she had really wanted, at that moment yesterday (it has something to do with a childhood memory, from a long-forgotten story), what she had wanted, was to go to an imaginary place where the end of the world might be found, to go there and jump off, into the unknown. But that moment has passed, as it had to pass, she considers. Then James stepped in! She smiled, looking at the back of James's head, looking at Robert's head, slumped against the

126

window, looking at the hedges and fields flowing past. How lucky I am, she thought, what good friends I have, what good companions.

Up ahead, a bridge appeared and just under or through its angle, Antrim Hospital came into view, with the blades of its big white wind turbine rotating jerkily. The road was virtually free of traffic, and they fairly sped along. Then, as they negotiated a bend on the road, she could see ahead to where the valley opened up, and there in the far distance was a corner of Lough Neagh. Even on this bright Sunday morning, it retains that horrible battleship grey colour, she thought. Ever since her school days she always thought of Lough Neagh as being in some way standing for the heart of Ulster she still remembered: a teacher telling them how Ulster was like a big dish, how it was a flat centre, surrounded by hills. 'The biggest freshwater lake in these islands.' How many teachers can she have heard saying that? What a claim to fame!

Soon the broad motorway inexplicably turned into the much narrower A9, a bendy, unsafe and slow bottleneck of a road that forced James to devote even more concentration to his driving. They passed a huge blue sign saying, 'O'Neill Arms Hotel Two Miles Ahead' and then a voice

'I spy with my little eye, something beginning with BBB.'

'Blue Bridge,' James replied, for the new bridge on the outskirts of Toome had just appeared up ahead.

'No!' replied the same disembodied voice.

'Big Blue Bridge.' It was Rebecca.

'Aye. Aye, ye' are right, there, so you are!' Robert sat up, looking around at the countryside. The road bypassed the old village of Toome and looking over the grassy spaces, intersected with water, Robert started to sing softly, 'Young Roddy McCordy, goes to die on the bridge of Toome today'.

With a laugh, Rebecca said, 'Talking of bridges and rivers, do you remember nearly dying, yourself? Do you remember the big fight you had with James? At the river – don't you remember?'

'No, I do not!'

'You – we – were young… it was down by the river.'

Robert habitually remembers his childhood only as one long summer. The sun was always shining, the fields rising up to meet the sky, birdsong and kites and ice cream. And injuries. Lots of them seemed to result from just falling down or being caught up in a barbed wire fence or entangled in a thorn hedge and having to run home to get the wounds attended to. The mothers then always had stinging antiseptic that they applied liberally to any cut or scrape before putting on a piece of skin-coloured sticking plaster. And by the next day at school the fresh plaster was always ragged, with black, knotty bits around the edges. Of course, he remembers that fight, but would rather remember the blue skies, the warm sunshine…

Rebecca's voice interrupts his daydream. 'You had been climbing that old beech tree that stood beside the small stream – the one that ran through the fields that lay beyond our gardens. Do you remember you had discovered if you climbed the tree, and then crept out along one of the long branches, your weight, once you got to the end, was enough to bend it towards the ground? Then, as it closed on the far

128

bank of the stream, you could drop to earth. Then by recrossing the stream and climbing the tree again you could repeat the exercise endlessly. Which you both did! For a whole summer! It drove Ruth and me to boredom!' She continued, 'It was a kind of flexible bridge, a secret bridge you called it, James. One that disappeared from view and became invisible to the untutored eye – it wasn't what it seemed...'

Yes, of course, Robert remembered. James too, remembered. Neither spoke, so she continued, remembering, always remembering.

'Only the boys did this. On this particular day James had gone first, followed by Robert.' While Rebecca's voice continued to narrate the story, James drifted off into his own realm of remembrance. The two girls – he can still see them, in his mind's eye – were sitting on the far bank, ignoring them. Yes, he could still see the scene, as he looked across the river from where he hung, upside down in the tree. Rebecca had been reading a book, Ruth was sitting still, deep in thought. He can still see the small yellow flower she holds in her hand. He watches as she inspects it. He had moved along then, inching his way out over the river. He remembers how Robert had quickly followed him closely, too close for comfort. Hanging on by his hands, legs grasping the branch and ankles crossed, inching his way along, he had shouted to Robert to wait for it had been their convention that only one crossed at a time, fearing the slender bough would not be strong enough to carry the weight of both. That day, Robert had ignored him and followed on too quickly. Then, what he had feared happened: with a sharp and sudden *snap!* the branch broke, and they both tumbled the few feet, perhaps it was as much as five or six feet, into the water. Simultaneously, his head banged against a large boulder and both girls laughed – with a wild yell James leapt to his feet and threw himself on Robert who was lying in a pool of water, soaked but with a wild grin on his face, hooting with laughter.

Even at that age, James was the heavier, but Robert was wiry and hard and when attacked seemed possessed of a demon. At last, exhausted, they gave up with common accord, and struggled to the bank where the two girls watched in silence. They were both wet through, bloody and bruised, as much from the fall as from the fight, or perhaps they had been bruised from the fall and bloodied by the fight.

The two girls took charge immediately. No, James thought, it was Rebecca who had taken charge. She had turned to him – she had been standing close to him – and, producing a handkerchief, began to clean his face, wiping away the blood from his split lip, peering at his blackening eye. Ruth, instinctively it seemed to him, went to Robert, who by now was sitting down a short distance away; she began to help him.

After they had been repaired the two boys continued to glare at each other. But Rebecca had stood firmly between them. 'It was Robert's fault the branch broke,' she said. 'But it was James's fault the fight started. So, you both are to blame, and both must share responsibility. Now, shake hands!' She was about nine or ten years old at the time. Yet, that day was established as a kind of template for the rest of their lives. In a strange way it cemented the friendship between the two boys, who never fought again, and it established Rebecca as the figure of authority within the group: she was the one who arbitrated on all moral, ethical and related matters. It set out the relationships, Rebecca and James, Ruth and Robert. No one ever mentioned it, but it was established that a natural affection existed between James and Rebecca and between Ruth and Robert.

They drove for some time without speaking. Then Robert broke the silence. 'Interesting display that the one with the buttons, the one I saw yesterday in your house.'

James continues to reflect on the awakened memory. That was how their first real fight, and their last fight, ended. Yes, he certainly did remember it clearly, just as clearly as he remembered his two weeks at Sandhurst, after he had joined the Territorial Army. Two significant rites of passage, one might say. He sat a little higher in his seat, his arms straight out, slightly bent at the elbow. Yes, that had been their first and last fight – the girls saw to that and then, after Ruth's death, there did not seem to be any point in fighting when there was nothing of importance to fight about.

'James! Are you asleep?' It was Robert. 'I was telling Rebecca about your father's collection of buttons.'

'Yes. Oh, yes. Buttons held a fascination for my father. He collected military buttons, did you know that? Catching Rebecca's eye in the car's interior mirror, he went on, 'Very colourful, highly textured… Great social history attached to them…'

'I didn't know that,' Robert said. He is being ironic, but the words sound sarcastic to his own ears and he feels sorry. Poor old James, he thinks, always so deadly, dully serious.

'Sorry Robert! I forgot I mentioned that to you yesterday. Yes, Rebecca, I remember, my father always used to say, 'If you want to discover the quality of a button, turn it over and look at the back.'

'I don't remember seeing such a thing in your house.' Rebecca interrupted.

'No. You wouldn't have seen it. He kept it in his bedroom. I hardly think you would ever have been in there. After he departed, it was put into a spare room, upstairs, until the recent past. I had it brought down a while back.'

'No, I don't suppose you did know about his hobby. He kept them in his bedroom. He had a case made - I must have been seven or eight at the time – by a man who brought it out to the house in pieces and assembled it, right there in the bedroom. He looked at it every morning, when he got up and of course he was always adding to the collection.'

'What did your mother think of all this, all this obsession with buttons?' Robert was slumped into the corner of his seat, his eyes closed, a red scarf wound round his neck and his cap pulled down over his eyes; he was still half asleep, and happy to drip-feed the conversation. He hardly paid attention to what James replied.

James, intent on negotiating a roundabout, said, 'Oh, you know... Well, he and I devised a display, together. The top of the cabinet was circular and covered in glass, so we created a huge round button, like a petal or bloom really, a flower, a highly textured, highly exotic flower.'

In the back, Rebecca sat upright, staring out of the window, only half-conscious of their voices. The houses had now given way to open fields, the hedges and trees flying past. A car nosed out of a side road; across a field she saw a man on a red tractor aim for an open gateway. A few cows stood by a wire fence. 'Apart from that, the world is virtually empty,' she thinks, 'we are heading west on an empty road.' The words of a song suggest themselves to her, but they refuse to materialise from behind the curtain of memory; it must be a country and western song, she thinks, an open road, heading westwards, something to do with running

132

away from love, or running towards love... or death... oblivion.

At that moment she reruns James's voice in her head: *so we created a petal, a flower, a highly textured, highly exotic flower* and instantly and completely she looks at the red tractor and the cows and the car and experiences the shock of remembering Ruth's final moment: the slow-motion release of the shape and form of her bending body, its slow, gentle, soundless transformation into a storm of black petals. It is so easy, she thinks, to die. One moment you are there, walking along, planning your next holiday, thinking about what to buy for your lunch, looking into a shop window, the next instant you are dead, and there is no going back. You can only exist again, doing these things again, if some living person takes the time to remember.

***

They are passing the car, nosing out of a laneway; the red tractor is crawling towards its gateway, the cows are behind them. She leans back into her seat but does not speak. James is saying, 'You haven't seen the display, yet Rebecca. I'll show it to you when you next call. I think you'll like it.'

'Thanks. I'd like to see it,' Rebecca says. She finds herself shivering, just a little. She notices more cows standing looking out over a wire fence. They drive on, past the new Creagh roundabout. 'Why are there so many new roundabouts?' Robert asks but gets no reply.

Soon they are on the open road and heading up into the Sperrin Mountains. Robert speaks to James, in an affected voice: 'I say old boy, do you think, can we have a comfort stop, please?'

'Well, if you must!' James replied. 'I'll look out for an appropriate place where I can pull over.' A few minutes later he saw an iron gate on the left fringed by a wide verge and stopped the car. They got out, Rebecca and James to stretch their legs and look at the view, while Robert went off, over the gate and behind the hedge. As he returned, he heard James swear:

'Damnation!'

James' hands were resting on the car roof, his head bent between his elbows. He shook his head, from side to side, violently.

'Damnation!'

'What's wrong?'

'I've locked the key inside the car!'

'Are you sure?'

'Of course, I'm sure! There they are, you can see them, there on the seat. I put them down in order to lift out the binoculars and then closed the door without thinking. What an absolutely dumb, stupid thing to do!'

Robert looked out across the valley. It was empty of houses. Even the sky was empty. The world was devoid of human life. He listened; it was silent. He looked up and down the mountain road. There is not a car to be seen. Even the fields and hillsides were empty of sheep or cattle.

'I thought modern cars had some kind of safety device that meant you could not lock the door with the key still in the car…' She looked first at James, then at Robert. James just shook his head but did not reply. Robert said, 'Well, if this one has it hasn't worked: I wonder how far the nearest garage is?'

'Not for miles, and anyway, all the garages will be shut. Don't forget, it's Sunday morning.'

'Do you have a spare key, you know, hidden in one of those magnetised boxes that can be placed under the car's bodywork?'

'No, I bloody well don't. I did have on my last car but somehow, I never… I'll have to break a window to get in!'

'No, look,' Robert said, 'people, children, break into cars every day; it's one of the community skills we have developed over the past thirty years! We just need to deploy a bit of ingenuity, a bit of imagination, a bit of the old hand/eye coordination, a bit of daring…' He beamed assurance. He is on one of his rolls, 'We need to develop a bit of creativity. And remember, as a last resort, we can take to physical violence, smash one of the side windows with a rock…' Rebecca looked at him coldly. James winced, involuntarily, his eye drawn to the immaculate coachwork.

Robert is immediately aware of Rebecca's response. He feels sorry and guilty; he has said what they never say; he has done what they never do: jokingly, he had come too close for comfort to something they never refer to: political violence, any violence. But then, haven't they been talking about their boyhood fight, and didn't she bring that up? Hurriedly, he says, 'But before we even think of doing that, give me a few minutes.'

Robert crossed the road, climbed over the low stone wall and made his way towards a wall-stead that stood in what had once been a garden but was now a place where, given the state of the ground, cattle or sheep were fed. He disappeared into the remains of the house to reappear a brief time later. He came jogging back to the car, a long piece of wire in his hand.

'See, we are saved. Now, just have patience. Rebecca thoughtfully left her window open just enough for me to get this wire in.' He set to work immediately, making a hook on one end of the wire, bending the length of thin metal with a care that seemed to the others to offer evidence of some expertise. He denied this when James made the suggestion, saying it was merely the result of watching too many films of the wrong kind. He carefully inserted the wire through the slight gap between window and door frame, fidgeted with the wire, manipulating it till, with what was a piece of luck, the hook caught on the door handle and with a little jerk he had it open. Just then, and before the other two had time to congratulate Robert a pick-up truck drew to a halt and an elderly man wearing a cap and scarf opened the passenger door.

'Are yees looking for help?' He had one hand on the steering wheel, the other resting on the open window ledge. 'He looks so real, so there, so much at home, sitting there in that old, rusted, mud-baked van,' Rebecca thinks. 'He looks as if he has been here for ever.. he looks as if he will be here for ever, he and his dog.'

'No, we have it covered, locked ourselves out of the car – but we managed to get it open.' Robert replied, tossing the piece of wire deftly and unseen into the long grass by the roadside.

'Right ye are. Well... good luck to ye...' and, touching his cap, the man drives off, his sheep-dog standing up, looking territorially proud, in the back of the truck, eying them suspiciously as he bumps away.

'I wouldn't like to meet that boyo up a dark alley.' Robert muttered as he opened the car door for Rebecca.

'It was very good of the farmer to stop,' was all James said.

'Yes,' agreed Rebecca, 'it was really very good of him!'

Soon, they are on their way again. They pass the highest pub in Ireland, but do not stop, despite Robert's half-earnest, half-joking drawing of their attention to its presence. Anyway, its doors are not yet open. The car runs smoothly along the open, virtually empty road; Robert looks out at the landscape: he finds himself responding to its flow; it's strange, how sensual I find it, he thinks – for some reason, the word 'voluptuous' materialises in his consciousness and he smiles - following with his eyes the rolling little hills, the curves and folds of land; yes, it's strange how feminine it is, how smooth, how attractive the texturing derived from heather and long grass is on the smooth, uplifting slopes. He feels relaxed, at ease, warm and happy. He feels as a poet must feel. He slips gently into a virtual slumber.

A little later they come down a long hill, sweep round a bend and start up the slope that leads into Derry.

'That's Burntollet Bridge,' James says, disturbing Robert. 'That's where the civil rights marchers were ambushed, back in 1968.' For a moment the other two don't reply, then Robert, now awake, says, 'Ancient history... now'. There is a pause, then Rebecca says, 'My father was invited to take

137

part in the march, you know. One of his patients suggested it to him. But he didn't... he didn't think it had anything to do with him... Ruth and I were about seven. I remember him talking to my mother about it, afterwards, saying how glad he was not to have been involved.'

Twenty minutes later, they were crossing the Foyle Bridge, skirting the city of Derry and driving out the Letterkenny Road. Half an hour later they had left Letterkenny behind and were driving westwards.

'I haven't been here for years,' Rebecca remarked, 'but there seems to be something different about the landscape... there seems to be an awful lot of houses.'

'I spy with my little eye,' James muttered sourly, 'something beginning with BB – he went on before either of them could answer, 'Bungalow Blight!'

Half an hour later and they stopped in Killybegs, largely to allow Rebecca to go into the hotel in search of what she called 'the ladies restroom', but also because the two men wanted to stretch their legs and to look around the harbour. James soon walked off, out along the roadway overlooking the sea, leaving Robert down by the water's edge where he wandered among the moored boats, noting the names. The *Obloin*, the *Largy*, the *Alpherax*, the *Emer Maria*, the *Girl Mareen* from Bunbeg, the *Fulucca* from Sligo, the *India Rose* from Dublin, the *Adina* from Burtonport – his eye was inexperienced and he read this one as a dredger of some sort, an old lady, he thought, her oversize skeleton arthritic and stiffly corseted by sheets of iron, her being expressed by dressings of massive chains; the cancer of rust was everywhere. 'If I were a painter,' he thought, in his ironic way, 'this could be a subject – the marriage of old age and gravity.' Then his abstraction was interrupted. 'Hoy!' It was

James, waving to him; Rebecca was back: James was keen to get on his way, again. Robert turned away. His hope for the romance of the sea suddenly dashed. He was glad to leave this decay behind him. As if he knew what Robert was thinking James spoke as he put the car into gear. 'The fishing industry is in bad shape, it has gone, really. No money in it, at all...'

Within moments they had left Killybegs behind and were heading westwards, with Donegal Bay spread out on their left, and suddenly the day became totally different: it became charged once again, enlivened with the appearance of bright sunshine; the sky was patched with blue and, in the mid distance, a light scattering of leaves rose on the wind. As they rounded a bend in the road the wind force increased with a sudden gust, giving the car a thrust on one side. James gave a grunt of surprise as he responded, reacting to adjust the weight of the car against the swerve. The wind played on the windows; to Robert, it had the sound of a muffled snare drum, and then just as suddenly as it started it was over, and there ahead the landscape fell open like a book before them.

James pulled in and parked on the grass verge. On the inland side of the road, the hillside erupted with bursts of colour; the ground rose from where they were stopped up to a huddle of whitened stones, all that was left of an old house; its remains sank into, or were coming out of, the earth. Around it, the mountain ash trees were hung with bunches of red berries and the fuchsia was in full bloom; the brown and green hillside was splattered with red and white and green and the wind returned to shake and churn the branches and leaves.

'It's like one of those paintings by Matisse,' Rebecca said, and then, 'It's so beautiful. Isn't it a pity we don't have one of those tops that come down and then we could drive on, into the wind...?'

'James, make sure the next car you buy is a convertible!' Rebecca continued, as James pulled out onto the roadway.

'You mean a *drop-top*!' Robert interrupted, adopting one of his Country and Western accents.

'I'll try to remember that!' James said wryly.

'Or, a convertible Rolls.' Robert countered. 'In British Racing Green! Rebecca would like that. It would appeal to her sense of tradition.'

'You are both so funny!' Rebecca said. Yet, she sounded happy, and they were glad: a warm feeling filled the car.

Within a few minutes the road suddenly ended. Robert commented, 'The road's intention has obviously been subverted by the presence of the Atlantic Ocean.'

'It's beautiful; it's so beautiful,' Rebecca said again. James parked on the grass verge, and she was the first out of the car, standing at the edge of the road, one hand shading her eyes.

Then, 'Look, a whale!' her finger pointed to the harbour entrance. 'That black rock, you could easily mistake it for a whale.'

'Yes, and the big' un behind it must be its ma.' This was Robert, standing by her side, one hand raised to keep the sun at bay. James, who had spent a holiday somewhere close by proceeded to tell them of a local fisherman's story about the two whales that guard the entrance to the harbour. Rebecca immediately saw what he meant and, quite literally, jumped up and down in delight; she is just like a child, Robert thought. James did not appear to notice. He said, opening the car door, 'Let's go, we are nearly there.'

Rebecca found the short drive hair-raising, or so she said. James turned off the narrow road and followed an even narrower road that soon skirted the land's edge, rising up steeply, with sharp bends and sheer drops off to one side. Even Robert remained quiet, apart from saying, as they passed a signpost in Gaelic, 'You would think we were in a different country!'

'We are in a different country,' James retorted, steering carefully. Each time they met another oncoming car he stopped. Away to the left Rebecca could see an old castle or fort, but she did not mention it in case James took his eyes off the road. Eventually they arrived at the top and parked the car on some gravel. Then they walked up to a little mound of earth, in order to get a good view of the earth's edge, the sea spread out below. Two great arms of sea cliffs protectively embraced the bay. They moved closer to the cliff edge. The sea rubbed against the rocks below. The dark openings of caves (they look to James, he says, as if they have been poked out by a giant finger) dark and red and black, mysterious but not in any way evoking danger, appeal to Robert's sense of adventure; there is something here that denotes fun. He can picture pirates, he says. It is a perfect picture of nature, Rebecca says, it is calm and serene. They stand there, using the scene to tell each other how they feel. Far below, three tiny boats are rocked; they appear so at ease in the embrace of the Atlantic.

'These are the highest sea cliffs in Europe,' James said. He stood there, hands on hips, urging the others to respond.

He was so proud of what lay before them; it was as if he had created it himself. 'It is beautiful,' thought Rebecca, resorting to today's favourite word, noting how it was capped by the mountain, heather and shingle, soft greens and browns nursing and cosseting the glints of slate. She repeats the words of her thoughts to James, looking past his shoulder, out across the water. Robert, who had wandered off again on his own to look at an outcrop of rock, came back.

'Did you know, the Sargasso Sea is the only sea in the world with no shores?' Nobody replied, instead, they looked away, in exasperation.

'That looks like caramelised honey' he continued, unabashed, pointing to the outcrop. He wants to capture in words the beauty of its texture, its colour; how it glows under the sun's influence, Rebecca thinks. He has startled her. She finds she doesn't like Robert's way of describing the scene: it is as if he is trying to take it all to himself. He is trying to *own* it. 'Honey doesn't caramelise', she said, tartly, 'it must be brown sugar you're thinking of, or sautéed onions!'

'Oh well, whatever...' he replied, confused by her response but refusing to be drawn into further explanation of how he feels. 'Onions!' he thinks, 'how stupid!' Instead, he said, 'The green shapes in the water, they look exactly like the speech bubbles you used to see in comics...'

Rebecca glanced down at the ocean but again did not reply. Without speaking, she moved off on her own, towards the edge of the cliff, and stopped to look out over the scene. The two men looked at each other, then they followed close behind. Robert sat down on a stone just behind her, James remained standing, alert to her every move.

She stood there, on the edge of the cliff, looking down on the sea. What a peaceful, restful thing it was. The very aliveness of it; the luminosity, the deep depth of it; the gentle, effortless lulling of it, the swelling of its body, the gentle rise and fall of its belly. One step, she thinks, and I too could be resting there, at peace forever, lulled and rocked and calmed. I could sleep there, she thinks; I could have some rest, some respite there; I could be the ocean's child. I could leave behind all this endless interrogation of conscience, all this trawling though and stirring up of memory. My memories could be allowed to fall, like silt, to the bottom. It all might just cease, it might merge into a blind contentment, induced by one long, long, thought-settling lullaby.

And then, rising up through her thoughts, and for the first time since last Thursday, she hears Ruth's voice, like a distant, muffled bell, calling out to her. She thinks sees her pale form move past, just under the surface of the green-blue fabric of the sea. For a moment, she believes she sees her hair, streaming behind her, spreading out, just like the hair she saw last Thursday in the Lagan. She feels faint; she closes her eyes. Again, she hears the distant voice calling her name; she sways; she feels hands under her elbows, hands on her shoulders. She feels herself grasped, lifted up and turned away. She takes a deep breath and then opens her eyes to look round, first into the pale, anxious face of Robert and then of James.

For a moment she pauses, rests in their hands, and then she stands up straight. She smiles.

'Let's have our picnic,' she suggests. 'I'm starving.'

****

143

They have had their picnic, beside the little lake that lies not far from the cliff edge. Now they have tidied up and are lying, or in James' case sitting, on the one shared rug, enjoying the late, bright – but, in terms of warmth, weak – sunshine. Hidden from sight in the long grass, they are looking at the sky. Robert has his trousers legs rolled up, allowing the sun to warm his knees. He had done that as a boy, he remembers, lying, alone and hidden in the long grass high up on the hillside behind the house, spotting animal shapes among the drifting clouds, chewing grass, dreaming, the sun on his knees, skylarks above – no, there had been no skylarks, it must have been blackbirds or thrushes – though he was sure the rest of the memory was accurate enough. He dwelt on the memory. On the way the sounds of summer had remained with him, how they melted into the smells he still associated with that season: the sounds of bees and distant yet close birdsong and the smell of warm grass and clover; the smell of wood smoke drifting up from an adjacent field where a farmer would be out burning hedge cuttings. Then, for some odd reason, he considers global warming: there is such a thin blanket between the earth and the emptiness of space. He finds himself stiffening. He thinks it all a bit scary.

'Do you know, the atmosphere is only about 18 miles thick? He went on, 'Nothing really. Many people drive as far to get to the shop for a tin of baked beans or for a night out in the local pub! James, if you were to drive your car straight up at a steady sixty miles per hour you would be out of this world of oxygen in no time!'

'Keeping to the speed limit! Rebecca replied, sleepily. 'I wonder, are there speed limits around the moon? I doubt it, somehow.'

'Not legal ones, at any rate,' James muttered, under his breath, but loud enough to be heard.

'I don't know about the speed limit, but you wouldn't want to do anything illegal, James. Anyway, if you pointed your car straight up and kept to that speed, and if my maths is correct, you would be outside the earth's atmosphere in less than twenty minutes!' A sudden thought strikes him. 'Can you imagine it, 'Major James' at the head of a flying column of light infantry vehicles. Can't you see it: the North Irish Horse, travelling straight up, vertically conquering open space! Colours flying. All set to establish a new plantation on the moon, a whole new moon colony! Now, that would be a sight for sore eyes! And sore hearts!'

'Don't be cruel,' Rebecca said, though she was trying to conceal a smile. James said, a bit abruptly, she thought, 'Well, I should tell you, it isn't Major any longer. I have to tell you that I have just been promoted to the rank of Lieutenant Colonel.'

Rebecca sat up. 'When did this happen? Why didn't you say?'

'Oh, a few days ago. Nothing to it, really. It's just a move away from my old command post to a staff job at Brigade.'

'Well, I think it's terrible, disgraceful. You never tell us anything.' She looked at Robert. 'Did you know about this? Did he tell you?'

Robert shrugged. 'No. Of course not.'

'It's just that I had to resign. My 'age,' you know. We are expected to stand down at forty-five. Anyway, I volunteered to stay on and was offered this staff job. Didn't want to leave.' James looked uncomfortable, shifty even, Robert thought. He could see that Rebecca was angry, or at least disappointed, and could understand why; he felt a bit sidelined himself. To break the unexpected rise in tension he said, 'So, no more light infantry, no flying through space in a tin tank? At least, you'll not collide with a flock, if that's the word, of angels!'

'A chorus… no, a choir, of angels would be good.' Rebecca said, trying to recapture the mood of a moment before.

'What about a host of Angels?' James joined in.

'Too conventional!' Robert replied.

'You know, I think I do believe in angels. How long do you think it would take an angel to travel that distance?' This was Rebecca, who had now recovered from the shock news of James's appointment. James glanced across the rug at her, glad that she had relented in her anger. 'Do angels travel like that? I can't envisage it, somehow: you know, beings, things, with wings swept back, diving like seabirds? It's a bit too, well, it's the marriage of a *physical* and a *metaphysical* concept – bit much for me to take on board…'

In the silence that followed, Robert replied. 'I have to admit I have never been considered to be an expert on angels; and I have never given much thought to what mode of travel they might favour. Did you know,' he continued, 'that distilleries have angels up in the roof spaces where they breath in the rising spirit fumes?'

'More useless information!' James muttered.

Rebecca said, musingly: 'Perhaps they don't travel, in that way I mean. Perhaps they are, somehow or other, everywhere at the same time.'

Robert replied, 'If indeed they exist in a space and time medium at all!'

'Don't be silly, Robert. Anyway, how can one entity, even an angel, be in two places at once?'

'Well, if I can be in the same place at two different times, what's to stop an angel being in two different places at the same time?

James snorted. 'Now you are playing one of your rather silly mind games with us!'

'Not really, if you take an angel to represent 'the good', it's just a way of saying that goodness can be universally present. Good is everywhere.'

'You might say that. But then, wouldn't you have to go on to say that evil is universally present? Evil is everywhere.' A cloud seems to obscure the sun. Rebecca felt its shadow. Then Robert said,

'I think it is. It's in the heart and in the mind of the evildoer. It's in his finger as he presses the trigger or presses the button or pulls the lever, or whatever. It pollutes the air through which the bullet flies and it's in the atmosphere where the bomb has exploded. It's present in that individual's action.'

'Have you ever cooked?' The question comes suddenly from Rebecca. The two men look at her. She carries on, speaking more and more quickly, the words tumbling out one after the other. 'I mean, *really* cooked, with ingredients and heat and time and all that. Well, I have suddenly realised life is like cooking, in the way we approach it. Some of us just put bits of what's to hand into a pot, heat it up and then throw in a few herbs, whatever might come to hand, just like this picnic here; whatever might be to hand, or not to hand, as the case may be! Boil it up, pour it out, and then consume it. Others,' here she looks at James, smiling now, 'others follow the recipe with minute concentration, they plan ahead, and they impose order on the process. A few of course just allow others to cook for them. Some people just go to the takeaway… You know, some are inspired, or just don't care, some are boring and mundane, some are simply lazy or just don't care…' She stopped, looking up at the men, again. She smiled, an odd, crooked smile. 'Is that trite? Is what I've just said just a tad trite…?'

'No. No.' James replies, looking at her with barely concealed concern.

'Well, it might be just a tad trite, to use your own expression,' Robert smiles, 'but it may be true, nevertheless. I'm sure where I'd fit into your hierarchy of good cooks.'

'Well, if cooking is like life, then I feel as if I have been 'cooking' with one arm missing!' Her voice has become lifeless. Robert shifts, as if to reach out to support her but James catches his eye and shakes his head.

They lay in silence for a bit, then the two men packed up the picnic and James took it to the car. Robert said, 'I can still hear the sound of the sea, even though the water itself is quiet now.' Rebecca replied, 'What does it sound like?' He concentrates; his eyes closed. Then he says:

'It's insistent; it is a noise that goes on and on; it's the noise of water lapping on stones with that insistent, circular, repetitive sound that turns slowly into a lullaby.' He pauses for a moment before going on: 'And underneath, the sound of the tide, the... I suppose the insistent *optimism*, of the tide, undermining the shingles with the ceaseless attacks and retreats, the movements of its ebbs and its flows. It communicates a sense of concord, to me...'

She thinks, by 'concord' he must mean outer calm, whereas I felt inner peace. She says, instead, 'I can hear it, but to me it's light and lyrical, like music...' She pauses. 'Can you smell anything?'

'I suppose the air is a bit salty?' he replies, running his tongue over his lips. He can't help remembering his own earlier thoughts about boyhood summers spent lazing among the scents of grass and clover. Rebecca carries on.

'Well, yes, it is but I was thinking, earlier, if I stand out on the balcony at home, I am almost always aware of a smell of dampness in the air! Here it is different: even though we are surrounded by water, the air is different, it is lighter somehow, and it smells of oxygen – light and life enhancing; oxygen and saltiness and the light in the sky: it all adds up to a kind of sensual music. I think Elgar would have made music from this.'

But she knew there was no watery concert available, what she could smell and see and hear was something given birth to by her own, innate emotional intelligence, by her inbuilt nurse's empathy, developed over the years: she knew it was all in her head, a memory given to her by numerous associations with water and rocks and wind. For, deep in her breast, she could hear the ocean's silence, now, could measure its void against her own experience of water and sea and wind and rock; yet from somewhere not here, she could hear its absent water music and then, from somewhere else, another kind of music and then out of the midst, a voice, the voice of a girl, like a bell calling. Swimming up out of the cacophony intermingling green and white and blue and grey that became black and blue, a face, Ruth's face, her own face, as if seen in a mirror. The sea's sound washes over her: again, she experiences a settling. A blanket of great peace descends upon her. Her eyes are closed. She is startled into abrupt wakefulness by Robert's voice:

I'm stranded at the edge of the world
In a world I don't know
Got nowhere to go
Feels like I'm stranded

Rebecca opens her eyes. The words rise out of the green sea. She stands up. The world rocks and rolls. She feels dizzy and reaches out to catch at Robert's arm.

'Steady on, old girl, or you'll be joining the angels,' says Robert. He takes her hand, and all is steady again.

***

A little later, walking along the cliff top, she remembers seeing, a long time ago, a programme on television in which a flower unfolds and comes into being unfolded from a tiny, tight bud into a wonderfully bloomed flower. What in reality took days, or weeks perhaps, had been captured and presented in a few seconds of what was, to her, wondrous visual poetry. She sees it again, in her mind's eye. The film speeds up. The petals increase in volume; they become a flower, black, they assume a mushroom shape; the mushroom slowly disintegrates in a mad, slow symphony of flying, coloured shards. To Rebecca's mind the colours and forms transcend into abstract images, they become the wrecks of shattered rocks and stars and planets hurtling through the darkness of eternal space. She experiences silence. She feels coldness, deep in her bones.

The silence and the coldness are one; she knows them – they are in her heart. She is back on that street; the scene recedes and then advances, the air is full of shards of hard, shining glass. They become thick, black feathers, soft... clouds of soft black feathers. She is choking, she cannot breathe. She pulls at the neck of her blouse. His attention caught by her sudden movement, Robert asks, 'Are you alright?'

She feels empty and exhausted. 'Yes.' Then, 'No,' she replies, 'No, I'm not alright. Or maybe I'm both...'

'Look,' she says, 'I want to take a walk, on my own. I need a bit of space.'

She moved off towards the cliff edge. The two men looked at one another; 'We'll go for a bit of a walk,' James said and they set off towards the longer cliff path.

She walks a little way before stopping to look at the white-tinged undulating waves. Unbidden, a picture appears in her mind. It is of two girls standing by the sea; they are looking out across the water, just as she is now in this moment, but they are separate and distant. She knows they are alien from her. She wonders idly how old or how young they might be. Six? Seven? Five? Part of her is aware that they are Rebecca and Ruth. They are holding red balloons, or rather they are holding onto the ends of long strings that are attached to two pulling and dancing red balloons. She recalls, without any conscious effort at remembering, how their parents had taken them to the seaside, how their father had bought them the balloons from a man who blew them up with stuff from a black cylinder. She remembers standing there, looking at the waves. She sees through the child's eyes a young man diving headfirst into an incoming wave and his curving pale body disappearing abruptly into its whiteness and greenness and blueness. She does not remember the string slipping from her hand. She experiences only the feeling of emptiness as she looks into her open hand, as she watches the red balloon speed away, higher and higher, lifting on the breeze, exploiting its freedom with amazing swiftness and lightness and agility.

She lives again the feeling of tears on her cheeks, the feeling of desolation she felt looking into the emptiness of her hand. She lives again the look in Ruth's eyes, the look of understanding, the feeling of empathy, and she sees again Ruth's hand opening, the string sliding through her fingers, red balloon rising against blue sky. They have perfect circularity, their precise definition between the red and blue, so cartoon-like, she thinks. For some reason she finds herself thinking about water droplets: the water being thrown by children at play. Another lurch of consciousness and she finds herself standing there once more alert to the wind on her face, to sea spread out in its watery solidity before her and to the firm earth beneath her feet.

She has no idea what has happened. All she knows is something has changed in an instant, and the world is suddenly crystalline. She no longer feels the old sickness inside; it is as if a veil has been torn in two in front of her eyes and life itself has been exorcised, abruptly. In short, she feels joy; she is joyful. She feels drunk, from joy.

James approaches: he has come back, feeling concerned about her. He looks happy but isn't. He remarks, 'What a wonderful view,' with just too much bonhomie 'What a prospect. It's so pristine; nature at its best.' He indicates all that lies below with a sweep of his hand.

She ignores him. She doesn't want to hear him.

Silence lingers and grows. He allows it to grow and grow.

'My hands are empty,' she says at last, holding them out for him to see.

'Yes,' he replies, gazing down into her bare, cupped palms. He wonders what on earth she is talking about.

'My hands are empty: but they have to be. They have been full too long. I feel I can now leave go of my self-regard. My ego does not exist, it has gone. For a moment there, before you came up, I experienced a most marvellous kind of freedom, a painful but beautiful vulnerability, so real it hurt!'

She says, in a rush, 'The awful truth is that it is just easier for us not to care *that* much, not to care *too* much, not to care *over* much. If we are to care that much, we have to be willing to *feel and accept* a connection with life that is so deep that it actually hurts. We have to be ready to live in our own experience in a way that is deeply committed, in a way that is unconditional, in a way that is authentic.'

James nods. He doesn't know what else to do. She is strange, different, he thinks. She does not say anything else and eventually they straggle to the car and make their departure, back down the disorienting sea edged, cliff-hugging road. James pays close attention to the road; Robert sits, stiffly, eyes averted; Rebecca takes in the glassy lucidity of the wide ocean, the far cliff, its dark tower, afire in her imagination.

***

Later, in the car on the return journey Rebecca says, 'Robert. Do you remember, the other day, when we were talking: you asked me why I was a nurse and all that stuff about why I stay committed to it?'

'Yes, I remember,' he replied, a bit hesitantly, but she did not notice.

'Do you remember asking me if I ever allowed my personal feelings to get in the way?

'Well, I was asking you, really, if you ever experienced, you know, pangs of doubt – in your own commitment, in particular situations, like...' He failed to finish the sentence.

'And do you remember my saying 'No"?

'Well, yes,' He replied, doubtfully, for he was still not sure where this talk was going and today, on a day that was to be devoted to Rebecca's well-being, he really had no desire to rerun a conversation they'd had numerous times in the past and one he believed would be fruitless. Better to keep things light, he thought.

It did not enter her mind to tell them of what had happened on the cliff. Instead, she carried on. 'Well, of course, that was not entirely true. I have been thinking about that, and many other things during the past few days. I think many things have come to a head. It has to do with Ruth and me and my seeing her all over the place, or rather, my thinking I have seen her. It has to do with Ruth and me and with the fact we are twins and it has to do with my meeting Ruth's killer and not being able to cope with that meeting. It has to do with me wanting to run away from it all, and it has to do with this journey to what we laughingly called the 'end of the world'. It has to do with me, really. And it has to do with your question, Robert, about nursing. And – I don't fully understand this – it has to do with the past and with my memory of it… and it has to do with the public and private worlds in which I live my life.'

Robert nods, looking at James, issuing an unspoken question: James shakes his head; Rebecca does not see him, or, at least she does not respond, she is so intent on what she has to say. James feels compelled to break the silence. 'Surely, it can't be about *all* of those things – whatever 'it' is! – I mean to say…' Rebecca appears not to hear. She continues,

'Well, let's take them one at a time: when I was a young nurse I worked with an older woman who was the best nurse I have ever met. She had this real empathy with patients and they loved her: what's more, they trusted her; they *believed* in her, she inspired *faith*. Every night, when we were on night duty, and when we got the patients settled down for the night, she would bring out their files and we would read them, together. We found out who our patients were. This man is a farmer, this man worked in the shipyard, this man is an accountant, this man is a widower, this man or this woman is an alcoholic… Then, when she was next dealing with that patient she knew who he or she was, where they were from and she could talk to him… about things that were real to him… she could connect with him, make contact… explain the treatment in his or her language; even if it was only a word in passing, it was *his* word…' James looked bemused, and then comprehends applauding in his mind the system he perceives at work.

'What she was doing was this – she was seeing each patient in a holistic way. She was one of the first people I ever saw doing that. She was one of the few people I ever saw doing that, even today! The point is, she wasn't nursing an illness, she was nursing a person, a whole, real person, not a symptom. That's what made her a good nurse. I have never forgotten that. I have tried to model myself on her. And I know she would never reject anyone who came forward as a patient, for any reason. And I do the same!'

Robert said, 'And the other day, when I asked you about... dealing with, nursing, if a really bad, evil person...'

'Well, there is my answer: but it's only partially true. What I am talking about is what happens in the ward, in public, if you like. It's like a mixture of politics and morality. But inside my head, in my private world, it's different, as I discovered the other day. There, I'm much less, if you like, tolerant of personal harm done to me.'

Rebecca tries again to explain, feeling they have not understood. 'Why am I telling you this? Or what am I trying to tell you? I think it's about balance: it's about proportion, it's about achieving harmony of some kind, it's about knowing that what's right is right when you see it. It's about love, selfless love... the instant I stood on that cliff top and surrendered to what my spirit, my soul, if you wish, had told me or had allowed me to see – I felt free... I was free...'

'I have been thinking about this a great deal over the past few days. The realisation I have come to is this: what evil is: it's a something, a thing, or an energy, it's a thing that takes love and subverts it.' She pauses, then continues in a very quiet voice: 'Whatever form it takes, it's there and its effect is this: it's like having the seed of a pernicious weed planted at the very heart of human affection, a weed of hate that destroys love. You are an instrument of that, or an instrument of love... that's the choice you have as a human being!'

'I think evil is the quality that denies other things the right to be themselves. It cannot allow another thing to be itself. Evil cannot tolerate another thing being true to its own nature. That nurse I spoke of, she wanted to know her patients, as people who were themselves: she accepted them, tolerated them, as people in their own right, not just a set of wrongs and weaknesses. She was able to grow love and respect in the heart of her patients in return. It's that sort of love that healing grows out of, like good garden loam. I tried to work like that, out of love, and: that's what is so hurtful about meeting that man... he made me confront that truth about myself...'

'I believe people have to forgive and forget,' James said, sitting up, straight and a bit stiff, Robert thought, in his chair. 'There has to come a time when we must do that. We cannot go on remembering forever, generation after generation... remembering and hating... hating and remembering...'

'I believe people, certain people, the perpetrators of violence, like the man who murdered Ruth, have to remember and repent,' Robert said; he spoke very softly. James could see his neck was flushed. 'No one else can be sorry *for* him... it's called taking responsibility...'

Rebecca spoke: 'Yes. If he said that, if he said, if he was straight and said to me, 'What I did was wrong: I am sorry' I would be able to say, 'what you did – I think – I know – it was wrong, but I am not able to forgive and forget, nor am I willing to condone it, but at least I can empathise with your feelings of guilt and remorse.' She looked from one to the other.

They sat in silence, then Rebecca spoke again: 'You see, what motivated him to plant the bomb, or the fact he put it in the wrong place or the fact that Ruth was the non-intended victim who was in the wrong place at the wrong time, these issues are of no consequence to her, or to me. She is gone. She is departed. She is dead. So, it is of no consequence to me. So, James,' she repeats this, slowly, as if knowing it for the first time, 'you see, your rational advice is of no consequence to me either: for it is of no consequence to her.'

'The more we talk about this, the more it seems to me we are living in a moral-hazard zone. No one prepared us for this, nobody handed out manuals for victims.' Robert said. He has become pensive now.

'You can love your enemy.' James said, harshly. 'There's many who would say there is a manual for your victims to look at and to consult; there is a roadmap that might show them the way out of the hazard zone.'

'And if I cannot do that, if I find I cannot trust that map…?' Rebecca asked.

'Well?' Robert asked, looking at James.

'The only other manual I am aware of is experience, the knowledge derived from generation learning from generation,' James replied.

'And what does this 'experience' of yours tell us?' Robert asked.

'It tells us is to pull up our socks and to get on with life,' James replied, tartly. Robert and Rebecca could see he was becoming irritated and defensive by the turn the conversation was taking. Robert sat back in his seat. He looked at James. He looked at Rebecca. For a moment, he considered history and the subtle, insidious impact of violence; one act and the impact it sends spreads so far, like the effect an old hen has, scratching and kicking among the dust, sending dirt flying in all directions, then caught by the wind and taken God knows how far away or how high up. He looked up to the sky. He smiled, and Rebecca became conscious of the vicious nature of his smile.

'It's amazing,' he says, 'it's only eighteen miles thick, the atmosphere I mean… Did you know, if the world was flat you could stare for ever and all you would see is infinity, over and beyond the point where the earth ends: but you know what they say, if the earth is round and you stare for ever you will eventually see the back of your own head.' James was silent for a moment. Rebecca wondered, suddenly exhausted, why men vie so. Eventually James responded with a laugh. 'Ah, a joke! Ha. Ha. Very funny. Still, if true, what does your parable tell us?'

'It tells me your 'experience' is strictly limited and what we can learn from it is limited! It tells me we are trapped, imprisoned inside space, and it tells me there is damn little we can do about it.' Rebecca interrupts him. She says, 'It's strange how you know the answers to all these obscure questions, but you don't know the answers to questions a bit closer to home!'

She sounds bitter.

'Well,' he said, 'it might be there are some questions to which there are no answers.'

Another silence grows. Then, in a somewhat lighter tone of voice she says. 'I don't know where you get all these weird ideas from! I don't know about your 'parables' but I do know this: I did not watch or listen to the Northern Ireland news for years. Each time I heard of another death, nearly always a young man it seemed, always pigeonholed into one camp or the other, it made me so sick. I couldn't cope with it. I just couldn't, I still can't cope with it!'

'There is no reason why you should have to cope with it. That's what we have politics for. Politics organises things without resorting to bloodshed,' James said.

'Yes, but they do it under the rule of law!' Robert interjects.

'But you must believe in the use of force, in violence of a kind,' Rebecca, says, 'You and your Territorial Army...'

'It's because I believe in a sanctioned army, controlled and disciplined, a force trained to engage with an enemy yes, but under the rule of law, that I believe, profoundly, in discussion, debate, argument and reconciliation. Fighting has to stop sometime; talking has to start at that point.'

'It's alright for you, James,' said Robert. 'You have your Territorial Army there as your support network. Every week, at weekends, a couple of times a year off you go for a couple of weeks' so-called training. Some salute you; you salute others; never a bullet fired in anger; the law behind you all the way. And on top of all that, you are paid for it! Adding to the family coffers, no doubt! But Rebecca has to cope with working in a hospital, and I have to cope with selling what I make with my own hands to what few tourists drive up to my door! But you, you have your boy-soldiers to play with.'

But James refused to rise to the insults. Though he was ruffled by the apparent bitterness, indeed the viciousness he perceived in Robert's voice, he remained unruffled. He has heard it all before. 'You are so right, Robert,' he said. 'We – me and my 'boy soldiers', as you choose to call them – are part of what the Elizabethans referred to as 'the great chain of being' of this human society, a necessary part; we welcome all classes and creeds. We provide discipline, order and yes, we use force, if necessary. We are there when needed. I remember Uncle Fleming telling me about...' He stopped, glancing at the look of incredulity on Robert's face. 'You didn't know Uncle Fleming had been in the Territorial Army during the war? Well, he was. I remember him telling me about his going on duty at night, guarding various areas of Belfast; the dark; the bombers overhead. In fact, he was sent for a while to Londonderry. And anyway, Rebecca has more than her work to support her. She has her choirs and a wide circle of friends from work. And she has us, for what that's worth!' He smiled at her while Robert replied.

'Well, that's true – she has friends galore. But it's also true, you do learn something new every day. I have known you – what, forty years – and I never knew your uncle had been a soldier! I suppose he was a 'major general', as well? Robert half asked, half challenged.

'No Robert, he was a private and proud to play his part. James replied. He paused, and then went on. 'Do you know, Robert, at times you can be a very irritating person indeed. If you were in the army I'd have you sent out as a sniper! You are very good at sniping.'

'Stop it! Both of you!' She is angry with them both.

***

When they reached the outskirts of Derry they decide to stop for coffee. James turned right and drove along Strand Road where they stopped at the first big supermarket they saw. It sits on the river's edge and the cafe looks out over the water and up the Foyle towards the city. Inside, they helped themselves at the self-service machines and found a table by the window. As soon as they sat down Rebecca started to talk. Unexpectedly, she said,

'You have both been very patient. So, I need to tell you about last Thursday: it's so silly, really but it shook me up, as you know. I walked in and sat down on the chair that was sitting there. As I sat down, the first thing I noticed were his hands. His hands were placed on the tabletop, one resting on the other. It suddenly struck me, they looked so peaceful. He did not speak, and I knew he was waiting for me to look at him but I did not want to look at his face or into his eyes. Then he shifted the position of his hands, so they lay on the tabletop, directly between us, palms upwards and slightly apart. The palms of his hands were pink and white, but I could see the crease lines, the lifelines, the wear and tear of a life. Despite that, they looked so 'unused' I suppose, but I knew they had been used: used for a wrong purpose! They were so ordinary. I could only think, 'These are the hands that made, or at least carried and probably primed and certainly detonated, that bomb.'

'Then I looked up. There was nothing else I could do. Our eyes met but still he did not speak, he just sat there, looking at me, with this calm, untroubled expression.' She was silent for a lengthy period. The two men waited. Then she went on, 'I found myself speaking, out aloud, 'What do you have to say to me?''

Again, she paused, before proceeding.

'He cupped his hands, somehow he seemed to lift them towards me though it was a very slight movement, a very modest movement, but I could see it; perhaps I somehow or other sensed it from the lifting of his shoulders, I could feel it as a kind of offering, resting there in his hands. It's strange, you know, even though I stared into his eyes, and something drew me to do so, I don't remember their colour – perhaps they were colourless – but I do remember his hands – the pinkness, the smoothness of his palms, the faintly etched lines, the shadows that lay around beside the veins on the backs of his hands, little patches of black hair along the tops of his fingers, the clean, square-cut nails.'

Once again she paused, sinking into silence. She gave a start, and then continued.

'Then, out of this silence that had grown he looked straight at me and spoke directly to me: 'I feel your pain.' That was all he said.' She pauses for a moment, and then goes on. 'I remember hearing the words, it seemed as if they were coming from round the back, over the top of the thought I had just had, the one about the 'pregnant silence', and I remember waiting a bit and the words staying there, in the air, or in the very centre of my head, and I remember counting the words, as I repeated them, inside my head, one, two, three four. Four words.' She pauses. 'And that was it, that was what happened. And I remember thinking, four words don't balance a life, they don't make up for a life and I remember standing aside from it all, in my mind, and thinking, it's not my pain that matters, it is Ruth's pain and all I know of her pain is this void that exists still – all she is not, all she might have been, all she would have done and made and contributed – and for an instant I could see – see is not the right word, I was looking into his colourless eyes, I was so cool, so calm, and at the same time, I was aware in my memory of the street, of the houses leaning backwards, opening up like two giant lips, her body lifting up, the silence, then the noise, the air filled with stuff – everything… stiffened, slowed down: and still I found myself standing watching his hands. They were still there, in front of me, resting, crossed on the table, I could see his hands – the clean, neat, uncalloused hands they said had made it and left

163

it…' She paused: 'Then, I just stood up, turned round and walked out. As I reached the door his voice sounded again 'We have all experienced pain…' his voice said… whispered…'

'It was as if the earth had opened, and I had fallen through and had kept on falling. I did not, I could not, reply. There was nothing I could say. I just walked through the door, left the building and into the street. It was all I could do. I don't know how I managed to get home. I barely knew I was on the journey.'

'It was the *falseness* of his hands…' she continues, so quietly they can hardly hear her. Then, 'So that's the great mystery solved. I told you there wasn't much to it. I met a man in a room, across a table. Each of us spoke a very few words. I left. Not a very dramatic story!' Robert responded, 'I think you were very… I know, it took a lot of courage to meet him, or to confront him, like that.'

'Yes.' James agreed.

'I keep on thinking, what if I had taken his hand? What if I had embraced him, if I had folded him in my arms, as a good nurse would have done with a patient, and willed nothing but good for him and of him, sincerely? I keep on asking this: but I do truly believe it would have served no purpose, even if I had done it, even if I could have done it. What he is, and what I am, are so different – I believe they must never become one. He must remain the black to my white, the malignant to my benign, and the evil to my good. It has to be like that. I can see no other way. And I cannot forgive him what he did. I can't forgive, for Ruth's sake; I don't have the right.'

The weight of her feelings seems to bear down on them all. Robert sits, his hands raised, cupping his forehead. Eventually, James breaks the silence: 'Of course, what he did was unjust: unjust to Ruth, unjust to you, personally. I believe it was also unjust, in other ways, but that's beside the point, now…' Robert says, 'Unjust, indeed! I'd put it more strongly! You talk about his hands, Rebecca. Those clean, neat hands took Ruth's life, but they did more, they hurt you. They hurt your family.' Looking at each in turn he continues in an exaggeratedly monotonous voice, 'they hurt you and they hurt us.'

She looks at them, across the growing silence: it is as if she had not heard them speak. She says, 'You see, don't you? I cannot. I could not. I am not able to forgive him. Even though he needs my forgiveness. Even though it goes against all my principles, as a nurse, as one who believes you must heal if you can. For her sake, I cannot heal him, if that is what he wants. And it's not for vengeance I say that it's not to make him 'pay' – for he cannot, he does not have the currency to pay for he is morally bankrupt, all he could do was to take life, life he cannot put back.

Rebecca sat up in her chair. 'It's frightening,' she said, the knowledge of how one moment can alter the flow of a person's life and what the effects of that can be. Something like an accident. A foot slips on wet grass: a fall, a leg broken that was whole an instant before; it's so simple, so quick, so irredeemable – once it happens, it cannot be altered or changed. The bone is fractured, and nothing can 'un-fracture' it. Like Ruth: a life was halted, stalled, and nothing can restart it.'

James replied, 'Yes, I know. After such a happening as Ruth's death nothing could ever be the same again. But it must be. Life must go on…'

'It has to be like that, life. I suppose I mean life; you cannot have a life that is all benign, just as you cannot have a life that is totally malignant. I mean, his hands, their cleanliness seems to have upset you. That and what he said to you... but isn't it time to draw a line under what happened in the past? It's the only way we can move on, the only way we can grow out of it...'

'You went into that process blindly, numbly, without thinking it through. You didn't even tell us about it!'

'I know,' she said, 'I'm sorry about that.'

Robert carried on: 'You were quite right not to allow yourself to be sacrificed on the altar of civic healing, or whatever justification this process has conjured up for itself. We are wrong to not say clearly when something is wrong or false!'

Robert interrupted, impatiently: 'Ruth's death was not the result of a slip on a patch of wet grass... it was no accident. Ruth was killed, assassinated from the shadows and by an anonymous hand. That man, his action was eight hundred years in the making, brewing away, an invisible thing but a powerful thing, moving down from father to son, leaching down, through all those generations... a terrible itch that cannot eased by scratching...

'Yes' James replied, 'but, that man is not alone; the world is full of political conflict... it's a part of our nature, to engage in conflict. They used to say, didn't they, that the land was barren, it needed the sacrifice of blood to make it fertile again...'

Robert again interrupted him. He retorted, hotly, 'Sacrifice of blood, my granny! The love of the old filthy

166

lucre, more likely! Have you any idea of the number of rich men we have running about Belfast in big cars, living in big houses, as a result of all this?'

There is a pause. They are both embarrassed by Robert's outburst. Then Rebecca says, softly: 'And so you think the strongest always win, win and prosper, that those most willing to exert the most violence will always prosper and do well? If that's the case, what's to happen to the meek: are they not to inherit a bit of this earth, after all?'

Robert frowns but remains silent. He shakes his head. He sits turning and turning the empty coffee cup on the tabletop. Eventually, James speaks, 'Yes, exactly, exactly so. But not everyone is infected by that virus of hatred that Robert has referred to, not everyone is prepared to take life in order to 'cleanse the land' or to change society or to make a political point or to make money or to gain power – only the very few do that, thank God!

'It may be more than you like to think. And, I don't think God has much to do with it!' Robert retorts. 'Even the Bible, to which Rebecca has referred, makes clear we human beings are the authors of our own destiny...'

'Yes' James agrees, 'we have been given free will. But within limits. We were given the ability to make choices, but I do think the scope to exercise such choice is limited, you know.'

Robert looks at him with an expression of incredulity commingled with exasperation. 'We all know your position on this: it's very well for you – you are the one who defines the limits – in your heart, you believe the world is going to hell in a handcart unless we are doused in moral guidance, given doses of strong government and watched over by police forces and large armies.' James is stung into replying. 'And what would you have us put in the place of social order? 'Love and do what you will!' Is that it? That's no way to run the country.' Then he smiles to lighten his words. 'You are an old hippy, an anarchist, at heart.'

'I suppose you would say that. Anyway, it only takes a few nutcases to cause mayhem. But that few are aided and abetted by the many who give silent support,' Robert mutters, darkly. 'And the only way to stop them is to get the people on your side, on the side of right.'

Rebecca asks, 'But then, who determines what is right?'

'Exactly! James says, 'There have to be absolutes, we must have lines in the sand. And these have to be set and policed by some form of authority... we can't leave it to individuals to do it by themselves...'

Rebecca has been listening to this and is becoming increasingly impatient. 'We keep getting away from the point I'm trying to fix on. You are being too rational; both of you have read too much, and I suspect you haven't understood much of it. I have been too rational also, I think, for far too long, but James is right: the world is full of examples of people committing terrible acts of violence and we need order imposed on that. And you are right too, Robert: not everyone takes that route – some people do the right thing, exist in harmony with their neighbours and love to do good... the question for me is, how do I respond to all this? Is the way I have responded the right or best way? I don't think so. I have to change; I have to change my understanding of things. And I think there is a higher 'thing' in charge – we always have to resort to a higher authority – it might be 'love' or it might be God or it might be something

I have no understanding of… I'm prepared now to rest on this belief… I think I regained possession of my soul today.'

She stops there, waiting for a response, but they seem not to have heard what she wants them to hear.

James continues, 'Otherwise, eventually, what that man did will destroy you, just as much as he destroyed Ruth.'

Robert interrupts him, 'Don't you think that is one incredibly good reason for holding such people who kill, randomly, for their own ends, to proper, moral, account for what they do? I do believe individuals make choices and they should be held accountable. Rebecca, you have been worried sick all weekend because that man asked for something you could not give, and why should you give him anything? Least of all, understanding, or forgiveness, or even recognition.'

Rebecca replies tiredly, 'You seem to be arguing against yourself, Robert. I believe that too, but now I think we are – I am – in danger of just keeping everything going – I mean, do you want someone sitting here in another eight hundred years' time killing someone because of what happened to Ruth and all the other Ruths in this horrible thirty-year attrition?'

Rebecca notices Robert's fists tighten where they rest on the tabletop, but he replies, quietly enough, 'Such people will find a reason.'

'No, I don't believe that.' James retorted. 'I have, what I believe, is a measured hope and faith and I have a belief in the goodness that resides in people – generally, I mean.'

'I was like that,' Rebecca said, 'but I changed. I believed in the innate goodness of humanity; but I also believed in the great need most human beings have for order and support and understanding and help: that is why I wanted to become a nurse. Now I need to rebuild my belief in the innate goodness in me, the goodness that is there, if only I can find it – because it's outside me, as well. That's what I felt, really felt, on the cliff top today. My corporeal body just drifted away, and I was joined with the sea and the sky and the cliffs… I said earlier – you didn't hear me – that I feel I have gained possession of something, my soul, perhaps, but it feels good, I feel good.

'My mind, sometimes, recently, it has refused to think – I think it suffers from a lack of energy, or something. It's suffering from a strange kind of inertia, but I have to work this through. Then, sometimes, I find myself thinking so fast, it is really scary.

'But back there, on top of Slieve League, I experienced something *real*. I felt alive and strong, but I also felt together – together *within* myself but at the same time I felt together with all that was *around* me. It was like a kind of religious experience, only not just religious, more spiritual… something like a new reach of reality opened up for me.'

Robert replied, 'I'm sure that this world of consciousness is only one of numerous worlds of consciousness that exist. Or we have access to multitudes of realms of consciousness, if only we pay attention…' Rebecca nodded. 'Yes, it's the intensity that matters…' But simultaneously she thinks back to that other odd episode on the cliff top. She must have dozed off while the two men went to explore the path. Oddly, for such a brief slumber, she had a vivid dream. In it, Robert turns to her and places the palms of his hands flat on his chest. He bows, formally, from the waist, and says, 'Madam, may I have this dance?'

She curtsied. She smiled. She replied, 'Thank you.' They joined hands and danced. Round and round they went, faster and faster. The world became a panorama. She felt herself to be as light as a shadow an immaterial thing in his arms. The sea, the cliffs, the hilltop, the flat land and then the sea again. Round and round he swung her; she felt herself carried in his arms, her feet barely touching the ground, until the landscape had become a blurred background.

Then, as if by magic, as if placed here by a great hand, James appears. He is standing apart, looking out to sea. Now she is in James's arms, or a copy of her is in his arms, and the dance goes on, then slows, and then stops.

She has had a strange experience, but she could not put into words what it was, or what it was like. It is like a revelation of the kind of relationship she has with the world that is around her.

She remembers all this but does not share the memory with the men. Somehow, it is too odd a thing to admit to having dreamed, much too embarrassing to reveal. Instead, she says, 'One moment I was dancing, or someone like me was dancing, then the next I was standing, looking out over the water, when I suddenly experienced the strangest feeling. I felt for a moment – felt isn't right, the word is not strong enough – I 'knew' for a moment that I was *wearing what lay all around me!*

'It was not… how can I put this… it was not my body that was wearing what was around me, it was me. Me, my identity, the real me, something different from my own body, was suddenly revealed, and was at one with the earth, with the universe. And that included Ruth... for that moment she was not lost to me... we were one again...' She pauses, but forces herself to carry on.

'I alone must face this challenge. I have been trying to live under the heel of inertia. I have forgotten what it is to be really human – I must succumb to my soul's demand for oneness, wholeness and completeness.'

James raises his head. 'It's the full implication of this that's exciting!'

'What's that? Robert looks puzzled.

James carries on. 'It's to do with Ruth, isn't it: if you are one with 'everything', you are at one with her, as well.'

'Yes!'

'That means you are not a victim!'

'Yes.'

They are silent for a while until James seems about to speak, but Rebecca holds up her hand to silence him.

'I want to just leave it: I suddenly feel at peace, and I want to savour it and enjoy it and just let it take its course. I don't want to think about it or to talk about it.' Nevertheless, she goes on, not allowing the silence to grow. Speaking quickly, she says, 'You know, for years I watched people on television, relations of victims of violence – mothers, fathers, brothers, wives, sons and daughters – standing there before the camera with tears in their eyes, saying, 'I forgive them' or 'I have no feelings of hatred for them' or 'I only feel sorry for them.' Do you realise how that made me feel… me, who felt so unforgiving? I certainly did not hate the person who killed Ruth – but neither could I forgive him, and if I did not hate him, I hated what he had done… I felt only disdain for him as a human being and totally disavowed what he stood for.'

They leave the café and go straight to the car. James immediately starts the engine, but before pulling away from the car park, and without speaking, he leans over to open the pocket on the passenger side and rummages through it. 'Ah!' he says, holding up a CD. 'We will listen to this. We have talked enough, for the time being. We will listen for a while and not talk.'

He puts it into the CD player and turns it on. It is the St Matthew Passion.

'Bach,' Rebecca says approvingly as the music starts, filling the car. They drive in silence, listening. They listen to the quiet voices raised after Christ's ordeal… Then the car is filled with voices, singing, 'Come ye daughters share my mourning…'

'Ah!' thought Rebecca, 'Humanity can overcome. I too can overcome… eventually…' She looks at James, 'Sometimes,' she says, 'you can be wonderfully perceptive.'

'Yes,' says Robert, turning to wink at Rebecca over the car seat, 'I agree with you: he is a really, truly wonderful human being! And always very good to his ma…'

***

It starts to rain as they leave Londonderry behind. The car glides along; they pass over a bridge. 'Burntollet, back to one of the places it all started,' Robert says. He appears to have forgotten their earlier passing of the bridge and the conversation they had had then. The others do not reply, and they travel on in silence, the rain now beginning to beat off the windows.

'Thirty-eight years ago,' Rebecca thinks.

'What a waste,' Robert thinks.

'Well, we have come a long way, since then,' thinks James.

As they top Glenshane they can barely see the great plain of mid-Ulster as it lies before them, half obscured. 'Do you see the downpour?' Robert asks reflectively, then defines his question, 'it's as if someone was throwing – or perhaps 'broadcasting' is a better word – huge handfuls of rain out over the plain.'

'The Rain in Spain Stays Mainly on the Plain.' He half sings, half speaks the line, in an attempt to lighten the mood, but Rebecca has again fallen into silence. Then, he says, 'You will both stop off at my place. I have some food in the house.' He takes their silence for acceptance and settles back into his seat. Each is engaged with his or her own thoughts. The music plays, the rain beats off the windows, the car speeds along into the east.

***

Two hours later and they have eaten what they always eat when it is Robert's turn to cook: steak, potatoes from the garden, vegetables he has grown himself. If it is out of season, he is happy with green peas taken from a can and potatoes from the local shop. On these occasions he habitually orders three enormous steaks 'well hung, as black as you can find them,' from the village butcher. This evening, he went to the freezer. His steak cooking skill is something he is proud of and he always cooks three steaks. He has one, Rebecca and James protest – habitually – the size, and share a steak, and the spare one is set aside to be used by Robert the next day. Tonight, however, they will eat what they are given, without protest.

James gets the fire going while Robert gets busy in the kitchen. Rebecca, who wants to be alone, takes the two dogs outside for a walk. Soon, James calls through the open door, 'Where are your napkins? Do you have clean ones?'

'Do you really need napkins?' Robert calls back.

'Yes, of course I do!'

'There might be some on the shelf of the dresser – under that pile of newspapers.'

He smiles when he hears James mutter. Then he realises Rebecca is still outside and opens the kitchen window to look out. He sees her sitting on a tree stump by the pond, looking out over the water, the two dogs sitting by her side. 'Rebecca, two minutes!' The dogs lift their heads at the sound of his voice, and Rebecca lifts her right hand in acknowledgement before rising to make her way back to the house.

'Wull thon dae?' Robert asks, pointing to the wooden kitchen table, and Rebecca replies instantly, 'It'll dae gran.'

'Yer a pair o' right glipes!' says James. He feels the brittleness of the mood but enters into it.

'The day,' Robert says, 'you two will dae justice to my cooking and you will eat a steak each. It's the sort of stuff will stick to yer ribs.' They demur to Robert's enthusiasm, James because he cannot find the energy tonight to protest (and anyway, he is hungry) and Rebecca because she is only half aware of the food's presence.

And they will have wine. Robert buys only red wine, always French. Usually, they have two bottles with some left over because James only ever drinks one glass and Rebecca drinks little. Tonight, and unusually, she has had three glasses and is now holding her fourth, allowing the glow from the coal to bring the wine to life in her glass. She is aware of its glow in her veins.

Still, she looks pale, James thinks. He is concerned for her. She is under a lot of stress, Robert thinks. He is concerned for her. He is angry that this is still going on; he thinks she ought not to have become involved in this scheme to meet Ruth's killer.

She herself now feels relaxed and slightly fuzzy; it has been a long week. It is her last week, she considers, as a woman who is forty-five. Next week, she thinks, I will be forty-six. Forty-six seems somehow different: it is a figure with great significance. It must mean she has passed the halfway stage – few enough live until they are ninety. This thought is accompanied by another, and the idea of Ruth re-enters her mind – she wonders is this an idea, or is it an image, physical in its emotional intensity? It certainly is a fuzzy black and white picture… or is it a word, her name, 'Ruth'. Whatever it is, it is as if a shadow is passing between her and the fire, and for a mere moment she feels an old familiar chill. Then it is gone, receding to the back of her consciousness. Today has changed her in some way, but she resists thinking about it: she will think about it later.

They have eaten and sit now by the fire. For the moment, the past is gone, and she feels half-asleep and very contented. She knows her moods change as swiftly as the shower of sparks that hasten up the chimney, their confusion caused by Robert's throwing another log of wood onto the fire. Sparks fly upwards, only to be swallowed by some invisible mouth. The fire illuminates the room with its long, sustained glow. The smell of burning wood and turf lingers in the air. Raindrops meander down the windowpane. The dogs make an occasional growling noise deep in their throats, out of the depths of canine dreams.

They are such good companions, she thinks, feeling drowsy and comfortable. This is so companionable: we are easy together, existing like this, comfortably between silence and utterance. I am so lucky to have these two as friends. Her head nods and she slides into instant sleep.

Robert is murmuring something to James when, without warning Rebecca leaves the room. She rushes into the kitchen. For what seems to be a very long time, silence, interrupted by the crackle of the fire and the sound of rain on the window glass, maintains its presence in the house, then it is broken by the sound of a cupboard door opening and a clatter of tin upon tin.

The two men look at each other, but do not say anything. Robert shrugs, lifts his hands and shrugs, a gesture meant to convey an unspoken question. James stands up and follows Rebecca into the kitchen. He finds her standing on a low footstool, carefully rearranging a few food cans in a cupboard. He knows well enough that they do not need ordering for he had looked into that same cupboard earlier in the evening – he was searching for something, water glasses, he remembered – and it had been perfectly neat and tidy.

He stands by her side for a moment, and then lightly touches her elbow. She turns slowly and looks at him and then reaches out her hand and, in what is such a fleeting gesture that he cannot be sure it has happened, her fingers brush his cheek. Or so he thinks, it happens so quickly, this touch and they are not really touching people. Now she has stepped down from the stool and is standing on the floor, looking up into his eyes.

'Go in and talk to Robert,' she says, 'He is on his own. I'll be there in just a second.'

When at last she returns, Robert and James are sitting at the table. They are talking about something, but she knows not what. Their voices are like the low rumble of pebbles on a beach. Her mind is numb, and she feels, rather than knows, that her body is cold. Then Robert speaks to her. It is a question, something to do with wine. 'I'm sorry,' she says, 'I'm sorry about just now, about leaving the room so suddenly.' And then, without preamble, she starts to talk to them. The words run out of her mouth, without pause, without punctuation. The words she spoke earlier were only a rehearsal for this, James thinks. She speaks, Robert thinks, as a shipwrecked man must swim to stay afloat, far out in the open sea: desperation is the only word he can find to describe it.

She tells them of falling asleep and then of a dream; she dreamt of her meeting with Ruth's killer. It all came back to her. She speaks of the shock she felt on looking into his eyes, so pale; she recalls the life-emptiness of his pale eyes, she speaks of seeing his neat, clean hands resting on the table; she explains the feelings of helplessness that pervaded her body and her being. She recounts her rush from the room, of her running home through the city streets, of the next few days spent in a confusion of competing feelings and emotions. She wants to explain how she has been trying to keep her feelings contained.

***

'If you don't mind I need to explain a bit more, and as much for myself as for you: I think now is the time to do it.' Rebecca sits in her chair, facing Robert and James. She absent-mindedly plays with the half-full, half-empty wine glass Robert has put into her hand. She takes a deep breath, and then begins. 'This all started on Thursday – or, at least, Thursday brought it to a head.' She pauses. 'You know, I always seemed to be the one who was 'in charge', I was the one who always 'took charge'. What I remember about this is the feeling of absolute helplessness that swept over me. I was imprisoned by it… it was as if I were frozen within walls of ice… looking out, through this barrier, seeing but unable to be seen, unable to stop what I could see, what I knew was happening… I think, now, that I never really recovered from that, that feeling of total impotence.

'And the silence – it was as if I were behind a wall that imposed silence on me. And the dust – I will always remember the clouds of dust that suddenly appeared.'

She has paused, again, and the silence grows heavy, but the two men maintain their patient waiting, each of them feeling in his own way that it is right to wait for her, that this is her space. This is the first time either of them has heard her attempt to describe that day's events in anything approaching personal detail. Robert is hungry to discover the truth of what had become – it has really grown, has been nurtured, he thinks, almost organically – into a secret, something they never speak of except in broad, general, third-party terms; a silence has been birthed, it has become accepted. He realises he wants this revelation as much for his own sake as for Rebecca's, for he too is self-interested. He too loved Ruth. He too misses her and feels her loss, perhaps not as much now, for human memory dulls with time, but still… he misses her. Rebecca is right, he thinks… it is Ruth's absence, it is the total absence of what might have been that is still there, a physical, concrete… absence… and the fact that she is not recoverable… she is gone… her absence is like a hurt that will not go away.

James, on the other hand, had always adopted a clinical, detached, watchful attitude to what one part of him thinks of as 'this business of Rebecca and Ruth,' and through Rebecca to Ruth's death. He has, in fact, he feels strongly, developed what he considers to be a fairly healthy stance to it. The result is, he believes, that he does not need to hear this, not really—but still, he remains watchful of Rebecca. She, now, is what matters. All else he cares nothing for.

Well, there are things he does care for, to be truthful. He believes in law and order – that reminds him why he continues to serve in the Territorial Army, after all these years: it is out of a deep belief in law and order, in democracy, and in strong, good government. Also, of course, he likes the life, the comradeship, the men: he likes the talk. This has helped him, it has become a kind of family, a source of conformity and a form of security.

For, in truth, his own life had been torn asunder that day. He too allows his thoughts to run on the past, for a bit. He recalls how they had begun to talk about weddings; the girls had wanted their weddings to be on their birthday. 'A double wedding – it will kill my father!' he remembers Ruth saying, referring to the cost. What had been killed, he thinks, his mind now overrun by a jumble of memories, thoughts and emotions, had not been her father. A man's hand had reached out of the sunshine of an autumn afternoon and set a briefcase down in a shop doorway: the man had walked away, safe and alive, firm of step and healthy, breathing, fit. He was alive. Moments later, Ruth had walked past a doorway and had died. She remained dead. It was as simple as that.

To him, there was no sense to what had happened, and no way of making sense of it. The man had been caught within days, but only because a sharp-eyed security man remembered him and came forward with his description. It transpired that he had left the bomb in the wrong place – but then, weren't all places wrong… Ruth had died, Rebecca had suffered terribly, the parents had suffered, he had suffered, Robert had suffered, their lives had been turned upside down. And whose fault it was is irrelevant, he thinks. It was that man's fault for leaving the bomb, it was the fault of those who sent him, it was circumstance's fault that Ruth was passing at that second, it was the Government's fault for allowing things to get out of hand, it was the police's fault, it was society's fault, it was the terrorists' fault, it was the 'securocrats' fault; why was it always someone else's fault? The past, history, society…

James sets these well worked thoughts out one more time in his mind. He orders them. He likes order, and order is coming – has come – he is sure. We have to move forward. The Troubles are over. The country is in great shape, business generally seems to be booming and buildings are going up all over the place, north and south. Look at Donegal this morning, he thinks, new houses everywhere. One of the dogs grunts – it is Blue - and shifts position. She likes to sleep over his feet and he likes to have her there, like a great foot muff. The clock strikes. He rises out of his reverie; he becomes aware the other two are talking. Rebecca is speaking, 'So, I have decided: I want to… explain. I know I have never talked about this… it's been difficult… first of all it was as such a… a… my behaviour has excluded you… the very last thing I would want to do… I felt it was too private… Ruth's death, I mean…

'It was a very public death,' Robert interjected, harshly, almost brutally, it sounds to Rebecca.

'Yes, and when that public part of it was over – and it was public in many different ways – and during all of that, the hours and days immediately after the blast, hospitals, the wake, the burial, the television news, the newspapers, the whole paraphernalia of evidence gathering, all the enquires, the repeated questions, then the police and the trial…'

There is a silence. The fire murmurs. The dogs lie like stones, unmoving. The two men wait patiently. The clock's tick fills the room. Robert notices the rain has stopped.

'On top of that, going home each day, into the family home, into the place where we had grown up with so many memories. Then there was my father and mother, sitting in silence –the house was desolate, they were desolate, I was desolate – the door shut and locked at dusk. Those long, long silences. After the initial frantic activity, I just… shut down… or a vital part of me shut down.'

'You had to protect yourself – that's understandable,' Robert said. Again, his voice sounded harsh. There was another pause, and then James spoke.

'You mentioned your feeling of helplessness earlier, remember...?'

'Yes,' she said, 'It was during those few moments when I turned round and saw Ruth and then the blast occurred and I could see her. I could see her die before my eyes and I could do nothing about it. And I was the one who always took charge, I always did things, I was always in charge, except when she really needed me... then I failed her. Out of that sprang all kinds of things. I have tried to hide them, ignore them.'

'What things?' It was Robert who spoke.

'Well, guilt, mostly. Shame, I suppose: you see, I think my self-image had been shattered. I felt worthlessness. Why not me? Why her? Even now, talking about it like this, is difficult – I feel I should be talking about Ruth, not me... Anyway, then I kept on seeing Ruth in the most upsetting kind of places and thinking about her. I know our being twins has been a part of it all... that, and my being a nurse, a healer! How can you heal others, if you can't heal, forgive...?'

Again, she sinks into silence. Then Robert stirs in his chair. 'You never seemed to be angry,' he says. 'I was angry, I am still angry!' He wants to awaken her from the dream she sinks into. One night, a few years ago, he had gone into the pottery. He told how he had been a little drunk and very angry. He had been frustrated and angry with James. James looks startled but says nothing. Robert carries on. He had been frustrated and angry with Rebecca and, above all, perhaps, he had been angry and frustrated with himself. And, perhaps, he had been just more than a little drunk...

For some reason he took down from the shelves four tall pots he had set up to cook earlier that day. Freud, he says, would have had something to say about all of this. He placed them on the anvil and looked at them. He took a heavy knife that lay on the anvil and proceeded to attack the pots with powerful, sweeping downward swings, the knife slicing through the air before severing the still damp pots into slices. He could still see the pots falling open before his attack. They looked like lilies, he says, their blooms burst ajar, their petals fallen in mute, innocent disorder.

He turned away, then looked again. The thin slices of pot lay where they had fallen, all a-tangle: it was like a mass grave, he says, a jumble of legs and arms intertwined, interlocked. The sadness of it made him cry. Blinded, he went out and left the mess where it lay. Then, for something compelled him to return, he came back into the pottery. He carefully composed and contained the four pots in one composite and unitary state, arm over arm, leg over leg, petal over petal, and carried them to the kiln. There he placed them, fired up the kiln and cooked the scrambled pieces until they were hard and firm. Later, he set the finished article; he never knew what to call it. One day a visitor asked him about it and he replied, without thought, that it was 'an accident' – the title stuck.

It is a remarkably ugly piece: objectively, he knows this, yet to him it exudes beauty. To him, it is beautiful. He says this to Rebecca, tonight, with James listening, because earlier today, all day, in fact, something has changed. He can feel it. Something in her has changed. He feels he wants to reach out to her. If he does and if she can hold onto that, he thinks, there is a chance we will all change, a chance our lives will change.

She does not speak for a time. The two men continue to wait.

Then she says, 'I think it is beautiful, also. It's how we are different. You have worked on experience: I have worked to experience.'

***

'No, I don't. Yes, I'm sorry. I'm rambling...' She spoke rapidly now, starting at the beginning again, as if remembering by rote. 'I had gone on ahead, alone, because Ruth had stopped to look into a shop window. I half-turned round, I think I called her name, then – it was as if my world just stopped suddenly, but somehow everything else kept on moving... and the silence... it was a very loud noise, followed immediately by this terribly intense silence – that was when the sense of not being relevant, of not being of any use, started, I think... I could see what was happening, but could not stop it.'

'When we were on the cliff top earlier today it was really quiet.' Robert was looking at her very intently. 'Is that the kind of silence you meant?' he asked.

'No, not at all – that's why I compare them, the two silences.' She hesitated, before continuing, 'Do you remember when we were little, you,' she looked from Robert to James, 'You used, both of you used, to catch flies... you went through a phase of it. Do you remember? You would catch a fly, put it in a bottle and screw on the cap. Then you would watch it, for hours. We – Ruth and I – used to hate you doing that. But the silence I imagine the fly experienced inside that sealed bottle must be similar to the silence I experienced that day. It's more than just the absence of noise...'

'I have thought about that moment a lot. It's the absence of time, I suspect. That is what makes the silence so

185

complete, that's where your helplessness had its roots.' This was Robert, speaking very softly. Rebecca glanced at him, quickly.

'Yes, that's right. It's like I was outside time… it's hard to explain, but what you've just said – that comes close to it.'

Time.

Once more, she finds her mind is wandering, following meandering thoughts. This is a form of behaviour she is not normally prone to. Is it the heat, the wine, the release of tension? Or is it that, for the first time, the walls she has erected to keep things apart and isolated are coming down?

'And do you know, the strangest thing… this has happened only, I think, three times: I might be walking along the street when, suddenly, I see – I think I see – Ruth, but it's like I see this so-fleeting glimpse of her, but – and this is the strange thing – it's as if I am seeing her in a mirror. It's as if I am seeing the mirror through a rift in the walls of reality and I see her image in it, or through it, but it's never her, it's her image reflected from somewhere else… She is there, but still, so far away, beyond my reach… she just slides into vision, then just as abruptly, slides out again… unhurriedly, but so quickly… it's as if she is there, just on the other side of something like a curtain, close but cut off from me.' She looks from one to the other. 'It is eerie, I know. When I speak about it now it sounds so strange. And again, though not so strong, this feeling – this knowledge of not being able to speak to or communicate with her – or she with me…'

'It sounds as if you are dreaming you are awake,' interrupted Robert.

'Yes. Yes. That's one way of putting it…' She is silent for a bit, then, 'It's uncanny, how you seem to understand these odd experiences of mine…'

'I don't know that it's so odd, really – we have shared…,' he corrected himself, 'we share, so much in common, don't we? It's just, we… well… don't express what we feel to others, very well… We all exist behind walls, just peering out, as you once described it…'

'So, anyway, last Thursday I went to meet – perhaps 'confront' is a better term – the man who killed Ruth. I walked into that room, looked at him and heard him say he understood my pain, heard him, I suppose, acknowledge my feelings, possibly ask for my forgiveness.'

James is waiting to speak, to support her: 'You weren't ready for it.'

'I sleepwalked into it!

'No!' Robert said, 'You were not ready for it. You have isolated yourself behind a protective wall and have grown used to it, you have existed behind a wall of denial for so long… denial about so many things…' He sounds so bitter, she thinks, and why shouldn't he be? But she went on, as if he had not spoken.

'I saw him so clearly. He was so real. He wore a white shirt, short sleeves, with a plain blue tie. His hair was cut short, very neat. His hands were clean, neat, workman-like; he stood up, I think, when I came into the room, and offered me his hand. I almost took it, but something checked me, held me back. He had aged since I last saw him in the court. He had become more solid, a man – then, he was really only a boy… He spoke… I ran out… I ran away…'

'You were ambushed,' James said.

'Ruth was ambushed!' Robert spoke quickly and instinctively, without thought.

'So, I won't be ambushed again. I won't sleepwalk again. I have decided, just today, when I stood up there, on top of Slieve League, I decided I will meet with him again. only this time I will be stronger. And I've decided… the meeting: it is about me, not Ruth. I have to express my love for her, my respect for her, my abiding sense of loss, the loss of a part of me, but I must not allow that to be contaminated by hate.'

'Do you feel hatred?' James asked.

'No. I don't. It's a cliché I know, but I don't hate *him*, I hate what he *did*. That's a distinction I keep having to draw, in my own mind. But, I want him to know – to realise, to understand – that I hold him responsible for what he did.

'Excuse me, for a minute. I want to be on my own, I need to be alone, just for a bit.' She stood up, her still-full glass in her hand. Robert reached out and took it from her as she left.

***

Rebecca stepped out into the yard and into the night. Having closed the door behind her she stood on the stone doorstep, giving herself time to adjust to the darkness. She became aware of the silence. Eventually, she could see the dark form of the tree and then the pond's lighter shape begin to materialise. This provided her with a point of reference, a marker against which she could start to place herself and her own position. She began a slow but steady movement towards the pond, both hands stretched out before her, her feet making a crisp crunchy-shuffling sound on the gravel. Across fields, on the road two cars sped past causing a startlingly great commotion in the rural night, creating a noise that darted itself into her consciousness. 'Boy racers!' she thought, as their twin lights disappeared over the top of the hill, departing abruptly from sight and then from sound.

She found that she had stopped, that she was standing in complete silence; she was conscious of a few stars now, appearing in the sky. She felt for a moment a great sense of peace, similar to the feeling she had experienced on Slieve League.

Then she became aware also of a noise: it was a small, insistent sound, not unlike that of a watch ticking. After all she has been through she could not but remember that Ruth's watch had a very loud tick. The feeling of peace evaporated. Then the back of her hand was touched by something wet and rough – it is rough, wet skin. Involuntarily, she shrieked or screamed and immediately the house door opened allowing a flood of light to fall across the yard. In its light she saw one of the dogs, standing beside her; behind it, she could just see Robert standing on the doorstep.

'Is everything alright? he calls out.

'Yes,' she replied, 'it was the dog, it licked my hand in the dark and startled me and I shouted out, that's all.' He closed the door and she could hear his footsteps as he approached her. They were standing close together, in a silence within silence, watching the stars sharpen in the sky. Clouds shifted and swathes of starlight became visible. The moon moved out from behind a distant hill; the wind had risen and a tree moved. They are in concert with the universe, she thought. Then, Robert's voice enters into her consciousness:

'Oh, God, make small
The old star-eaten blanket of the sky
That I may fold it round me and in comfort lie…'

'That's beautiful,' she said. 'Who wrote it?'

'I don't know,' he replied. 'I remember reading it, or learning it, at school. It always comes to mind when I see the stars on a night like this.'

She observed the shape and form of him for a moment, out of the corner of her eye. She remembers, once, they talked, a bit like this, about Ruth. She remembers him saying, 'There is a hidden rage in me. I feel it. I keep it disguised. Good manners… you know.' 'It's strange,' she thinks, 'how I forgot that.'

She thinks, she remembers so much, too much.

'Do you remember that day, a long time ago, when you and James fought? It was down by the river. You and he climbed out on a branch, on the big chestnut tree…'

'I do, vaguely. Why do you ask… I mean, what made you think of that, now? You asked us earlier… this morning, wasn't it?'

'It's just that James mentioned it a few moments ago. He never did before. It was just now, just before I came out. He said he had been thinking about it, earlier. It reminded me. That's all.'

'Oddly enough, I don't remember the fight so much as sitting on the river bank afterwards. It must have been early autumn for we had just gone back to school. It was our last year at primary school, I think. Anyway, we were sitting on the riverbank looking at a crop of mushrooms that were growing beneath the trees. I remember the smell of dampness, of mud and water and the mushrooms – the colour of sand, they were. You know that sand you find, isolated between rocks at the seaside? It has a strange, dead, deadening, colour. I found myself looking at them – at the different shapes and sizes – and this colour and texture drew me in, and then the sun shone, quite suddenly, and they were transformed into bronzed things, gleaming, blazing with life. Then Ruth came up to me and started trying to give me some more 'medical help' – I remember that's what she called it!'

'Yes,' she said, 'I had done the same for James. I remember that because my mother could see us from one of the upstairs windows and she was watching. She said we would make a pair of fine nurses… It's strange how things work out, isn't it…? Maybe that's why we became nurses…'

'Yup! Instead of doctors, or dentists or…..'

'Or potters!' she replied, laughing.

'Or potters, or button manufacturers.'

'Well, it wasn't much of a fight. We weren't great fighters, either of us – although James did become a soldier,' he laughed too and added, 'Of sorts.'

'Yes, a Lieutenant Colonel, no less. James is a good man. He just lacks… imagination, sometimes. But then, so do most of us. I know I certainly do.'

'Yes,' he replied, 'He certainly is a good man. And, he certainly lacks imagination!'

'You are good, too,' she said, smiling in the darkness.

'I have decided,' she carried on. 'That today was great: it allowed me to think, standing there on the cliff tops. I have taken a decision: I will meet him, to confront him, to tell him how I feel – how I feel about what he did and how I have no right to pronounce forgiveness, if that is what he asked for, or wants. But I must, I will, clear it up. I am the one who is alive but Ruth was the one whose life was taken.'

'I think we were all hurt. Maybe we all had our lives, or bits of our lives, taken in one way or another,' Robert replied, speaking softly but not totally disguising the bitterness that rose up through his words.

They stood there for a few moments, looking up at the tail end of a moon in the sky, just over the loneliness of the treetops. Then, somehow, her hand and his hand found each other. They remained there, together, yet alone in the dark, palms squashed, fingers tightly interlocked. They floated at the centre of a silence that stretched from Cave Hill to the Giant's Causeway, which stretched from there to the other side of the moon, filling all that might be in between. Robert could hear words striving in his head, they came there from his belly, from his chest, from his heart – but he did not utter them. Rebecca could only feel; she felt consumed by something that was both inside and outside her being. How long they remained suspended there they did not know. Then James's voice rattled out across the dark yard:

'Hello, you two; are you there? Are you alright?'

'Yes,' called Robert. Then he felt her shiver; he said, 'It's getting cold. You don't have a coat. Do you want to go in?' His voice sounded strange: their hands no longer touched. She thought, my hand is on fire. By now, James had crossed the yard to join them. Rebecca stood for a moment, between the two men, looking up to the sky.

'Is that the dawn breaking?', she asked, adding, 'It's very early,' pointing out over the trees to where a pale gleam has appeared.

'Yes, it is,' James replied, 'Or at least, it's the start of the dawn. The dawn and sunrise are two different things, you know.' She looked at him oddly, then.

'It's been a long night, a long day. It's time we went home and left you to a bit of peace and quiet.'

Once inside they gathered up their coats. As they were about to leave Rebecca turned to Robert.

'I've noticed we're rather good – when we speak at all about these things – at telling others how we feel or how they ought to feel, but only about certain things. We're good on the surface facts of feeling, not good at sharing our real feelings or acknowledging their existence. We're not so good at getting below the surface of how we feel, or asking others how they really feel. I want to ask you, do you not think we are all caught up in a collective memory thing, a bit like a root system of intimate sorrow, with big and small roots all intertwined, all feeding off the same sorrowing food system? I think that's how I see it all, now.'

'By gum, you're becoming poetical!' Robert said.

'No, it's nothing to do with being poetic,' she said. 'There you go again... you see, you are avoiding the real issue: you are engaging in the great Ulster defence, shrug it off, make a joke of it, ignore it… 'it can't be all that bad, we've lived with it for years… whatever you say, say nothing meaningful'…'

'It's just that it's easier to do that – it oils the wheels of cultivated society… blood oils the wheels of an uncultivated society!' Robert replied.

'No!' said Rebecca. 'Be serious! What we need, we three, isn't oil: what we need is good companionship, we need to experience courtesy and respect; we need the security of love; we need to understand each other fully and we need to be understood fully; we need to maintain the strength to keep on going, as individuals… and collectively…'

'We do give each other that, I think,' Robert said. 'But we can do that only because we find ourselves somehow outside society, cultivated or otherwise: we have been forgotten by the world, we are of no importance, we are not even merely 'disappeared', we have been erased from the general consciousness: if our kind was ever noticed in the past, we aren't now.'

Rebecca replied, 'That's because we have allowed ourselves to be made up, to be put together, by others, out of recycled parts. What I am talking about is something real. This is solid, solid ground I'm talking about. It's to do with integrity, authenticity, transparency, and conscience – things all people truly rise out of, or aspire to rise out of: I am talking about the only solid ground in the universe. I experienced it at Slieve League. It's about letting go, it's about emptying the hand… leaving go… seeing what is important and committing to that…'

James interrupted. 'I don't follow this at all. One minute, you say that we, whoever 'we' are, have somehow disappeared, slipped under the radar of perception, so to speak, the next you say it's about 'letting go'. To me that all smacks of self-indulgence: what about human will, what about imposing a bit of *will* on reality... on the world, or whatever... that's how progress is made... that'll make people see us.'

'No! No! No!' Rebecca was on the verge of screaming in exasperation, while Robert smiled but appeared unwilling to join in further discussion. 'Look,' she continued, 'I'm happy to engage in internal negotiations with myself, but that's because I recognise I can't impose my will on anything, even on *myself*: it just doesn't work – it obscures the underlying reality. I am willing to *accept* my susceptibility to my own strangeness. And letting go is an essential part of that acceptance...'

'That might be why we are where we are,' Robert spoke now, slowly, almost reluctantly. 'Imposing *will!* Look at the Twin Towers, look at our own thirty years of mayhem, look at the Arab/Israeli conflict – just look at America's history of imposition of its will, its brute force. Look at what went on in those insatiable detention camps fed by invisible plane-loads of blindfolded and shackled humans!'

A sudden frisson moved through the air and Rebecca looked away. She thought she had never before known Robert so animated, with such pent-up anger. He went on, 'Your 'order' James, has a lot to do with social and political inertia – that which moves and keeps moving, but which remains as stolid and stiff as old mud. I agree with Rebecca.' He paused for a moment before continuing, 'We have to transcend the conditioned mind, the mind... the mind that rests on a given order, the imposed rules of a commanding authority, secular or otherwise! I believe that the only truly sustainable authority lies in the freedom of the human spirit...'

James muttered a scarcely audible 'hmm' of disdain, which was, for James, almost but not quite a sneer. Rebecca felt Robert stiffen, felt him rise in his seat and expected another outburst but he seemed to slump. 'What's the point!' he whispered, 'What is the point!'

Silence fell over them like a thrown cloak and then, as Robert had in effect acquiesced, they settled back into their accustomed modes of social quietude.

**

It is late. Or is it early? Robert considered he must be a bit drunk, for the others have slowly and mysteriously increased the distance between themselves and him. Yet, he reassured himself, firmly, they are still here – it is only that he has to concentrate on them, across this enormous gap, so that it appears to him that he is looking at them through the wrong end of a telescope.

For a moment the background music creeps into his consciousness, then fades away.

He watches them while they talk. Now he feels lethargic; their lips are moving, but he cannot make out what they are saying.

A women's voice drifts out in melancholy song; he assumes it comes from the radio in the kitchen. Simultaneously a man's voice murmurs from the CD player that is switched on softly on the other side of the room in which they sit. The three sets of words are indistinct and muffled yet incessant or insistent; they appear to him to be like velvet chains, the words linked together and then woven and interwoven, one with another. The result is a blanket of sound that lies heavily across the room.

And then the question poses itself, instantly and without pre-thought,

Where do words come from?

He finds himself sitting in his big armchair. He considers,

I mean, ultimately, where are words conceived and born, where are they filled with life, puffed up with stuff. Who was the first to impregnate sounds with meanings?

Babel, he thinks, *Babel.*

Lips part, a mouth opens and words appear. Or don't appear: they are invisible. Yet they are real, real in their consequences. They can inspire love or hate, hugs or the hurling of hand grenades.

Here am I, looking at James's mouth, opening and closing. It opens and closes and little puffs of air emerge; before it appears, the air crosses the vocal cords. Then it emerges as sounds, noises.

But how do words come into it?

It's not the acoustics of words, it's where they spring from, emerging out of that little thing, the skull – what is it? A small, dark, bone-encrusted cubby-hole filled with smoke and mirrors, so distorting it can contain within its close confines galaxies, universes, worlds of things… moments, weeks, centuries of time…

When I make a pot it's there: it is derived – derived is a good word, it has a good sound – a pot derives from clay and water and the wheel and my hands and heat. I use material that undergoes a process. At the end of that process, I have a pot: something I can touch and feel and put water into. Something with a beginning and an end. Words have no beginnings, no ends. Once spoken…

He watches with interest as his hand reaches out for the glass. He has not instructed it to move. It moves of its own accord. It grasps the glass and carries it to his lips. The river of thoughts start moving again; thoughts come and come, they are a weakness, running through his head, a diarrhoea of sounds run through his mind… meaningless noises.

Words are different, strange, magical, like liquid, yet they are so hard.

And while there is always a word for a thing, there is always a word for its opposite:

Black and white…

Up and down…

Tomorrow and yesterday…

Orange and green

Nationalist and loyalist

Good and bad

Right and wrong

We used to go through all this at primary school – drawing up lists of similes and opposites. Or was it synonyms, not similes…

I don't know the difference!

He thinks: he wonders:

What is the difference?

Language is just another way of imposing order – it's just the imposition of consistency on inconsistency. It's a way of imposing order on chaos.

Or is it?

Words are like bricks, we erect prisons with brick-like words, we build cells for ourselves, eventually they become fortresses from which we cannot escape...

We build cells for others.

Why should we perceive orange and green as opposites? Why opposites? Why should Loyalist and Nationalist not be similes? When we touch them, they are only people, after all... buying cheese and wine, combing their hair... putting on their boots; we are all the same...

Because... he pauses and squints at Rebecca and James. They both come into focus, briefly, then slide away,

...because words are nothing to do with what they represent, they come from inside our heads, they are to be found in that cavernous place where the whole world resides, that is, inside our heads. He is looking intently at James's square head. *There is a head that has fixed dimensions, buttresses and double locks and moats and God knows what, fixed points of reference, walls of granite, like the stout, sturdy stone walls that surround his house. Words do not respect order, they do not respect time or place – they live there inside our heads, dangerous little rascals, like mischievous angels they play with the furniture of our minds, they are furniture removers, who can shift things to any place at any time, or move them so they are in different places at different times, or at the same time!*

***

They are at the door. They say goodbye, hurriedly, for it is late. Rebecca speaks.

'Thank you. Thank you both for being so understanding, and for coming with me. It has been an important day for me, more important than I can say.' Robert stands, swaying gently, a little distance away from the doorstep.; He is caught between the light from the porch, as it slices outwards from inside the cottage, and the departing, confined, lighted bubble of the car. The car pulls away. He watches its red rear lights until they disappear round the bend of the loanen. He listens to the crunch, crunch, crunch of the wheels on the gravel. He notices the slight hiatus in the sound as the car stops at the lane's end and then he listens to the muted roar of its engine as it takes off, as it gains more momentum. He follows the vehicle's curving journey as its lights cut through the half-dark, half-light of early morning, as it gathers speed along the road. He watches it till, ultimately, all evidence of its being vanishes over the hill.

He stands there for a while, listening to the silence of the night, consciously building up his sense of loneliness. Then he calls the dogs and attaches them to the chains that are mounted on two wooden kennels standing at the side of the cottage. He goes inside and pours himself a last drink. He leans his two forearms on the mantelshelf and rests his head on the backs of his interlocked hands, his body spread-eagled over the grey, cooling ashes. That is what he remembers.

He starts; he finds he is in bed. He lies there, half asleep. He remembers: through a familiar anger he reviews the day, the weekend, the life he has lead, the life he will lead. Gradually, the emotion of anger is washed away, though the reality of it remains to the fore. His thoughts ebb and flow against the borders of his consciousness. The image of the four pots rises... *crudely sliced and spilling out and down, like the*

petals of an over-ripe flower, a nice image, a good, strong metaphor;
whatever you say, say nothing, he never ever told either of them about
how his anger grows till sometimes it gets the better of him, of how, at
least twice before, he had gone into the workshop and had hurled every
piece to the ground, smashing the entirety of his work, the pieces lying
spilled, for days, waiting for his brush and shovel, waiting for their final
resting place in a ditch beneath a hedge across a field, far away from
sight.

He sleeps then and dreams and sleeps again. Someone stops by his bed; a cool hand rests on this forehead. It is Rebecca who moves though his dreams.

***

The inside of the car quickly warms up. Rebecca snuggles into her seat and within a few minutes appears, to James, to be asleep. They travel in silence. He glances at her occasionally, but does not attempt to speak to her; he has no wish to disturb her. Instead, he thinks about what has taken place over the past few days. He has found it a confused and confusing period. He doesn't really like confusion: he knows he prefers certainty, he likes order, he thrives on routine. I am just a very boring person, he thinks.

Rebecca is lulled by the continuous murmur of the engine, but not enough to sleep. She is soothed by the motion of the car. She recalls, with feelings of pleasure, standing on the great cliff edge at Slieve League, the sea at her feet, the temptation, the choice before her, the feeling of pure freedom she experienced there. She remembers the sense of inner calm, of outer concord with all around her, that she experienced there. I don't think, she thinks, I don't think there is an answer to it. And if there is no answer to it, what can I do? I can choose: I can stop, give up, lie down, stop breathing, die – or I can go on, go forward, inch by inch.

Maybe, she thinks, that's where Ruth and I have grown to differ. She was an idealist, a romantic – she did not have time to change. In that moment she became history. She did not have time to accommodate her dreams to reality. She sits up, 'James,' she says, 'does the word 'compromise' ever enter into your way of thinking? Or into your way of acting?'

James is silent for a few long moments. *The road is straight. There is no traffic at this time of night, or morning. His car fairly hums along, the embodiment of controlled power, with more beneath his foot, waiting to be released; he knows he only has to press downwards against the pedal for the surge to occur.* He glances sideways at her and tries to catch her eye. She is looking straight ahead.

'Yes,' he says, eventually. 'I do believe that compromise, as you call it, enters into my way of thinking, into my actions, quite a lot, actually. I suppose I have come to regard it as a necessary if unpleasant fact. I would prefer to call it negotiation, though. It's what grown up people do, all the time.' He thinks of what he has: his home, his factory, his life in the army, his life with Rebecca and Robert.

Robert knows, he thinks, *Robert knows about the empty sham that is the button factory and about my uncle leaving what he regards as tainted money to me. He never mentions it, directly – or not often. He snipes at me now and then, when he is in bad mood, but when he looks at me sometimes, I can see it in his eyes. There is something vicious beneath that radical non-conformity, beneath all that individualism he preaches – it is that viciousness that gives him the energy to know, but not to say. There is cowardice too, otherwise why not say what he feels? To judge, but not to speak judgement.*

'It's strange, he never speaks of it…' The words are spoken before he can put a stop to them.

'What's that?' she asks, looking across at him.

'Oh, no, nothing. I was thinking of something else.'

It is indeed a strange mixture of honour and viciousness... Rebecca, on the other hand, is all honour. She is also, possibly, the essence of naiveté. She is asking him again about compromise. With a jerk he pulls the car in to a lay-by. He twists round in his seat to look into her surprised face.

'I am going to tell you something I have never told anyone else. You know how I love the Territorial Army. It's a huge part of my life, really.' She gazes at him, how intense he is.

'It has been for years. And I'm good at what I do. But I'm not a fighting soldier and I know that and accept it. Twice I have been called up to go abroad, into action zones. Each time I appealed the decision and was allowed to stay at home.'

'How did you appeal. On what grounds?'

'Largely, on the grounds that I have a single-man business to run and people whose jobs depend on my being here, to run it.'

He pauses; she waits.

'There is an appeals process. I made use of it. It's perfectly above board. But yet, if I were a better human being, a better man, I would have gone – I should have gone, I know that – but I didn't and that's that. I live with that awareness all the time: but I do live with it and get on with the rest of my life... That's what I mean by compromise: I negotiate the best deal I can and just get on with it. You see, I accept I'm not perfect... None of us is...'

No, he thinks, *I am far from being perfect.* He turns away. Something has come to him that he had buried away, out of memory's reach for many years. He thinks about the New Year's Eve before Ruth died. He remembers… *we had all been to a party. Rebecca had not felt well and had gone home early. I stayed behind, as had Ruth. I can't remember where Robert was. We had been drinking. Even I drank in those days. I had gone to the bathroom. I opened the door. I bumped into her, literally bumped into her as she was coming out — just as I entered. I pushed her inside, laughing. The door closed behind us. Then, she was in my arms. It had been, I knew, no more than a fumbling contact, a blind kiss in the dark, even though it was with my girlfriend's sister. It was nothing — yet, I never told Rebecca about it and I knew, and I felt absolutely certain, that Ruth would not tell her about it either. And yet, how I cherish the little spasm of guilt the remembrance of that night always gives me. I have no idea how Rebecca would respond, were I to tell her. In truth, I am afraid to think about it.*

'Thanks for telling me,' she is saying, then seeing the surprise on his face she continues, 'You are in a strange old mood tonight! Thanks for sharing that story about the army — or have you forgotten, already? It certainly is truth and reconciliation week, isn't it…? Anyway, it has helped me, finally, finally decide: I believe I have a lot to do, a lot to think about and I believe, a lot to change…'

'Maybe, maybe. I mean, yes, certainly,' he says to her, not really knowing what he is saying. He feels dislocated, mentally off-balance.

'I think we should go, now,' Rebecca says. His right hand is still resting on her left hand and she puts her right hand on his. She recalls the feel of Robert's hand no more than an hour ago, but says nothing. Instead, she pats James's hand awkwardly. He feels the pressure she applies as she squeezes his hand between hers. He feels guilty; he feels elated.

'Yes,' he says. 'You are right. It's very late. Let's go.'

Despite the lateness of the hour, when Rebecca got home, and after changing into her nightclothes and putting on a dressing gown, she sat down at the desk in her living room. She took out the book and began to write. She had no idea what she was going to write. The pen in her hand seemed to lead her thoughts, rather than her thoughts directing the hand and through the hand the pen. She allowed the pen its head.

Sunday.

This has been an amazing day. I want to remember it. We went to a place called Slieve League in west Donegal. The sea cliffs here are over three hundred metres high with breathtaking views out over the Atlantic & the surrounding cliffs and headlands. We could see sea cliffs that a man told us were near Bunglass (the same man told us this means 'the end of the cliff'). We could see as far as Donegal Bay & the mountains of Sligo. There was an old watchtower at the end of Carrigan Head. James knew about this (he seems to know about everything, or so we tell him!) & informed us it had been erected to help defend the coast against attack by Napoleon's ships.

It has been a terrible few days but that place helped me to recover.

I think I did have a kind of revelation. It may have been to do with the nature of the place — it is so dramatic — I don't know & I don't want to think about it too much. I am just happy that I feel more positive tonight than I have for a long time.

I feel real peace, for the first time for years. I feel as though I have been in a cage for years, & now I am released, the cage has simply disappeared.

I know I have found it so difficult to explain to Robert or James how I feel, or what my feelings are. I know Robert feels things very deeply, more so than James. He is capable of a very great passion but hides that side of his being.

I am just afraid he feels for me more than he should, more than Ruth would be capable of dealing with. I don't want that to interfere with my sense of peace. Is this my being selfish? I have so many important things to deal with. Maybe I don't understand what feelings are, really. Perhaps I need to know, too much.

I want to understand where my present sense of peace came from. I think it lies here — I am aware, and am able to accept, how temporary this thing called life is, how little control we have over it — it's not just me feeling that. It's the same for everybody… only, I think, so few people are aware of how vulnerable we all are — they are so, they **feel** *so … impregnable … so inviolate … so indestructible… What I felt grow inside me was a feeling of dignity, up there on the cliff top, I felt a sense of dignity that had been taken away from me. When Ruth's life had been taken so arbitrarily, her poor body tossed into the air and dumped down, like a rag doll, onto the chewing gum, pockmarked, spit-bedewed tarmac of the public street, dignity had been stripped away from her and from me. That is what I have lived with, all these years. That and my feelings of guilt.*

And then, I found myself standing, feeling free and uncaged, with this great, solid piece of rock under my feet, looking out over the soft sea, carrying the boats on its swells, like babies on mothers' breasts, and I felt so like a child… I gave in: I think that is the secret, I felt myself give in to the water, to the sea, to the sky, to the wind on my face, I gave in to the great openness at my feet & to all that lay stretching out before me… I gave in to the hills and cliffs I could see, embracing all this in

206

their arms, they were covered in greens and blues, in patches of colours, delicate and liquid and limpid in the sunlight, & I thought, this is now, today is today: I accept I am just standing on this rock, with rock and water all around me, for a little time, I am in this body for a little time and then I too will step out and off… And there returned to me a real feeling of dignity and strength. & Ruth and I were one again.

I can't explain it any better than that.

Rebecca closed the book and, leaving it where it rested, went to her bedroom. She lay down on the bed. For a while she dozed, still in her dressing gown. Then she got up and went out, past the desk where the book lay. She did not pay any attention to it, but walked into the kitchen to make a hot drink. Her head was alive with thoughts and memories.

Monday

It is Monday morning. Although he had been most unusually late last night, James got up at six-thirty, as usual. He looked again at the clock; he reckoned he got to bed a little after four. He shook his head, but smiled. It had been a good day, a good night: he feels pleased. Something had been released; somehow, somewhere. He feels freer, looser. Slieve League, the 'end of the world', the drive west, then east: all a great idea. Cleared the air; somehow or other it had diffused that meeting Rebecca had with the bomber and the mood she had been in afterwards. And the talking they had done... it had let in a new breath of life, really – a breath of new life, perhaps that is a better way of saying it. For a moment, he considered the complexities of the English language as a means of communicating emotions. He stood, looking out over the garden, watching the swaying of his trees. Rain yesterday, storms today, winter is approaching, he thought. He felt ready for it.

He walked in the garden, enjoying the freshness in the air. He likes days like this. He finds they invigorate him. He looked at the seagulls, battling against the wind out over Belfast Lough. Eventually, he turned away and went to take his car from its garage, parking it by the front door, ready for the journey to the office. He prepared, then breakfasted on, prunes and freshly squeezed orange juice, unbuttered toast and a pot of tea, each utility set out in its accustomed place on the table. These days he forgoes milk and sugar, as well as butter. While he is engaged in these routine activities he reviews the weekend he has now left behind, outdated, academic, really. He considers Robert – strange, how that thing about their fight came up. He had forgotten all about it though he recalls the sheer red, blinding hatred he felt for Robert. He considers, above all else, Rebecca. He considers their lives together, the little society they have created, their weekly meetings, their by-now habitual various meals together. It's strange… perhaps it's not so strange, after all… how their friends have drifted off over the years: some leaving the country for good, some to get married, have children…

He considers once again, and this time finally, the journey to Slieve League. A very good suggestion, that. He mulls over the things Rebecca said last night. He does not speak, for there is no-one there to hear, but he allows himself a little shrug, a little lifting of his shoulders, for still, he does not fully understand. He does not understand this – to him – futile concern with the past. He is aware, still, that she has assumed, and holds onto, responsibility for Ruth's death. Indeed, she positively experiences guilt, she always has. To his mind, the only person who is guilty is the person who planted the bomb: he was caught and has paid the price – not as much, certainly, as he, James, would have liked. But, at least, the law had been satisfied. Released a bit too early, possibly: politics, certainly lay behind that, the 'Good Friday Agreement'… but still…

Still, we must, he considers, raising his shoulders, on balance, put the negative things behind us and build on the positive things. But still, he reminds himself, it is difficult to forget… it is dangerous, also, he fancies, dangerous in the larger scheme of things… The danger, he concludes, lies in using 'forgetting' as an aid to political expediency and then finding the violence erupting again, in the future. Everything out in the open, strong, transparent government… that's the answer… not necessarily compromise – rather, an easing of the way…

He clears away the few dishes. Good. The word compromise has not entered into his thinking, even though he would be the first to say he sees nothing wrong in compromise. He goes to the corridor that leads off the kitchen and walks to the window. He takes from his pocket a neatly folded paper napkin. He opens it and looks at it. A reddish flush radiates across its middle. This is where she drew it across her lips, last night. They were at the table. He had been watching. Watching as she drew it across her lips, as she tossed it onto the table, where it lay, unnoticed among the empty plates. Later, he had lifted it and put it in his pocket. He puts the paper tissue to his lips, feeling its texture – a slight crinkliness impinges on his skin. He closes his eyes. He feels a tremor coursing through his body; he feels a tickle, like a minute electric charge stimulating his senses. He senses the sweet aroma of cinnamon.

He stands there, staring out of the window. The thick, old, lead-heavy glass distorts everything on the other side, making it fuzzy and distant, but this does not matter since he is not seeing what lies before him. He stares at nothing, for a long time, while sinking deeper and deeper into a pit of soot that slowly numbs his senses.

Then, at some point, he does not know how long he has been standing here, the clock in the hall behind him strikes and he is recalled. He is released; he emits a long sigh and reaching out places the napkin that he has been stroking and stroking on the window ledge. Slowly, he turns away, leaving the napkin where he set it.

A moment later he returns, picks up the napkin and takes it to the kitchen where he places it in the bin beneath the sink.

A moment later he puts on his tweed overcoat, lifts his thin, black leather briefcase from where he had stowed it on Friday beneath the partners' desk in the library, and arms the burglar alarm. He closes the little mahogany door behind which the alarm controls are discreetly hidden. He glances around the hallway; everything is tidy and in its place. For a moment, he closes his eyes; he feels tired, somehow. It must have been that long drive, yesterday, that and the lack of sleep. The windows are securely shut? Yes. In his mind he affirms to his own satisfaction that he has turned off the gas cooker. He is certain he does not need to return to the kitchen to make sure.

He steps out into the day and pulls the door shut. It is an elderly door, slow in its movements and very heavy, and makes, to his ear, as it does every time he draws it shut, a satisfactory thud as it marries securely into its frame. He senses, rather than feels, the air in the hallway vibrate. For a moment, the silence inside and the silence outside achieve a state of equilibrium that hangs there; why, he wonders suddenly, does he feel the recurrent return of this sudden and unexpected sense of weariness that has plagued him recently? He shakes off the momentary doubt and steps out.

As he approaches it, he notes again that the car is grimy from yesterday's journey. He makes a mental note to have it sent out to be washed and polished later this morning. Meantime, the day stretches ahead. Already, he is looking forward to it: he is anxious to get into his office with the big desk and the new, high-tech digital telephone. He pines for the security of the wood panelling and his framed certificate from the Society of Dyers and Colourists. He looks forward to his early morning consultation with Harry; he looks forward to the hum of the Dumb Dryer with its 200,000 buttons rattling away inside; he looks forward to the muted rattle of the polishing machine with its little parcels of bamboo shoots, placed there to shine the buttons. He looks forward greatly to reviewing the month's sales figures with Dorothy, his secretary of long standing.

As he eases the car down the driveway, he wonders again about the weekend and about today: at weekends he feels – and this morning he considers this carefully – he feels rather like he felt when he was a child; sometimes he feels like he did when he was a teenager, or perhaps, it is the world that feels to him now as it did then. He pulls himself up short: this is the kind of contorted thinking that Robert, and even Rebecca – take yesterday, for example – love to engage in. This is a new Monday and he has things to do; he has things to accomplish.

He stops for a moment while the gate swings open. He takes the opportunity to look around him: the gardens are looking good, neat, tidy, everything in its place. He smiles. In his head, he is already making a plan for next weekend's gathering with Rebecca and Robert.

***

Robert sits at the kitchen table. He too woke early, moodily thinking of last night, of yesterday, of the last few days, of the last lifetime. But he thinks mainly of last night. Now he remembers hurling his glass into the fire. He goes to the fireplace, picks up a few bigger pieces of broken glass and carries them outside to the bin. The air is fresh but not cold. The room feels cold when he re-enters. Grey ashes lie in the fireplace; he will clear out the ashes and the remains of the broken glass later. Empty wine glasses sit on the table, dirty plates sit stacked up in the kitchen; he will attend to all these things later.

'You're an untidy, throughother person,' he says out aloud, looking at himself in the mirror. 'But no matter, for nobody is there to see the mess but yourself!' There is a hint of weariness in his words and the two dogs seem to sense something is wrong, rising to their feet.

'Good dogs,' he says, leaning down to pat them. But his mind is only partly on them. He is remembering a word that remains elusive, even as it rises up into consciousness.

Then the sense of what he has been seeking comes to him. 'Purged.' Yes, 'purged' is the word. I feel purged. *Purged* in the sense, he reflects, *in the sense that my personality feels emptied. My being is only my body, is a kind of shell, something to be thrown away when no longer fit for purpose.* The anger he experienced earlier has left him, drained away, as if by magic. But there is nothing left in its place. The gash in his soul that was Ruth's death has gone, for his soul has gone. *It withered away and I didn't notice.* Is that why he feels released? Is this the result of some kind of penitence, an easement? All those childhood beliefs – well the fear, nightmares, guilt, at least – gone. Or have they?

It's a strange word, he thinks, purged, a word as strange as the feeling it stands for. Disconcertingly, it has religious connotations, connotations he does not feel entirely at home with nowadays. He has made coffee and now sips at it slowly, for it is hot. His thoughts change tack. He considers Rebecca, then James, then Ruth. She is the focus of this weekend's attention. He supposes it natural she should have been; this is her birthday, she would have been 45 had she been alive.

He wishes he could bring to his mind's eye what Ruth looked like, exactly. He can, in a way, but only in a way, and not exactly. He cannot exactly recall what she felt like when he held her in his arms. He cannot recall the weight, or seize or feel of her body in his arms. He can remember the feel of Rebecca's hand, last night. He can smell *Lily of the Valley*.

Strange, when he looks at Rebecca he can see what Ruth would be like today, for they are still identical twins, but he cannot recall exactly what were her features, then – when she was a teenager, when she was in her early twenties. Yet, he thinks, she is as real to me as this floor, this ceiling, it is just that she is beyond my reach. Is this how the mind tidies itself?

He gets up and goes to the bookshelves that stretch along one wall. He reaches to a top shelf and takes down a Bible. As it falls open in his hand the title page is revealed. He glances at it. A bookplate tells him it had been presented to Robert Orr for excellent attendance at Sunday School. It is dated 1971 and signed by someone whose writing he cannot decipher and whose being he cannot now remember. Another winnowing job, he smiles, somehow pleased by the thought.

He leafs through the Bible and takes out a single photograph that lies concealed within. It is a colour photograph, but strangely there is no colour in it. The paper it is printed on has become hardened over the years, and yellowed on the back. A yellow stain has crept round one edge and is beginning to slightly disfigure the image.

The electric light is switched on but he goes to the window. The early morning light seeps through the glass and he stands with his back to it, holding the photograph up so that it catches the cold light fully on its face.

In the clinical light of early day, those caught in the snapshot assume an alien presence. James is leaning against a lamppost and looking towards the camera. He is wearing a dark suit and white shirt, and a thin vertical line indicates he is wearing a tie. He is very un-plump: not thin, exactly, but not filled out, as he is now. A glimpse of sea can be seen, lying flatly behind him. He, Robert, must be the one holding the camera. The two girls stand between the lens and James; they stand side-on. Their captured slenderness is touching, for the girlish state it represents is now beyond reach. They are both wearing what appears in the curling photograph to be nondescript grey coloured cardigans and pencil-thin black skirts; they are both wearing white or cream blouses. One girl's head is slightly turned away, towards James, the other has her head averted so her features cannot be seen. The two nut-brown heads of hair are exactly the same and in the same style – short, bobbed affairs that could place them back twenty or thirty or even more years.

They had gone to Helen's Bay, he remembers. It must have been 1980 or 1981. He knows which of the two is Ruth as she is holding the handful of wild flowers he had collected and given to her earlier on their walk. It could have been early summer or late spring. It could even have been early autumn; he cannot now pin the time of year down with any precision.

He looks at the photograph for a long time before replacing it in the Bible. Ruth is the one whose head is turned away. Even then, he thinks, she was beyond my reach; she had moved beyond the ability of even the camera to catch her. Elusive. In his memory, always there but never quite there. Unlike Rebecca. Or unlike how Rebecca had been.

He takes the Bible back to the shelf and puts it in its place. 'It will rest there until the next time I want, momentarily, to halt this un-detainable slithering slide in my memory of who she was,' he thinks. He feels the momentary rise in his breast of the vicious old snake: hot emotion. He goes out, shutting the door behind him.

He finds and places a partly used block of sketching paper down on the bench and takes up a pen. He is not a natural writer. Now, he chews the pen, as he did in school, before starting; he stands up; he sits down. Eventually, he begins:

Dear Rebecca,

You are very unhappy. You have been unhappy for a long time. Odd as it may seem, I believe your quarrel is with Ruth. It is not with the man who murdered her. Who that man was, why he did it, whether or not it was a mistake – these questions essentially are irrelevant to your happiness, or to your unhappiness…

He asked to meet you; why he wanted to meet you is irrelevant.

When you met him, you did so without thinking about it. If you decide to meet him again do so because you want to, not because he wants you to.

You are not a leader, even though you think of yourself as a leader. James is a leader. I am not a leader. As you hinted, you are a healer. That is something, something important. Steer by that. All we have to guide us, all we have to steer by, is our own sense of direction, our own sense of right and wrong.

You are a healer.

You deserve happiness.

Why don't you have it?

Your quarrel is with James.

Your quarrel is with me.

Above all, your quarrel is with yourself.

You must heal yourself, then you must heal us.

He reads what he has written, then he writes:

Your quarrel is with Ruth. You must struggle to take that dead, cold hand off your life, off our future... she is strangling you... she – her shadow – has blighted us.

He looks out of the window. The trees move, sedately, from left to right and back again. He writes:

You must heal me.

He sits for a bit, then tears the sheet from the block and crunches the paper up into a ball and throws it onto the cold, white ashes in the grate.

'Infantile!' he growls at the two dogs. They do not move their heads but both wag their tails, slowly in a half-hearted, half-expectant way.

'Who am I,' he says, 'to apportion blame? Who am I to offer advice? Responsibility: yes, responsibility always comes back, in the end, to an individual person: this weekend's discussions have all come back, repeatedly, to that same conclusion.'

He feels the rebirth of his old, native cynicism. He can sense its presence as it rises up, growing inside his skull, filling his brain's shell, blurring his vision; instantly, he recalls an image, a memory seen on television of a flood of the blue-black ink spilt into the crisp, clean waters of the ocean by an octopus coming under attack, defending itself in darkness, contaminating the clarity that had previously existed all around it. Now he feels disgust. He thinks, that is what I am like, producing darkness all around me.

He goes outside. He stops for a few seconds, allowing himself to be caressed by the wind. Across the valley, on the hillside opposite, he can see a few straggling groups of people playing an early round of golf. 'The middle classes,' he thinks, 'out spoiling their early walks!' He hears the sound of cars passing on the road below: men and women going to their work, parents taking their children to school, golfers going to play golf... His day has started. He shakes his head and sets off towards the old forge. The two dogs follow him.

As he walks, he passes the pond that he habitually thinks of as his lake. He regards it along with the sky, the earth, then the sky again, for it is bluer and whiter now and the wind continues to rise steadily, and the clouds are speeding; the trees are bobbing their heads and curtsying. He stops to look at the pond. In its glassy surface he can see the sharp images of four crows as they flap past on their way north; four others cross at an angle, heading west. His world, he thinks, is nothing but grey clay and flat water, all slate and stone, earth and water and wood and leaf, all clay and water and air; this morning, it is quivering with life. It all lies before him and for the moment he feels elated and free and light. This is all his; he is happy to enter into it, to forget the rest while he can. It is men who make him angry. This thought somehow soothes his breast.

'Come along!' he commands. 'Come along you good dogs... let us see if we cannot get things moving here. 'Dare to be honest and fear not labour', that's the motto here so go to it...' The two dogs agree, with him: their eyes tell him so. He laughs and they laugh in response.

There is a sharp nip in the air this morning and he decides it is cold enough to justify his lighting the wood-burning stove. As he carries an armful of logs into the pottery his eye rests briefly on 'The Accident'. It is a test he takes every day: yes, he still finds it beautiful, in its way. He passes on.

He is all anticipation: soon, he knows, he will sit down at the wheel, then, unbeknownst to him, as it were, the day will settle over his bowed head and shoulders, its hours will knit and wrap around his being like a blanket, and he will know comfort. He is aware of all this, but is aware without consciously knowing, and is happy so.

He purposefully does not allow himself to think again about last night. In a recess of his mind, or somewhere, buried deep in his being, he is aware that something has changed, profoundly so. They have made a start, a beginning, that is all, but it is a start. They will talk again. But he will not think about it, just now. Later, he will. And when he does he will feel the return of a deepening emotion, his anger at so much waste. Anger at the impossibility of justice being done, because justice is not a human thing, after all. Justice is a dream.

This morning, now, however, he feels energised, empowered, ready, as he says when in this mood, to take on the challenge of the clay.

***

It is early. Rebecca stands on her balcony, overlooking the city. She sips her morning tea. It might snow tonight, she

219

thinks, but why she thinks so, she does not know: it is not the season for snow. And anyway, it will be too stormy for snow. Before snow comes, the world grows calm. Then the world turns white and becomes quieter and quieter; silently, the world recedes beneath a blanket of soft, white calmness.

Still, she finds herself shivering for she has sensed a barely articulated threat in the air. She thinks, again, that the day has that disinterested, obtuse, alienated quality she associates with the first snowflakes falling; she thinks of childhood times, of the wonder of snow falling; there is a quietness all around her, here, this morning, that is somehow removed from the moment that lies around and before her.

She loves it here, she considers, looking out over the city. She is so raised up, so elevated, so removed from the river, from the streets, so imperially, regally, positioned above the people, be they on foot or in cars. She always feels safe here, she thinks, in this eyrie, perched on this shelf of concrete: she feels how grand it is, how impossible it is for any of them to be aware of her existence. She is invisible, she cannot be seen, she cannot be touched. She cannot be blamed.

She turns away; she must prepare to go to work. That is her other place of safety. Even though it is a public place and she is open to constant scrutiny there, in many ways it is more comfortable than her private world has been recently. She wears her ordinary clothes; she will change into her uniform when she gets to the hospital. Soon, she lets herself out of the flat. It certainly has grown colder quite quickly, and a storm has started and she finds herself catching her coat more closely, hugging it to her body for warmth.

She moves past cars caught in the traffic jams, purring quietly like a choir of satisfied cats. Comic-strip puffs of smoke escape and rise up from numerous exhaust pipes, their anonymous occupants smoking, listening to radios, using their telephones – swearing, no doubt – the lure of home fires, the lost weekend insistent in their heads.

She turns right to walk beside the Lagan. Perhaps it is all really very simple, after all, she thinks. Perhaps I have just made it more complicated than it is. She observes herself, as if from a distance. For years, she has avoided the issue; she has avoided confronting the issue, she put her head down and kept it down. She has got on with her job, which is to care for people, and she has done that well, everyone will say so, if asked.

And, yes, she has cared for Ruth. Except on that one day! Now Ruth is dead. Ruth who is related to her by birth, by gene, related physically and emotionally, bodily and mentally, and in every way conceivable. Ruth, her other half, who has been absent from her life for more years now than she had been present. Ruth whose very absence is a physical space, left empty, a vacuous place, a gap left in her life; her half-life, since she is only half a person.

But is that the issue? And if not, what is the issue, or what has been the issue? The issue has not been my feeling of loss, my experience of absence, my awareness of that missing part of myself; it has not been, even, the feelings of guilt, or unshouldered responsibility, real as these things are, the overwhelming knowledge of my lack of power to alter how things were, or are... or will be.

She gives herself a shake, her shoulders rise, her head signals, *no, no, no: I am doing it all over again! I am starting to repeat the past, the thing I have decided not to do! These ideas, these feelings, must go: they have been my companions for too long now, leaching through my defences, I have become their victim... I am not to be a victim. Perhaps I have made a companion in victimhood of Ruth. Perhaps I have been unfair to Robert and James, who have been true*

companions to me: I have been putting the dead before the living.
Momentarily, the future looms: her choir friends, her hospital friends, James's army and masonic friends, Robert's few crafts friend – they are all gone and she sees the three of them, sitting together in the twilight of their lives, silence shrouding them like mist. Clouds of mist, shawls of silence, resting on their shoulders. She starts, then smiles. How melodramatic! Even for me, she thinks.

For the first time since last Thursday, she passes the big blue fish, giving it a cursory glance. She turns left, across the road. They will just live quiet but full lives from now on. James has said he will retire from the army business soon and she expects he will use the time to travel more. I might travel with him, she ponders. This is something she has always refused to do, for she has her work at the hospital where, she knows, they depend on her.

And Robert – what of Robert?

She is passing the water fountains and gradually grows conscious of her surroundings. I walked this way, she thinks, but in the opposite direction, only last week. What a lot has happened since then. I have had what I can best think of as a revelation. But what was it really? What happened, really? I find it so difficult to put it into words. We went to Donegal on a day trip, that's all… and I confronted my demons, that's all.

But what of the others?

James is fine. James is self-sufficient. James will survive. But Robert; Robert is different, she thinks. Robert has not confronted his demons, yet. Robert has not used his art to confront the things he gets so angry about, sometimes. And he drinks too much, she thinks. He drinks and potters! And what do potters do, but potter? She smiles and as she does so bumps into someone, or someone bumps into her, on the now-crowded footpath. It is another lady: they both smile; Rebecca says 'Sorry' and the pale lady says 'Sorry' and then they carry on in their separate ways. This is where the lorry almost bumped into me last Thursday, she recalls. I'm just like that yellow lorry, she thinks, growling along, bumping along. And like the lorry, I carry a tremendous load of stuff around with me. She smiles, I carry the good and the bad, I carry it all.

That pale lady she had literally bumped into – the one whose complexion she realises so reminded her of Robert – she recalls this while remembering glancing at him last night, in the cottage. He had looked so… so *bleached*, she thinks. It was with surprise that she realised she had never before perceived him in this way, had never envisaged him before in any other way than his being just Robert, the boy Robert, merging in some hazy way into the teenager Robert. And there he had stayed, in her memory of him, locked up tightly. It is as if she had not seen him for the past thirty years.

She considers him. He has aged: he has become a mature – a middle-aged – man.

It was as if all the colours of childhood and youth had been drained away, along with the playfulness and vigour she associated with him. He stood there, leaning over the table, half turned away from her. He was wearing his usual cords, held up loosely by braces. He looked lean to the point of being skinny. She saw the beginnings of a slight stoop. She allowed her eye to scan the closely cropped hair, a few, faint streaks of grey beginning to show. She took in the closely-shaven jaw. She noted, again for the first time, the *monkish*, yes, that is the right word, *monkish*, for there is something rigorous and hard about him; she noted the monkish, stretched, tightening of skin between cheekbone and ear. He had turned his head and looked into her eyes. She felt strangely disconcerted.

'Are you eating properly?' she had asked. To her ear, her voice sounded harsh, but he appeared not to notice.

'Of course I'm eating properly: I've been eating properly for the past forty-five years! He replied, 'tartly', she thinks. She noticed how his lips have become thinner.

She thinks: one weekend past and another round the corner. On Friday she will walk to meet Robert who will be waiting by the bridge. And then the blue Jaguar, containing James, suited and tied, James whose lot has been to patiently wait all these years, will be pulling up to the pavement at eight precisely. He will have the heater running, the radio barely audible. It is his turn to host their weekly dinner and they are going out, something they never do when it is Robert's turn and only very rarely when it is her turn.

'Do you know, I fancy something Italian,' James had said as he dropped her off last night. 'It's time we tried something different... I hear there's a new place, on the Golden Mile. We will give it a try, if you don't mind... if you want to...'

'Sure,' she had replied. 'Yes, of course... you're right: it is time we tried something new!'

She stops to look back towards the barely flowing water. 'This evening,' she thinks, 'when I get home from work, it will be so different: I will walk by the river, then. Alone.'

She thinks, 'I will spy on the reflected lights winking to their shadow-lights on the water.' She pictures the scene, and then another image enters her head, unbidden.

She imagines, as she has done so many times before, the conversations they might be having now, if Ruth were here. The shared concerns about patients... perhaps, even, about husbands, about children...

She imagines, once again, all the laughter they might have had. All the songs they might have sung are in her head.

'I must stop this,' she says, again. 'I mean to change...'

***

She will walk now to the City Hall and catch a bus there. She takes the long way, approaching the river and stopping beside the blue fish; again, as she always does, she wonders if it is pregnant, and if so, what will happen to the little fishes? She thinks of a poem that speaks of wisdom and of fish. The words stir in her memory but do not come. Later, close to the pedestrian bridge, she looks towards the place where she saw the women's hair streaming out on the water. Is it still there? Will the little fish swim through that hair?

The wind stirs in her own hair, plays on her skin. Where, she wonders, is Ruth, on this newly minted, wind-stirred Monday morning? Is she down there by the stream, under the tree where the two boys fought, down behind their house where their mother kept an eye on them, all those years ago? The years melt away. She sees the curtains of the room slowly move to one side; she can see her mother's face there, its paleness materialising out of the darkness of the room behind.

She is taken over by the image of that face. Then, the magic of memory creates something new: something moves, two elements in her brain click together, gears engage. Imprinted words float to the surface: another poem, taught to them by their mother, all those years ago, enters her mind, unbidden and in its entirety. Like spring water rising, the words stream:

As from the house your mother sees
You playing around the garden trees,
So you may see if you will look
Through the windows of this book,
Another child, far, far away,
And in another garden, play.

The words fail to materialise. She stops, her mind blank, then they come, in their fullness.

But do not think you can at all,
By knocking on the window, call
That child to hear you. He intent
Is all on his play-business bent.
He does not hear; he will not look,
Nor yet be lured out of his book.
For, long ago, the truth to say,
He has grown up and gone away,
And it is but a child of air
That lingers in the garden there.

She savours the sounds of the words and the memory of the words and their movement from all those years ago: that and remembrance of their mother come together. 'Like the white and the yolk of an egg, dropped into boiling water to poach,' she thinks.

Then, 'Lured,' she says, softly, 'what an apt word.'

She looks at her watch. She has plenty of time to dawdle, there is no rush on her. She stops by the wall that protects the city from the river and leans on it. She is thinking again about Robert. She understands in a clear way how intense he is, and how private he is about the nature of that intensity.

As she walks she considers. Words, poetry, people. Words like Intensity. Focus. Relationships. Robert takes a physical part of the real world, and there, in that indefinable, immeasurable space between his hands, he coaxes into being something that is new in the universe. He *lures* (there is that good word again) meaning and shape and form and space. In essence, she thinks, he assists at the birth of a new shape and form and space, but he is more than a midwife! Or a sculptor. Unlike a sculptor, who hacks out of a rock the form hidden or imprisoned within it, Robert introduces form and space into what before had been a void. He is engaged in transcendence, she can see that, and in some odd way, the core of his work is about that. She thinks she understands now, in a way she never considered before, why he will not, or cannot, talk about these things, for they are, in their essence, she can understand quite clearly, beyond words. She remembers something he said as they passed Cave Hill yesterday. In the proper meaning of the term, what he does *is* radical.

James, on the other hand (and she loves James), James she can see, with his reliance on order and law, with his reorganisation of things that are already there – buttons and dyes, collections of pictures, his house and gardens, his soldiers – simply imposes a structure on the surface of life, oblivious to the vital and alive, the squirming and heaving world that lies beneath, leaving it to get on with it. He ignores, is ignorant of, what lies beneath the surface of reality. His head is heavy with what it contains and it contains all the imposing structures and edifices of a commanding church. There is little room left for the free flight of swallows around the belltower.

So long as people conform to the letter of the law, he will be happy. He does not *live*, is not attached to his values in the way Robert is, he is attached in a different way. She can see that now and her job will be to help him see that, also. And to let Robert know she understands something of what drives him, of his engagement and commitment.

But what of me and my own life? she thinks. My role is with the living: the dead and the dying will have my sympathy, but I must attend to what is important. My role is to mediate with these two people whom I love, giving freely to each whatever I can, giving whatever each of them can accept. For a moment the image of the swallows comes back to her: my job, she thinks, should be to point out the circling swallows to one and to help the other to apply his mind's eye to the swallows' cousins, the swifts.

Rebecca walks on, one woman among many, alone. She is conscious of feeling the convulsed earth shifting beneath the smarting pavement of this stretch-marked city as it creaks and groans once again into life on this new Monday morning. She holds her black coat close around her body, like a shield. She looks at the river, remembering again the long tresses she saw in the water – was it yesterday? She remembers seeing them in the ocean: that was yesterday. The freedom she felt as she stood on the cliff top, looking out over the ocean. Then, hearing Ruth's voice. Looking at these flowing waters she repeats to herself the lines: 'It is but a child of air that lingers in the garden there…' Perhaps James is right, perhaps it is time to try something new, to try to forget the past. Anyway, she has made a decision. Standing there on the cliff top at Slieve League she had made a decision. She will make arrangements to face the man she can think of only as

Ruth's killer. She walks on, her heart heavy. *'What,'* she thinks, *'does it all matter, now, now when all I can feel is this sense of aloneness, I am more alone than I have ever been.'*

The past squats on her shoulders, it bows her back, her head. She can physically feel its presence. The old feelings rise up. She feels so tired.

She gives herself a shake; *what would James say*, she asks herself: *'Pull up your socks,'* is what he'd say. She finds she is smiling a little. She thinks of Robert. What would he say? Probably the same: something like, 'knuckle down' or 'roll up your sleeves' – they are so alike, yet so different: like brothers, or cousins, she thinks. She turns to leave. If she doesn't hurry, she will be late for work.

***

To any casual observer who has known them, they are as close now as they have ever been. The months and years pass and continue to pass. James's eyes are narrowing, his black hair thinning, prematurely. Robert, he will tell you, once described his hair as 'fuliginous', a word he was unfamiliar with and had to go and look up. Soon, he will leave the Territorial Army and he will retire from the business. He means to travel; he has hopes, as yet unspoken, that Rebecca will join him. Robert's perceptive good humour long ago turned to irony, and that in turn is now slowly turning to silence. Of them all, his anger hardens, it sits like a weight on his tongue: many things, many feelings, are unspoken, and he becomes more and more taciturn; he cannot be sure why he is angry. He works. Often, he jokes and smiles and is happy. If you asked him, he would pause and smile and say, 'it's a queer thing, life,' and leave it at that. And Rebecca. Rebecca's lips too are thinning. Rebecca will carry on nursing, a vocation she carries out wonderfully well.

The years will pass, more and more quickly. They will grow old: most likely they will grow old together, as they have grown to this stage, together yet, being alone is the inheritance their history has passed to them.

***

Before bending to the wheel Robert glances out of the window. He notices the ash trees along the loanan are beginning to lose their leaves. He looks at them and thinks, *They look so sad, so mortal. One by one they will die. Yes, one by one they will die,* he thinks, *leaving no children's voices to break the silences. They will leave only empty spaces that the days and weeks will curl in on and fill with alien voices, their only legacy, silence, absolute.*

He spins the wheel.

Postscript

A Friday in September 2006

It is a cool Friday evening in September. Rebecca comes into her apartment. The rooms have changed little during the past year, save for the introduction of spots of colour here and there: a bright rug adorns the floor of the hallway. A big, almost surreal, painting of a cup and saucer, given in sprawling reds and greens and by Neil Shawcross, hangs against the living-room's far wall, directly opposite the entrance door. It is what Rebecca considers to have been a rather extravagant Christmas present from Robert and James, though, in a sense, she chose it herself, having seen it in an art gallery on the Lisburn Road, and then extolled its vibrancy. A bunch of cut flowers stand in a glass vase that she carefully placed on the table earlier. Half a dozen plant pots stand on the balcony, still in bloom.

She takes off her shoes and goes into the kitchen barefooted. She returns with a glass of white wine and sits at the table by the wall. She opens the drawer and takes out her book

My book.

My diary.

Ruth's book.

She leafs through it until she comes to the pleasing, chaste whiteness of an untouched page. She remains still for a little, considering how to start. A smile curls and softens what has become the rather thin, tense line of her lips. She runs her fingers through her neatly cut hair. As she does so, it shines under the light: in the old way, little mahogany tints spring into life briefly, before dying away.

She gets up, goes to the kitchen and returns with a cigarette, a saucer for the anticipated ash, and a box of matches. She lights the cigarette. Briskly, she takes up her pen. She inhales the illicit smoke, her head inclined to one side, her chin lifted. She begins to write.

Dear Ruth,

It's close to midnight on the night of our 46th birthday. We spent our last birthday together. Do you remember? I remembered earlier tonight and felt so guilty that I had somehow deserted you. I want to share this birthday with you, in our own way. I am now sitting at my desk. I want to write.

I've a glass of wine to hand, as usual! It's my… I don't know how many I have had! And, for once, I don't care! James and Robert took me out to celebrate. James chose the place, a new wine bar in east Belfast – a few years ago, who would have thought one could put the words 'wine bar' and 'east Belfast' in the same sentence? It was great, though: bright, light, full of life and really, really, good food. It makes me feel happy, just to see the city buzzing with new life.

It's been a long since I wrote anything 'substantial' in our book. I think I should try to put down some thoughts, a kind of overview, on what has happened during the past twelve months. So here goes.

Before I start: death is such a close thing. Death is such a real thing. In the midst of life, it is just around the corner. I walked on the street with you, then I was there, touching your body, the texture of your skin, its coldness. The smell of death on your cold body. I dressed you, with our mother's help. What a thing it must be, to dress one's dead daughter. I brushed your hair until it shone. I brushed your hair until our mother led me from the room. I have been selfish. I need to say that: for a long time I shut her out of my life.

It's been a year since my 'conversion' at Slieve League – conversion, epiphany or whatever one might wish to call it. Try as I might, I have found it impossible to put the experience into words. I cannot quite capture it. I remember using the word 'crystalline' to describe how I suddenly saw the world around me as I came alive in that marvellous place. 'Crystalline' is a lovely word.

I remembered how if felt when I learned to swim. Our parents took us to the swimming baths at weekends, we must have been eight or nine at the time, and you took to the water with great ease. I kept sinking and then, one day, quite suddenly I was floating. I remember the sense of oneness with the water, a feeling of total ease; the water belonged to me and me to it. At that moment, I could have swum across the Atlantic to America. In my mind, there was such clarity around the relationship that had just emerged, yet I did not know how or why I could float – I only knew I could, because I was…

That is the best way I can find of describing the indescribable.

The important thing was, at that moment I was enabled to see, for an instant, the interconnectedness of things, I became aware of a perfect harmony running through the universe. For the briefest moment I saw it; I was part of it, connected to it; then – it was gone. But one moment was enough. I knew! Somehow, I understood enough to give me hope. I remember, I perceived this unity as being there to serve all the parts it united, not the other way round.

It was a bridge, of a kind. It existed, if only for a moment!

But what is a moment? How do we measure time?

I have discussed this with James and Robert, of course. We are an odd lot: increasingly, you know, we cannot live together, nor can we exist apart. We cannot agree nor can we agree to disagree! All we can do is bicker and argue! I'm sure that we are disagreeing more than we are agreeing these days.

I think they initially believed I was mad. Perhaps I was. They felt, I think, that the explosion and your death had deranged me in some way. (I think we are all deranged. It's what makes us all distinct and different: how else could we be normal and not remain clones?) Anyway, we keep on going along, as friends. Robert, despite — no, because of — his anarchistic inclinations, is sympathetic to my idea that we're all a bit crazy, so he is forbearing. James is willing to humour both of us, but he holds firm to his own 'sane' views and will not be budged. And yet, we have remained companions, friends, colleagues in this messy business of living amid (forgive me) the dead who surround us, whose shoulders we stand on, whom we rub against, as we rush about our daily duties.

What is a moment? How long is a moment?

Dearest Ruth.

Am I being morbid?

Sometimes, I suspect I may be.

Mostly, I don't know. Sometimes, I don't care, really.

Anyway, that experience allowed me to look. It gave me the hope necessary to be honest, or to try to be honest. To examine my life. It's been hard, but worth it. Honest about myself: about my sisterhood, my daughterhood. To face up to my womanhood. To face up to my selfhood, above all else — and to face up to all the various and numerous and different and diverse and often conflicting dimensions of my existence and experience. And those who share my life...

Companions?

Yes, but what has been the nature of our companionship?

We have functioned more as a family, really.

A dysfunctional, contingent family!

Each one of us, trembling in the balance.

Nine months ago, I changed jobs. I discovered I had been drifting for decades! After nearly twenty-five years training and working — and if the truth be told vegetating, hiding, in the same hospital — I felt I had been compliant, too submissive; I merely consumed what was given to me. So, I have taken on a new challenge. I am now a new person in a new job, a Nurse Specialist, working in the community with GPs and hospitals, working with and for patients, developing care pathways for people with respiratory diseases. I believe it is really useful work, I know I am making a difference in peoples' lives and I love it! Somehow, I am beginning to love me!

As I said, I have tried to be... what have I tried to be? 'Better', I suppose — I suppose! I am not an angel, though. Who is? Not James or Robert. Nor were you an angel. But neither were we bad or of evil intent. I suppose the four of us were naïve: we were young when you left us. We were essentially young and ordinary — we were self-effacing people, like our parents; when you went away we were little more than teenagers. We were naïve not just because of our years, but because we believed in something that was not there; like our parents we believed we were under siege, all the time! We believed in the authority of rightness to protect us.

235

Recently, I have come to believe we really were the proverbial sacrificial lambs. Another set of victims, self-selecting. That's been Robert's line for a long time, and for a long time I resisted victimhood but now I think I'm beginning to understand this view, at least partly. All those who held power ever wanted from us was our vote and our loyalty. In return, they promised they would keep us safe. Maybe they believed it, too. They kept us safe from the unknown… safe, I suspect, from being too generous of spirit. That was how we grew up. We are beginning to come to terms with it – it's taken us thirty years. It has cost us dearly, as we both know. I have looked back in the book and have come across this account of one important conversation we had.

She opens the book at a new page.

***

It is now October and the evenings are drawing in. I have been drawn back to my journal, again.

It's been two weeks since we went to Donegal, though the repercussions are still present.

Robert and James were here for a meal tonight. After we finished we sat at the table and talked. Coming when it did (just at the 'apex' of my reaction or response to that fateful meeting and at the height of Robert and James's attempts to sustain me), I felt it important that I make a note of the conversation. It got very, very heavy at one point (I suspect Robert had been drinking before he arrived). They left, earlier than usual and rather abruptly (I'm sure they will make up afterwards – they always do).

I will try to write down what was said, as far as I can recall it. When I read this, as I shall do, or as someone else may do sometime in the future, I or they will have to remember that I am the narrator and I may have got some parts of it wrong.

Our talk moved from the usual gossip to my intention to meet the killer for the second time. I am still sure I have conflated the conversation, but here goes. Robert was trying to needle James – that is the only word for it – and was saying something like:

You are a loyal, natural-born subject James! I, on the other hand, am not! I don't believe there are many of what I would call morally natural 'subjects' in life. I believe that institutions, states and churches, and those that head them, especially those that head them – kings and queens and popes and archbishops – ought to exist only to provide support for, and to be servants of, the people. James replied, somewhat brusquely, (I remember, he raised his shoulders, in that way he has, and leaned over in a very aggressive manner for him):

'These are questions I don't feel qualified to express an opinion on!'

'You can't divert me like that! Tell us what you really think: share your thoughts with us.'

'One can only insist on what one sees to be the truth! In my experience most people have a deep, in-born need to be governed!'

'I am not to be 'governed!' I don't have to have a 'boss!'

This is more or less what they said, then there was an angry exchange here... I can't remember, exactly what was said. I remember Robert continued, 'They should not exist to dominate and feed off the weak and the needy!' James shook his head, but didn't reply.

Then I intervened. 'I don't know about that: I suppose there's always a boss, somewhere. But I agree with you, Robert, to this extent. When I was on Slieve League, I had the sense that I was surrounded by, and was part of, a great, cosmic, universal 'oneness'- but I somehow know that the 'one' – the feeling it existed just flashed into my consciousness, then was gone, and I was left only with the memory of it

– was important only because of the presence of all the other pieces. It did not 'govern' the elements, but existed, I felt – I think – because of them; it got its strength, its 'oneness' from them.

Robert said: 'Yes. In a very real sense any king figure, or boss, is only as good as the people he serves…'

'But it's more than that,' I replied. At this point James broke in, angrily:

'This is all cloud-cuckoo-land stuff! Rulers rule! That's what they do. You must have law and order; it's the glue of a civil, democratic society. Of course, people have to have a head of state, a head of an organisation; people need someone to lead them, someone who can take decisions. To me, that's the basis of a lawful and ordered country and society.'

'You can call it 'balderdash' if you so wish,' Robert replied, 'but I believe profoundly that we have to have law and justice – not just what you call 'law and order', but something infinitely better. Look at what your so-called 'law and order' delivered for us here! It produced a palpable sense of injustice and unfairness among one section of our community and pushed most of the rest of us to one side, ignored, left as tongue-less mutes, as bystanders! We were stranded on the empty stage playing the fat castrati; dumbfounded, while the proletariat took to the streets. We existed for decades, always on the edge of peace, perpetually on the edge of violence. We existed on the edge of fear and were kept there, deliberately so!'

James replied in a very quiet tone of voice, in fact, he spoke so softly it seemed menacing: 'I think you are entering into very dangerous territory, Robert. Firstly, your criticism of what happened here is ill informed and ill founded. Second, what you're suggesting as an ideal is a recipe for disaster. A tyranny of chaos!'

Robert broke in here with, 'That was always the response! I know it well! However, your Paddy is the only chaos I can see around here!'

James simply shrugged and said, 'It's not somewhere I have any desire to go. I think we should drop the subject!' He paused for a moment, before saying, 'Except to make this point: it was the maintenance of order and a reliance on law that got us through the past thirty years, and it wasn't easy, despite what you seem to think. Government did respond to public demands and would have done so sooner if violence had not hampered it. That's what a democratic society does, it moves continually and that's what the authorities did, and I am proud to have played a part in it. Now let's ...' But once again Robert interrupted: 'I know you've always been an apologist for the bosses, for the status quo. But you're old enough now to see beyond that. Take a look at the consequences of your whole system – it always ends up with some Caesar or other lying with a knife in his back! The King is dead, long live the King! It's a vicious kind of system, don't you think? I want to stop people being victims of their own insatiable lust for money and power, and hurting the rest of us at the same time! As a society, as a people, I have to have a vision of something more. We must be able to anticipate something beyond all that greed for mere transitory power. Remember, Burns had a pretty sound vision of radicalism and internationalism: he put it quite simply:

'For a' that, and a' that,
It's comin' yet for a' that,
That Man to Man, the warld o'er,
Shall brithers be for a' that.'

James glared at him and then got to his feet. 'I don't want to carry on this conversation. It's futile and childish. But I'll tell you this, before I stop. What you're articulating is nothing but a fairytale. When you get up on a dark winter morning and press a switch and the light comes on, when you go to your larder and open the door and you find food there, or when you turn on the tap and clean water flows, that's the result of things being ordered. When all races and creeds can walk along the street without fear of attack, that's law. When society says if you are ill or old you are entitled to be taken care of, that's security.' He looked intently at Robert, then turned his gaze towards me ('me', for other eyes, is Rebecca), as if for support. He went on: 'I know it sometimes fails, but it works a lot of the time and when it fails to work we acknowledge that and we make a change and we move on, and we rely on people who can take responsibility to ensure these things happens. That's the reality!'

Robert shook his head: 'It was your sort of law and order that bolstered up those cliques who loved power and who clung to it. Just as your new, improved system will bolster up those who are moving into power. Where will the poor and needy be? They will be under the table, searching for crumbs! While people like you and me and Rebecca here, avert our eyes while we are neatly pushed off to one side! It's just the way things are...'

'But doesn't Robert have a good moral case?' I asked. To which James replied, 'No! It's so naïve! What he preaches is moralistic in the most simplistic terms imaginable! And of course, like all such things, it stands in danger of turning into a dogma, and very quickly so. You both talk about me and laugh at me. Yes, I know you do!' he said, bitterly, seeing the looks of credulity on our faces. 'You talk and laugh about the black and white tiles on my floor. You act as if they are some kind of representation of how I view the world. In some forms of thought, they could represent the presence of good and evil as opposing forces in the world, but that does not represent how I see things — including people — at all. I don't see some men as good and some as evil. I do believe there's good and evil in all of us, just as there are positive and negative things in most societies, in most governments...'

'Robert.' I said, 'Isn't what you're saying this: that ultimately all actions have consequences and that each individual has to hold himself or herself accountable for those consequences? First of all to himself, then to his or her fellow human beings? And this is where real justice is to be found?'

I remember Robert telling me about hearing a man preaching on the street corner. He told me the preacher quoted from some English poet or other, Donne I think, and how wonderful it was to hear someone like that being spoken of in our mean maze of streets. The pain of Donne's story caused me to remember an incident from childhood, the fire we must all go through in this life. I must have been about ten at the time for I was still at primary school. We were in the playground, just this girl and me, I cannot remember why we were alone, but we were, eating our sandwiches and talking. It was over in the corner, in the shade of the big ash tree that grew there. Do you remember it? Out of the blue, she started to tell me about her father and the things he had been doing, was still doing, to her and making her do to him. And then you came and joined us. She stopped and I remember her looking at me, a pleading, imploring look. The bell rang and on our way in to class she made me promise not to tell anyone and I never did. Not even you. Why I remembered was her father was a lay Baptist preacher, a local farmer; a man who was highly regarded and well respected.

I see her occasionally. The last time was about a year ago, in Belfast outside the City Hall and she smiled and said, 'Hello' and we chatted for a bit. I wondered, does she have any memory of those things. She is married now and has two children. Over the years, I have often wondered what happened to them, between her and her father and their family, I mean. I am very sorry I never told anyone, my mother or my father; after all, he was a doctor and could have done something. But I had promised, you see: a child's promise to a child. I never told. My word was my bond! Indeed!

When I think of it now – when I think of her father doing those terrible things, my promising to keep it a secret and keeping it... Then I think of Robert's romanticism, his idealism, about the goodness and sovereignty of the individual, and then I think of James and of his unswerving belief in good order, and his corresponding lack of faith in human goodness, though he would not admit that. Even to himself.

What snares we create for ourselves with memories and with words.

241

I am like you. I have never had a life, a real life.

Take that word I used earlier, 'sacrifice'. It's not a word I would have used a year ago but one whose connotations I feel inclined to explore now. I have become more interested in the concept of class since I took up this evening course. Not in the old, narrow sense, but in the sense of finding out about the class with power and the class without power. Who are the leaders and who gives them the power? Why is one group poor and another rich? How can one person take power and others can't or won't? Where is 'justice' – Robert's question – to be found in all of this?

What about Love? What about Hate? Yes, I went back to talk to the man who killed Ruth. I had to and after that long weekend last year I felt empowered to do just that. It was much the same as the first time: I went into the room, he was sitting there. I told him I could not forgive or even begin to understand why he had done what he had, how his killing of Ruth had taken not only her life, but how it had taken away from me part of who I was. I told him how I had had to live with that. I told him how it had destroyed my family, hurt my friends and affected all of our lives. I told him how much I hated and despised what he had done.

He said nothing. He just looked at me, without expression. So, I turned and walked out. Then, just as I stepped through the doorway, I turned on my heel and walked straight back in. I sat down, facing him, and asked him why he had killed Ruth: I asked him to explain. What gain did he hope to make from such an action?

He attempted to separate things out: Ruth's death was one thing, an accident and he was sorry for that. Many people, he said, had died. He said again (hateful words) he could feel my pain. What he was about was to bring change in this country and he would not say sorry, would not apologise for that.

As I left, he asked me to meet him once more, a week later. He said he would try to explain; he needed time to think it through, to put it in a way I would understand. I agreed.

Two days later James called me at work, an unusual thing for him to do. I took the call, thinking something was wrong, perhaps something to do with Robert. Then it all collapsed into chaos in my head. Had I heard the news? No, what news. A long pause, then: 'Peter Bond, the bomber, is dead!' The world stopped. I hung onto the phone. Then James continued. 'Bond had been killed! A stolen car, driven by a joy rider, a youngster, had hit him. He was dead. An accident…'

I looked up the newspaper that evening and to find out where the burial was to take place. I had decided to go to his funeral. And I did go. At least, I went to the graveyard and stood watching over the wall, but did not go in. I watched his wife and three children; they were in tears.

Afterwards, as they came away, I approached her and said who I was. She looked at me. Then she opened her arms and embraced me. And I embraced her. We didn't exchange a word. Somehow, we didn't need to: there was no need, or no room, for words.

I did not feel sorry about his death, but neither did I feel joyful or even mildly satisfied. I felt nothing, really, certainly not that justice had been done.

I think, if I felt anything, I felt cheated. I felt cheated out of a final meeting with him. I was denied an opportunity to find closure, and just when I had finally willed such an ending. It all seemed so unfair: first I was denied my sister, and then I was denied closure with the only person who could have granted it.

When I think of him, which I don't much or often, I think mostly of that last image of his wife and children weeping by his graveside. I can see there was no harmony between his role as a father and a husband

and his action, or even between his political ideals and his actions. It's not what I understand by republicanism. In the few words I shared with him, he did not appear to see how his violent action has soiled the legitimacy of any aspirations he might have had for this island we all must share.

I feel cheated but I also feel vindicated: Ruth never gave me permission to speak on her behalf, to seek vengeance or to bestow forgiveness. I don't feel anything else. I am agnostic about it all, or I try to be. I don't feel good about his death: death provides no liberation, and what small liberation I have, I have worked for, for many years, and paid for during many days and nights.

I feel I am making a difference, a real difference: I am enhancing many lives by my work. I despise his contribution and I feel justified in feeling that. I have left guilt and hate behind me. It's just a sad fact that I feel I am right. I wish it were otherwise.

But I believe we, my community, were wrong in some way, too. I believe we are all interconnected. That's why I am trying to understand, to see things more clearly, to be less innocent than we were about life. The politicians are getting ready now for another big get-together to discuss the way forward. If they succeed, which I fervently hope they do, I do not believe for an instant that any one death, or the deaths and injury to hundreds and thousands of individuals over the past thirty odd years, can ever be justified.

It seems, as James said the other night, a very careless, inefficient way to effect change: Robert replied that he thought it a very inhuman way to effect change. To my mind they are both right: I also think it a very ignorant and bull-headed way to bring about change; in fact, I think it simply hindered change that would have come, change that was on its way. You can't stop change, but you can certainly slow it down. It was not done to bring about change, it was done, I always felt, looking at and listening to those people who talked on television, it was done to

244

further the cause, to bow the knee to history, to honour a past: I want us to honour a shared future, not a blighted, divided past.

I have just been to the kitchen to refill my coffee cup! And I am about to have another cigarette! This reminds me (seeing the white saucer I have taken to using as an ashtray), when I was at James's house last Christmas I noticed, for the first time, really, the black and white tiles on his hall floor. Robert always claimed they have some sort of wider significance and James has always refused to say. I do not know really, but if they do represent two opposing forces in life (good and evil), I do believe that that human life and experience cannot be represented by two sides only, black and white – it's much too complex and complicated for that. It struck me, looking at those tiles, that they stood in opposition to my experience of last September – which was that everything in this diverse, multiple world is all part of the one thing, everything is interrelated, interdependent. Although the tiles had harmony, of a sort, they seemed to me to represent a very thin, shallow nature. To coin a phrase, it's too black and white a view.

No. That statement of bi-polar opposites represents too simplistic an analysis, it is only a stepping stone; increasingly, I see little point in swapping one form of naïveté for another, and I intend to try to understand what this means, not just for people here but for – and this is where I may have had too many glasses of wine tonight – but so I can understand us, humans, people, everywhere… There! Forty-six and I'm still thinking and feeling like a teenager! Robert would love that – love me*. James would hate it, but would still love me.*

My love for them has grown stronger.

I still don't know what to make of life. For one brief moment on that one day, I had this cosmic, universal insight: I became aware of the existence of an unbelievable beauty, a unity that holds everything together.

245

We talked about it at the time, but gradually we stopped having discussions. There was no point for I couldn't fully or clearly explain to the others what my experience had been. We just kept on repeating what we'd already said. And then, almost immediately, the memory began to fade, and soon I had trouble recalling it: we were just having unrelated conversations...

When I went back to see Peter Bond I remember Robert saying, 'How can there be such a unity as you talk about if such terrible, destructive things exist in the world?' Ultimately, the only unity, he argued, is the simple one of individuals living their lives and being accountable for their actions.

Bond had not repented. How could anyone forgive him, in that case? If he did not feel sorry for what he had done, how could I forgive him?

This reminds me of Hutchinson. Perhaps, this is the difference between art and life. I suppose there must be a difference? This thing about stains and perfections. It may be that art is perfect whereas life isn't... Or it may be that art is a lie, the idea that it articulates truth may be just a great falsehood. It may be that the unity I saw and the harmony Robert talks about are very different.

Or they may be the same.

I keep being tangled up; I think too much. That's where James is a great help to me: he brings me back to mundane reality with words like 'duty' and 'public service' – he helps keep everything in my life in good order, or in as good order as is possible.

Such odd thoughts to have; such odd things to write down. But then we are strange creatures, we humans: so individualistic, such strange companions to ourselves before we are companions to others; we live entirely inside our own heads, when all is said and done.

I sometimes allow myself to think, if things had been different I might have married James; sometimes, if truth be told, I think I might have married Robert. But I have grown to feel that to marry one and not the other would be a dishonourable thing to do. As it is, I have the best of both of them and they have what is left of me.

But I know there is more, there must be more. I don't really know them.

What we have will have to do. For now, at least. Who knows what tomorrow holds?

Still, I feel good. I'll end now. No. 'End' is the wrong word. There are no endings. To me, endings are like a great gathering of snakes, all writhing and wriggling in constant motion in an enormous circular pit. Each one has a beginning and an end, a head and a tail. A billion tails and a billion heads, all constantly slipping past each other. Destined to make constant repetitions of their journeys, their meetings and their departures.

What a strange conceit to devise! Still, it's how I feel just now, so I'll let it stand. Tomorrow, I may feel differently. And still be true to myself. There are so many truths in this life.

I feel sane. I feel balanced, somehow. I'll finish now.

Book Two

Autumn, 2006

(Belfast, Enniskillen, Belfast)

If a man be overtaken in a fault...restore such a one, in the spirit of meekness.'

Galatians 6.

Belfast

Her name is Rebecca.

She sits at her desk. She prepares to write. She tells herself she will try to be truthful. In the end, she thinks, truth is all I have.

Although her thoughts are now on the beginning, she is writing this at what is the end. She thinks 'I hadn't known I was going to create a narrative history.' Which is what she supposes this is, partly, at least. She feels a strong desire to reconstruct what happened, or what she remembers happened, or what – she supposes – she imagines she remembers of what happened.

She determines she will try to be truthful for she was brought up to honour and value truth and truth-tellers; in the end, the thought is still with her. Truth, as we see it, is all each one of us has.

She writes.

When you read this, if you do – read it, I mean – it will transmute into your head, for good or ill it will alter your mind. Your imagination will make it your own. In other words, you will find in it your own truth and then it will no longer be mine; yet, as mine, it is precious to me, as I hope it will be to you, as a starting off point. Respect it if you can.

Despite what you will, it will change you. It will become part of you, or you will become part of it; it may take you over. In this sense, I know that it's a dangerous thing in which to engage, in which to invite another to engage, this challenge of saying what is true.

At least, I'll do it with tenderness. Don't be alarmed of my intentions. At a time of cynicism and suspicion, that is all I ask: give me the grace of suspending disbelief; believe in the truth of my name, at least.

I fear I am being too pushy too early; as my mother would have said, I am being melodramatic.

Whatever.

I will begin now: I am starting to write this a week after Easter, 2007. All around me, people are parading generosity of spirit, tentatively yet hopefully – the papers and the radio and television, they are full of it.

Now is the time for generosity. Of spirit.

***

I am sitting here, alone in a quiet room, looking down on the city. I sit in an enduring silence. I recall having said somewhere, perhaps many times previously, I like to be alone. Then I am myself. Now, I find this speaking out of what has been a silent life difficult. How or where should I begin? I will begin by breaking the silence at the hardest bit, the hardest bit for me.

No. Not silence. Or not silence, or not silence, alone.

Simplicity, perhaps. Simplicity. Simplicity.

I remember. Hot water. A razor.

The hot water encompasses my body. The razor rests on the bath's edge.

The alteration of a body, of a body's state, the shift from life to death is so simple.

The razor, sitting there, within hand's reach.

People talk about crossing the divide, they mention passing away; they speak of passing over; they whisper, slipping away.

It's as easy as… falling asleep; falling dead; falling out of life; falling into death. Then we are gathered up. We are to be called to eternal rest. Everything taken care of. I sink.

I allow myself to slip lower, beneath, under; deeper into the warm cosset of welcoming water until only my lips, my nose, my eyelids are uncovered. I allow my mind to rest, to drift, and drift; I allow it freedom. It assumes its own freedom of being.

I lift an arm up out of the water, I raise my eyelids and watch with dulled interest as it lowers itself, slowly, until it is resting on the water's surface. It floats. Then it sinks. It sinks out of view. My hand descends through the water until it comes to rest on my belly, in the V between my thighs. My eyes close. My fingers bend, my hand cups my body. My fingers slide inside, they infiltrate my body.

I float. My mind concentrates, it drifts, existing variously.

Robert and James. They are at the bath side. They are close to me. Whose hand is it that rests heavy as thistledown, light as rock, on my body, whose bony fingers are working their way inside me, ever so gently, so imperceptibly, so insidiously, so unstoppably?

My face smiles. I feel the smile. It is like a hard mask. Hardening.

Now, I feel the water grown cold; it has lost its warmth.

I open my eyes. At the end of the bath the white tiles rise up in uniformly clinical, unblemished rows to where they meet the white ceiling. On the window, the white lace curtains sway, slowly, gently. Through the partly open window comes the sudden, noisy, chain-saw call of my blackbird.

I hesitate. I decide. With my free hand I reach out to grasp the hot tap. I turn it, allowing the water to hurtle out, violently so, roaring as it comes. I wait a little, gauging the spreading heat. When it is acceptable, I turn the tap off. I sink back under the water; my ears are covered once more. All about my womb-like state the outside world grows mute. Slowly, I raise my head. Again the blackbird's call clatters through the evening air. This time it is muffled, smothered, behind padding. And it comes from a place very, very far away. It comes from another world.

I feel safe and secure and protected here. Buried in this water. I am not in control because there is nothing to control. Nor am I controlled. Yet, I am not out of control, merely beyond control. I am. I am but am not what my body is. My body does what it alone does. My hand moves, it follows a

252

circular motion; around and round and around and round it goes.

My body is cold and hard as rock; my body is soft and liquid as warm milk. Waves gather; wave follows wave; faster and faster, they swell. My back arches. The blackbird's call lives on and on, it is in a far-off, different place. I forget everything; I know nothing; without knowing, I join, I become one with the blackbird's noise; under the heavy, pressing water past and future are one.

***

The bathroom is full of steam. I wipe loads of condensation off the bathroom mirror with a towel and handfuls of tissue and do a quick survey of my wet body before the glass mists over again. Here I am, a forty-seven-year-old spinster, I think, looking at my body's image, doing unspeakable things, having unspeakable thoughts, being totally unspeakable, even if it is in the privacy of my own bathroom. 'You are a disgrace to your upbringing,' I say out aloud, addressing my other self, standing there, beneath the glass behind the hazy and running wetness. 'And you don't give a damn,' I reply. For a moment, I feel elated, the razor forgotten.

But that's not true. My gaze lingers. I do care. I know that because I do feel pangs of guilt on these rare occasions. The guilt passes, but still, I take time to look at my body with an admiring eye if, these days, it is condemned to be an increasingly critical eye. It is a trim body, no (not much) unnecessary bulk, no unwanted rolls of flesh. Just, perhaps just, a little bit of a bulge growing on my tummy.

I rub myself dry and slip on a dressing gown. I am just emerging from the bathroom when the doorbell rings and I go to answer it. I peer through the peephole and see the back of James's head. He has turned away but by the time I open the door he is looking at me, full in the face, a broad smile crinkling his eyes. Quite nice eyes, I think, as I often do.

'Hello.'

'You're early,' I say.

'The early bird catches the worm!' There is something in the air, I can sense it, a lightness and I find myself responding.

'Am I the worm? I reply, teasingly. I hold the door open to allow him to enter and as he squeezes past me his head swoops down towards my breast, in a motion that reminds me of a horse grazing. I realise he is eating my smell, with his nose.

'You smell nice.'

'Thanks. So would you, if you had just spent half an hour lounging in a nice, warm, spicy, bath.' I go off towards the bedroom to dress. 'I won't be long. Make yourself coffee.' And James strides off briskly, obedient as usual, towards the kitchen, calling out as he goes, 'Do you want some?'

'Yes please.'

Since his recent retirement James is a changed man. For example, today he is wearing a sweater and jeans! A form of clothing that has not, until recently and as far as I am aware, adorned his body since circa the mid-1970s.

I like that word, 'circa' – I have been making a conscious effort to use it as much as possible, no easy task, given the fact that I don't precisely know what it means and nor do most of my friends. (I have researched this, at work, and have had some odd looks.) I like it because it conjures up in my mind's eye an image of a wobbly old picket fence irregularly circling a house, moving closer here, and further away there. For some reason, it reminds me of the *Little House on the Prairie*. I absent-mindedly consider James's sartorial alterations and improvements while I stand there, simultaneously considering my vast wardrobe of clothes.

'What shall I wear?' was not a problem until recently. Recently, and I mean the past six or nine months, I too have taken to buying colourful attire, so much so I cannot always decide which bright garment to choose. Today, just to be contrary, I avoid anything with any hint of colour and take down a black top, black jeans and gather up a pair of black runners from the wardrobe floor.

When I finally appear, I find James out on the balcony, a mug of black coffee in his hand and a mug of white coffee waiting for me.

I greet him. 'Hasn't it been a glorious day? Only the second of April and it's like summer.'

'Yes. It does make a difference, doesn't it? Makes us all feel better, brighter, happier!' He is looking out across the river, sniffing the air. He is doing a lot of sniffing today. 'Makes one feel it's good to be alive. I hear on the car radio they've started to pull down the Maze today. And the parties have started to nominate ministers to the Assembly. So things are looking up! On all fronts!'

I take time to consider this rather broad, holdall statement, the one about politics and the weather and human feelings. It's the politics one that slightly dampens my mood.

However, despite my reservations, I don't share my considerable doubts about the universal truth of what he is saying. Rather, I remain silent, allowing his words to hang there, in the air, between us. Then, still in silence, I sit down and reach for my coffee.

Later, as we drive along the back roads that James has chosen to take – for despite his earlier hurry we are a little early, we have time to spend – my mood darkens. I think; I feel a compulsion to try to get back to the beginning. I want to make it clear to myself what I am. I decide I am a witness.

A witness has to act, to witness, she has to tell, otherwise she or he is a silent witness, an invisibility, or merely a potential witness, a near invisibility. To tell, he or she has to issue a report.

A report has to be – to be, it has to be… it has to be *made*, all the disparate bits brought together; the thing has to be constructed.

But before I can do that, I have to be sure of what is the truth – I have to get under, or behind, this patina that I'm sure we all, or most of us, use as camouflage.

When we arrive at Robert's place the others are already there. At least, as we approach, we can see through a gap in the hedge and across a field, the big, shiny four-wheel drive and the smaller, sleeker BMW sports car parked outside the cottage. In a moment we turn in at the entrance to the lane and prepare to meet the gang. Not that there are many others to be there, just Robert and Liz Dickey and Ursula Doherty and Patrick Mooney.

I always think Paddy and Ursula make an odd couple. But I realise they are 'odd' only in relation to the rest of our group and I'm sure my attitude reflects on me rather than on them. Paddy is older than us, in his mid to late fifties, I would say, and separated, I have learned by putting bits and pieces of information together, from a wife he found in London and left there when he went to America, years ago; Ursula is quite a bit younger, in her mid to late thirties and is divorced. Unlike the rest of us they live together as partners and appear to exist in a state of blissful and continuing sin. They are good fun, lively and rather unlike the kind of people I normally socialise with.

Still, while they are good fun I could not do it, I mean, live like that. I don't have the inclination or the energy, the demonic energy as Robert once described it, to live in sin.

Ursula drinks gin like a fish, swims a vast number of lengths of the pool daily, and has a figure most men would die to get their hands on – or so I have been told. No, truthfully, I am well aware that it's a figure most women would kill for, not including me, of course! I am so different from most women. Or so I would like to think...

Ursula is an estate agent who works incredibly hard and plays equally hard. According to Paddy she is very successful at her job, which is selling houses. A skill much in demand now. Paddy drinks gin like a fish too, never takes exercise, and shows it for his girth is expansive and seems to continue to expand, almost daily. He is a property developer. Another occupation that is much in demand. He seems to have become hugely wealthy, due, Robert and James say, to Belfast's recent but unrelenting upward and onward economic boom.

I don't know how we became friends with these two. It seems to me now that they were always there, but that is not the case. I think James knew Patrick years ago through some sort of business dealings they had, and then later when Liz and Robert became friendly, she and Kate knew each other, and we all just linked up. We fell into friendship. Organically, as they say: we simply drifted together, and inertia keeps us together. It's a small world.

James turns left at the Forge Pottery sign and the car crunches heavily up the lane. James is a very sedate driver, and we proceed elegantly in his big, heavy vehicle. As soon as we turn the bend we see them, down in the grass area between the cottage and the pottery. I can see Paddy's head, emerging out of what appears to be a clump of tall grass. He is sitting on a low bench by the pond and gets up when he hears the car. The others are standing around, in the sunshine. When he is opposite them, James stops the car on the laneway, and I get out leaving him to drive up to the cottage where he will park.

I stand for a moment looking down towards the knot of people. They have formed themselves into a group, positioned close to the pond. They appear to be like strangers to me, strangers in the sense of their seeming to belong to another age, another time.

The tree overhangs the still water, its shadow stretching now to darken a good bit of the grass that surrounds the pond. Oddly, for this is Co. Antrim after all, each of the four figures is wearing varying shades of white, if you can have shades of white. There they stand silently and in strong contrast to the green grass, the greening tree, the darker shadows that lie behind them, yet they themselves cast shadowy forms on the grass. The scene reminds me of something. Something alien, though I can't think of what. Something remembered from my childhood, perhaps. Or from a photograph. Then, as Robert raises his hand in welcome, I suddenly recall a similar scene, or a similar grouping: what springs to mind is something to do with a Chekhov play. I must have seen it on television, years ago.

I try to recall that scene as I write this; it rises in my mind and remains there and brings with it a sense of peacefulness, a mood of tranquillity.

Or was it just something latent, something unforeseen and unforeseeable, something waiting to happen?

A sense of stillness rests upon them.

The sense of stiffness emanates from them.

The sense of their being caught between one moment and the next, holding and maintaining their balance on the fulcrum of time, halted in motion. The two women are seated, the two men standing – both have their arms raised in anticipation, in welcome. What do they anticipate? Do they really welcome me?

The others watching, waiting.

For some reason, I think of that story in the Bible, the one about the woman whom God turned into a pillar of salt.

What thoughts, if any, I wonder, move, dance or meander within their distant, unknowable heads? What a potential for a multitude, for hordes of unreachable, unreadable, images, all milling about, locked within those skulls, as the men and women remain there, motionless, yet collectively the possessors of virtual worlds, of universes, comprising small and large dramas, glorious celebrations and grim realities.

All those worlds, not one but many, existing in each head, unbeknownst to the heads around it.

I start. I wonder, why do I have such odd thoughts? At the same time, I smile.

'Hi. Hello.' My call interrupts the moment, and they bloom, turning, rising, like loaves in an oven, rising in slow motion, calling back, expanding, and moving in little choreographed squalls of movement. Then Patrick, who else, bursts into a quick flurry of movement, of action: bending down to leave his glass on a small plastic drum that acts as a table, one-handedly hitching up his trousers while darting over the grass towards me, his free arm outstretched.

'You're looking bloody smart!' he says, embracing me in a great bear-hug. 'Come and have a drink.' His huge hand is clamped on my elbow as he half-guides, half hoists me down the slope.

'I'll have a glass of orange, or anything soft,' I say. 'It is only just after six o'clock, after all and I have to work tomorrow and…'

'Nonsense! You are here to enjoy yourself. You'll have a glass of wine, at least.'

He knows me too well, does Patrick, I think. One glass will lead to two. Over his shoulder I watch the glint of light on water. I see a dead leaf float, stationary and brown, its fragility evident as it nods and bobs, even in the lightest of breezes.

'No. Honestly.' I affirm. 'And anyway, I'd prefer to wait for James.' I say this, desperate to avoid any large-scale dispute, but instantly a glass of white wine appears, hovering temptingly before my eyes, floating on air, as it were, and my hand closes helplessly around its thin stem. Ursula, who has delivered it, smiles, steps back and then moves forward again in an insinuating kind of way, takes me by the same elbow that Paddy has so recently released and draws me to one side.

'How are you?' she asks, and then without waiting for an answer says, 'Have you heard about the new shopping centre?'

'Not really. Where or what is it?'

'Well, it's just opened, this morning in fact, and it's supposed to be fabulous. I'm planning a trip there, tomorrow, do you want to come?'

At this point Liz breezes over to us, asking me: 'Have you heard about the great new shopping centre...'

'Yes!' I speak quietly.

'Yes, she has,' Ursula says, 'I've just been telling her.'

'Yes,' I continued, 'but I only just heard about it and I haven't the faintest idea what it is or where it is or why it's so great!'

Then they both began speaking at once. This is a habit they have developed, having known each other for years. They met when they were students together and they appear to have thrived on what seems to me to be unnecessary competition for voice space.

'It's called The Outlet and it's quite close to Banbridge and it cost £70m to build!'

'And took ten years to conceive and build, I've been told!'

'And it sells oodles of designer clothes, all at discount prices!'

'And Paddy has some special gift vouchers that someone he knows gave him and he has offered them to us. We are both planning to go tomorrow. Can you come, too? We'll share the vouchers and we can have lunch there.'

'Yes, we can make a day of it. A girls' day out!'

'That sounds really lovely,' I say, faintly, 'but I'm afraid I have to work tomorrow. Sorry.' In reality, I wasn't a bit sorry. In fact, I was very glad for I loathe shopping and these two, I have discovered, are recreational shoppers *par excellence*.

At which point, and just in time to forestall any loud expressions of disappointment that might have been, James appears and immediately greets Ursula and Liz. He addresses them fulsomely, especially Ursula, I noticed. Within seconds Paddy too is beside us, 'What will you have to drink, James?'

'Something soft, I'm driving!' And, of course James, being of a more commanding disposition than me, has delivered to his hand a glass of orange juice, without argument or comment.

Then Paddy begins by asking him if he has heard about the new shopping centre. And of course, James has heard of the new shopping centre even though it has been a complete surprise to me. During this we have somehow or other moved down the slope to where Robert stands. I notice him suppressing a yawn before we exchange glances.

James is holding forth to Paddy. 'Yes, I understand it's likely to create 400 new jobs in the Banbridge area; it'll do wonders for the local economy.'

'Well, I think it will do well; I know they are hoping to attract customers from a very wide area. They have an all-Ireland orientation in their marketing.'

Listening to these two grown men talking about a shopping centre that's situated miles away and going on about international fashions and top fashion names and so on makes me edge closer to Robert. He is listening to this conversation with a look of incredulity on his face.

'Fascinating!' I whisper

'Aye, indeed!' he retorts, before, would you believe it, taking me by the same elbow the others have used (I am beginning to feel as if it's being adopted) and drawing me off to one side.

'Are ye all set for this big holiday?' he asks me.

'Well, I am!' I reply and oddly enough I have been feeling excited about the break. This will be the first time we have all been away together (by all, I mean the three of us and the three of them) and while apprehensive I must admit I'm looking forward to it. Robert grimaces and mutters, 'I have a funny feeling about it. Too many of us, all on one small boat for, what is it... three days? We could have ructions galore!'

'It will be alright. It will be fine. And if there are fireworks, as you seem to fear, they will probably be your fault! Just take things easy and don't get involved in heated arguments.'

'I don't have plans to do any such thing – but if others start…' He paused for a moment before going on, all the time looking away. 'I have to admit, I have been feeling a bit on edge recently.

Just then, I noticed James had moved closer and was listening to this with an expression of thunder on his face (there I go again, mixing my metaphors! There is one of those unexpected lulls that happens in every conversation and we all move about, but within a very small space, brushing against one another, aimlessly, all the while nibbling at nuts and crisps and sipping our drinks. I see Paddy move towards the pond; I see him standing there, looking at the water, then stooping to pick up a handful of gravel. He begins to throw individual pieces of gravel into the pond. I see he is trying to hit a brown leaf that is floating there. It must be the one I saw earlier. All alone. 'All leaf alone.' Idly, I wonder where that old saying comes from.

'Are you trying to sink that ship?' Ursula calls out. I turn and see that the entire group has stopped and is watching. He does not hear her or appears not to: he keeps on tossing little stones at the leaf. Each one misses but with each plop as it falls into the water the leaf moves further and further away, spinning as it does so. We all watch this, fascinated in a strange way, oddly mesmerised by such a simple activity. Is it the challenge of hitting the leaf that fascinates us, or is it the potential destruction of something essentially inert and thus innocent?

Then there is a great big splash: a large stone has landed on the leaf, causing it to disappear under the water. I now turn to see Robert rubbing his hands together as he stands there, looking on.

'It was a boat, not a ship,' he says. And then Ursula shouts: 'Whatever it was, it's not sunk yet. Look!' Sure enough, the leaf had bobbed back to the surface.

'Ship, boat, Noah's Ark... whatever it is, it is unsinkable!' James broke the tension with an accompanying smile and they all clapped and then Liz called out, 'Come inside and have a bit of supper.' And we all obediently trooped after her.

I have not said much about Liz. And that is unfair of me. Liz is a very serious person. By that, I mean she has a serious demeanour. I think it has something to do with the way she wears her hair, but perhaps she wears her hair as she does because, inside, she is serious. Since I have known her Liz has worn her hair pulled tightly back and drawn into a ponytail. I have never seen her wear it any other way. It is always pristine. The look always strikes me as extremely severe: the hair pulled tight, strained tautly against its roots.

A bit prim, really. But she is not prim person, not at all prissy or proper or aloof. The very opposite, in fact.

Still, I often think, watching her, that she must have a hair fetish.

She habitually runs the flat of her hand over her hair when she is thinking, patting and running her palm back along as if searching for one hair that might be out of place, a miniscule furrow might be found there, marring that smooth plane. She does this with her right hand. Then she uses her left hand. Then she runs both hands along the smooth surface of her hair, feeling with her long thin fingers for any offending blemish. Finally, she adjusts the tie on her ponytail. Then she goes about whatever other business she might have – until the next time!

Her hair adorns her head like a close fitting helmet. When she is away from me, at a distance, and when the sunlight catches it, I have noticed that its auburn tone reflects the light and the whole, the hair and the reflected sunlight, takes on a deeply rich sheen. It has the glossy quality of butter, but is not buttery; it has the glowing colour of old mahogany, the sheen of young chestnuts just out of their casings. That and the close fit to her head, her head raised, chin up, makes her appear like an ancient warrior; that, and the trim figure and the belted jackets, of which she is very fond, make her seem like a boy warrior.

Only she is not a boy warrior, she is really from the 1950s I sometimes think, an escapee from *Breakfast at Tiffany's*.

I often think she is not a 'Liz' at all – you know how some people seem to fit perfectly into their names, people like Harry or George, people like Beth and Sadie. I think of Liz as really being a cool Carol: Liz is too flippant a name for an icon from another decade. Or, one from another world.

She is seriously pert, (which is not the same as prim) like an attentive young mother bird, then she laughs and everything about her changes. I have often heard of people who have what is called an infectious laugh (though seldom have I met one) and Liz truly has an infectious laugh. And she uses it to make Robert laugh when no one else can. At the beginning, when they first met, I felt jealous of how she could command and control him, with so little effort. Occasionally, I have noticed how peevish she can be, how

266

her mood can swing from being jolly to being the opposite; how she can be poised and pert one moment and unsteady and vulnerable the next; how she can appear tired and old and can I say this, ugly in an odd way, her face heavy, and then suddenly lively, young and beautiful.

Cool is the word. Although, sometimes, when she smiles or when she laughs, her eyes sparkle and her face lights up and her whole demeanour changes, totally. She is a very nice person, an attractive woman. I can see why Robert likes her, but increasingly I find myself wondering what she sees in Robert, he who is becoming more and more grouchy the older he gets.

I have noticed recently that Robert does not laugh as much as he used to. I noticed his dullness – no, not dull but a new, quite strange combination of maturity plus sombreness – has become quite marked.

Someone mentions supper and we all troop inside where Liz, for the first time in Robert's house, acts as hostess. She, with Robert's approval if not his enthusiastic help, has laid on an informal supper of bits and pieces from Marks and Spencer, together with more wine. She superintends our plates and sees to it that we form an orderly queue while, even though it is Robert's home, Paddy takes on the role of wine waiter (or sommelier, as he termed it), and helps everyone to more drinks. I know Liz has planned all this, though no one mentions her role; the food is simply laid out on the kitchen table, and we all help ourselves before going to sit at the big table in the living room.

I must admit, the food was very good: fresh salmon (a change for Robert, who normally cooks only steak), beautiful fresh vegetables and some lovely potatoes cooked with herbs. Full marks to Liz, I thought.

Shortly after we sat down, James used his glass to gently tap on the tabletop, before announcing the agenda for the evening. 'We are here, as you all know, to make any final changes to our plans for the long-awaited weekend away.' The boat had been booked and was, even now, awaiting our arrival on Good Friday. He, glancing at the other two men as if expecting a challenge, would act as 'informal Captain', being the only one to have had previous experience of sailing. Slight pause. Silence. 'Essentially, we were going to enjoy ourselves by having a break and relaxing' and James was very willing to take the lead, if this was what others present wanted. I happened to glance at Paddy during this and was a bit taken aback by the glint in his eye. A vicious, mean look, but then it disappeared, and he smiled and nodded in agreement with James and I was unsure of what I had seen. I remembered it later, though. We all agreed then with all of James's proposals, including the one where we would form three teams of two to a team and each team would cook and wash up breakfast and dinner on an agreed day. At this point he paused, opened a file that had appeared and handed out a sheet with detailed instructions, lists and details.

'Very good, James. Well done, James,' we all chorused. James beamed. The big baby, I thought, reaching out to touch his arm in a spontaneous gesture of support and thanks.

It's strange how potent a new influence can be. Take James, for example. Paddy has certainly jazzed him up a bit, has helped change his attitudes, made him a bit more adventurous in what he eats and wears and – this is the amazing part – a bit more democratic in his attitude to women. One of the things we established was what James and Paddy called 'an informal cooking and washing up rota'. We all agreed to work in pairs: Paddy and Ursula, James and me and Robert and Liz supplying and cooking one evening meal each – and doing the washing up, afterwards. The theory behind this was that on all other occasions we would be totally free of all domestic responsibilities. Paddy and Ursula were to have the Sunday evening, Robert and Liz the Friday evening and James and me Saturday. Breakfasts and lunches were to be simple, ad hoc affairs, left to individuals to cook, eat and wash up as the mood touched them. Later on, when Liz called me with the suggestion, we both go to St Georges Market early on Friday morning, I was a bit surprised but readily agreed since I had not made any great plans to shop. To be truthful, I had not given it much thought.

Liz had it all worked out, but only in theory; I think she wanted my support because Robert had refused to engage in shopping and I think she lacked the confidence to undertake the purchases on her own, unlike Ursula and Paddy, who, she said, were doing their own thing. What that was she did not know; Ursula had been very secretive about it.

I arrived at the market early; it is more or less across the road from where I live, though I do not often go there, being at work when it's open. The place was very busy, full of people, normal, ordinary people.

Men and women, but mostly women. Old and young, but mostly middle-aged or older. Tall and short. White and yellow, light and darker than light; housewives and businessmen out on the ramble, between appointments. Cooks and chefs out buying food and materials for their kitchens. Housewives buying provisions; lovers buying delights for Friday evening cook-ins with candles and wine and blazing coal fires. I waited by the entrance for a bit, before venturing inside. The first stall I saw was selling fish.

Fish from Portavogie and Kilkeel – monkfish and plaice and north Atlantic cod; hake and silver hake and prawns and live lobsters, lazily waving to passers-by, shrimp and trout and thick slabs of tuna the colour of boiled rhubarb, scampi and sea bass and winkles and oysters.

There were three huge salmon lying on the counter, facing me. To my shocked eye they were grotesque and beautiful. Beautiful, simply because they were, to me, simply magnificent. Grotesque because to see animals of such beauty dead was shocking.

So whole.

So intact.

Such perfection.

I stood there, gazing, people easing past me, the noise of the market receding into the background. So big, and so blackly dark with dulled silver and mottled creamy white patches. I just looked, taking it all in. Recording it.

Lifeless.

Motionless.

Spotted.

Spots – like snowflakes seen against the dark of the night sky.

Eyes – smaller than I might have expected.

Skin – luxuriant and smooth as Venetian glass.

270

Bodies —so sleek, so powerful. So motionless.

Even so, so together.

People were pressing forward, shouldering me out of their way. I stepped off to one side of the narrow walkway and waited until the crush lessened. I moved forward again; voyeuristically, agnostically eyeing the three big fish as one of the fishmongers lifted a hosepipe and sprayed the stall with water as I stepped back, even though I wasn't in danger of getting wet.

The water fell, sparkling like shards of glass.

Everything glistened.

I found myself eyeing the markings on the salmon's lower bodies; they reminded me of something, they or perhaps it was the water, but I could not immediately capture what it might be.

Then Liz was at my side, in triumph holding aloft a large white plastic bag for me to see; it was bulging softly; strangely, *sagging-ly*, heavy and full.

'You look very pleased with yourself,' I said. 'You look as if you had caught that yourself – I take it you've got fish in that bag.'

'Yes, it is fish. I got here early, so just started without you. Do you mind? And, well, I feel as if I have a good catch, a good bargain. Lovely fresh plaice. I was going to get oven chips but I don't know what kind of cooker we will have or even if this boat has such a thing, so I'll just get some potatoes and boil or bake those. That and some asparagus should do the trick. Have you got anything, yet?'

'No,' I admitted, 'I'm so fascinated by the variety of produce on sale. I'm just gawking, I'm afraid.'

'Well, gawk away,' she laughed, half opening another bag. 'Look, I got some prawns, as a starter and I want to get a few avocados to go with them. Do you want to come while I look for them?'

'Sure. I'd love to,' I replied, adding, 'and I can think about what I'll do while I am about it.'

We crossed the floor, blindly, not really knowing where the avocados were to be found. The floor of the building was covered in rows of stalls and trestle tables that stood underneath the criss-crossed metal rods that held up the ceiling and that in turn were held up by old cast iron columns. We made our way around the inner edge of the building since that seemed to be less crowded. Underneath those tables immediately in front of us were stacks of cardboard boxes, old, crumpled newspapers spilling out onto the concrete floor.

The tabletops were crowded with cups and spoons, boots and shoes, balls of cord and string, aprons and dresses and second-hand toys. There were old cameras and records stacked up beside CDs and music cassettes, hammers and wrenches and ancient and brand new saws, old stools and ancient mahogany and pine plate racks, boxes of boot- and shoe-laces, linen tablecloths and old green-glassed bottles that once held remedies for numerous illnesses.

Even the food seemed endless.

Soda bread and rock buns and carrot cake and chocolate cake and cherry cake and corn bread and brown bread and wheaten bread and white, crusty bread. Potato bread and apple and cinnamon cakes and roast vegetable quiches and steak and onion pies and rhubarb tarts.

Home cured bacon and peppered chicken from Co. Antrim; organic, farm-fresh, jumbo eggs from Co. Down; pears and apples from Co. Armagh; roasting chickens and boiling fowl and fresh strawberries from somewhere.

A couple of huge metal bowls of paella were cooking away before my eyes: Spanish rice, swimming in golden, oily liquid, rich with the browns and greens and reds and yellows of sliced vegetables. The smells were adorable; scrumptious, Liz said.

Next door there were hard and soft cheeses, creamy cheddar, Cultagh goat's cheese and Gubbeen cheese. I couldn't resist this, having read the card beside it that described it as being 'overlaid with scented mushroom flavours and the flowery tones of grass and savoury herbs'.

So I bought a big lump of that. And then we were off again!

Sweet potatoes and big, white roasting spuds and fresh Comber potatoes, coated still in their Co. Down soil. Then suddenly there they were: the avocados, great-heaped piles of them. Avocados and mushrooms and plums and bananas and cabbage, green and leafy, together with carrots and turnips and parsnips. And next door to them, glossy sirloin and fillet steaks, Aberdeen Angus roasts and ribs and sausages and black puddings and white puddings and chump steak and frying steak and stewing steak. Big butchers with bloody aprons, knives and eyes flashing, bantering with their customers, all the while working at top speed.

While Liz bought her avocados and lemons, I fought my way into the butcher's level of vision. I left here with six big sirloin steaks, a paper bag of mushrooms and a few onions. I resisted the Comber potatoes, appetising as they were since I did not fancy carrying a bag of spuds all the way back to the apartment and from there to the car when James arrived. I can always buy potatoes on the way through Enniskillen I said.

The air was thick with noise. Everywhere, the calls rang out:

'Buy one, get one free!'

'Get your bananas here. Get your bananas here. A big bunch of bananas for a pound!'

'That' holding the banana aloft, 'was on the tree this morning, you can still taste the dew on it!'

'Give me fifty pence and it's yours, I can do no better than that!' Everywhere, the air is thick with the buzz of conversations.

'Jimmy brings me here in the car and I get the bus home.'

'Very good. That's very handy.'

Purposive, intent on sourcing a bargain but with good humour and ordinary, normal kindness and warmth; people with focus, yet, prepared on the whole, to stand aside and allow another first choice in a place of plenty. Young and old, but mostly old. Silver hair and no hair. White and black, but mostly white with a good sprinkling of Chinese people. The odd businessman, suited, sneaking a few minutes of his boss's time, just popped in, looking for something fresh to take home to the wife. Workers and retired people, but mostly retired. Blackmailers and hairdressers, men and women in drag, transvestites and lesbians and gay men, abusers and housewives and cooks and chefs, prostitutes and ministers of religion in mufti, fathers and mothers and grandparents, out-of-work gunmen and retired chiefs of staff of illegal organisations. They are all here. Irish and British and Ulster people and immigrants, mid- and west-Europeans, others, of many hues. Planter and Gael, Catholic, Protestant and Dissenter and backsliders and unbelievers and believers in many Gods. They make this a real melting pot of diversity and pluralism and difference – but they have this in common: they are ordinary people; they are not those with expensive haircuts and Armani suits.

I wished Robert could have been there to see it, as I saw it, just to share it. He sits out there, elbow deep in clay, and doesn't know how much this place has changed over the past few years. This, surely, is what he dreams of.

I ended up leaving with six steaks (and three pounds of Comber potatoes – I couldn't resist them, after all), half a dozen onions and half a pound of fresh mushrooms. I planned to pick up a couple of tins of peas I had at home, to complete what would be my contribution to the culinary delights of the forthcoming weekend.

Liz suggested she should buy me a cup of coffee at the little coffee stall, and I agreed, readily. We got the coffee, in plastic cups, and sat down at a vacant table. We were companionably silent for a bit, just looking at the crowds of people passing, back and forth.

An obvious thought had struck me. Why were *we* here, why not Robert and James? When I reported this thought to Liz she just smiled and shook her head and shrugged. But I pursued it: once I get on the trail I never give up, even I if I do say so myself! Even when I know the answer, I sometimes feel compelled to ask the question, anyway.

'They should be here,' I said. 'Look at this place: it's heaving with new people – well, not heaving perhaps, but it's different – why have our Ulstermen not caught up with the twenty-first century?'

Liz ran a hand over her hair, pulling at her ponytail. 'Because we are the victims of their self-delusion. But it's our fault: we let them off the hook too easily. We pander to their whims.' We parted soon after that, but I thought about what she had said on the way home.

***

It is a Friday evening at the beginning of spring, and Rebecca is on a bus on her way back to her home. She has been to the supermarket; such has become her weekend habit, and two plastic bags lie at her feet, bursting with goods.

Outside it is winter-black, though winter is long past, and squalls of rain are falling, rattling off the windows and making the falling night even darker.

She is lost in a magazine she has just bought, head down. The bus suddenly grinds to a halt, forcing her to tumble forwards colliding heavily against the iron bar on the seat in front.

The bus doors slide open and a group of men crush and crowd inside. They are masked. One has a hammer held aloft, another has a gun. Of it all, Rebecca sees only the gun. Years, time, Belfast and her life, Ruth's life – everything amalgamates in her mind in that split second.

It is as if a black cloud has reappeared from her past and descended about her head, smothering her. She cannot breathe.

Or perhaps it is to be likened to a windscreen wiper crossing and recrossing her mind. She thinks of this later, rerunning the scene in her head as she explains to Robert what had happened. She watches as one of the masked men peers into the body of the bus, head lowered, scanning the faces of the few passengers. He shakes his head and without a word the men turn as one and jump off the bus. The driver sits for a moment, his head in his hands then apparently recovered from the shock, he shrugs, shuts the door, engages gear and the bus moves off.

Rebecca remains in her seat until her stop is reached. She forces herself to her feet and climbs down from the bus. Her plastic bags remain on the floor by her seat, forgotten.

Later she tells Robert, attempting to explain the significance of the event. How she felt at that moment, how she feels now, how she will always feel. He considers her, for a long moment. Then, resignedly, he speaks. It's simple, he says; accept it, he repeats, as we all accept it. Accept it and ignore it: it's of no importance to you. Do not make more than it is. He pauses, then quotes something,

Homer's ghost came whispering to my mind
He said: I made the Iliad from such
A local row. Gods make their own importance.

Patrick Kavanagh, you know, he continues. He was a man who knew a local row when he saw it. Take my advice, try to forget the bus and the men on it. Forget rows, local or otherwise. Don't allow what happened to change you – you have come so far! Rebecca looks at into his eyes. She thinks, he is out of sympathy with me. Even as she thinks this and even as she understands why after all this time he has grown weary of her, another part of her is swamped by a great wave of grief. It arrives and departs and then it is gone.

For a moment a collage of images crowds her mind: Ruth's death; the man on the bus with the gun; Robert who moved away after so long by her side and who has just now moved again, even further. A dying passion; a catalogue of losses; her life.

Besides, she does not agree with what he has just said. She does not believe in gods. She does not believe in devils. She believes in truth, she tells herself. She doubts he really believes what he has just said. She smiles at him, then reaches out and touches his shoulder. The west, she says by way of reply, I think I need the west. The clarity, she explains, reading the question on his face, I want the clarity of air and sky and water. You are right, no more clouds…

Enniskillen

We are off! into the West! I feel so excited, like a child
again... and, oh! That night in Belfast, when those men
stopped the bus... the memory of it has almost gone.
Perhaps Robert was right. Look how the sky gets clearer and
brighter the further James drives.

The sky seems to lift. It expands; it feels like we are
entering a new realm.

Next morning – Good Friday – James and I drove down
independently to Fermanagh. We choose to do this because
we are independent, or so James asserted. We couldn't pick
up the boat until mid-afternoon, but I wanted to arrive a bit
earlier than the others did since I wanted to have a quiet stroll
around Enniskillen. I have always liked the town: I find there
is something inviting and interesting about the layout of the
streets, the river and the bridge, the Clinton Centre standing
in its modern and austere contradistinction to the mixture of
shabby gentility and rural, 19th century low-life that to me is
epitomised by the variety of buildings. I like the way each of
the shops still seems to have a name that is real and local and
not just the result of some ad-man's universal and abstract
imagination, the result of fleeting inspiration and not decades
of plain hard work. It remains a rooted community and I like
that.

Robert often says that Blakes of the Hollow is his favourite pub in the world, even though he has only been in it a couple of times. And he always goes on and on about Beckett and Oscar Wilde being educated locally.

'It was a beautiful day: just like a summer day,' James said. We parked the car in the first car park we came to and walked down the hill and through the town. The streets were busy and everyone seemed to be infected by good humour and happiness, and we caught the mood instantly. James kept stopping to look at the houses for sale in estate agents windows. At each one he exclaimed, 'Property is so cheap here!'

After lunch we went to the local bookshop and pottered around the castle and along the water's edge, before getting into the car and wending our merry way from the town and out through the Fermanagh countryside. I enjoyed it; it seemed so natural, so relaxed, so without strain or stress, and James was in great form. He kept on talking about the price of property down here, about how it's so much less than Belfast, how he might buy something close to one of the lakes, close to the water. Just for the odd weekend, he said, and I could feel his eyes on me, watching, waiting for a response. But I refused to be drawn and just nodded and said, 'Ah' and 'Um' and 'sounds like a good investment,' and so on. Eventually he gave up and I had a little peace to look at the trees and hedges and fields. I even spotted a few lambs on a hillside.

It is a ten or twelve mile journey to Tully Bay where the marina is situated, and we arrived in good time.

Indeed, we did arrive in good time for we were the first, and so we got our stuff on board. We had a scout around on our own and I selected a room, a cabin is what those who know about these things call it, and got settled in before the others arrived. I should say here that there was no question of James and me sharing a cabin, though we knew Paddy and Ursula would do so. At that stage, I had no idea what Liz and Robert had planned, though in the end they did share.

Before we were allowed to set off we had a little bit of instruction from one of the boatmen on how to handle the vessel. The next thing we knew, we were on our own, on the 'high seas' as it were. The men took the boat out while we women got settled in. We had already decided that each couple would cook an evening meal and it fell to James and me to take the first stint. James came down to the galley at seven and we set to. By eight the boat was anchored and we were all sitting at the table. James had to go twice to call Robert and Liz, and when they did arrive they looked rather dishevelled. The steaks were beautiful and James's selection of wine was decreed excellent by all who partook. That is, by everyone, including James. By nine thirty we had finished our meal and were deep in conversation, another bottle of wine opened.

The conversation roamed widely and was good-humoured – at least to begin with.

'Let's look on the bright side,' Ursula kept repeating and every time she said this Liz would smile and nod and answer, 'Absolutely!' For some reason, I found this extremely irritating – this evening I found Liz especially irritating, for some reason – now, it seemed to me, looking at and listening to Ursula and Liz, that they had been mandated by some higher authority I did not know, or was not supposed to know or could not imagine, to be always positive and optimistic. I suppose they fitted in with the mood of the time – it was morally wrong to be doubtful, pessimistic or critical.

For years, I had believed that the barbarians were at the gates and I was instinctively cautious, I suppose.

For my part, I felt like asserting myself by pointing out that I was neither optimistic nor pessimistic, however, I decided to remain silent. I recalled the gist of Liz's theory about us women 'pandering' to men's whims. I also recalled a remark I had heard Robert make, earlier in the day. We had been sitting on the deck of the boat. The sun was just going down. For a few moments there was silence as we all looked out across the lake. It was so peaceful. Then, quite unexpectedly, Robert said, 'You know, it's strange but I didn't realise I have been actually and actively engaged in a form of resistance – of passive resistance – for all these years; quite simply, I was not aware of it. Now, I have nothing to resist and I am empty. I feel lost. And I have gained nothing. How did I lose all those years? Wasted time!' He looked across at me, for a moment, before continuing. 'I am like a judo player, I have been gently led off-balance by the manoeuvres of a superior tactician and I feel as though I am on the verge of falling over.'

I can still see him. He was just in front of me, sitting there unmoving, his face turned away, his eyes directed towards the shivering water. I glanced across at James and he looked directly at me and raised his eyebrows. It was such an impassioned little speech, but little as it was, it was also so forlorn. For a long time, nobody spoke.

I watched the water rippling under the fading light. The others began a bit of banter, a bit of chit-chat. I thought of all the years that lay behind us, the decades that lay behind me.

The water reminded me of something; it reminded me of the skin of a nervous young foal.

Nervous.

Fearful.

I too had been emptied; I had felt that a hand, a fist, had come inside me and had ripped everything out. But then, I had felt like that for years. Robert was different: now, here, he was desolate, like me

Emptied.

Crippled.

We sat there in the gloaming for a long time, all the excitement and expectation of the holiday suddenly gone. It is strange how a few words can change everything. From across the water a blackbird's sudden antisocial, raucous, nerve-jangling call burst out; it existed for a fleeting moment, and then it too was gone. And with it the bird, back to where it existed. Back to another world.

Eventually, I reached out and touched his arm. He ignored me.

'What were you resisting, Robert?' I spoke softly, in case the others should hear. He just shook his head, but did not reply.

Even Paddy appeared suppressed but now he sprang to his feet, suggesting everyone have another drink. With his bulk moving between us the mood seemed to change abruptly, and as a result Liz and Ursula began talking to James as soon as their glasses were refilled and Paddy had eased himself out of their way. I was the only one who did not have anything – I find I am naturally or instinctively abstemious – when I'm with people, but Robert held his glass out, automatically. And that, I think, set the tone for the remainder of the holiday.

'There you are old fella. Get that down you! It'll do you good!' Paddy said, topping up the glass and then turning towards James and raising the bottle as if in a question, but James shook his head and Paddy went back and sat down in his seat.

At this point Ursula suggested we all take our glasses outside, 'to toast the night', as she put it, so we all trouped out behind her. We sat where two benches met, so the others could continue with their conversation.

Under cover of this movement, disruptive in such a confined space, Robert, still refusing to be diverted from his topic, turned to me, saying, 'Why did you ask that question? Don't you know what I was resisting?'

'No, not really,' I replied, feeling cold and hard as I spoke the words, then realising that what I really felt was vulnerability. But I also felt remote from him as his question issued out and hung there in the void that lay between us.

Now, looking back, I think those words marked the unremarked ending of an era. The coming down of a curtain. Their utterance was an act of vandalism. The unthinking snuffing of a candle. The crushing of a fly. The denial of friendship. A slap in the face.

Trust.

Faithfulness.

Loyalty.

What did these things mean? Suddenly I felt tired. I couldn't take any more self-pity. I thought, I have not the energy to fight against this constant questioning. Then his voice came into focus, once more penetrating my thoughts. 'What I was resisting was murder, thievery, stealing, lying – for political ends. Murder, thievery, lying – for personal gain. What I was resisting was the opposite of truth.'

'I say, old fella...' Paddy's voice carried through the air.

It was as if a ballet, or an opera, was being performed, with me on stage, at its centre, but not really part of the cast. Life is made up of so many bits and pieces, parts and layers: so many fictions and so many realities.

'I say, old fella, that's a bit strong!' Then he turned, unusually appealing to James. 'Wasn't that a bit strong, James?'

'We have had these discussions, many, many times,' James replied, answering him but staring at Robert. 'We can have them again, if you wish, but I see little that might be gained from repeating the same argument endlessly.'

Ursula tossed her head, looked detached, and then took a swig from her glass. Liz got to her feet, so gracefully, and left, without speaking. Her head was held high, her face pinched, crimson tinges at her ear lobes.

Yes, it was as if a ballet, or an opera, was being conducted, all around me. The cast was performing its set roles. However, this performance means nothing to me, nothing at all. I could not allow it to do so, I realise that, immediately.

When I get home, I wondered, to whom will I relate this performance? Once, Ruth would have been my listener, my sounding board, my other half, but not now. Now, there is only a vast emptiness.

Emptiness.

Coldness.

Hardness.

Febrile?

Brittle!

That's the word I want.

For Robert.

He cannot bend; he will break in two. He must stay as he is.

'Gain!' How scornful that word sounded on Robert's lips. 'What I'm talking about is moral resistance! But none of you would know little about that. Gain!'

Before James could reply, Ursula stood up. 'I'm off to the loo, boys. I don't know what the agenda is here, but I feel there's more to this conversation than meets the eye, or my eye at least. I suggest you all ease back a little.' Then she smiled. 'Coyly' is how I would have described that smile. 'For my sake?' As she passed him, Paddy slapped at her behind as she gave a little skip, so his big hand missed her and he almost overbalanced, almost toppled off his seat, laughing.

Laughing, now slapping his thigh. Out of this ruckus James spoke, as though for the first time.

'I have some sympathy for Robert's point. I hadn't thought of it in these, possibly extreme, terms before but there is the possibility that the parties will have some difficulty at some point in agreeing on common values, on finding common ground, with the best will in the world, on some issues. Christian Fundamentalism and a form of, ah, possibly, a form of Marxism wouldn't appear to have much truck when it comes to – well, when it comes to agreeing to agree on a set of, ah, agreed, relative values… What I mean is, they would not appear to believe in relative values, but in absolute values and in different absolute values, even if some of those coincide; so… and if they did agree to compromise…' At this point his voice melted away into silence.

The boat rocks. Another boat lumbers past, leaving in its wake a surge of water.

I feel dizzy.

The two girls return together, now laughing and giggling over some private joke perhaps.

'It's getting chilly. Should we all go inside?

They disappeared, leaving the four of us sitting there. Paddy remained silent and carried on drinking. Eventually Robert spoke, unerringly going to the thing that was on my mind, the thing that was always on my mind: without looking at me, his words came, almost too quietly spoken to be heard clearly, yet spoken with a firmness of tone that suggested he was saying by rote sentences long learned by heart.

'The thing is, Ruth (to take an example) died for nothing: no cause needed her death, nor did any cause gain anything from her death. The cause itself did not succeed in any stated aim, it succeeded only in gaining another victory for inhumanity and in providing another victim for itself, another thing for it, the Beast, to consume, for the man Bond, the bomber, was also a victim of this madness. Even if her death had been, in some strange, unknowable way, instrumentally beneficial, it would not matter, for any change her leaving this life might have brought about is so infinitesimally minute I doubt it could be measured on any scale known to common humanity.'

He paused for a bit, looking past me, towards the horizon. He lifted his glass to his lips and then thought better of it and put the glass down, before going on. I was glad, for I thought I had detected a slurring of his words. Later, I thought how strange it was that I should notice such a small thing in the middle of such a speech and in a speech that touched on something of such value to me. But while one part of my brain was thinking this, another was attending to Robert, while yet another part was remembering that day, that scene, remembering how, as I turned to glance back, looking for Ruth, how this horror opened out before my eyes: it was as if I was looking at a scene from hell, a make-believe battlefield abruptly established in front of me, painted in tones of grey. What appeared before me was devoid of colour; the darkening whites and the near blacks stood out, clouds of dust lay thickly, slowly swirling in the air, as if tossed there in giant-sized handfuls, carelessly. My eyes found Ruth. Robert's voice disrupted my flow of memory.

'Those who supported the legitimate rule of lawyers and politicians, those who acknowledged the right of men of money and men of conviction to speak for them, right or wrong; the men who consistently said no, the men who were always right, what was Ruth's death to them, to those infallible ones? Would the cost of her death be measured on their scales? If it were so done, would their word, their accounting, carry any more weight?'

The floor sways beneath her feet. Someone – is it Robert? – his mouth is somehow inconsequentially opening and closing – and he is looking at her, is speaking to her, but she does not understand what he is saying.

She feels suddenly lightheaded. She experiences recurring flashes: images that come and go, that swirl, that form crazy collages that become silent kaleidoscopes of that street where the bomb exploded, the terrible silence, and the body of her sister rising, swimming in air; the men on the bus, the gun, the silence, Robert, and is that James, beside him? They are harlequin figures receding, moving away, beyond her reach. She sees a world with only emptiness, only colours out of focus, like mist, a place of silence. She is alone under this thick blanket of mist.

And then it ends, and she is surrounded by people and voices and the clink of glass on glass, and the sky is clear and the light is reflected as if through shards of glass as it skitters off the little waves.

And she is recovered and suddenly happy.

What could I say? What could any of us say. We sat there for a while as the day faded, me listening to the water striking against the boat's hull and to the beating of my own heart, then I went to an early bed. Lying there, I pulled back the curtains and looked out into darkness. Holidays! Away in the distance I could see a light flash on, and then disappear. Repeatedly, it came into being, and then died away. Its routine was monotonous, yet reassuringly so. A warning light, not a lighthouse though, perhaps a buoy of some sort. As I watched it, I felt gradually hypnotised and something stirred in my mind, but lazily so, and eventually the memory of my epiphany on Slieve League rose up before me. I opened my arms and ran towards it but it drifted away, drifted away. It was then, I think, that I must have dozed over.

I woke up the next morning, instantly feeling as if I was in some kind of enclosed box. I was in total darkness; it was very black, and I was shrouded tightly in somewhat constricting material. 'My God, am I dead? I must be dead! I am in my coffin! I'm in a shroud!' The next thought to flash through my mind that this must be a nightmare. I tried to call out, aloud. Simultaneously, all of Robert's words about Ruth came flooding back, filling my head. I heard my own voice and immediately realised I could both speak and hear. Irrationally, I believed I cannot be dead, then I remember this was a holiday. I was on a boat, on a lake, I remembered putting my coat over the window – then, irrationally, I found myself saying 'Sorry, James!' Why, when in this frantic state, did I take time to apologise to James! – last night before going to sleep. I could now see a faint glimmer of light and reached out to drag the coat away. However, my arms were still pinned to my sides, but with a few twists and turns I had the sleeping bag loosened from where it had bundled around me in the night and finally, I got one arm out. The coat came off the window – sorry, again, James, porthole! – and then I got the thin curtain pushed to one side. I wrestled my other arm free, and then released the rest of me before crawling the few inches on my knees to peer out. Quickly, I rubbed some moisture off the glass. Through the remnants of grey dampness on the windowpane, I could see outside to where the grey bath water of the lake spread out and away into the greyness of the near distance. Unfortunately, there it met an equally grey sky. The grey water shivered, suddenly: there must be a slight breeze blowing up. I stayed there for a bit, taking in all this Irish early-morning-ness. Taking it all on board. 'On board!' I could so easily have felt depressed. But I refused.

Yes, I could so easily feel depressed, I thought, but I grew into a wakefulness that, more and more, I determined not to. I am on holiday after all, I thought. However, I felt distinctly cold and shivery and so, even though it was very early, and I was sure no one else was up, I decided to go and make a hot drink. I put on the coat that has hung across the window during the night. It felt distinctly cold and pretty damp. I remembered some thick socks I had packed away in my rucksack. I found the rucksack, found the socks, put them on with my pyjama legs tucked securely inside, and thus encased in heat-retaining coverings headed towards the deck, the water-laden air and the dreaded grey day.

A narrow corridor led to the facility most people would call a kitchen, but I remembered James referring to as 'the galley'. I put water in the kettle and turned on the gas ring. There was no one about, so I buttoned up my coat and headed out onto the deck to look around. Yes, I said to myself, I can indeed confirm that the world out here is grey. The trees are limp; they too have surrendered to the wetness and to the greyness. The outside drove me in, and I returned to the kitchen where I had already spotted a radio. Waiting for the kettle to boil, I fiddled with the knobs until it sprang into life. A man was talking about the significance of the day – it's Easter Sunday, he says – so I listen and remember and nod, and then, when the kettle starts to bounce on the gas ring, I find a mug and make a cup of coffee.

A few minutes later I am sitting behind the shelter of Perspex in the top front cabin, a rug around my knees, nursing my hot mug and looking out to where the greyness is lifting. I begin to see how the water spreads out beneath me and away into the distance. I can see a flock of birds lifting off the water, silently and swiftly skimming the surface, before abruptly disappearing into the haze. Then, silence that is not silence. As I sit and listen I begin to discern the different noises: the sound of birds, a dog barking away in the distance, the low mooing of cows in some nearby field, the low, indistinct sound of water and, somewhere close by, the sound of leaves moving in the slightest of breezes.

I sit, enjoying the peace but intrigued by the sounds of life as the world shook itself awake, listening in peace while recalling what the man had said on the radio: how, early on the first day of the week, while it was still dark, Mary Magdalene came to the tomb, how she had seen that the stone was removed. And then the great kafuffle with Simon, Peter and the disciple Jesus loved, all running to and fro, searching for the body, and Mary crying and then her confronting the two angels who were sitting there, quite naturally, one at the head and one at the foot, and the grave-clothes lying, empty on the ground between them and then them conferring with Mary, and finally Christ startling her by speaking to her from behind her back. 'Do not hold onto me because I have not yet ascended ...' Just then, and out of my brown study, I sense a movement behind me. Ruth! I think. I turn quickly, but of course it is not Ruth, it is only Robert. Only Robert!

'You startled me!' I accused him, still feeling a little shocked.

'Sorry.'

He sat down beside me. He too had a mug of coffee, or possibly tea, and was fully dressed. Last night's whiskey did not seem to have harmed him in any way. He sat close to me on the small bench seat and I felt so much comfort from his presence that a surge of warm feeling welled up inside me. I leaned over and rested against him.

'It's been a long time.' I don't know why I said that, and he replied, 'Yes, it has. It's been a long, long time.'

Unusually for me, I inched closer to him and now rested my head on his shoulder, and we just sat there, like brother and sister, staring at the lake. What I meant, I thought, is it's been such a long time since I first met you; we have known each other for such a long time. It's been so long, my whole life, practically, and I feel you are a part of me. How is it, I wondered, how is it he seems always to know how I feel, or what I mean, even when I put it badly, or only half say it? Or, when I don't myself know what I mean. And then, I wondered, how can I tell? Perhaps it's all an illusion; perhaps it's just a trick, like a trick of the light at dusk when you think you see something that isn't there. Perhaps he thinks I meant something totally different from what I really did mean, or he hasn't a clue and is just playing a game by pretending.

'What do you think I meant just now?' I asked.

'About it being a long time?'

'Yes.'

'Oh, I don't know.' He looks straight into my eyes. 'It's a long time since we left Belfast.' Then, seeing the dismay on my face he laughs. 'I think you meant, 'It's been a long time since we played at little houses by the river'. And of course, so it is, well over forty years!' And that is exactly what I meant.

Do I find that comforting or do I find it depressing? 'Well over forty years!' Our lives, I think miserably, are mostly in the past; for us, the future diminished while the past rises up, waiting to overwhelm us.

'I am not sure I want to think about that – it's too much,' I say, eventually. 'There should be an awful lot of living in forty years and I don't feel I've lived at all.'

'You mean, you've led a good, clean, innocent life?'

'Oh, yes! No sin, at all! No fun!' I replied.

'Except all those male patients you flirted with!'

'A bit of flirtation is part of the treatment, there's no harm or sin in that.'

'No, of course not. You know,' his head leans against mine, conspiratorially, 'I read somewhere recently, the average person – someone actually sat down and worked this out – the average person sins about two billion, five hundred million times during his lifetime.'

'Amazing! His lifetime... I suppose 'she' comes into it? I don't suppose *women* sin as much, or at all?'

'No. No. That's each *person*, of course. Imagine, on this boat we have six people, that's an accumulated sin count of, say...' he screws up his eyes, while continuing, 'fifteen billion sins!'

'Goodness!' I say, 'It's a wonder the ship is still afloat!' Robert laughed at that. He likes to play these statistical games, and who am I to spoil his fun? So, I play along.

'It's strange you should say that,' he replied. 'Do you know about air? I mean, do you know how much it weighs?'

'No, Robert, I'm afraid I don't.' I said, setting my empty, cold coffee mug on the floor.

'Well, each person has about two and half tons of air, weighing down on his – or her – head.'

'Is it any wonder I always feel exhausted.' It's Ursula voice. She has come into the cabin. She looks anything but exhausted, fully dressed, painted and no doubt perfumed. She is too far away for me to smell – anyway, the air is full of the smell of water and damp air.

At this point we all stood up. Robert said, good morning and she said good morning and she, and I, of course said good morning, said good morning again, and then the boat rocked a bit and James appeared from the landside, wearing a tracksuit and running shoes! Good morning we all said, you're up early and he replied, good morning and not at all, just out for my usual bit of a run in fact I'm a bit late this morning and then, just as he says the word 'late' Patrick moseys out, crushing his way through the narrow door, stretching his arms in the air, yawning, unshaven, wearing a pair of very black trousers and his horribly yellow and orange striped pyjama top. 'Well, you are all up very early, all very bright and frisky!' he said.

'We were just discussing sin and sinning,' Robert remarked, reverting easily to our previous topic of conversation, as if the intervening minutes had never happened. 'Just telling you, in case you 'keep fitters' should try to contaminate everyone else by your healthy lifestyles.'

'Some rise by sin, and some by virtue fall'. Shakespeare, you know.' Ursula smiled. 'You didn't think I could quote Shakespeare, did you, Robert?' Robert smiled and bowed, in that extravagant fashion he sometimes adopts.

After that, we all milled around in a confused state. Robert said he understands he is on the rota to make the breakfast, and Liz is to help him, but Liz is nowhere to be seen. Reluctantly, I said I would stand in for her. Robert and I gathered up the empty mugs and retreated to the galley. I had discovered the fridge the previous evening, camouflaged behind what looked like a simple wooden door, so I showed Robert its whereabouts and its contents. We both look in awe at the said contents; the fridge is absolutely stuffed with food. Paddy and Ursula's doing!

'There's enough food here to feed the five thousand: and there's only six of us and we are only here for a few days!' Robert exclaimed. We explored various cupboards and the story continued in the same vein – tons of food in boxes, tins, jars and plastic bags. We discovered one cupboard given over to the demon drink, loads of bottles of wine, an extra-large bottle of whiskey and two litre-bottles of Plymouth gin.

Less than an hour later and we were all sitting down to bacon, eggs and sausages, fadge (as Robert insists on calling potato bread), toast, coffee and a pot of tea.

'You're a great chef, Robert.' Liz said, looking at her heaped plate. She'd had Robert fetch her from her bed, and she still looked sleepy.

'Aye. He'll make some lucky man a great wife!' says Paddy, grinning and cutting at the same time. He pops a piece of beef sausage into his mouth. 'Delicious! I'm a man of the world, as you know, but sometimes you just can't beat

the homegrown stuff. These are made in Newry, you know!'
Robert looked at me and raised his eyebrows but did not say
anything. During this little interjection, James was deeply
engrossed in the contents of the plastic wallet of maps and
papers and charts.

***

I can see myself as I was on that morning as I remember this
now. We had finished the washing up, James had investigated
his maps and charts, and we were under way. The sun had
emerged and it was beautifully warm. James had taken the
helm, of course, and we were cruising gently across the lake. I
was sitting on a deckchair, a rug around my knees, reading my
novel. Oddly enough, a novel is a work of fiction that tells the
truth. On the face of it, that appears to be a contradiction. I
stop reading to consider what I have already read. I think this
book tells the truth, as Robert might say, but does so by
skellying at it, by viewing it from the corner of the author's
eye. That, I decide, is fine with me and I carry on reading.

But I soon grow weary of being awake. For a little, I
struggled with my book and with wakefulness, even though it
was only mid-morning. Still, I find I have become tired of
reading. I see my head, nodding: my head grows heavy. I am
half-awake; I am falling into a kind of dream. I listen to the
sounds of water, to the music of roosting birds on an island,
and to the lullaby of the wind in the trees, to the sounds of
water. A thought comes to me, seeping into my consciousness
like smoke crawling under a door: we can have too much truth.
I need more fruits of the imagination, more fancy, more
dreams. More fiction?

It is as if I am falling under a spell.

The lake now is quiet, the water's coolness surrounds me. My mind is still, it is... demure. I dream; I decide I am a child, I am a young woman, I am an eager young woman, I am something that exists in a far-off place.

The sky here in the west is high and light filled and bright. Today, there are no clouds. I feel contentment.

I conjure up pictures in my mind of apple blossoms, of a pond, of water, of a tree, of a tree reflected in water; my mind brings into being and then considers pink and white apple blossoms; I watch them falling, drifting, settling gently then floating on the water in my mind. They do not make an impression on the water or on the water's surface; they do not enter the water, at all. Everything is surface, or appearance. What might lie beneath, behind, beyond that soft, wet grave? What is real? Where is truth to be found?

Only the silence through which the blossoms fall is real.

I find the rug has slipped off my knees and is lying on the floor. I reach down and tug at one corner. I hoist it off the floor, tuck it in under my thigh and press my weight downwards, trapping the rug between my leg and the chair. My knees are securely covered. The word 'chaste' rises once more to the surface of my mind. It is a word I remember that is used in my novel. It is the last word I remember reading there.

In my half-awake state my mind considers this term – it presents itself for consideration; I do not invite it – what does it mean, to be chaste? How can one *be* chaste? Am I chaste? I have been chaste all my life. I have been nearly chaste all my life. I have been chaste nearly all my life. Which of these statements is true?

Chastity. How can that be real? I mean, what is it and how can it last? The water laps against the boat's hull. Emily Dickinson, I believe, was chaste, from what little I know of her. I fancy she was chaste, in body at least. Perhaps in mind, in heart, also.

I wonder, can a man be chaste? Really? Can he be chaste in the same way that a woman might be chaste? A woman like Emily Dickinson? And what of virtue? Are the two linked?

When a man lies with a woman, does he lie like apple blossom, on water, lightly, hardly making an impression on what is beneath?

Chastity is a feeling, a sense of the untouched self. Now I find that I protest to myself, in my dream-like state. I don't mean physically touched or untouched, I mean the real self, of its not being touched, at that time. I suppose it's a kind of poise, achieved, and maintained, it's like achieving and maintaining perfect balance.

Danger is the thing: the possibility of being toppled off, the possibility of not being toppled off. For what is time, after all? Surely, virtue and chastity exist through time, through all time, outside time, beyond time. But still, there is a beginning, middle and an end, to everything. Everything starts and finishes; everything has a something that exists in between, the meat in the sandwich, the jam filling in the sponge cake, the fig in the fig roll...

When a man lies with a woman, does he fall down upon her, like an apple off the tree, hard and firm and unchangeable, falling onto the pond's yielding surface, sinking in the opening water, sinking deep, without trace?

Is that how chastity is lost? Is it lost through the fact of the apple lying there, in the water, or is it lost though the grace of the blossom, settling imperceptibly, on the water's surface?

Am I talking of love?

Why do people equate chastity with youth and youth with innocence? Young girls are so hasty, so greedy, and so hungry for experience. Young girls are eager: eager for what might be beyond the moment, they are eager for life to begin... as Ruth was... as I was...

The rug slips, finally, to the floor. I let it lie there. I have no more energy to struggle with the gravity that continually pulls it away from me. My head is heavy, my mind is light. My head nods and I let it nod until it stops.

I am half asleep when through the silence voices emerge, low voices, men's voices. Robert and James and Paddy are active in the real world.

Through the mists of sleep I can hear their separate voices. I hear a match strike. I smell cigar smoke.

'The parties are very cordial now, at any rate.' Paddy's voice, smooth and relaxed.

'Yes, everything is very cordial now; but just wait!' Robert's voice, tense.

'But there is so much common ground, so much shared interest and mutual benefit: that must prevail.' James's voice, casual, disinterested perhaps.

'Of course, the infrastructure is in pretty bad shape, but it's getting better, and look at the opportunities that are now presenting themselves. The two governments are behind us on this. Regeneration, that's the name of the game; change is the name of the game; even though there will be battles, no doubt.' Paddy's voice

'You are right. Regeneration means change. We have an opportunity now to look outwards, to search for good – for excellent – role models…' This is James, but he is interrupted by Robert's ill-tempered voice.

'What do good roads matter, what does a decent health service matter, who cares about providing excellence in education – what do bureaucratic battles signify when those battles are about mundane things like these? How can such issues matter when you have the twin itches of geography and history permanently irritating us, egging us to go to war with ourselves? Robert's voice.

'As usual, you are too pessimistic, Robert.' James's voice.

'What do you mean? The twin itches?' Paddy's voice.

'I mean half the population with one eye turned to the east, the other half with one eye turned to the south, that's the geography of it. I mean each lot loathing everything the other stands for because what they stand for is rooted in another past, that's the history of it.'

'Do you not think we've moved beyond that?' Paddy says, and there is a smile in his voice. I can hear and see it, his question sound reassuring, confident. 'Don't you think times have moved on: the guns are beyond use, the two governments have committed substantial financial packages to help us get on our feet, and anyway, the people generally are tired of violence and conflict. They have had over thirty years of it!'

'Forty years, three hundred years, eight hundred years! Who is counting?' There is silence, and then he continues, answering his own question.

'Everyone. Everyone is counting! That's the problem. I would be very surprised if there was not, even as we speak, some group, or perhaps groups, of people sitting out there, under cover of darkness, beneath roof and behind wall and beyond wooden, painted doors, dreaming, considering, discussing; planning mayhem, murder, blood on the streets, wanting change.' Robert's voice.

I listen to these words, words that are enlivened by the men's beings. I am inclined to wonder a little, for I find they are wondrous, dangerous, words. For some reason I wonder again about virtue. Are the people who are going to work together and govern together – are they chaste? Are they virtuous? I mean, are they chaste and virtuous because of their talking to one another, or were they chaste and virtuous before, when they refused to talk to one another? Is it possible for them to be chaste and virtuous at all times? Can they retain virtue, having acted in direct opposition to what they had previously decreed to be right and proper conduct? Does virtue change, as the circumstances change, as the context changes? Had I been chaste, then not chaste, then chaste again, does this mean I am always now unchaste?

In my mind I put these questions to James, and in my mind I hear his voice replying, 'Compromise, Rebecca, compromise.' I want to reply in turn, 'How can virtue or chastity be issues of compromise – they are or they are not, surely?' In my mind, I hear Robert's voice say, 'I agree: if we compromise, will we be whole? If we compromise with those who have themselves compromised how will we know what truth is or where it is to be found? Will those to whom we have given power now lie on us, will they use their power to bear down on us? Will they make their morality our morality?'

'Perhaps we are all complicit…' delivered in a voice so low I could not discern who spoke.

Silence answers these silent questions.

Yes, I thought, rising from my half-dream state, these are big questions, worrying questions. I was now more or less fully awake and decided they were too big for me. I needed a cup of tea. Suddenly, I wanted to talk to Ursula and Liz; I felt the need of female company. I felt contaminated by maleness.

Without being noticed by the men, I slipped down to the galley were I found Ursula and Liz: they were sitting at the little table with a bottle of Alsace, two glasses of wine, a bag of crisps and a bowl of olives resting crowdedly on the narrow surface.

'Are you awake, then? We looked out a little while ago and you were fast asleep.'

'Yes. I think the men woke me. They are out there, talking politics!'

'Again?'

'Yes. Again!'

'Great big children,' said Liz.

'Big weans!' said Ursula.

303

'Of course, we are entering a period of considerable change. We can't just ignore it… we all need to be involved…' I said this weakly, feeling the need to defend the indefensible.

'Let's forget about it now; I'd much rather talk about sex and decadence and good old-fashioned bad behaviour!'

'Well, I can tell you, Paddy wasn't talking about politics or even thinking about politics last night… we had a really fantastically great shag!'

Immediately I went over to the work-surface and lit the gas and put the kettle on and began searching for a mug. I am always in two minds about this kind of conversation, and I was not sure which mind was in the ascendant at that moment.

Ursula, of course, noticed my discomfort and looked up at me intently, a queer smile on her face. 'Rebecca. Can I ask you a question? And tell me if I'm out of order.' I thought, she is a bit tipsy. Then she carried on, 'We were both wondering, just before you came in. It's this: I know it's cheeky but then I am a bold thing, or so my ma always says, do you and James sleep together?'

I don't say 'yes' and I don't say 'no' – instead, I say, 'Occasionally.'

The word hangs in the air, between us. And I blush! I can feel the blood rushing up to my face, as I stand there, feeling like a great fool. I mean, I've only known these two women for about ten minutes, or so it seems, and here they are, shining spotlights into the dark corners of my life.

'What does 'occasionally; mean? Does it mean once a week, once a month or once a year?' Then, impishly, 'Once a day?'

304

But by now I am back in control again and I smile and say, 'I never discuss James's private affairs with third parties.' But they are hardly listening. They don't really care. Liz interrupts, 'I must say, Robert is a bit slow at times. I mean, he hasn't laid a finger on me since we arrived here. I thought we were coming for a dirty weekend, but it seems I thought wrong!'

For some reason I was delighted to hear this and cheered up quite a lot. I cannot bear to think of my Robert, (my Robert! Where did the 'my' come from?) and this scrawny, middle-aged woman, all bronze-from-a-bottle skin and toned-flesh stretched tautly around jutting bones being, intimate.

Bitchy? Yes, I can be as bitchy as the next one.

Having said all this, she is rather attractive, I have to admit. Still, I don't want to share my own, inner thoughts just now, but I must say, even though I have never, ever done it, I do like the *idea* of sharing such intimate moments with other women. To me it seems like a combination of gossip and feeling like a schoolgirl again, discussing things one ought not to think about, never mind speak of in public.

I enjoy and savour my enjoyment at these thoughts. Like Ruth and me, at night, in bed, under the blankets, the lights out… whispering, holding hands, giggling…

'You are very quiet, Rebecca.'

'Sorry. I was just thinking of something, remembering something…'

'Well, anyway, look, to get to something serious: we are planning a shopping trip to New York – just Liz and me, no men – and we wondered if you would like to join us? We plan to make a real shopping blitz of it!' At that moment, and before I could answer, the door burst open and the three men came thumping down the short stairs.

'What are you three girls up to?' Robert asks.

'Just chatting.' Ursula replied. 'We were saying how lucky we've been with the weather. It's been like summer!'

'A different realm,' Rebecca replied. 'A different realm altogether.'

***

Later that day, Robert suggested that he and I go for a short trip on the rowing boat. After a bit he lifted the oars out of the water and laid them to rest across the boat's stern. We sat there, peacefully, listening to the sounds coming off the water and from the trees on shore, content to just take in the beauty of the evening and the warmth of the sun. We did not speak. It felt so companionable, just like it had in the past.

I looked at Robert. He was now laying back, his eyes closed and his face lifted to catch the heat of the low sun. His hands were at rest, folded across his stomach. He looked so much at peace. I examined the tilt of his face, the gesture that was inherent in its response to the sun's warmth; I look at his lips, at his chin; I look at where he has missed a bit shaving, a little dark spot of stubble, alive on his skin. I want to reach out, to touch it, to touch him, to be closer to him; suddenly, I want to bring comfort to him, to know him fully and to have him know me, suddenly, I want him to know me better than he does.

But I don't speak.

I cannot.

Instead, I lose myself in the walled garden of thought.

In the shelter of ideas, of dreams.

In the hidden glade of what-ifs...

Perhaps Robert faces the same constraints, the same containment by what was, and remains, around him, by what he learned to love and how he learned to love – by family, by what makes us, if these are the things that make us what we are.

This acceptance of things given, surely, is what I am, is what I do, is what I have done, always. It is what has shaped me, made me what I am, today.

It's strange, I think, we have never, as far as I can remember, spoken of this, not openly, directly, honestly, and yet it's been at the very core of our friendship. Or rather, of our acceptance of our friendship: the four of us, then the three of us. We did not choose one another, we just accepted each other as being there. Comfortable, like old jumpers, cosy when frost is on the windowpane.

How is it we have never moved past that, I ask myself. Others have: others have lived together, have married, have had children and have been happy and unhappy. Is it that we were too honest, too attached to romantic ideas of truth? Are we just not adult enough to live in an adult world...?

For once I forget about Ruth and myself. I think of Robert and of his conversations over the years; of all the things he is passionate about and I just tolerated: his attachment to his Scottish ancestry, the links he feels to the Enlightenment and to freedom of thought, his belief in the values of the United Irishmen and of their vision of Ireland, of what he calls true republicanism, his loyalty to his family and his respect for their rooted-ness in this place; I think of his own attachment to the cottage and to the forge, I remember his sense of responsibility to all these things. I keep glancing – 'skellying' is the word he would use! – at him, seeing him as though through freshly opened eyes.

But then, perhaps it is best that such influences be resisted. Perhaps they form too strong an impulse – that is built into each of us – to conform to the given.

Perhaps these things stand, in his case, for what Ruth stands for in my life.

But if they are not there, who do we become? The authors of our own beings. And there are so many veins, so many little interconnected roots, hairs, webs of inter-connectivity…

I oscillate, between one idea and another.

Yes, I oscillate. The boat rocks. I oscillate.

Sitting there in my small piece of wood on the lake, bobbing on the water's surface, surrounded by liquid life, I am well aware that so many important things exist only in the past, they are of the past. They *are* us, but as we were, yet we remain attached to them, and them to us; it is as if ropes of elastic connect us, pulling us back, eternally pulling us backward, while we eternally attempt to step into the future.

That is where the tension is to be found.

The future does not yet exist.

And we are not wholly the authors of what is to be: it may be we can never be. I may suffer from chronic writer's block.

Maybe, without constraints, we would go, spinning like men and women in space, away from base, out of control.

I have begun to go to church again, after all these years. I find it comforting, in a way, but what I find comforting is not the content of what happens there but the form. I don't think that is a good thing. I'd prefer, I think, to leave go, or to be let go, freed to go spinning out of control though space, free from commands and controls.

Eventually to be lost. But that would require courage.

Too much control.

Too much governance of our inner lives.

That is a difference between Robert and me, and this is it.

Robert has courage of a kind that is far beyond what I can muster. Even when it is wrong-headed.

Sitting there, on the little boat, at a distance from the big boat that in turn lies at a distance off the land, I could see clearly that this is where freedom lies: it lies in being free of all the things that bind us, all the anchors that bind us, all the things that claim custody of our imaginations, the things that chain our allegiances to others, right or wrong. It's achieving a kind of poise, a kind of balance.

Or, perhaps, freedom is living in harmony with the rules, accepting the facts of life and just getting on with it.

Yet, time is always ticking away.

Like throwing a pot.

With time, ticking away.

Like maintaining a position between... like standing on a boat, rocking, fishing with one hand while flying a kite with the other. What an image! I become quite excited by it.

Impulsively, I reach out to waken Robert, to tell him, to share with him my amazing insight – of how I stand between him and James – but then I see he is asleep. I am afraid, suddenly, to wake him. So I leave him be. I just watch over him. I love him. I love his good instinct.

For he has a good instinct.

He understands.

A few minutes later he awoke, stretched and looked directly at me. 'Ha!' he said, 'I must have dropped off!' Then, smiling, then asking, 'Anything happen while I was away?'

I should have told him then, at that moment, about the amazing clarity of insight I'd had, but somehow, just as his eyes opened, just as he stared into my eyes, my thoughts, I fizzled out of being myself. Like an exotic desert plant, flowering and dying away in the space of a few moments I'd had my brief time of bloom and now it was past.

'No.' I replied, glancing down at him. His eyes, I thought, are brown pools. Of course I didn't say that to him. I just replied, 'I have just been sitting here, enjoying the peace and quiet. Daydreaming, I suppose. Or perhaps I was in a brown study.'

On the way back Robert rowed, steadily and smoothly. I was rather surprised for I did not know he could row. After a bit, for no reason, he began to hum, then he half-sang, half-spoke a song: I listened, trailing my hand in the water. It was odd – unreal, like something from an old Hollywood musical, but very, very pleasant.

My love's an arbutus
By the borders of Lene,
So slender and shapely
In her girdle of green;
And I measure the pleasure
Of her eye's sapphire sheen,
By the blue skies that sparkle
Thro' that soft branching screen.

And so, in that way we made our return journey: the falling sun, the creak of the boat and the fall and rise of the oars in the water, with Robert's voice, raised in song. I did not know it was to be one of the last beautiful moments we would share.

***

And so, in this fashion the weekend progressed. On Sunday evening it was Paddy and Ursula's turn to cook dinner. We berthed at a wooden jetty at about five and had all gone off to do our various things (like sleeping, in my case), and were told to be present and correct at seven o'clock. I could see no sign of any preparations for a meal, and no one else mentioned anything about it, so I decided to forget all about food and leave it to the two who had been designated cooks.

I went to my cabin and lay down on the bunk. I dozed for a bit and then was woken by the noise of a car arriving and stopping outside. My bunk was nearest to the land. I heard car doors bang and voices raised in conversation and so I looked out, being nosey, and saw a man and woman carrying two large baskets towards the boat.

Then I saw Paddy coming down the gang way

'Hello Patricia, Hello Brian,' he called out.

'Hello, Mr. Moran.'

'Come in, come in! Get yourselves sorted out here. Will you be ready for, say… seven for seven fifteen?'

'No problem, Mr. Moran. Everything is more or less ready, just need access to an oven and gas top.'

So there we are, this is Paddy and Ursula's idea of providing a meal for the rest of us. Outside caterers! I decided to get myself afoot, washed and ready to hit the deck.

'Crew! A little aperitif?' This was Paddy, a little later coming up onto deck with a bottle in one hand and a cloth in the other. Ursula, carrying a plastic tray containing six thin glasses, closely followed him.

'Absolutely!' Robert said, leaping to his feet. The rest of us followed suit, crowding round the little table.

'Why not?' replied Paddy, proceeding to take the wire off the Champagne bottle – yes, Champagne bottle – and before that the black metal foil covering; he covered the cork with the cloth before twisting it off, or out, like a magician performing a trick. He had that air about him; I've noticed it before with Champagne: it nearly always happens when men are put in charge of it – they grow in stature!

'Don't want anyone to lose an eye,' he explained, as if he were dealing with an unexploded missile. A bang, or rather a weak flopping noise, issued from beneath the cloth. 'This is how the world ends,' I thought, 'not with a bang but with a whimper.' I did not say anything. The truth is, I don't much like Champagne, it always makes me sneeze.

A few minutes later we are all standing there on the deck of our boat with filled glasses, waiting for Paddy to place the empty bottle to one side.

'May I propose a toast?' he says, lifting his glass. We all agreed, yes he could make a toast. After all, it was his Champagne.

May the road rise to meet you,
May the wind be always at your back,
May the sun shine warm upon your face,
The rains fall soft upon your fields,
And until we meet again,
May God hold you
In the palm of his hand.

Of course, 'may the road rise up to meet you!' Very appropriate, I thought, coming after my idea of the unexploded missile made me again think of my sister Ruth. In the middle of my reverie I heard Robert's voice boom out.

313

'Another toast!' Then, drawing himself up to his full height, he raised his glass heavenward.

Here's tae us
Wha's like us
Damn few,
And they're a' deid
Mair's the pity!

In an instant we were seated (we had little menus, handwritten on white cards. From this I could see we started with Goose Foie Gras Entier en Gelée, translated by Paddy as whole goose foie gras in aspic. (I noticed that his speech was already written on the glass jar). Then Ursula started talking her way through it, about how she loved the subtle, delicate flavour and the creamy texture of goose foie gras, how delightful it was. I have to admit, it was extremely good, served on little crispy pieces of toasted bread, cut very thinly. It was quite delightful – so long as I could forget the production methods. Paddy passed among us with a bottle of Sauterne and the goose liver soon disappeared. I noticed that Robert, who said nothing during this time, was not really eating his portion, so I caught his eye but he gazed back rather coldly, remaining impassive.

Next, the menu cards told us we were to have *Chateaubriand A La Rosenbad*, served with a salad and a few (oven, but you can't have everything!) chips. Robert made a big deal of asking us how we liked our steaks cooked but I think he got a bit mixed up for mine was very rare, bleu in fact, and I believe I got Ursula's portion (she has such exotic tastes and probably got my mundane medium rare) though it was big and beautiful. When they were served Robert and then Paddy made a big thing about the sauce, how it was made from brandy, sherry, truffles, butter. Then we all just ate. From this point things settled down and Robert got into

314

better form. Perhaps the wine helped him along. It was a bottle of Pomerol, followed by another bottle of Pomerol and then by a third bottle of Pomerol; even I could tell it was good, so dry it seemed to evaporate off the tongue.

To finish, Robert and Patricia brought forth a Cheese Brie de Meaux, a 2.6 kg wheel, said proudly by Paddy to be 'the most famous French Brie.' He instructed us to watch out for the 'mushroom and hazelnut flavours.' All the while, faithful old 'Robert' sallied around filling our thirsty glasses from a bottle of white Cotes de Beaune.

'Heaven,' I sighed. All this, and no washing up to do!'

Before departing, 'Robert' came once more among us with six little glasses and a bottle of crusted port (Graham's Jubilee, 1977, as Paddy took time to mention). Then Brian and Patricia were off the boat in a jiffy, with their various cases and boxes; so fast and silent that and we were hardly aware they had left. Later, I glanced into the kitchen and found it was spotless. I don't know how they did it! I reported to the others. 'They are professionals.' Paddy retorted. 'What else would you expect?'

***

'Let's look on the bright side.' This seemed to be Ursula's favourite saying and every time she repeated it Liz would smile and nod and respond with, 'Absolutely!' For some reason, I found Liz's behaviour extremely irritating, and especially so when it was allied to Ursula's in this way – it always seemed to me, looking at and listening to the two of them, that they had been mandated by some authority I did not know, or was not supposed to know, or could not imagine, to be optimistic.

I suppose Robert is correct in his beliefs. For my own part, for years, I have been told that the barbarians were at the gates, and I am instinctively cautious. I suppose now, caution (which in the past had been highly regarded) will be considered negative.

For my part, I am neither optimistic nor pessimistic: just cautious. I must remember to explain this distinction to Robert.

I have just recalled a remark I heard Robert make, earlier. We had been sitting on the boat. The sun was just going down. For a few moments there was silence as we all looked out across the lake. It was so peaceful. Then, quite unexpectedly, Robert said 'You know, it's strange but I didn't realise I was actually engaged in a form of resistance – of passive resistance – for all those years, but I was. Now, I feel I have nothing to resist and I feel...' he paused... 'I feel useless! Redundant. Set to one side, again.' He looked across at me, for a moment, before continuing. 'I am like a judo player, I have been gently led off-balance by the manoeuvres of a superior tactician and I feel as though I am about to fall over.'

I can still see him – he is just in front of me, sitting there unmoving, his face turned away, his eyes directed towards the shivering water.

I glanced across at James and he looked directly at me and raised his eyebrows. Nobody spoke.

I watched the water rippling under the dimming light. I thought of all the years that lay behind each of us, that lay behind me. The water reminded me of something, yes, it reminded me of the skin of a nervous young horse.

Nervous.

Alert.

Fearful.

I too had been emptied.

I had felt that a hand, a fist, had come inside me and had ripped everything out.

Emptied.

Crippled.

I reached out and touched his arm. He ignored me.

'What were you resisting, Robert?' He shook his head, but did not reply. Then Paddy sprang to his feet and started offering everyone another drink. With his bulk moving between us the mood seemed to change, abruptly, and as a result Liz and Ursula began talking to James as soon as their glasses were refilled and he had eased himself out of the way. I did not have anything, for my glass was still half full, but Robert held his empty glass out, automatically.

'There you are, old fella. Get that down you! It'll do you good!' Then, turning to the company he lifted his glass. 'May I propose a toast, *To the Future'* Paddy spoke solemnly, holding up his glass for a moment before touching it to his lips. We responded with embarrassed mumblings though I noticed Robert, while he lifted his glass with the rest of us, did not drink.

Under cover of the accompanying movements, disruptive in such a confined space, Robert turned to me, saying, 'Why did you ask that question? About resistance. Don't you know what I was resisting?'

'Not really,' I replied, suddenly feeling cold and hard as I spoke the words. At that moment I considered him to have become a very reactionary person. I felt so remote from his concerns as they issued out into the void between us.

Now, looking back, I think those two words marked the end of an era. The coming down of a curtain. Their utterance was an act of vandalism. The unthinking snuffing of a candle. The crushing of a fly. The denial of friendship. A withdrawal.

Trust.

Faithfulness.

Loyalty

Suddenly, I felt tired. I felt I couldn't take any more self-pity. I thought, I have not the energy to fight against this constant negativism. Then his voice came into focus, penetrating my thoughts.

'What I was resisting was murder, thievery, lies – for political ends. Murder, thievery, lies - for personal gain. What I was resisting was the opposite of truth.'

'I say, old fella…' Paddy's voice carried through the air. It was as if a dance of voices was taking place all around me. 'I say, old fella, that's a bit strong!' Then he turned, unusually making an appeal directly to James. 'Isn't that a bit strong, James?'

'We've had these discussions, many, many times. We can have them again, if you wish, but I see little that might be gained from repeating the same argument repeatedly.

Liz got to her feet and left, without speaking. I had a sudden strong longing to follow her, but resisted. It was as if the informal dance was turning into a formal ballet: a performance taking place, all around me. I was a part of it, on stage, but this dance meant nothing to me, nothing at all. I realised that. When I get home, I thought, to whom will I relate these events? Who is there to listen? To show interest? Once, Ruth would have been my listener, my sounding board, my other half, but not now; now, there is only emptiness. The old descent started.

Emptiness.

Coldness.

Hardness.

Febrile?

Brittle!

Brittle. That is the word I want! Despite, perhaps *because of* his radicalism, Robert cannot bend. He is a single oak in a forest of willows. He will break in two; he must stay as he is, even if it kills him. There is no change in him. 'Gain!' How scornful that word sounded on his lips. 'What I'm talking about is moral resistance! But you would know little about that. Gain!' Before James could reply, Ursula stood up. 'I'm off to the loo, boys. I don't know what the agenda is here, but I feel there's more to this conversation than meets the eye. I suggest you all ease back a little.' Then she smiled. Coy,

319

is how I would describe that smile. 'For my sake?' As she passed him, following Liz, Paddy slapped at her behind. She gave a little skip and his hand just missed her causing him to almost overbalance off his seat. Laughing.

Laughing, his big hand hanging there, free and loose and useless in the air.

Then James spoke, for the first time.

'I have some sympathy for Robert's point. I must admit, I hadn't thought of it in these terms before but there is the possibility that the parties will have some difficulty at some point in agreeing on common values, on finding common ground, with the best will in the world, on many issues, I should imagine. Christian Fundamentalism and a form of, ah – possibly Marxism wouldn't appear to have much in common when it comes to, ah – agreeing to agree on a set of, ah – agreed, relative values... What I mean is, they would not appear to believe in relative values, but in absolute values and in very, extremely, different, absolute values, so...'

The boat rocks. Another boat is labouring past, leaving in its wake rolling surges of solid water. I feel quite dizzy. Paddy is speaking: 'I hear it's a real love-in at Stormont. I believe it's not uncommon to hear, 'After you.' And, 'No, after you,' Or, 'No, no, I insist, after you...' During this little speech the two girls return, laughing and giggling over some private joke or happening.

I thought, 'there's more love then at Stormont than there is here, among this small group!' and then, again, another, fellow-thought followed the first: I thought, 'those people up there are at least trying, they aspire to change and that's more than we are doing, more than you are doing, Robert!' But, of course, I did not say this and we all sat there until a voice broke the silence.

'It's getting chilly,' Ursula said, from the doorway. 'Should we all go inside?' Obediently, we all got up and went in. I looked back. Robert was still seated, his head on his hands. He looked so isolated and lonely. I almost went back to comfort him.

It must have been about one o'clock when I finally staggered down to my cabin. It seemed as if I had only just climbed into the bunk bed when there was a knock on the door. I decided to ignore it but it was repeated. I never knew a simple knocking on a door could convey such urgency.

'Who's there?' I called out, too exhausted to ignore the noise any longer.

'It's me. Robert.'

'What do you want? It's very late and I have a sore head, or I will have a sore head – very soon, tomorrow… I've just got a spinning head at the moment!' I switch on the light…

'My eyes don't focus!'

'I need to talk to you. Can I come in?'

'Yes. Of course.' I replied. Rather reluctantly, I have to admit. The door opened, in he came and down he flopped, on my bed. Then he started.

'A little while ago I went out onto the deck, to be on my own; I was feeling a bit fed up, to be truthful. I was standing there, and for some reason, I was dying for a cigarette! Then

Paddy appeared. He came and stood beside me, very quiet, puffing on his cigar, playing with it, you know, rolling it between his fingers, holding it out over the water until the ash fell off. Never saying a word. He appeared to be playacting, to be behaving like some Mafia hotshot. It was absurd! I decided to wait him out. Then he spoke:

'What do you think of this new set up at Stormont?'

'Well, I hope they can make a go of it. I hope they succeed: we all need a bit of stability in our lives, here, now. Though I am sorry to see the middle-ground disappear so abruptly.'

'Yes,' he said, 'I agree with you.' Then more silence. I found it a bit weird, to be honest. Then: 'How's the pottery going? Business good? He caught me a bit off-guard and I replied without thinking about it too much: 'Ah, it's so, so. Could be better, I suppose.'

'Does it clean its face?', then, seeing the look of bewilderment on *my* face he moved to explain, 'I mean, does it pay its way, does it produce any kind of an income for you?'

What a cheeky bugger, I thought! I was about to tell him to sod off and mind his own business when I thought better of it. After all, we are here to enjoy ourselves. I didn't want to cause bad feeling, so I just said, 'Oh, yes, it cleans its own face, alright.'

'I was staring out over the water, leaning on the rails but I could sense him looking at me.'

'This Stormont business – I think one of the things they might do is to ease up on planning restrictions, you know, give a break to the development of new rural dwellings, and so on…'

'I still didn't get it. I must be getting really slow in my old age! I just said, again without thinking, that that might be a useful thing to do, provided they retain a lot of green belt areas. And I said I thought there are too many single dwellings going up in haphazard ways all over the place. Probably better to develop brown field sites, in town centres or on the edges of towns and villages.'

'That's true,' he said, 'but take that place of yours, that might be a grand site for a nice little development – I've noticed there are a couple of primary schools close by and it's on a bus route into Belfast. It would be a grand place for a little development for first time buyers…'

'No. I don't think so,' was all I said, sharpish, but still, he didn't give up.'

'It's your decision, of course. But, you'd get a tidy sum. There'd be enough to set you up for retirement!' That word 'retirement' really jumped out at me! I remembered how, just the previous evening, James had said something about my retiring and I suddenly knew they were in this together! The pair of them, plotting to steal my bit of land! 'You've got the wrong man!' I said, and I walked away.'

I listened to this but didn't say anything for a bit. Then I said, 'I can't believe James would be involved in anything like that. I mean, he knows how much you feel about the forge and the land. And your grandfather. I mean, you are always talking about him and the old forge.' Even while I was saying this thoughts flashed through my mind… like, well, James is

323

very fond of money and now he's sold his own business he is looking for opportunities to make investments; he has become very friendly with Paddy recently; it's an unspoken fact that Robert's pottery is barely keeping going. Maybe it's not such a bad idea, after all. Immediately, I felt guilty; I looked up at Robert. I felt I had betrayed him by even thinking such a thought.

I reached out and took his hand in my two hands. His flesh was icy cold and I almost dropped his hand in surprise. When I looked at him more closely, I could see, even in the paltry light in the cabin, that he was a grey colour. I must have betrayed my surprise, something a nurse should never do, but it's so different when it's a friend who is presenting all the symptoms of a potential heart attack! All the professional distance seems to disappear.

'Are you alright? Do you feel all right?

He laughed, only it wasn't a real, hearty, outward laugh, but an inward-turned, ironic kind of laugh that made me feel even more tense.

'If course I'm all right. I'm fine,' however, he looked suddenly tired, exhausted. He had slid down across the bed, across my legs and now lay, his upper body slumped against the wall. I remained where I was, trying to smile reassuringly, while wild thoughts raced through my head: should I get James? But if James comes Robert will lay into him and there will be a big argument and if he is on the verge of having a heart attack, that certainly won't help. Heart attack: should I phone for a doctor or an ambulance, even if only to be on the safe side? But where do I telephone to; and how do I telephone – we are on a lake, and I intentionally left my mobile at home.

Lying here, imprisoned under Robert's weight, bobbing on the black waters of a strange, dark lake, I feel quite isolated, dislocated and away from all my familiar levers of power. In Belfast I'd have an ambulance here in a few minutes. Here, I'm sitting on this lump of plastic and wood in the middle of nowhere and all my support systems might as well be on another planet, so, I tell myself, it's only natural I feel both helpless and useless. This sense surges over me in an instant and I decide I must take action, calmly and with authority. But I knew Robert and as soon as I thought of the idea of acting with authority it suddenly seemed a remote possibility. Ever since Ruth died, Robert and James have taken control of my life; to be truthful, both have bossed me – not in a nasty way, at all, but they have sort of taken charge of me in a different way .

Now I decide I'll take control, for once. But while I am deciding Robert levers himself up and off the bed.

'I'll confront James tomorrow. I can't let this lie! Goodnight.' With this he marches out of the room and shuts the door behind him.

I leap out of the bed and am at the door in a flash. I call out, as I open the door. He halts and spins round. I approach him, putting my hand to his brow. His temperature seems all right. I look into his eyes. He seems quite normal, if a bit pale. I shake my head, bewildered. We stand there for a moment.

'Goodnight.' I say, slowly and hesitantly, not wanting to leave him. He looks at me strangely, then turns away. I give up. I go inside, close the door and crawl into bed. Before I know, I slide back into a dreamless (and, considering it the next morning, a seemingly callous) sleep.

***

The next day turned out to be very peaceful. We spent the time going up and down the lake, the men taking turns at reading maps, navigating and steering the boat. The girls read or just sat about idly, enjoying the sun's unusual heat. Robert looked very well and no one mentioned the row of the previous day. I do not know if he did confront James, or not. It was early on Monday evening, or possibly late afternoon, when we pulled in close to an island. Robert dropped the anchor overboard and we all wandered about the deck, sampling the view, drinking coffee, and feeling in a holiday mood.

'It's a bit like a taster menu,' someone said; I think it was Ursula.

'Trust you to be thinking of food!' Robert said this as he came up to where I stood, gazing across towards the island.

'I meant the views, stupid! All the little bits, they are so beautiful.' He ignored this.

'Do you fancy going over, in the dinghy?' he asked me, nodding towards the island.

'Yes,' I replied, 'I'd like that.' He helped me down into the dinghy, then climbed down himself and soon he was rowing us across the little bit of water towards land. It was a glorious warm, peaceful evening. It is a strange thing to say, but the very light was warm. The air dripped with millions of little insects, gold and silver, dancing against the dark water's background. By the water's edge a sycamore tree had just burst into leaf; each branch was tipped with little butter-coloured leaves (they were the bud casings for the new leaves, Robert explained, noticing my looking, I suppose).

The sunlight, though it was late in the day, was very strong and seemed to set the whins afire and everywhere I looked I could see many shades of green.

The air seemed vibrant with life. I was afraid to breathe in case in doing so I took life. The evening brought back memories.

I have come to see that a part of me acts as a kind of witness to what goes on inside my own head. I am no longer in the custody of my imagination. I can audit my imagination.

I do not – could not – know if anyone was aware, but for years after Ruth was killed I imagined she was around and about me, wherever I went. The air was filled with her presence. Or rather, I knew she was there. I believe that what I experienced was like an echo. This realisation had come to me the previous night, before I went to bed, when I was standing on the deck, looking out across the water. It was late in the evening. We had finished eating and the others were sitting around the table, chatting. I had gone out to get some fresh air, for I found the cabin was stuffy. I was standing by the railings at the back of the boat when I heard the call of birds, somewhere in the distance. The sound seemed to come from an island that I could only dimly see, a black shape in the darkness. Each utterance was single and plaintive, yet each one seemed to be accompanied by an echo, like an auditory image of itself. I thought, how beautiful, how haunting. I found myself moved by it. Then, somehow or other, memory kicked in and quite suddenly, I found thoughts, almost like auditory images, of Ruth welling up. The thoughts were indeed like echoes. The fullness, the completeness of sound and echo caused another coming together and into my mind came thoughts and images of Slieve League. We had gone there, a year ago almost. Standing on the cliff top, looking down at the Atlantic, far below, I had an overpowering sense of oneness with everything around me: it was like listening to echoes of God's omnipotence reverberating out of every molecule, every cell that lay before me, and in me.

Ruth.

How does she fit into all of this, for fit she must: yet, she never changes, yet, everything else changes.

If, in the past, I imagined I saw her, and she was not there, could not be there – that meant, surely, that I could not take the experience seriously. But it was real to me, the experienced of her being present was real, to me. But, how could it be real to anyone else? That's where Robert and James were so important to me: they took time, they listened, they never queried or questioned or criticised, never laughed, never lost patience. Never once questioned my sanity.

So there I stood, on the clear, clean wooden deck. The birds had quietened, just the occasional piercing call, from far away. The water lapped against the boat's hull. I was mulling over my, I suppose, to some, dark thoughts, when I heard a sound behind me. I turned round and there was Robert.

'Are you alright?' he asked.

'Are *you* alright?' I replied

This is more than a rhetorical device. I remained genuinely worried about Robert. He looked thin. In fact, he looked a good bit worn. He was drinking too much. I knew his pottery business was not going as well as it should and that he is surrounded by all these people who seem to have unlimited money I think he feels like a failure.

'Oh, yes,' he says. He is close to me and I think I can smell whiskey on his breath. Then I see a small glass in his hand.

'Are you drinking spirits?' I ask, for he seldom does, when I am around at least, and he has always said he prefers wine.

'Aye. Just a wee dram.' He is grinning now; his face lights up when he smiles like this and I impulsively put my arms round his waist. Just then, I couldn't help myself: I suppose it was a mixture of concern, of love, of sympathy for his aloneness and for his loneliness.

'You shouldn't drink whiskey,' I whisper, 'it's bad for you.'

He puts the glass down on the flat bit of the railing and returns my embrace. We stand like this, for a long time. Then we pull apart; he reaches for his glass and takes a sip.

'I was listening to the birds, out there, across the water.' I say

And now, twenty-four hours later here we are, in a different boat, listening to different birds. And in between, last night's unexpected row about the land! We rowed in close to the island but decided not to attempt landing for the reeds were thick and the banks were steep.

We stayed a little, drifting. Then, eventually, Robert rowed us back to the boat.

***

It was no big deal, really. James lost his temper and that's all there was to it, or that was the start of it.

It was our final day on the lake and we had to get back to the yard to return the boat. We were supposed to have it returned before noon and it was now nearly twelve. Ursula and I were in the gallery, doing a final clear up, and the others had gone to help James with the ritual of casting off.

I was just putting some mugs back on the shelf when a shudder ran through the boat and I heard the sudden deep hum of the engines, as they started up. I could envisage James at the helm, the Master of the ship! Then I heard his voice ring out: 'Cast of fore; cast off aft.' It sounded, well, 'professional', but I did not have a clue and was only half-listening when I heard him call out again; this time, though, and there was panic in his voice. 'Who moved my charts? Where did you put my charts?' Then the engines stopped and the boat kind of swung, or began to swing. Through the window I could see that its nose was drifting away from the wooden quay where we had tied up the previous evening.

Ursula and I had almost finished our tasks so we climbed unhurriedly up the stairs to see what the matter was. I could see immediately that James was in a bad temper (his face and neck were a deep Victoria plum colour, you know a combination of deep red and purple) and the others were standing there, in a semi-circle, just looking down at him. He was on his knees, peering under the wheel, then poking under the cupboards.

'Someone moved my charts. I had them prepared and left out last night. I had notes with them. Now, they are not here!'

'Well, I didn't seem them, or touch them,' Robert was the first to speak up.

'Nor did I,' Paddy said.

'I certainly didn't see them.'

James eyes turned towards Robert and me. We both shrugged and denied any knowledge of the charts.

'Where's Liz?' James demanded. Nobody knew.

'Look. Does it matter? The marina is only just along the edge of the Lough here: ten minutes will take us there.' This was Robert. Being helpful, as usual.

Eventually, we set off with James at the helm, but still minus his charts. The rest of us stood around for a bit, savouring the morning light on the water. There was a stiff breeze blowing up so I soon decided to go to the cabin and get my bag ready for off-loading. I hadn't been there for very long when I noticed that the boat ride was becoming very rough. We seemed to be rolling from side to side quite a bit while at the same time we were being bounced up and then down. The result was a kind of corkscrew effect with a regular loud slap as the boat fell back onto the water.

'I hope we don't sink!' I remember saying to myself as I zipped up my bag. I was huddled over the bed where the bag rested and holding onto the window ledge with my free hand. Then, unexpectedly it happened: one moment we were merrily bouncing along, the next I heard this awful crunching sound that seemed to go on forever, then we stopped abruptly, then the sound of the engine stopped.

For a long moment near-silence reigned. All I could hear was the slap, slap of waves hitting against the hull of the boat, just outside my porthole. I leaned over the bed to look out. I looked at the water; it was very choppy. I had not realised until this weekend that you could find waves on lakes but you can. I've discovered that the wind creates them. Then the great roar of James's voice broke the semi-silence: 'We've run aground! We've run aground!'

Of course, everyone was in his or her respective cabins but we all raced to the deck. There was poor James, standing to attention, holding onto the wheel and looking devastated. I really felt for him at that moment. We all crowded round him, asking what had happened. Had we run aground? Were we going to sink? Then I asked in a plaintive voice, 'Is the water cold?' That seemed to bring everyone to his or her senses and gave James the opportunity to explain himself. He 'thought' he said, that 'we are stuck on some rock or rocks that lie under the water,' and he had 'stopped the boat and turned off the engines to prevent us tearing the bottom off.' As he said this, a gust of wind rocked us and nudged the water into even stronger and more frequent motion. The horrible grinding sound rose once more from the innards of the boat.

'Look! You went on the wrong side of the marker!' Robert said, 'You should have kept to the left of that marker, over there!' Pointing, 'Instead, you kept to the right!'

'Someone took my charts! It's not my fault!' James retorted. He was almost in tears. At this, Paddy stepped forward and took James's arm and moved him to one side. He said, 'If we don't get this boat moved the wind will keep rocking her and she will grind a hole in the hull and we'll all get our feet wet! I'm going to start the engines and reverse off.' And that is what he did. Initially there was a further and alarming grinding noise and then a bump but that was it and in no time we were off the rocks and heading back to the marker where James had taken the wrong turn. Paddy turned to him and said, 'Here, you take the wheel, James. I'm no good at docking and we will be there in a few minutes.' Without comment James took over and the rest of the voyage was uneventful. Well, uneventful apart from Robert and Paddy being at each other's throats, again.

'Well done.' Robert said when Paddy stepped away from the wheel and stood beside him by the railings. Then he went on: 'You know, I couldn't help thinking, we must have been a wonderful sight there, for a few minutes.'

'In what way, wonderful?' Paddy said.

'Well, there we were, a small pocket of humanity, contained in a boat, sitting on a rock surrounded by water, within shouting distance of dry land but with no-one out there to hear us. It made me think how alone we are in the universe.'

'Do you know what I think? I think you think too much!'

We took the boat in, docked her and while Paddy went off to the boat owner's office to take care of paperwork, we watched while a man in a little rowing boat went round her, searching for damage in what appeared to be a routine manner but was, to us, a slow and nerve-wrecking procedure. None of us spoke a word. I noticed we all avoided each other's eyes. After a little, and while the others were fussing about seeing to their bags, I walked a little way along the path that ran beside the lake. I stopped and stood looking out across the lakes, in one last farewell. There was a trace of a moon in the sky, but I thought it must be a mirage. Robert dumped his bag beside mine. It landed with what can only be called a dull thud, cliché though it might be. We are all clichés, after all. We have all been used so many times, we gradually become repetitive and commonplace in our manifestations of who we are. Thinking about it later, that 'dull thud' was a statement, an angry utterance as old as mankind itself, I fear. He dropped the bag and stood beside me, in silent companionship, or so I thought, contained as I was in that moment.

I felt at peace. I gazed across the lake. The water was still now and unbroken; a short time ago it had been so rough; indeed, for a short time it had felt like being on the open sea in a storm.

'What I love about the lakes is the way everything you see can be seen twice!' I said, as much to myself as to him. 'It's so beautifully – it's so symmetrical! Every island, every tree, every bird in the sky, every cloud, is accompanied by its double, its image in the water. Especially things close to the water. Do you see those reeds over there, the way they appear to grow in two directions at once? Two things emerging from the one root.' I could feel his eyes on me, as I carried on, in a rush to get it out, 'And then a little breeze comes along and everything ripples and merges…' As I said this I turned. He was looking directly into my eyes. After a moment's silence he asked 'Has it started again, this double, this twin thing? This, this seeing things?' Without waiting for my answer he continued. 'It's time it stopped! Do you hear me?' His voice was so hard, so cold. I had never before heard, or I had never before noticed, such a hard, cutting edge to his voice, not at any time. Then, as if forestalling any reply I might make he bent down, picked up his bag and walked off towards his car, leaving me – well, I can only describe it as breathless and paralysed from shock. Recovering, I ran after him and caught him by the shoulder. He stopped and turned to stare at me.

'How dare you speak to me like that!'

'I'll speak any way I want! And anyway, to whom am I speaking? Do you know? I certainly don't!' And with that he shrugged and turned away towards his car.

'Don't walk away from me!' How often, have I heard that line spoken in films or read it in books? I never thought I'd be saying it myself.

Ursula, Liz, Paddy and James materialised. They had witnessed what had happened and, while at a distance and not being able to hear what had been said, were aware that Robert and I had just had a disagreement. They were full of unspoken understanding, and hugged me and left quickly and quietly.

James and I drove straight back to Belfast. We had half-planned a stop in Enniskillen but after Robert's attack – what else can I call it – I didn't really feel like doing anything apart from escaping and forgetting. James seemed to understand that.

I repeatedly ran over all that had happened during the past few days. At the core of my concern was the question of Robert's behaviour and its erratic ebbing and flowing; his moving from closeness and warmth to anger and aggression baffled me. In truth, I now felt numb and alienated from him, and oddly, from James also.

James did his best. After an initial silence of half an hour he conducted a monologue most of the way back to Belfast. I can't remember much about what he said; I do recall his trying to mount a defence, or at least an explanation for Robert's behaviour.

'You know,' he said, 'Robert is under a lot of pressure at work, in his business. But this is not about that.'

'Well, can you tell me what it is about? I certainly don't know.' And that is when he started on his long monologue.

'It's partly to do with the political changes. Robert feels strongly and honestly about these things, but not at a political level. It's more instinctive with him, more idealistic. And he seems to pick up on the feelings of lots of ordinary folk. I must say I don't agree fully with him, or them. I don't think we want our politicians to be more radical, as Robert wants; we – I – do want them to be more relevant. The danger is, Sinn Fein may prevent the DUP from being truly relevant, or vice versa. We need to look outwards; we need our Assembly to look to the south and to the east and further. We have been left behind economically and we are too small a unit to achieve much on our own.'

'It's been forty years of murder and mayhem and economic starvation and for what? We have a lot of catching up to do and I'm not sure if our politicians are up to it. It will need vision and belief in ourselves and joined-up thinking among all those involved. And leadership. Leadership that is not afraid of change and openness and the giving of freedom to individuals.'

'Robert is afraid of what might happen. He's afraid he might lose his business. I think he is afraid Liz is more serious about their relationship than he is.'

I had been half-listening until now but this caused me to sit up abruptly.

'What makes you say that? I think they are very well suited.'

336

'What makes me say it is that I believe it to be true. Robert is a transparent person, for all the shenanigans he gets up to. You must know, he is upset with you not because he dislikes you, but because he likes you too much!'

This certainly gave me a jolt and not because this is the first time I have ever heard James say such a thing; but I refused to respond. As I have always refused to respond, I suppose.

This time the silence descends fully. The words 'because he likes you too much' hang in the air, like a barrier between us; a great conversation stopper.

When we got back to my place James carried my bag up to the door and then said goodnight. No, he replied to my invitation, he would not come in for coffee; he preferred to get straight home.

There he left me. Shaken and stunned. I had never before heard him give such a sustained analysis, or was it a criticism? And was it of Robert, or of me? Or of both?

I went to the window of my empty room and looked out. It had started to rain and I felt miserable. Though it was not yet dark I drew the curtains and sat down in the nearest chair. I had so much to think about. The weekend, just past. The lake with all those currents swirling unseen beneath the surface. Us.

***

She is standing on the boat, her hand rests on its cool steel railing. She is looking towards the quay – or is it a wharf? She realises she does not know what its proper name is. Then the cloudy, haze and shimmer, of a crowd of people passing like birds in flight, half obscured by the shadows. There! There! It is Ruth! Surely! Dissolving into the crowd! Only for an instant – only for a fraction of a second. Was the image real, already it is gone, a trick of her eye? Could it have been real…? The familiar shuddering heart-stop! The surge of recognition, then the raised expectation followed by the familiar icy grip of grief, clamping once again about her heart.

But only for a fraction of a moment: a blind was raised and as quickly it is lowered.

All around her, she senses the trees swaying in the breeze, the boat rocking in the water, a sunbeam shining through clear air, and the lake water rolling, reflecting the blue of the sky above. In her heart she senses the lilting of Bach's Brandenburg Concerto as it accompanies the swaying, curtsying trees, their tripping shadows, the boat rising off its flat footedness and the lake waters lifting and falling. The world is suddenly alive, and dancing and she is dancing with it.

She is lifted and shifted by all that surrounds her, by the life that embraces her body and her soul. There is lightness in her bones.

Belfast

It was just two weeks after we had come back from what had proved, for me at least, to have been a less than successful weekend on the lakes. Now, inevitably, the three of us were together, once again. For fourteen days there had been silence, then tonight my doorbell rang twice; within minutes of each other Robert and James were here. No explanations, nothing. I assumed they had planned their coming and had synchronised their arrivals, but asked no questions. I invited them in, opened a bottle of wine, which remained untouched, and made coffee.

Although dusk was fast approaching, we were sitting out on my balcony for it was an unusually warm spring (the results of global warming, according to the ever-gloomy Robert.) For a bit I hoped we were enjoying the warmth in the air and the view over the river; there was something of the old feeling of being content, content just to be together. To be truthful, we have not made up, or otherwise, because I had not raised the issue, being too much of a coward. And neither had James or Robert. The result? As always with us, the issue was set to one side, or buried partly, but has been neither resolved nor forgotten – as I was about to discover.

Dusk was descending and through our small talk I heard the blackbirds call out again abruptly, shattering the peacefulness of twilight, the sudden, raw sound reminding me of the blackbird we had heard on the boat at Easter. Then, another memory floated into being, rising effortlessly out of the depths of the darkness that, increasingly, is the past: I was a small child. I was out in the garden, at home, Ruth and I together with our father and mother. The closing evening was bursting with birdsong. Our father identified the call of the blackbird, so stark among the others, and my mother said something, unusual for her, something about its being, despite its clarity, a sound from another world. 'It always sounds to me like a warning, sent from across a divide. There is something alien, yet comforting about it.' That is what she said, or something like it, and I recall the tone of her voice and her warning each time I hear this sound.

'Across a divide.' There are so many divides, so many worlds, with each one resting, each one on top or lying below another, like sheets of paper, or bundles of dried leaves, blown on the wind and randomly settled in a pile. Settled, until the next puff of wind comes along and settled so that one can never read all that is written on any one, just the bits that stick out to be glimpsed by the observer, in passing. So it is with our realities and with us.

I am in that world which, now, for this moment, is so clear and alive in my mind, my father on one side, Ruth and I in the middle, and my mother on the other side. The four of us, content and safe and secure, promenading on the lawn as night fell over the turf, our footprints black on the dew, listening to birdsong. Although bound together by the same experience, each of us is isolated, alone, marooned on his or her small island of selfhood. How little we knew. Still, that moment was, and it remains, a constant amidst the chaos and flux of time and tide, and is as real to me as this scene now spread out before us.

And this too is real, this present moment. James is sitting by my left hand. He is the personification of easement. I think James was always part of what Robert referred to as 'the contented majority'; Robert said (he is becoming increasingly bitter and very personal, I think, the animosity shown a few weeks ago apparent once again.) 'that's why you are such a supporter of law and order. That's why you protected the status quo for so long.'

Robert went on to say that is why he, James, loved to remain living there, alone in his big house, the gates closed and locked, 'clad in self-conceit and self-adoration' – all that stuff James argued for as 'heritage, turns out to be your heritage, your house and all the art work you purchased and collected is yours – it's all about self-identification with something you have no real appreciation of, you just buy into it'. These are the things Robert said, his voice growing louder and louder.

Eventually, he stopped. We sit in silence. James does not respond and I dare not speak. I don't say anything but I think Robert is caught up in what he sees as this modern predicament of buying and getting. This offer on his cottage is a case in point. And, after all, he makes pottery that people buy. Well, I think, bitchily, what if only a few people buy only a few pieces of Robert's pottery: it is hardly his fault more people don't appreciate what he makes! Now he leans forward. He breaks the silence, his voice lower now but more intense.

'Freud's thesis, that we have traded freedom for security, is just so true in your case, James! It's unbelievably so!' James just smiles and rubs his chin with the back of his hand, still refusing to respond.

'What about you?' I asked, worrying that this is getting out of control, thinking Robert's manner is just a bit over the top, even for him. And how did this start?

'I'm just the opposite… I have always been willing to trade security for freedom: for the freedom to accept personal responsibility for my actions… at least in theory…' I struggled to think of an example of Robert's trading security for freedom, but could not think of one. Is that it – is it all theory?

'James here is a good old fashioned liberal capitalist – I'm not so sure about your friend Paddy, I'm not so sure what he is, but since you are asking these questions, what are you? What, or perhaps a better question, *who* is Rebecca?' I could hear the edge starting to creep back into his voice, so I decided to take things easy and answered as lightly as I could.

'I don't know, I'm just a woman who wants to lead a quiet life. Potter… you know…'

'Quietism! The worst sin of all!' Now it is my turn to respond and I do so, tartly. Tartly yes, but I did try to say it with enough lightness and apparent warmth not to make it sound aggressive.

'Why is that? Why do you say such a thing? I do no one any harm with my pottering!'

'Because you are essentially a pessimist; you don't believe anything can be altered so you just go, feebly, with the flow. You debilitate those of us who look for change, real change. People like you rest, like a dead weight, on the aspirations of the rest of us…' I looked at him, trying to ascertain his state of mind. For once, I couldn't see beyond the words. Perhaps this was what he really does think of me.

'Do you truly believe that?' I asked, offended. He must have seen the incredulity on my face, or sensed the hurt in my heart, for he immediately softened and grimaced and smiled a bit and reached out, all at once, in what for him at that time was an unusual gesture of reassurance.

I smiled at him. Weakly, but I smiled. However, I noticed he did not retract one word of what he had said. Then James spoke for the first time, quietly but firmly. He surprised me with the directness in his voice.

'You have been a bit unsettled recently, Robert. Rebecca and I spoke of this on our way home from Enniskillen. She took what you said, ah… rather personally, so I made the point that you were, ah… perturbed by other things – you know…' He allowed his voice to trail off, inviting Robert to respond. Which indeed he did: in fact, he seemed pleased to be given the opening.

'I have been – I am – worried. I know none of you seem capable of understanding why. It's the general tone of this community. It's what we are becoming. It's the so-called, so-lauded 'new way' in which we are to be governed. That and this dreadful change of values – everything is for sale, everything can only be measured against money and consumption. I hate it. I hate what we are becoming!'

'Politics is about government enabling citizens to make choices, it's not about imposing choices on them. The big picture is what matters…'

'You know, it's old hat but social conventions do obstruct the possibility of human liberation. Tribal conventions do obstruct the possibility of human freedom. I think we are still trapped. I think we are going to miss a great opportunity. We've had a new body set up and imposed upon us – a

343

governing system that expects two diametrically opposed forces to work together. One of them wants to close the book on years of criminal activity, while holding everyone else to account for their actions, legal or not. You realise,' he said, looking at me, 'Ruth's death will no longer be a tragedy but will become an embarrassment, at this time when lots of people will want to engage in collective amnesia.'

James shook his head and seemed about to speak, but Robert continued.

'If there are such things as crimes against humanity – and as someone who believes we can only be measured against our ability to be whole human beings – I believe the actions of those who have taken life have to be named, explicitly, as crimes against humanity. And we must not forget these crimes, nor should we forget those who carried them out. It is, quite simply, about honesty and integrity. The way of quiet compliance with mis-remembering being the rule cannot be allowed to come into being; it is evil, insidious; it is a cancer that will lie dormant for a while, but it will emerge.'

He stops for a moment, then continues, the words spilling out in a rush.

'All those unsuccessful attempts in the 1970s and 1980s to have international courts give political status or prisoner of war status for terrorist convicts were unsuccessful. Yet, now they and we are, in effect, being told their crimes will be forgotten. But they can't be and they won't be!'

James looked troubled and shifted irritably in his seat. Then I broke the silence.

'Robert, I know you care terribly about this but what you are doing is making a private thing public. Are you not turning private loss into some matter of great public or political or philosophical principle? As one individual I have not the personal energy to take all this on board! It's too big, too complicated for me to cope with. I can barely cope with my own sense of loss, never mind the loss of the whole of humanity.'

To be fair to Robert he stopped at that point. I could see the sweat on his brow, gleaming. He just sat there, shaking his head, despairingly. He looked at me. 'I know,' he said. Then James started talking about something else; it was at that point he told us about Paddy's invitation for us all to come out for a meal. I think we were so upset we simply agreed, in order to settle things down. Then I made fresh coffee and soon after they left. As if nothing much had happened.

***

So that is how I found myself the following Friday evening out with James and Robert and Liz and Ursula and Paddy. We were in a little Bistro, not far from where I live, just off Victoria Street, and at well before eight o'clock it was almost empty. Paddy, of course, held the floor, treating the place like a stage setting on which he could glow and shine – and speak loudly. Sometimes he is larger than life, but in a burlesque way, playing it for laughs, one minute very much over the top, the next, very low key. As in, *Paddy's eyes narrowed*, I thought, looking at him. Always the performer.

Paddy's eyes narrowed.

I've never written that down, or even said it before. It sounds quite an American way of describing a person, it indicates a touch of toughness, meanness, even.

Behind the sheen of his rimless glasses, his eyes narrowed.

And I suppose that's appropriate for I do think now that Paddy is a tough person; I suppose, compared to me, or even to Robert, he has emerged out of a tougher background. What do I mean by 'tough'? I don't mean a person who would pick a fight in a pub or on the street and beat up his opponent. Paddy is not like that, at all. In fact, I think he is probably a bit of a physical coward, but tough, mentally. Yes, Paddy's sucker punch, as Robert might put it, is his smile and how his smile masks a competitive, tough mind.

Behind his shiny, rimless glasses his eyes narrowed; for a moment, a sardonic smile played about his thin lips.

I describe him like this because, somewhere, somehow, deep down, I have come to think of him as the direct descendant of American gangsters: a real tough guy; a bit of a swank, yet, underneath naïve, a bit innocent. I have hardly ever seen him disagree seriously with anyone; he never takes up an important argument on a point of principle, yet he always seems to come out on top. Because, and this is the secret of Paddy's success in life, his real, real, sucker punch, I believe is this – he does not care who or why he hurts, his aim is to win. He is focused on that and on that alone. He measures winning by the simple criterion of money. The creation of accumulation of money is what motivates him – that is what drives him and consumes all his energy. Perhaps he is no more than a man of his generation. I don't know, but I suspect there are many like him.

There in the restaurant, which I realised is his natural environment, for a moment, I saw him as I surmise Robert sees him, as one of the new rich, the gold ring, the open necked shirt, the pink, plumb fingers, and the heavy, lazy yet watchful arrogance of the ignorant. As I observed him, I thought you are right, Robert, as usual you are right, he is from another world, far from the one we inhabit. But it's more than that. He is always looking out, beyond the here and now: he is orientated to the future while we look to the past.

I can remember once, it was on the boat, I think, wondering whether or not I was *real*, to him; I still cannot say whether or not I am. That is how I thought, as I considered him, as I sat there, listening to him. Despite his show of good fellowship and his manifestations of good cheer, despite all his open-handed, loose hospitality, he did not care for me as a fellow human being for he did not know me as such. And that, I realised, quite suddenly, (it was like a small epiphany) was where his success had its ruthless roots. That and his innocence.

He has empathy, of a sort, that's why he can make, and seems to have the ability to keep, friends so quickly and so easily, but he does not care if he causes hurt. As and when a friend can be bartered for a profit, I suspect he will be sacrificed. I also suspect, sometimes, that he might verge on the psychopathic; behind the ready smile there is a coldness that, when glimpsed, is just a bit scary.

Only once did I see his guard drop. And that was an important occasion, as you will see. The last time we were all out together, just after Christmas, we had been invited by Paddy and Ursula to eat at a new up-market and very expensive restaurant in the city centre. This was by way of celebrating the New Year. This place is housed in a vacant big bank building that had been bought and turned into an up-market hotel-cum-restaurant.

'What do you think? A prestige inner-city destination!' Paddy claimed, looking round at the decoration.

347

'It is a bit over the top, isn't it? A bit of a rip off!' Robert retorted, throwing the price list he had been scrutinising down on the tabletop.

'Ah, come on Robert; you don't begrudge paying a decent price for a drink, do you? I mean, this doesn't come cheap, you know.' He spread his arms out to indicate the room's admittedly luxurious décor and sat back in his chair, waiting for our affirmation. Robert beat the rest of us to it.

'Yes, I do begrudge spending money in places like this. They represent consumerism for the sake of consumerism; they represent all that's shallow and crass in what we are becoming.'

That's when I noticed Paddy's eyes narrowing. But he did not lose his temper.

'I hate to disagree with you, but I think this is exactly what Belfast needs. Places of recreational quality that will attract people with taste, people who exercise fine discriminations, and yes, people with money to spend and who know how to enjoy themselves.' Robert should have left it at that but of course he has no sense at times like this. He just let go, again.

'Money to spend! Stretch limos! How ugly! Discrimination! How vulgar!'

'Vulgarity! Good old-fashioned vulgarity: something your average, solid Ulster citizen used to shun in the same way that he shunned sex!' Paddy retorted. He was obviously stung.

'I'm not so sure about the sex bit, but your average, solid Ulster citizen took great care not to advertise his wealth, if he had any. I used to know people around Larne who had holes in their trousers' backsides and were worth a fortune!'

'You are right enough there. But do you remember when the odd one, and there was always the odd one, do you remember the vulgar individuals who used to build a huge, vulgar house, it was invariably built just on the skyline, on a ridge so people on both sides could see just how vulgarly wealthy a brute he was? Well, now it's not regarded as vulgar to build a massive house, everyone yearns for such a house, and it's not at all vulgar to build it on a hill top, if you can find an empty one.'

'Yes, and once you have built it, you must make sure you have at least four new cars parked outside – a four-wheel drive for your wife, a good big, heavy saloon for yourself, a soft-top sports car for your son and a modest Mini Cooper for your daughter who is still at school. If you can manage it, you should also have a speedboat parked by the gable wall. Then, you must install a really powerful set of lights, preferably down-lighters all around the eaves and a battery of powerful spotlights to light up the front façade.'

'Yes and a good big bit of decking around the back. With under-floor spots built in.'

I was watching Paddy through my lowered eyelashes while Robert and Ursula and Liz were going on and on in this fashion. Paddy displayed no emotion, but I couldn't help wondering if he was drawing any parallels between these descriptions of vulgarity and his and Ursula's style of hospitality.

Then Ursula laughed. 'Do you know, you have just pretty much described Paddy's house, except he only has two or three cars parked outside. Oh yes, and he does have one thing you forgot to mention, he has a hot tub, in the garden naturally – he's wild keen on nature!'

Paddy grinned, unashamedly pleased by this. 'My motto is, if you have it flaunt it'

'There does seem to be something wrong, though. While some people are building or buying large houses others are practically disallowed from buying any kind of house, small or otherwise. Look at the number of homeless people, look at the number of young people who can't afford a deposit on a house. It seems to me we are creating a whole generation of poor young people. They can't get onto the housing 'ladder' as it's called, and they have little or no access to pensions; they will live poor and die poor.'

'It's always been the case, nothing changes; there will always be winners and there will always be losers. It's the way of capitalism.'

For once, James joined in the discussion, debate, or dispute – however one would wish to describe it.

'I think you are going a little too far, Paddy. I couldn't agree with you when you put it as bluntly as that. And I do think Robert has a point when he says, as he has in the past, that our expectations of this new administration are very high. They must put in place policies that promote the economic wellbeing of the vast majority of the population in this part of the world. If they don't, we may well see violence once more on our streets – not today, not tomorrow, but at some point. Mark my words.'

Paddy shook his head. 'Well, I shrink from disagreeing with you, but the question is, how do you achieve this? To me, capitalism – though I don't think of myself as a capitalist

– is about maximising profit and building up capital, and to do that I have to compensate others with whom I do business. But I have to compensate them carefully – if I don't someone else will maximise his profit and I'll finish up on the dole.'

'It used to be that capitalism was about owning the means of production, but since we produce bugger all now it's about owning everything else that's valuable, and making what's of no value appear valuable.' Robert said.

'No, be serious both of you. We live in changing times. We have had here the 'third sector', the 'social economy'…'

'Yes,' Paddy broke in, 'an army of do-gooders, a class, if you will, of professional beggars who constantly have 'do-goodery' oozing out from the sweaty palms of their ever-outstretched, ever-expectant hands…'

But James carried on in the same vein, 'we have a third sector who, in truth, produce very little real benefit of a sustainable nature, but who do spend quite a bit of money. However, if Government could harness their creativity, their…'

'…you mean, if the Government harness these people's largely mercenary instincts!'

'No. Be fair now. Ordinary people must be able to perceive and relate to the entrepreneurial spirit demonstrated by their fellow men and women, but that means – and here I do agree with Robert – that they should not lead lives of conspicuous consumption. It seems to me, they could lead lives of quiet decency, lives that inspire admiration and not greed in their fellow citizens. I'm sure there are many ethical persons among those in the third sector.'

Occasionally, just occasionally, James can come across just a tad pompous.

Robert said, 'Nothing ever changes. If I remember correctly it was Adam Smith, the great Scottish thinker, who drew the distinction between sympathetic and mercenary capitalism. I certainly think that today we are becoming very well endowed in the North of Ireland with the mercenary type, and if we must have capitalism – and at this moment, I will admit I do not see any alternative, I have to say – I think we could do with a bit of the sympathetic kind. I think that's the challenge that's facing our policy makers. Is facing each of us.'

Could I sense behind the poker-faced delivery of this a slight parody of James's way of speaking? Sticking to my usual policy, I kept very, very quiet. Discretion, I thought...

I can't help considering, what a socially dysfunctional group of people we are, or were. I fear we cannot continue like this for much longer. How we got together in the first place, or how we have stayed yoked together like this for so long now, I will never fully understand, but recently the fun has gone and we always seem to end up having serious disagreements. I forget how that particular conversation finished but here we are again, a few months later and we are still on the same, or similar, topic. I suppose I blame Robert, for recently his habit of always bringing the conversation round to politics has become even more exaggerated. He did the same now in the Bistro, and I remember Ursula becoming a bit tense, saying, 'I know you lot are always having arguments about politics but while I wish the politicians all the very best I can't help thinking – and I know nothing about politics – I can't help thinking Robert is right, that there are deep and bitter divisions among the various parties up there and I can't see how it can go on for very long.'

'Well they do seem to hold a number of irreconcilable values – beliefs and visions for this country that are inherent in their different philosophies, if you can call them that,' James said, looking at Robert.

'It will be a case of the long siege holding while those who oppose it dig away with their teaspoons at the fortified foundations!'

'They build up, all those years of attrition against apathy…'

'Who will be the first to blink?'

'You are taking this far too seriously. For my part, I can't take it seriously, at all.' Paddy said.

'I see you are taking the economic benefits of peace seriously enough.' Robert replied.

'I don't think the economic benefits have a lot to do with who is in power here. I suspect that is down largely to international capital. The world has changed a lot in the last ten or so years.' Paddy replied.

Silence from Robert.

Normally, if some argument like this broke out within our group, someone would interject as peacemaker and everything would settle down. On this occasion an unspoken decision seemed to present itself. It was there, ready-made and uninvited, having arrived like an unexpected stranger, it sat down at our table. Both sides were right; who could arbitrate between two truths?

Silence took root and grew. It spread over everything; it manifested itself like the proverbial damp blanket. I mix my metaphors. We gazed at the tabletop. We looked off into the near distance. We waited for Robert to make one of his sharp retorts.

After a bit he did speak, softly, addressing Paddy. 'A while back you made reference to my da' and his farm.' He paused, before going on. 'What my father did with his father's few acres is none of your concern, Paddy. My family has 'sat on its arse' there, to use the elegant term you once adopted, for at least the last three hundred and fifty years. They were weavers and they were cobblers and they were blacksmiths and they were small farmers and I'm a craftsman potter, and proud of it. We worked for what we had, what we have: we never stole it from anyone. We have never been put off our bit of land by anyone and we'll not sell our inheritance to some fly-by-night speculator.'

Paddy's eyes narrowed, then narrowed even more. His face was immobile, otherwise. Inscrutable. The rest of us sat there, shocked into silence, not so much by the words as by the constrained passion in Robert's voice. Then Paddy leaned back in his chair. I could see his body physically relax. I thought, we have just avoided a terrible row, then he spoke, a little smile on his lips.

'You keep saying 'we' did this and 'we' did that: that's all in the past. What about the future – you've no family of which I am aware. Who gets your inheritance? Sell it and enjoy the proceeds! Invest your money in a venture like this,' waving his arms to indicate the room in which we sat. 'Invest in a pub – you've invested quite a bit in quite a lot of pubs, or so I'm led to believe.'

Robert just sat there. Silence moved in to its dreadful ascendancy once more, and squatted there.

We waited for the waiter, but he or she had still not appeared, so we just sat there, eyes focused on the place where a glass should have stood. The silence grew and grew, and with it the tension. Then, standing up, Robert said. 'I think I'll leave, now.' He stood there, for a few moments, looking directly at me. His look was an invitation to me to come with him and I looked at James, for guidance. But James kept his gaze firmly fixed on his knees. I looked at Liz but she, too kept her eyes averted, and anyway, Robert did not pay the slightest bit of attention to her. I looked at him and just shook my head, in the tiniest movement, and with that he turned away. So that was how we let him go, alone out into the night.

Of course, the only one who showed no emotion or upset at all was Paddy. I must say, after Robert left, Ursula and Liz appeared a bit put out and Ursula frowned and shook her head at Paddy while attempting to catch his attention. He just carried on, as if nothing had happened. James tried to respond to Paddy's gusto performance at conversation but failed, miserably, his face ashen white, while I just remained quiet and invisible. A waiter came eventually and Paddy ordered a bottle of wine, without consulting any of us of course, and when it arrived I noticed it was a Vieux Chateau Certan, Pomerol, and knew at once that it was very expensive. For a split second I wavered in my resolve, but in the end I had the strength of character not to drink it: it would have been a betrayal of Robert, I felt. 'The water of life!', Paddy said, lifting his glass high in the air. The others lifted theirs and sipped and made appropriately appreciative noises but I simply lifted mine and put it back on the table, untouched.

'He is a bit down. I can see how his life is all in turmoil: there is all this stuff about a new political order at Stormont, his own business not going at all well and I think, between you and me...' here he stopped and looked around to make sure that Liz, who had gone in search of 'the powder room' was not close by, '...between you and me his relationship with Liz could be better.' Paddy pursed his lips and I interjected. 'You have to understand Robert is a very rooted person.' Paddy snorted. He actually snorted. 'A spade under his roots would give him a bit of a lift! Maybe that's what he needs! Dug up and moved into fresh soil. Ha! He needs to be re-potted!' James compounded the situation by murmuring, 'He's potty enough as it is...' causing Paddy to laugh ever more. As he spoke and jerked about, laughing at his own humour, his new John Lennon rimless glasses gleamed and flashed, hard and cold, under the lights and the glasses on the table bounced light; my senses felt assaulted, my eyes felt bruised and my heart felt... nothing, nothing at all. If Robert was being mocked and laughed at it was his own silly fault. That immediately made me feel mean and disloyal and guilty.

Despite Paddy's best efforts the conversation from then on remained stilted and disjointed. Eventually, I couldn't bear the tension any longer and said I felt I needed an early night and I was sorry but I wanted to leave. 'But surely,' Paddy said, apparently surprised, and turning to motion to a passing waiter, 'you will want to eat: the salmon is fresh.'

'Yes.' Piped up Ursula, 'I had it here the other night and it was superb! Do stay!'

'You haven't touched your wine!'

'No, thanks, Paddy, Ursula: I don't really feel like wine and I just don't feel hungry and I wouldn't do the food justice.' I stood up.

'Goodnight, everyone.'

'Let me get you a taxi!' Paddy was on his feet. James remained where he was. What's wrong with him, I wondered. Why can he not give me a bit of support, when I need it?

'No, thanks, Paddy,' I found myself saying for the second time in so many seconds, it seemed. 'I prefer to walk.'

***

When I got home I phoned Robert's cottage, but there was no reply. Three days later and I had heard nothing from Robert, and, even odder, nothing from James, despite having called both of them a few times. This was very unusual – it must have been the second time in twenty or thirty years that I had not spoken to one or other or both on an almost daily basis. However, things change. We had recently broken the habit of having our weekend meals together, and when we did meet it was with the other three present, and our get-togethers always ended up with Ursula and Robert and often Liz and occasionally me and usually Paddy having too much to drink, and normally ended with us all being stressed out by steadily increasing feuds and arguments. This was becoming very different from what I was beginning to think of fondly as 'the good old days' when we argued but in an intimate, soft-hearted kind of way.

Something had altered. During our Easter holiday I was aware of a change-taking place and especially so between Robert and me, between James and me, and between Robert and James: we, who had been so close, so compatible. Now, we are strangers.

Then it struck me: we were the reverse image of that which Robert railed about so much, the political settlement where previously irreconcilable interests were meshing and feeding off each other. We who had been so compatible were now apparently irreconcilable. We were the old order, dying! Our present state was merely a forerunner to what was to come.

Sometimes I feel lost, out of control; so small, so unimportant, so ineffectual.

History certainly ends with a whimper.

Patients I have cared for, gone. So many.

Patients; their last breaths, rattling breaths.

Such waste.

The old order dying. What a grotesque thought! But then I thought, what is odd about that? I swim in deep waters, moving between the murky cold depths and the bright sun-warmed surface.

A couple of days later, I had just come in from work when the doorbell rang. I opened it to find Robert standing there. I was a bit surprised, mostly by his calling at that hour, but smiled and said 'hello'.

'Let's go for a walk. I need to get a breath of air.'

'Robert! I've just got in from work. I have things to do...'

'Did you hear? Let's go for a walk.'

'Sure,' I replied, stunned by his insistence and manner.

'I was thinking. Why don't we drive up to Stormont?'

'Sure, if that is what you would like,' I replied.

'We'll have a bit of a walk in the grounds.'

'Sure.'

At my third 'sure' he looks at me, a bit oddly, but without further ado he nodded. I told him to come in while I got my coat and a pair of proper shoes. He said no, he'd just wait where he was. He had the car (he is still driving the old Volvo) parked down one of the nearby side streets and soon we were striding along, barely speaking. He drove out along the Newtownards Road, then swung left, up through Belmont. The Volvo made frightful noises every time he accelerated, but neither of us was in the mood to comment. Once, such a noise (I think it was the exhaust) would have inspired a whole conversation, jokes, puns, remarks about his meanness in not buying another car, a proper car. On that day, there was only silence.

We passed Strandtown, a place I had not been to for years. I observed it as we passed through: nothing seemed to have changed since I was last there. Well, apart that is from the number of little bungalows in big gardens and big houses in big gardens with *For Sale, Development Potential* notices or *Large Garden* notices decorating their fronts. This is a new phenomenon. As if reading my thoughts, Robert spoke for the first time: 'Developers! Greed, pure greed. They are destroying the place.' I agreed, but merely shrugged. He went on.

'Do you remember, in Donegal last year, when we drove up to Slieve League? All those new bungalows, and all the new, huge houses. They were absolutely everywhere, and with no infrastructure to support them, just individual septic tanks, spilling out into rivers and streams, making their way into reservoirs. Look at Galway, at the moment: no drinking water; everywhere is becoming contaminated! It cannot go on for much longer!'

He is off on another rant. I feel my reserves of strength are being rapidly depleted. 'Reservoirs of Dogs,' I say, thinking to divert him. I find I just can't be bothered to argue anymore, I hate all this negativity.

'Reservoirs of shit!' The words explode about my head. For some reason I remembered him asking me those silly questions he used to ask, something about the Sargasso Sea – did it have shores or not? How things change; how people change.

'It called progress,' I say very quietly but he just makes a grunting sound. I find myself thinking back to Easter and about that moment on the little boat, out on the lake, when I almost told him about my understanding. Now, I'm glad I did not confide in him. He has changed. Or perhaps, he hasn't changed; perhaps he was always like this. Perhaps he was always crass and rude and inconsiderate. I find it difficult to remember, and while I'm trying he speaks again.

'It's called lining the pockets of people like Paddy Moran. And his friends, his new friends. Celtic Tigers, indeed! Gombeen men, if you ask me!'

'Now, you could hardly call James a gombeen man and you know he and Paddy are planning on setting up in business together.'

'Not on my land, they're not! And it wasn't James I was thinking of. Where is this new business being set up?'

'Well, over in north Belfast. They're buying some big bit of land out in the suburbs.'

Robert replied immediately, 'I wonder, will James ever sell his own house and grounds to allow blocks of apartments to be built? I very much doubt it!'

I sighed. 'I shouldn't think so, Robert. But then again, you never know.'

In a further attempt to divert him I said, 'Look! We are almost there.'

We were now driving up Massey Avenue. As we turned the bend we could see along the wide avenue – it's still fairly early in May but the regimented lime trees are coming into leaf; they look so young and tender, the light seeping through the translucent young foliage. The cherry trees are in full blossom. Dotted at regular intervals, great bushes of Camellias are spilling over garden walls, keeping their drooping, fragile pink heads well clear of the shadowed tarmac.

Robert parked just at the rear gate to Stormont Park. Two horrible yellow signs adorn the outside of a former gate lodge. I recalled it had been used as a bank at one time. 'Development Opportunity' on one, 'New Office Accommodation Available' on the other. I look quickly at him just as he looks at me, but neither of us says anything about the signs or their meaning. However, as we leave the car behind Robert cannot contain himself.

'Wasn't there a local branch of a bank here?' he asks and goes on without waiting for an answer, 'Typical! They don't want customers any more, they can't be bothered dealing with people. Everything's shunted into 'telephone banking' and 'web banking' and such rubbish.'

The park gates were open and we walked through, between the high pillars and the elegant wrought-iron railings. We passed the security man and nodded to him and walked up the avenue. We stopped as soon as we saw Parliament Buildings, grand and white and still, to me, a most imposing vision on the hill top. The sun was shining and there was warmth in the air. People were out walking their dogs, a few children were playing with a ball, a jogger ambled past, wearily, earphones jutting from his ears. The occasional car sped along the avenue. It all felt so normal. Then, Robert broke the spell. 'Let's get away from all these people,' he said, nodding to indicate we should take a path that ran off to the left. He did not see the irony in this remark, following on from his last statement. I think he really is becoming a tetchy old reactionary. I think this warmly: I feel I am beginning to defrost.

We retreated back down the hill and took a path that leads off through a stand of mature trees. We stopped by a group of old Cedars. A plaque recorded that they were planted by someone in memory of the 36th Ulster Division. The date is given, 1914. Presently, we walk on; we move in silence through a tangle of trees and shrubs. Robert darts off to look at a figure set on a plinth. I walk on until I come to a water feature that forms what is termed on a plaque a 'peace garden'. Robert joins me. Two kneeling figures, resting on their knees, leaning forward, embracing, their heads touching, and their arms locked into an embrace with their bodies supporting each other. I look at the plaque and see this has been donated by the people of Coventry, and then I remember the bomb that exploded there and the dead of that city. I read aloud 'These statues remind us that human dignity and love will triumph over disaster and bring us together in respect and peace.' Robert listens. He stands quietly. He is looking on but does not respond in any way.

We turned away to sit on one of the two benches. Within sight, two memorials stand, erected to the memory of people who have died violently. All around, the pathways and the grass lay under a pink and white carpet of fallen cherry blossom. Birds were singing close by and when I listened closely I could hear that the sounds were multiplied by layers of other birdsong, coming from varying distances, but all clear and vibrant. The layers overlapped and supported each other and blossomed outwards, filling the day with music. It was like an orchestra. Against this cacophony of sound the falling water played endlessly, yet lightly. It had the quality of a flute rising up from another world.

I remember dreaming – recently it was – about apple blossom, about water, about birds singing. I feel the warm air on my skin. I feel elated. I say to Robert, 'Isn't it a beautiful place we live in? A wonderful place to be alive in! And it's about more than physical beauty, though it has that in abundance.' I gesture to what is around us. 'It could be the scene set for a marriage celebration. It has all the elements – they all come together, somehow: confetti, music, celebration, awareness of death but awareness too of new beginnings, the need for respect, the acceptance and acknowledgement of a role for suffering and pain in human life.'

Robert did not respond. He sat there, mutely, glumly staring at the scene before him. I found myself wondering, does he see the same world that I see? Eventually he spoke, 'The daffodils are dead and gone.' He pointed to where, behind the two embracing figures, I could see the remnants of a daffodil garden; the flowers' yellow heads entirely wilted, some gone, the green foliage beginning to turn yellow.

I felt cold towards him.

'So what? Daffodils die, something takes their place, they come again. They don't die, they just retire for a season.'

He pointed to the figure I had passed a few moments ago, the one he had walked across to look at. 'You didn't come over to the Gleaner statue: she is holding, she is looking down at, a sheaf of cut corn, or maybe it's wheat. There are words carved around the statue's base. They say, 'There is the gleaner behind all human endeavours.' That's a sentiment I concur with, this evening.'

'I didn't come over to it because you ran on ahead and left me behind.' I decide this has to stop. 'Look, what's wrong with you this evening? These past months, if it comes to that? You're in a bad mood about something and you are determined to take it out on me. Well, you can go and find someone else to be miserable with; find someone else to *make* miserable!'

He just sat there, staring at his boots.

'We are in this idyllic place, the sun is shining: why can't you just enjoy it?'

'Because, there are rats in the grass! If you listen you can hear them, rustling about. If you look, you can see the grass shiver and shake. The Pied Piper of Hamelin has been here! He has led the rats here and has left them here, fending for themselves When they grow hungry, mind your toes!'

'You talk about weddings, marriages. That white wedding cake up there,' he says, gesturing towards Stormont, 'is full of them. They are nibbling at it, nibbling away at it, from the inside. And the Pied Piper brought them here!'

I listened to him, thinking. One interpretation of the Pied Piper story is that he didn't care about the rats, it was the children he wanted rid of. I realised I was fed up with all of this. I was fed up with these constant ruminations. I got to my feet.

'Look. This is stupid and silly. Rats in the grass! Rats eating cakes! Pied Pipers! I want to go home. I can't cope with this! I can't cope with you, when you behave like this!'

'There's a song: I think it called the *Turkish Reverie*, it's about a man who is asked by the captain of one boat to sink another boat, to 'sink her in the lonesome water' and he swims out with an awl and bores nine holes in her bottom. Then he is betrayed by the Captain who commissioned him. That's a prediction and a warning for you: the world's a dangerous place, and this place is as dangerous as any other part of it: there's an example for you, an example of corruption, skulduggery and intrigue everywhere!'

'Robert,' I sat down again at his side. 'I want you to stop this wild talk! Are you insane? What's got into you? Are you crazy, or what?'

'Crazy! You are a fine one to talk! You've been...' he stops, obviously exasperated, struggling to find the right word, 'You've been an *enigma* for years! The rest of us have had to cope with you and all your moods. Your seeing ghosts. Your guilt!' His face is pale. I can see tiny beads of sweat on his forehead.

'An enigma?' I repeat the word; I felt shaken.

The sweat beads on his brow look how I think acid rain would look. As I look they grow bigger, they are eating holes in his skin. 'Cope with?' I have been coped with, all these years; not loved, merely coped with! I refuse to acknowledge the word guilt. Or whose guilt. I will not allow my mind to dwell on this. I stare at him. His pale-skinned face appears to be contorted into a snarl. I turn away, my heart pounding in my chest. The world lies behind a mist, the trees obscured, the landscape has been taken apart and badly put together again, by a person who cannot see. I hear his words, floating in the air, following me.

'A real riddle, yes. Playing James and me off against each other. A real cock-teaser, all these years!'

I turn, in disbelief. Now he has risen to his feet. He towers over me. He continues: 'A smile here, the touch of a hand there! What a beguiler! What a fool you must have taken me for... taken both of us for!'

The language! A beguiler! Playing James and him off against each other! The language! An enigma! Seeing ghosts!

All of these words rolled together in my head. The sun cast long pale shadows on the grass. Silence; words; silence; I burst out: 'Ruth was pregnant. When she was killed. She was pregnant.' I have never uttered these words before. I whisper this message to him. My voice roars out across the grass. It is as if I am afraid the grass, the trees, the birds, the two kneeling figures, might overhear.

'Pregnant?'

He cannot take in what I mean. I can see his blankness, I can see how his expression changes from simply not understanding to incredulity, then to disbelief, then into anger and finally horror.

Had I done this to him? But at this moment, I am beyond caring: I am cold.

'Pregnant.' I repeat the word. Or is it, the word repeats itself.

'I never... We never... How can this be? You are wrong... or lying!'

And so I told him. After all these years. Without preparation. Without forethought. Both of us standing there, face to face, by the garden of peace, the water bubbling up, falling down into its pool, without preparation and with no forethought, of how it happened when we were student nurses. I told him how we had gone to a party; how we had drunk too much; how we had become separated; how a medical student had taken Ruth, or how she had gone, to some room on her own. How things had got out of hand; of how he had raped her. How, for three days, the police kept referring to it as 'the alleged incident'. I told him of how, as the weeks progressed, we talked it over and over and over, endlessly. How could she, how could we, manage with a child? How could she have got an abortion, even if she had decided to take that route? And, how could we tell our parents? Of how we agreed to keep it a secret. I told him this,

367

and more. Finally, I told him how, three months later, she was dead, a post-mortem and the secret was revealed to our parents.

I did not speak of the collapse of my world, far beyond what he already knew.

When I stopped, Robert's silence was all-pervasive. It prevented me speaking further. So, we just walked back to the car, wordless. My stomach felt like a ball of steel, my head was reeling. Otherwise, I felt oddly calm. In truth, I felt a great sense of release. I glanced occasionally at Robert. His face was still an ashen grey colour and I began to feel concerned. We got to the car and he spoke for the first time since we left the peace place.

'I don't feel at all well, Rebecca. Can you drive?'

'Yes, of course.' I did not have to ask what was wrong, he was rubbing his upper arm and that, together with his colour, told me it was his heart.

'I think you'd better drive to the hospital,' he said, and then, after a pause, 'I think this is serious.'

I suppose I panicked a little. I do not remember how I got to the hospital, or indeed much about the drive there. I remember I kept talking to Robert, keeping his attention alert, wondering if I had any aspirin in my bag but not wanting to waste time stopping to search.

Once I had him there, screeching to a jangling, noisy halt outside the main door, just like they do in the films, things were taken out of my hands immediately. The triage nurse played calm to my concern, then eased me out of the way and off went Robert, sitting up in a wheel chair and looking sorry for himself, though his colour had returned and he now seemed to me to be a bit better. He did not wave or smile as they wheeled him round the corner and into a corridor.

I decided to go home, and having told the nurse and after giving her my phone number in case of an emergency, I set off. I was almost at the gates of the hospital when I remembered the Volvo. I scuttled back and there it was, sitting where I had left it, engine still running, outside the front door. I took the car home and parked it in the same side street we had collected it from only a couple of hours before.

Once inside I telephoned James, telling him only that Robert was in hospital, then I filled the kettle and put a teapot and mug beside it. I then had a shower. I dried myself and put on a dressing gown. During all of this I kept my mind utterly blank. The only thought I allowed myself was that Robert had had a possible heart attack.

I made a pot of tea and carried it out to the balcony. It was too chilly there so I came in, shut the glass doors and sat beside them, at the little table. I sipped my tea and gazed out at the river. I kept my mind blank. The bell rang and then the door opened. It was James stood in the open doorway.

'You say Robert is in hospital? What's happened?'

'It looks like a heart attack.'

Then followed a barrage of questions and answers: When had this happened? (About two hours ago.) How did he get to hospital? (I drove him.) From where? (Stormont.) Stormont? What were you doing at Stormont? (just walking about, just looking at the park.) Hm! How serious was it?

(Impossible to say.) Who is with him, now? (No one.) No one? (No one.) Why had I left him? Why had I not stayed? Why had I not phoned him immediately?

'Look James, I took him to hospital; he is in perfectly safe hands. I came home to have a shower and wait till he's ready to see visitors. I intend going in about half an hour. You can come with me, or you can stay here and be quiet or, if you must, you can leave and shout outside.'

That set him back on his heels, I could see. He is not used to me standing up for myself I thought, perhaps a bit bitterly.

'It's just that it's so sudden! It's all so strange! And you were with him, up at Stormont? By yourself?' He looked at me when he said this and I could see he was suspicious. I said nothing. Let him wonder. I sipped my tea. He moved to a chair by the table, unbuttoned his light, bright white raincoat and sat down.

'A new coat,' I observed.

'Yes. I got it in a sale. Half price.' But it was evident his mind was not on his coat, for he answered automatically.

'Do you want a cup of tea?'

'No. Thanks. Do you think we should go, now?'

'Yes. I'll get dressed.'

Then, as I moved towards the bedroom, another thought struck him. 'Have you told his family? His father or his sister?'

'No, I haven't and before you start again, it's too soon to phone them when we don't know what's wrong, if anything. It could be a just touch of angina. It could even be indigestion' I waited for a response. There was none so, 'Now, I'm going to get dressed. Excuse me.'

I went into the bedroom and shut the door. I leant my back against it and just stood there. My insides were cold and hard. I could see myself in the mirror. My face, my features, were calm. I felt no emotion. It was as if an ice age had settled on my heart, on my mind. I felt nothing. I was unaffected. It was no wonder James had looked at me strangely.

My mind was a vacancy. I was unable to consider what had happened, or to think about what the future might hold. Yet, even while this chill lay on me, I was aware there was something I should tell James, before we saw Robert; something.

But I told him nothing. I did not know what I could tell him.

A little later we arrived at the hospital and found the ward in which Robert was being cared for. James, of course, insisted on bringing grapes but I took nothing. I should have brought toothpaste, a toothbrush, pyjamas, and a bottle of water. But no, I'd had no thoughts of what he might need or want.

So there I stood at the bedside, empty handed, feeling empty-hearted; Robert laying on the bed, wearing a hospital gown, ghost-faced, impassive.

***

It was two or three weeks later and we were gathered in Robert's cottage to gently celebrate his recovery. After the big scare and all the drama, and following many tests, they could find nothing medically wrong with him and he was told to rest. Here he was, sitting at his table, giving out as usual. 'Houses are no longer places in which ordinary people live and rear children and from which they go about their ordinary day-to-day lives. Their ownership has become the *purpose* of people's lives, the final object of endless struggle and endeavour and sacrifice.'

I replied, 'What's wrong with people wanting to live in decent accommodation? What's wrong with them wanting to invest in their future and their children's futures?'

And then it started, the banter with question following question.

'There's nothing wrong with that: what's wrong is that the agenda is being driven by those who simply want to make money. I mean, who needs six bedrooms, four of them en suite and a main bathroom and a shower-room or wet room or whatever it's called?'

'Who really needs a sunroom? In this country!'

'Yes, who does the cleaning of all these bathrooms?'

'And who pays the window cleaner?'

'And who pays the gardener?'

'And where does he dump the cuttings?'

'And...'

'You are quite right,' James said, interrupting the flow. 'House building has become the engine that drives our economy. There's no doubt about it. But it's working; our housing stock is vastly improved, people are investing in their own homes, in their own lives and happiness, and that's good! There's more prosperity and more security and that's a good thing.'

'Well,' Robert replied, 'it's good in one sense, that is, that people are no longer blowing buildings up, but *putting* them up! But it's the value system that we have allowed to underpin this, that is what I object to. Take the town centres: they are full of super chain stores, all competing and all full of people pushing overflowing trolleys. Yet, when I go out, rarely it's true, but when I do go out, I can't get a seat in a restaurant. The whole world is eating out, Monday till Sunday – what do they do with the shopping they buy? What do they do with their kitchens and dining rooms in these vast new houses? They certainly can't be using them to cook and eat in!'

Paddy has been nodding and smiling and now, rising to his feet, he says, 'Your glasses are empty. Anyone for a drink?' There was a mini-clamour of 'yes, pleases!' for, in truth, everyone wanted to get away from this topic of consumerism that seems to obsess Robert. Robert, however, wanted have the last word: 'Babel!' he muttered, 'You are all living in the Tower of Babel! It will collapse. Just wait!'

So there we sat, elbows resting on the table-top, contented. Outside, the garden lay tame enough, with the fields billowing verdantly beyond its boundaries and beyond that the Antrim hills and then the world.

It was as if nothing had happened, or would ever happen.

So here I am, here once more at my table, at my desk. My glass of wine sits beside me, full once more. Perhaps I drink too much. I have found that it makes a dull world seem bright, an unimaginable world appears more real. For a short time, yes. But what is time?

I find my fingers itch to get at something, at the thing that's inside me, to get it out and down, in doing so, to make love to the keyboard, to feed those magical black marks into the maw of the every-hungry screen. Yes, I have bought a computer. Times change.

Yet, I am fed up with flux. I feel I want to stabilise reality; I want to pin the bits down; I want to make sense of things.

I want rock under my feet.

I want to have a relationship: with the past, with God, with certainty with the future.

This desire, this itch, this seeking, could go on forever and ever and ever. Or while I'm still sentient. Or, for as long as I'm alive. Two very different states of being!

It will never be the four of us, Ruth and me and James and Robert. That, too, is the past.

I know well enough it will never be the three of us, Ruth and her baby and me.

Whatever – as Ursula would say. I can say that now; I can think it! You know, when I come to consider it, I have very few friends; very few real friends. Acquaintances, yes.

Friends, no. What a lonely place this universe is. What a small thing a life is.

Whatever. I've come to realise that I have a very small circle of what one might call 'reference' as far as friendships are concerned. I think that is why I find myself remembering, thinking about, mulling over, and repeating what a few people say.

People like Ursula, for example, a person for whom I do not have high regard.

It's just that I have so little else to draw on.

I do have the past. The past often comes calling, but nowadays not often and erratically so. When it does it surprises me, like a stranger in the night.

I digress, as they say. I want to get this bit down, even though it happened after the time when I really did intend to stop writing.

It was just before Robert's shocking last letter (which I will come to later when I feel calmer, less agitated) and just after our walk in Stormont. It was in that little hiatus of calm, lying there between two storms. We were sitting, talking. We were in my living room. Idling. Just the three of us. Conversing. Convalescing. Then a sudden squall hit me.

As I said, we were on our own and it was as if it had been in the old days: just talking. Or rather, Robert was talking and James was talking. I was thinking, quite deeply, not really listening to what the others were saying but just enjoying the feeling of easiness, of closeness, of companionship. Allowing the sound of their words to lap around me and over me. Like a rug, a comfort blanket. Perhaps, I wasn't thinking but daydreaming, in a bit of a brown study as my mother would have called it, when I was young. Then out of the depths the words emerged, '…when I was in London…' It was Robert's voice speaking and I knew, somehow, that he was talking about a contemporary event; quite suddenly his voice rose up and moved into focus.

'There are lots of ways to disorientate people – nasty ways, no doubt, but this isn't one of those, it is the sago of social terrorism, the soft custard and hot milk version.'

'Humph.' James's lower, deeper voice emerged and then submerged all in one murmuring motion.

'We may need a real, painful social crisis to make people see clearly, but to my mind this is a poor substitute for that.'

'Humph.'

'I remember coming down some stairs and seeing a set of big windows directly in front of me. I could see some of his Lilliputian figures on distant rooftops and so I moved across the floor, towards the window to be able to see them more clearly. I think I counted seven figures, all in view from where I stood, spread out all across the London skyline. I was thinking, I have seen this many times before, on television, in the newspapers. This man is taking over the world; his presence is everywhere. He is like a human virus, spreading and growing, replicating himself at enormous speed.' Robert stopped for a moment and looked at me. Then he resumed his story.

'That's one way to tackle global warming – populate the world with replicas of this fellow and look how much energy we would save – they can even be sent to the seaside for us, that'll save us making the journey!' James interrupted.

'He sounds like a one-man supermarket – he sounds like the Tesco of the creative world!' This was James, chuckling in an unusual show of humour. Robert more or less ignored him, as he usually does when he is on a verbal roll, merely saying 'indeed, that's good James, very good!' before carrying on. Now that he had caught my attention he was speaking to me, his eyes fixed on mine.

'Then a woman's voice murmured in my ear and a hand took my arm, easing me past something. She was a gallery attendant and what she guided me past was one of the artefacts – I was about to bump into it. I had not seen it. It was a wire figure, life size, with spikes sticking out of its body. I had simply not seen it! That was the nature of its presence in that space. And his work is about space! I didn't even thank her. My immediate instinct was to say 'sorry' and 'thanks very much' but I quelled it. The thing did not belong to her: she was being paid the bare minimum wage, I would doubt if it was more, to protect something that belonged to someone else. All in the name of art.'

I'm afraid at that moment I was not much interested in all this talk about art. I was more concerned that Robert had been away and without my knowing. He had not spoken a word of this trip to me.

'But I didn't know you were in London!' I managed to interrupt the flow of words, 'When were you there? Why didn't you say anything about it?' He looked up at me.

'Last week. Just for a few days: Tuesday until Thursday. And I did say, a few minutes ago.'

I couldn't fathom this. I tried to recall the last time he had been to London, or anywhere else for that matter, and couldn't. He is just not the sort of person who leaves home – I know that may sound strange, but he has always been a bit of a home-bird, like me, but unlike James who has always had an urge to travel and who has always gone away – not often, but fairly regularly. I'm sure I must have looked a bit nonplussed and that, together with James's glaring at him, made him explain himself pretty quickly too, I noticed.

'I suppose I should have told you earlier, but it was a last minute thing. I just fancied a couple of days in London. I went early on Tuesday and came back late on Thursday. Anyway, what's the big deal? Why shouldn't I go wherever I like? Surely, I'm big and old – and ugly – enough!' He smiled. Such a sweet smile and not often seen.

I just sat there. I felt… I don't know… I felt… nothing. I don't mean I felt *nothing*, it was rather that nothing was there to be felt… an absence of sorts, but so real in its presence. I felt empty and hollow and then, when I considered it, I thought I could feel a thin line of pain, or rather of hurt, stretching across my lower stomach.

And I was suddenly tired, enormously tired. I couldn't really think. All I could do was passively enjoy – what a word! – the sensations that were there to be felt.

Looking back at it, I think I was trapped, imprisoned. In prison, in the strange sense that I felt excluded, expelled, put outside the fold, sent to Coventry. My terms of reference had been shifted when I was not looking.

The shock must have shown for James leaned over and took my left hand in his right hand. It was so unexpected. And, in company, even if it was just Robert, but still…

I continued to sit there. Or rather, my body just sat there, immobile. My mind both whirled and was numb.

Even I have to admit that this description of my reaction seems a bit over the top. It only lasted a few seconds, perhaps only a few milliseconds, and then I was my normal self again. I still remember exactly how I felt during the episode, though.

James was explaining. 'Robert just was over to see a few exhibitions. He has been telling us about them. Just now. I think you might not have been paying attention. There is an exhibition on at the Hayward of Gormley's work. You know, the sculptor. Robert, you were about to been tell us about the light box.' So Robert described the light box to us – how it was a clear box filled with water vapour and how, when you went inside you became disoriented.

'The way you describe it, it reminds me of the Ghost Train at Portrush,' I said, vaguely recalling the feeling of unease I had experienced when taken there as a child.

'Exactly!' Robert replied. 'Only this is a bit more static than the Ghost Train. It's like being inside a stationary motor car with snow-covered windows – you know how it is when you get into the car on the morning, after a big snowfall, and everything is white and you can't see out.' James nodded, sagely, but I found myself very, very not-interested in this line of conversation. I...

'Was it interesting?' James asked, brightly, interrupting. 'Did it offer inspiration, at all?'

'Interesting? Well, yes. Inspirational? No! You know, I think nature's secret attraction is its randomness; it's the human being who has this thing in his head that needs everything to conform to a standard pattern. Like one body being set up as a sort of benchmark. Maybe that's what is wrong with his work – to me at least. Oddly enough, the night before I saw that exhibition, I had gone to the Barbican to catch a film called *Ten Canoes*. It has a very simple plot: it's just a story about a story about indigenous Australians. It's about their ideas of accountability and justice. Now, that I did find enjoyable and real and true. Very different.'

'What is it about? James asked, valiantly trying to keep the conversation moving along. Meanwhile, his eye, I noticed, was firmly on me.

'A member of a tribe is killed by a member of another tribe. The first tribe demand justice. They get it by claiming the right to kill the killer – they are allowed to throw spears at him, while he stands there, waiting. Eventually, one spear finds him. He dies. Immediately, both sides agree to forget the incident. It's over. The matter is closed. Memory shuts down.'

I think of Ruth. I look at Robert and he looks at me. I know what he is thinking.

'What is the past? What is time? How can memory be shut down, and should it be shut down?' The questions hang there, in the air between us.

'What is space?' James asks unexpectedly. Nobody answers. 'I mean, what do they mean when they talk the space around those figures? I never know.'

'Space, time, memory, grief, joy; they exist only when I am there to experience them,' I say, vaguely remembering one of my philosophy lectures. 'Trees in the forest, falling;

does the falling tree make a sound when I am not there to hear it?'

Nobody answered me.

I sat there, waiting for the blackbird to call out. Robert walked over to the balcony rail where he stared moodily out across the river. Meanwhile, James went off to the kitchen, to 'make a pot of tea'.

**

I came in to the apartment at about seven o'clock. Work had been rotten; meetings all day, problems all day, no resources, no cooperation from anyone, no enthusiasm, just a feeling of impassivity all around me. I left work that afternoon feeling I was alone on the planet. I really felt, to be honest, that I applauded Robert in his lambasting of indifference and the way in which that mood seems to be spreading.

My head was aching and I wanted to get something for it from the bathroom cupboard, but as I crossed the living room floor I noticed the light flickering on the telephone answering machine: someone has left a message. I paused; this was such a rare thing to happen – few people telephone me at the best of times and those who do always leave it until I am home from work.

I stopped and switched on the machine. Robert's voiced issued forth – ha! I thought, good man: you're calling to apologise and to make up, at last. But he was doing no such thing! After a moment of listening to this I reconsidered: it's a big, angry rant!, I thought, alert and growing angry now myself. However, it was not an angry rant – even though he *was* angry and it *was* a bit of a rant. It felt, I admit, from the tone of his voice, to be an honest rant. And one that had its genesis in love, I knew. Anyway, I sat down on a chair to listen to his words, again and again, still wearing my raincoat.

I kept the message on the machine for days afterwards and then copied it down, and I am going to reproduce it here. I want to record this defining moment as accurately as possible.

Rebecca, it's Rob here. (Long pause) *You said Ruth was pregnant. Why you said such a thing, and after all these years of silence, I will never understand.*

To be truthful, I don't care to understand, or to know.

I don't care whether she was pregnant, or not. That sounds so hard. But it is the truth. If you are telling the truth – and I have no way of knowing whether or not you are telling the truth, or even if you're capable of telling the truth, or of knowing the truth if it reared up and bit you – if you are telling the truth, and she was pregnant, the simple matter is, it was not my child, it couldn't have been, and I have no idea whose it might be.

And I don't want to know. I don't need to know. I cannot allow myself to care, one way or another.

And if you are telling lies – what a terribly vicious thing that would be to do! – it means you are carrying on doing what you've been doing for years, living out a life that is entirely made-up. A scheming little drama of your own. And I have been nothing more than an extra...

Why should I believe you? You have become engorged on this fantasy world; I think it must be your equivalent of a real relationship.

You have become a figment of your own imagination, a thing created out of guilt. I used to think Ruth was the figment of your imagination but now I know differently. I used to feel sorry for you, but now I don't.

There was more, but I cannot, yet, share it. Then he finished:

I am going away, today. I'll be away for a few months. I am going to Japan, to work in a pottery. I want to learn something more. I want to grow a bit. I want to learn about Japanese glazes. And I want to be free...

The message stopped there. At least, he had the good grace not to say he wanted to be free of me, I thought. I was remarkably calm. I called him back immediately but the phone line was dead.

He must have planning such a major thing for ages, I thought. And keeping it a secret, just like that trip to London!

I listened carefully to the message, repeatedly. Listening to his voice I could never decide whether he had been drinking or if he was stone cold sober or, for a dreadful moment, if he had been taking drugs. I could hear the anger and the sadness in his voice. But his language! I considered it quite unbecoming; unfitting.

I discovered I was shaking and my mouth was dry.

This was the first time he had mentioned the pregnancy in all the weeks that had passed since that day at Stormont.

***

I remember, when Ruth died there was a... a little eruption of news... a little flurry of items on the television, in the papers, on the radio, but only for a short time. Apart from that flurry, nothing. She had dwelt certainly among untrodden ways. She left no monument to her being in the world. Only those of us who loved her carried the mark of her love for us and of our love for her. But that is an invisible mark and has as much to do with her death as with her life.

After the funeral, I never went to see her grave.

To the best of my recollection.

Even before I write this, I know it may sound morbid, but it's not really. It's just practical, good sense.

I have not seen it but I know what is there. A grave marked by a plain granite headstone with her name. Ruth Porter. Born 1961. Died 1983. And below that there is another name, mine. Rebecca Porter. Born 1961. Died... I insisted on that and it was done.

There is no mark to show she was pregnant.

Even he did not know he was a double killer.

I have come to believe that you have to grow to understand what drives some people to kill; you must enter into their mind-set, even though that mind repels you.

I grew to this view too late. Bond, the man who killed Ruth, was himself killed before I grew to fully understand his motives, or to enable me to make him understand the import of what he had done to others.

If Robert or James died, what would I do? I mean, what would I do to remember them, what mark would I make in remembrance of their lives? Apart from remembering them, that is. Scratchings in dust.

Ruth's baby has no name. It is not named. It is a concept rather than a fact, yet it was a fact; yet it has no name, not even the name of 'baby' – Baby Porter.

I remember feeling it kick inside Ruth.

It is not there, yet it is there. It is here, now, with me, in this room, in my head. Sometimes, I feel it move in my belly.

Yesterday (I think it was yesterday), I heard on the radio that a Minister in the new assembly had issued instructions to his civil servants that the words 'Northern Ireland' should not appear on any communication issued over his signature. It is strange how such small things matter so to people.

I remember begging him, but my father would not allow any reference to the baby to be inscribed on their gravestone. That my name be there was his only concession.

It is strange. I am sitting here, writing this, a glass of wine on the table beside me, the radio playing in the kitchen. This is normality. The apartment is so calm and I am calm and peaceful, really. Peaceful but also sad...

James, who loomed so large in my life and for so long; Robert who played such a part in my life, for so long; now, they are both receding. For years I did not pass a day without speaking to one or both of them, and now they have shrunk in my memory.

I have begun to remake my soul.

This revelation has altered everything. It is as if my soul is alone.

I know now that I must turn away, away from James who is a man I love deeply but whose values I really question. He loves social style and status, he loves money too much. He has never written, nor will he ever write, a cheque for ten thousand pounds to go to a charity, even though he could easily do so. He desperately wants to make more money. That is how he defines himself, as a money-maker. I know he truly believes in the law and in good order, yet he bends with the wind, he bends to accommodate authority. Robert I love truly and he truly loves this place in which he has lived. He loves the touch of water and clay, I know how he loves the form of a pot emerging under his hands; he loves the shape and feel and weight of the trees that grow around his cottage; he loves the life of the senses; he loves childish things, like walking on dew-wet grass with his shoes strung around his neck. He loves freedom. I suppose, he loves youth; he remains a child, yet a child whose essential characteristic is generosity. Living in this place that he loves has robbed him of that innocence.

Yet he hoards himself. He does not share himself or his love with others, apart from me. Instead, he condemns, he will not move; he is stubborn and opinionated and silent when he should speak and speaks when he should be silent. Does he love people? Does he love the Polish women who beg on the streets, clasping their hands in silent prayer, asking for a penny; does he love the immigrant children who play their accordions on Castle Street corner; does he buy a newspaper from the foreign men who patrol the traffic lights selling papers, silently, mutely? Does he see them or is he too busy thinking about Henry Joy McCracken, who is dead, to even see them, who live?

I don't fully know. Is it love, or is it hatred that makes him rant and rave? I know he loves too much; he is too passionate, yet his love makes him fearful, and his fear makes him weak and increasingly his weakness makes him strike out when his love alone would make him strong.

I know, for I was like that.

That is how things are, with us.

The life that is history is stifled under that terrible, suffocating quilting of the normal and the mundane and the ordinary.

**

Ever since Ruth left me, I've not been the same. I know it. I don't feel the same. She was my other half, you must see that. She was my laughter and my tears. Ruth was lovely.

She and I were one.

What more can I say?

Do you know, I gave myself a present on our birthday. That's why some people might say... something hateful. Are you sane? Are you insane? Well, I might say in reply, it is just a way of remembering, it is my way of effecting remembrance. Of not surrendering her to the destroyers.

Last year, on our birthday, we ate together. I liked that.

A present from me to her. And from her to me.

But I don't think we will do that again.

For a long time after she died I wore her old woollen scarf, at night, in bed. I loved the comfort it gave, the warmth it closed in. I loved its smell — it carried the smell of her hair and of her body. I could close my eyes and know she was close.

I want to write this down. Even though I don't know how to do it. I mean, I don't know how to write it down, properly, so that it is beyond misunderstanding. I'll just write it, as it is, in my memory.

We used to lie together, in bed, in the night, in the dark. We used to cuddle.

For a while, when we were very young, we would take it in turn to pretend the other was a boy.

We were innocent. We did not know then what boys were. They were an illusion.

We did not know they became men. We did not then imagine the things men are capable of...

That is my secret. That was my secret. That and Ruth's unborn baby. My secrets, our secrets. Now I have spoken them.

The wind blows, the rain falls, the earth crumbles away under our feet. All hidden things emerge, eventually to lie under the sun.

Life to me remains a strange, complicated thing: some days it is bitter and sweet, some days it is savoury and sour; it begins and then goes on and then it ends. Life is constructed from lots of little things and a few big things. Knowing which is which, that is the trick. Knowing how to differentiate the inconsequential from the crucial, that is the hardest thing of all. Or, perhaps the thing is, knowing that each one, big or small, is as important as the next. Perhaps that is what people used to call wisdom.

One big thing befell all of us in 1983, when the bomb exploded and Ruth's life was brought to an end. My life went on, as did James's and Robert's, but life had been changed, transformed, blown off course, for each of us. My existence became imbued with a toxic mixture of grief and guilt, enabling a cancerous growth to form somewhere, deep within a huge pit of vacancy, of loss that lay inside my head, inside my body.

My existence became imbued too with the crutch of friendship, something I took too much for granted. I took Robert and James too much for granted and I sometimes think that their love and concern fed that cancer. To this extent I can now see how destructive that friendship, committed as it was but blindly followed, became for each of us.

Then all the other things, small or big in themselves, it is no matter, they were nevertheless important: that first, short and abortive meeting with Peter Bond, my blinkered walk through the city, the trip to Slieve League, the holiday in Fermanagh, the walk with Robert in Stormont grounds that culminated in his feeling so unwell. The amalgamation of each little incremental accretion of life and its mundane routine. Even Ruth's pregnancy falls into this category: our parents' mute response to that knowledge, even in death. Robert's ignorance of this reality – that was my fault, my weakness, my guilt: he should have been told and he wasn't.

Looking back now I can see that each of these things, tiny as each one was in itself, when viewed against the great hardships fate throws up for millions of people each day, helped introduce change, and that when taken together they represent a considerable impact on one life. My life has not become a better life, but it has become bearable. It has not become freer (I will never be free, for my loss takes the form of a great gap that cannot be filled, and a great guilt I cannot redeem). I remember Robert saying once that I instinctively opposed change. That may have been true, once, but it is no longer so. My life has become less constrained, less tense – not because these things happened, but for some other reason. I think the reason is this: I have changed, imperceptibly and naturally, for I have become older. Certain things have fallen away. And Ruth has remained the same. In that simple way, we have gown apart.

I have grown up. I am able to accept things that once I could not accept. I can see how things are related, one to another. I think I first became aware of that on Slieve League when a little light blinked in my darkness and then was gone.

The realisation has gradually come to me that one can so easily give away one's power over oneself. Slowly, it has dawned on me that when such basic but fundamental authority is lost, the question is, what is left?

An answer is the will to live, the will to survive. If only you can recognise it.

I know this for I have seen it in another form so often: in my work in hospital wards over all those years when patients handed their power over themselves to us, to the doctors and nurses. I knew it then but did not consciously acknowledge it. I did know about the will to live, for I saw it when it was there and I saw the consequences when it was absent.

My fellow Ulsterman Peter Bond voluntarily planted the bomb that killed my twin sister. By the simple action of callously, clinically, setting a timer he took her life and, realistically, I know there is nothing I could have done to prevent that abrupt lurch across that one-way bridge between life and death.

I cannot rewrite history. There is nothing I can do to give her back her life, nothing anyone or I can do could bring her back from among the dead. Subsequent to Peter Bond freely choosing to plant and detonate that bomb, it was as if I had voluntarily handed over to him total power over my life, and even though he did not know it, I left it with him, for so many years, years of investment in experiencing loss, of feeling grief, of living with constant guilt, of lies and illusions and evasions.

It may be I have had to go through this and work my way out of it. How did I do this? How did this outworking occur? I cannot give a direct answer, for truthfully I do not know. I believe it has to do with the accretion of experience, like the lime-grey deposit that builds up in my kettle. Sometimes, when it is late, I sit on my balcony, ruminating, looking out across the night-time river. The occasional car passes and where the traffic turns I often become aware of the flashing indicator lights, spitting sharp bursts of coloured energy out across the dark. Life is full of strengths and weaknesses. So many things, often small in themselves, have acted on me as those fleeting lights act on the darkness. It is as if these positive things that have happened to me, and have formed into a strong deposit in my soul, have given me the will to live.

The terrible thing is experience is not personal to Peter Bond and to me, and it is a matter of wide principle, of universal truth. The terrible dilemma is I allowed it to be and to remain personal to Peter Bond and me for, in reality, it was a matter of the deepest personal significance. I was trapped. By offending against the principle he made it impossible for me to keep authority and power over my own self. I grew to understand this, even dimly, and I now believe that is why I eventually wanted to meet him, to confront him and to regain power over my own life. His accidental death, before I could meet him, robbed me of that possibility. However, I can now acknowledge that I was ready to take such a leap of faith and when I embraced his wife and she embraced me a great lightness fell across my soul and heart and body and mind. Even though it was by proxy, I felt resolution.

**

Suddenly there, I needed an escape. So, I have been to the bathroom and then I smoked a cigarette out on my balcony. These are deep waters indeed and I don't feel I can swim in them: now. Perhaps one day.

My life has become pliable, looser. I feel I am becoming open to new experience.

Ruth recedes, but grows no less important.

And what, then, of James and Robert – are they changed, too? James! I always thought of James as having all the dogged staying power that anyone could ever want, but I always considered he lacked ardour, while I perceived Robert as being exactly the opposite. Yet, I was wrong: they too were amalgamations of many things, many talents and many riches I opted not to notice. Yet, I kept them as friends, but denied them access to my inner self. I pretended, to myself, and to them, that they were true allies in life while keeping them frozen out, standing there, annexed in an outer waste.

The inner place was too full; crammed with shadows and fleeting images and voices, so full of memories, so full of the past there was no room for the future. Yes, I suppose memory and remembrance are two very different things. Memory is just the things that happen to you and it becomes who you are – in a sense, you are its instrument, its slave. So many people are victims of memory – remembrance is somehow more positive. It's something you engage in... you direct remembrance – honest remembrance of all the hurt, all the pain, all the joy, all the laughter, all the bone and sinew and muscle of true celebration.

In short, I have been dishonest. I don't know if that can be changed. I don't know if I can change, I know I shall try. I don't know if the redemptive power that I experienced that day on the cliff top will materialise again. If it does I will welcome it, however, if it does not, so be it.

Nothing is as it seems. I am learning to live with that certainty.

For a long time now, the ground over which Robert and James and I have repeatedly peregrinated has resembled nothing so much as a maze – our wanderings orchestrated by these sadistically conceived pathways, the product, apparently, of a twisted mind, a cul-de-sac built with walls formed from the ambiguities of language. Each time we thought we had found a solution it proved to lead only to another dead end: this was a search whose object was to find the truthful answer to the question 'why did Ruth die?'. A search in pursuit of justice, truth, accountability, responsibility. Perhaps what I sought for so long is simply a desire for permanence, a fear of change, a denial of the nature of how things are in the flux of time. For many years James, Robert and I achieved, or thought we had achieved, permanence, of a kind, but then that too altered. However, before I tell you about how that chain snapped and how the anchor was lost, can I tell you about another kind of permanence, and how I became aware of this?

Only once was the grey mist that habitually fogged my vision rent in two, and from what I can only describe as a transcendent state I beheld the world that lay before me, in all its splendour and integrity, and for that split second I had an intense glimpse of what I can only think of as the divine. That occurred that day on the cliff top overlooking the sea, at Slieve League.

Yes, the memory has been released, yet I have to struggle for words that explain. They do not come easily but as mere approximations whose meanings only half materialise, the most apt, I think, is the word beauty. In that moment, as I viewed what had materialised, and as I meditated on what this was, and as I contemplated the universe in all its manifold relationships, including mine to the earth, its hard rocks and its soft creatures, I became aware that what I was realising was the reality and the nature of beauty, not beauty as an adjective but beauty as a noun, as the thing that pervades all else. This is not to say that what I perceived was awesome for it was not, though I did feel a wondrous, wonderful sense of awe: I was too much part of what I sensed to be awed. Nor had I any interest in taking possession of what I perceived; my viewing was disinterested in all but the feeling of being, of observing – and yet, of being an integral part of what I observed, and what I observed was real and yet unreal, diverse yet balanced. Everything was symmetrical, poised, unified, with purpose, yet without the greed of success that purpose presupposes.

I do not know how long this sight – perhaps I should I call it insight, for I did not apprehend it through my senses. All I knew was, it was present. I knew it in my body, in my bones and in my blood. So – insight, or outsight, or perhaps, rather, I should term it outsight and insight combined. I do not know how long it lasted but it did end: as abruptly as it had materialised it was absent and the greyness once again rose up to corrupt my vision.

I am aware I saw it, but not what it was: that knowledge has faded. Only the vaguest of labels now make themselves available to me. Words like helix, or rather perhaps, helical, suggest themselves. Words suggestive of a reality within which everything was seen as intercoiled but not convoluted. No, it was not that, exactly. Everything was serenely simple and clear and visible, like a sky with a star seen in the moment of its appearing before its disappearance, dancing in harmony with the movements of the sun at dusk, and again at dawn.

I sometimes think it was all in my head. Was this just me, casting my thoughts upon the world?

There is that old, recurring question: if a tree falls in the forest and I am not there, to see or hear, how do I know how it fell, and if it fell, did it make a noise?

I desperately want to know again what I apprehended in that instant, but it has moved beyond reach. I wonder, repeatedly, did it happen, at all? Then the memory of the memory comes back to me, and I believe I know it for what it was.

This glimmer of hope has proved enduring. My experience on that cliff top enabled me to see clearly how these ambiguities might be negated through understanding. That pure, serene moment led me to be able to accept Bond's action and Ruth's death and his death. The power, the energy of that moment enabled me to breathe again, and to feel free. I know now how any other reaction would have led to my living death. I accept now that this is not a betrayal of Ruth, nor an easy acceptance of the very opposite of truth, but reflects another truth, the reality in which those of us who live must exist.

Another truth emerged. Robert called me, the last time we spoke before he left for Japan – indeed he may well have called from the airport. The telephone rang, I picked it up and his voice blossomed up out of the silence.

'Rebecca?'

'Yes, Robert?'

'Have you heard about James?'

'No,' I replied, thinking something terrible had happened.

'You mean he hasn't told you? I suspected he wouldn't have! Too much of a coward. He has sold his house! His family home! To a 'consortium of buyers' as he put it to me. He has allowed himself to be seduced by the new order. So much for his regard for the old order! He has just left me at the airport and he told me, calm as you like. I just hope he and Paddy are very happy together. Well... that's it... I'm off now... goodbye.'

That was it. A single word, 'goodbye', and the line went dead and he was gone. And with him all that I held dear for so long.

And James – he did tell me, eventually, about selling the house. He and Paddy Moran had set up a company and he had sold the house to this company – in effect, he sold it to himself, or at least half of it to himself. 'Tax benefits' was the only explanation I was given and I did not ask for further information. I know Robert would undoubtedly regard the sale as the act of a traitor, but who am I to judge him? Was his selling of it a rejection of everything he professed he had stood for and believed in, or was it an honest acceptance of the way things are, of how things change and move on? I just do not know.

***

I hardly saw James after that. He was busy buying a new house and moving into it and making plans for the development of the site where his home had stood. Yes, it had been demolished and the trees cut down, and when I did see him there was a palpable frostiness in the air, stiffness had developed between us. Despite myself, and without analysing it, I felt he had betrayed something that had existed, unspoken, between us for years. Remembering Robert's various outbursts I think I blamed Paddy, as an individual. Not what Paddy represented, for that was just commercial or financial interest, but some insidious, slippery, serpent-like thing I had come to see in Paddy's influence, something not quite right. Behind the ready smile, behind the ever-open hand there lay something – it sounds melodramatic, I know – something life threatening, something the opposite of life enhancing.

To exist may be just to breathe, nothing more. I slowly found I want to do more than just exist. I wanted to live. But did I have the energy? After Robert's departure, for a time, I felt so tired. I just wanted to be alone. That is a strange thing for someone who lives on her own to admit to, but for ages I had felt pressurised, always at someone's beck and call. So much pressure was building up at work – targets: targets, set, targets to be met, targets missed; new targets being set daily, staff shortages, endless tension. Everything about quantity, not quality, and quality was what I had supposed my job might be about. So, I just stepped out of my flat, locked the door behind me and caught the train to Portrush.

The landscape the train passed through pleased me greatly. From feeling I had to escape from something, I found I had escaped to something that suited me. The fields through which the train passed were bare, scraped clean and devoid of life. The harvest had been taken home, though I could see a few laden apple trees and lots of berries still in the hedgerows. The bird-nesting season was over and many hedges were already cut back, giving a trimmed look to the landscape. There was a feeling of work completed, and a sense of lull. A sense of waiting. Perhaps it was because I was escaping, if only for a few days. Perhaps it was because the sun was shining, but I had a sense of richness, a feeling that the bounty had been collected, the harvest had been brought home, as much a joy for me as for the farmers, for was I not a member of this community also, and all this for another year. Life was, after all, full of goodness, it contained a secure pattern of certainty and hope.

When I arrived at the railway station a few hours later, I immediately set off to look for accommodation and knocked on the door of the first decent looking bed and breakfast place I saw. The landlady, a Mrs Cunningham, viewed me rather suspiciously, I thought. A woman on her own is still an object of suspicion here, even though the world has moved on in so many ways. I arranged to stay for three nights and occupied the time by looking at the sea, sitting on one or other of the many benches along the front, and by walking along the seaside pathways. When I left 'Sunset View' (the rather optimistic name of my residence, given that it faced east and never saw the sun set) I could turn right, along the path and then across the beach as far as the White Rocks, or I could turn left, skirting the harbour, passing the amusement park and out by the coastal path to the West Strand. Once, I found a set of car keys lying on the path and set it up on a flat rock in case its stranded owner should come frantically searching for it. I smiled at and spoke to numerous elderly men and women walking their dogs. In the evenings I ate fish and chips, sitting on windswept wooden benches overlooking the sea, and in the afternoons I drank tea in rather dreary cafes. This quickly established routine was a comfort to me, and initially I used my time to just be.

Best of all, I liked the time when, at dusk, I walked, alone, by the land's edge. At these times I found it easy to commune with the sky and the sea and the beach all coming together, melting into lightness and darkness, into what I described to myself as egg-white whites, and then there were numerous tones of grey. At these times I became it and it became me. The sound of the sea, in its coming and going, so seductive, so insinuating, so sleekit and modest in the manner in which it issued its deadly invitation.

I resisted these invitations. Instead, I lived in the landscape and in my head; the place helped me think a lot, delving into the past, fabricating images, working at crafting individual memories into cogent wholes. I remembered our weekend on the lakes, all that preceded that and all that came after. I remembered Slieve League, and I think it was that memory that helped me resist the sea's seduction, and helped me in other ways too. I thought some more about the difference between memory and remembrance.

Delving in among such thoughts and sensations and images, I came to realise the once-sharp memory, the once always-present image, the once vibrant lines of Ruth's identity, has all but leached away from wherever such things exist in our minds; it was as if she had been bleached out. In reality, my picture of her had been weathered beyond recognition by the intervening years. I discovered, when I searched my mind, that all of her defining edges were dissolved, thawed, melted into fuzzy outline. Only when I really concentrated and really tried to recall her face did the shades and shadows begin to take form and rise up out of the cloudy void; those and the curve of her cheek, the line of her jaw, the up-tilting tip of her nose, the pink lobes of her ears, the rise of her eyebrows, her lips, her eyes, her hair. It was such a task!

In my life of unexamined memory, I had grown to accept her as an idea, not as a fact; an abstraction and not a reality.

I realise now that my complaint is not solely to be placed at the door of memory, though that is a part of it, for I find my memory, generally speaking, becomes muddier as time passes. No, what happened was that the lucidity of the image has gone, the years have indeed blanched something inside me, but not my heart or my soul or my brain. It is as if the thing itself, the thing I want to remember has become thin. A certain pallidity had slowly emerged, not just in me but in it.

How am I to explain this?

I am not alone. Those who know about these things say the universe is expanding at a tremendous rate. It may be that this is a universal function of the ageing process, of physical things growing older, a consequence of the death process. Dying begins the moment we are born, or the instant we are conceived. We do carry the seeds of our own destruction within us; it is something that I suspect is present, even before we have been conceived. The seed of death is bound up with, attached to, is an integral part of, the seed of life. We speed away, away from what we are, away from those around us. For a while this process is invisible, yet it is present, lying dormant only.

Or apparently so, for then there comes a point when those bright, vivid, intense days of our youth are over, never again be achieved. As well as dying in ourselves, we are also dying to each other, slowly.

A blackbird calls out at dusk, generation after generation, year after year. The once-slow days become the speeding years. The seasons come and go. Flowers bloom and wilt and die and rise again. Coastlines crumble into the sea, galaxies move away, the universe changes.

It is how things are.

In my months of mourning I grew fat, I know that. I became large, swollen with grief, not thin as I had been but heavy and slow and staid and without energy or volition. And then, in time, I grew thin again. But now I was thin, a bundle of sharp harp bones in a bag of skin. Physically, I became badly provided for, not slender or willowy, as I had been, but scratty and scrawny and puny looking.

And not only that.

There was a time, when I was awake, my head was full of other people's voices. As I moved into each bleak new day, they grew closer, louder, like the clamorous roar of a great waterfall approaching through stands of trees, the source of the noise unseen, but the roar ever-present. Omnipresent.

During this time, when I tried to sleep, I entered nights that were silent caverns, cut from black rock and empty, apart from one fleeting figure, elusive and ethereal, yet to me real and solid and ever-present.

In these dreams, or rather, in these nightmares, she – for it was a she – was faceless. I could not put a face to this invader of my nights, except by waking and looking at my own face in the mirror. And when I saw her – for I did see her, eventually – it was in outline only, the contours of her face fitting neatly over the contours of my face, in a mask so perfect that I could not be sure who or what I was seeing.

For a long time my attempts to find rest failed consistently. I was left, alone and lonely, in the hours before dawn, cold and shivering, staring into the hard glass of that reflective mirror. With no living glance, no human smile, no comfort available to me.

How can a face be given to the faceless, a voice to the voiceless, and a body to the body-less, a life to the lifeless? I could not then find answers to these questions.

Only time could tell. I waited. I was nothing if not patient.

I can recall this one thing, but only if I concentrate, and focus hard: it is a warm summer Saturday morning, and just as I made this journey northwards to Portrush, I have come to the east, to Bangor, by train. I am alone. I walk by the sea for a bit and then find a café. I sit at on outdoor table and drink my coffee and cut and butter and slowly eat my scone, and add jam and eat that also, and look out at the water before eating another. Imperceptibly, I became aware of people at the next table. A man and woman – no, rather, a boy and a girl. They were Indian, I think, no more than nineteen or twenty years of age and both were drinking water directly from blue bottles, the unused glasses they had been given casually pushed aside and left, dry and idle, on the table top. The boy – I could think of him only as a boy, I decided, even though I was aware of something about his demeanour that conveyed sophistication beyond his years – the boy wore a checked shirt with a black waistcoat. His hair was neatly trimmed, indeed it was more than that: I could see that it was well cut and carefully brushed back from his narrow forehead. The term 'razor-trimmed' came to mind, the words rising out of some dim recesses of my memory, but I had no idea whether they was applicable here. I know nothing of men's grooming. The checks on the sleeve that covered the arm that lay across the chair back were precise and clearly delineated, in a manner that I instinctively knew spoke of quality. The waistcoat was wool and definitely not cheap. Across the back of his chair hung a black leather jacket; it had that soft, supple sheen that I knew denoted high cost. I knew he was different, that he came from money and not money as James knew it. I could tell – his money had given him such confidence and self-belief.

They had grace and poise.

He was talking – presumably to the girl, but not looking at her. She too had very densely black hair, worn long and loose. She listened to the boy. In the sunshine, she was lazy, easy and relaxed, one hand toying with the blue water bottle while the other, her left hand, moved constantly but easily, casually, from cheek to chin, then stroking her neck from her chin to the point where the high-necked white cotton blouse stopped. She wore black jeans and long black boots and was slender, almost unbelievably so.

This was in the days when I felt fat and slow and heavy and anything but casual, anything but relaxed.

It was late afternoon and the mild sunlight caused the sheen of her skin to take on a luminous quality. The long, white-painted fingernails added to this sense of lightness and of luminosity. Then she turned her head, looking abruptly and directly across at me. At that same instant he too turned his head, following her gaze. Their eyes were like dark pools, deep and unfathomable. For an instant she took in my presence, then as suddenly as if she had taken me up as a subject for study, and before I had time to divert my gaze, she dismissed me, turning away to attend once more to the boy. I felt I had been in the presence of some alien, animal, presence. Cold and cruel and disinterested. I felt a stirring, oddly enough, of jealousy – I felt locked out, rejected, abandoned, surrendered up. I felt terribly alone.

You had not to look very carefully to get the message, if message is the correct term. Now they were standing up, the boy passing the girl a small leather purse, his other hand reaching out to guide her, protectively, past some empty chairs. Everything about them denoted the fruitful marriage of ease and wealth, but not in an ostentatious way; it really was so understated, it was so right. No, I reconsidered, everything about them indicates health, not merely wealth, but a unity of good health, physical and mental and social and cultural.

Passing me there in the sunshine they seemed so well. In their poise and easy grace they seemed without the secret, half-buried cancer with which I was so familiar.

Their physical bodies were so actual, so earth-bound, so centred and balanced. They moved with such easy purpose. To me, for that fleeting moment, their bodies seemed like sacred vessels. They evoked such feelings, a sense that life was sacred. Life as it should be.

And then I sat back in my chair, with a jolt. It sprang from behind some dark curtain, a glimpse seen fleetingly through a tear in reality – an image of Ruth, of how she, of how her body, must look now, at this instant, lying there in her coffin, the dank earth weighing down on her, caressing her, like a living blanket. She who had been so alive, now inert, lying there in that dire state. I could not bear to think of it, so I did not think of it, this image, or this thought, or this insight that came to me as the boy and girl moved past my table and out of my life, forever, leaving me such an insufferable gift.

But now, here in Portrush, sitting on my bench before the sea (for I have quickly selected a bench I think of as mine) or walking by the sea, I think today of other things. And I do so with a new freedom. I feel good. I have learned lessons. I use my memory to good ends. I remember good things, like how it felt to sit in my favourite chair, at the scrubbed table in Robert's kitchen, or to stand on my balcony in the morning, sunlight streaming across the wakening city.

For now, I sit here by the sea, but not seeing it. I am looking blindly ahead, staring into a mirror hanging on a wall opposite. Behind me is a window. I see its reflected Georgian bars, how they are arranged in perfect symmetry, offering twelve little white-painted frames that admit to the mirror chequer-board images of a world beyond.

Later, on my return journey on the train, this memory is still with me, and the memory of Robert's window returns with it. The world seen though this memory is green. In the lower half of the window-in-the-mirror I see again the wooden fence, painted a green (that is, the colour of that sea I walked beside this morning) and that still undulates before me. Above this there are the apple-green leaves of a hedge, dappled darkly with shadows. Over it all, the movement of darker, dancing shadows, the coming and going of the images of un-see-able tree branches, their leaves curtsying and bowing. The light that washes over it all is the colour of the purest olive oil, black and green and luminous and warm.

It is a perfect picture, or rather, it is a picture of perfection.

It is so soothing, so peaceful, and so beautiful.

I am lulled into dreaming.

I dream often, and sometimes when I dream, I believe I become like Robert, when he washes his pots in impenetrable glazes. At such times, I also am: I have become. I am an artist, I am a painter, I am a poet; I am a maker and a part of creation; in the making I am made. At these times I am resolved. I will accept this. I can never see the truth, in memory or in reality: always reflections and imaginings and shadows and dreams.

I cannot be sure if I am awake or if I am dreaming. Then the ancient train bumps and grinds and I lurch in my seat and awake from my doze with a start; I look out to find the landscape changed, again. Perhaps it is because it is now almost evening and the sky is grey, the hedgerows in this part appear raggedy, they needle-work and stitch the landscape into tightly bound but uneven acres, the enclosed small fields coated with uneven tuffs of short and long grass. Mist lies over the fields (I think we are crossing the bogs that lie somewhere near the village of Clough) locking together the sky and the earth. Neither man nor beast move within this slumbering landscape as I speed across it; I consider how different it looks now compared to the way it seemed only a few days previously; how things change, how change is present everywhere, how change is the only thing of which we can be certain. Consciousness alters, constantly, like boiling liquid; always the same, yet always different, constantly in motion, always changing. And so it is with the world, as we accept it and understand it.

And what of the 'how' we are to live in such a world, now?

We have had enough of the denying hearts. Yet, who among us can speak for those years when we allowed ourselves to be corralled and made into such a pottage of pulped humanity? I have heard Robert say we need a true people's prophet, a woman or a man, a poet of humanity, a person who can encapsulate our most fundamental desires and give them back to us, reconciled in the glory of their unity and integrity, like the stars and the moon and the sun, the sea and the wind, the clouds, the day and the night. Robert may be right, though I am beginning to think we, each one of us, must become his or her own prophet.

But then he is here, with the sun, like a red coal, hanging there, behind him. And she is here and I say I am sorry and then she is not there.

***

As I write this, I ask you – you who have travelled this long way with me, you who have kept faith with me through illness and in growing health – do you really think such a thing as peace is possible? I would love to think so, but I feel fearful. Two such opposites, as we are – how can they be reconciled? How can they be reconciled, completely?

The door is open. I hear a noise, is it the wind? The beginning of a storm?

Cymbals clash in a Belfast street and the sound echoes across the universe.

Still, it is my hope that what I have come to recognise as complex and subtle forces may still exist, together, behind the shadowy veil, each recognised and honoured. For what is, is; for what resides in one, resides also in the other.

Is it too much to hope we can learn to live differently, amicably side by side, giving and taking? I pray we may grow to be like that, like the star that advances and then retreats, fades and is gone, leaving the sun to do its work until, in its turn the sun too retreats and the moon appears and the star comes back. I hope we can learn and grow to accept that everything has its place and its time.

My heart, bruised but beating.

Scratchings in dust. I know we are dust, dust given life – ah, the wind has risen – I hear leaves scuttling on the balcony – I must rise now, I must brush the tiles, I must brush the balcony, I must leave it clean and tidy...

***

The year is turning in upon us: spring, summer and autumn have come and gone and now winter has arrived. Rebecca takes what has become her customary early morning solitary walk. She climbs to the top of the road and turns to look back, out over the slated rooftops beneath which the people's sleeping hearts beat as one, out over the web of winding narrow streets that bind all this together. Cave Hill stands there, seeming to buttress – or halt – the city's sprawl. The sky is a gunmetal grey, and a few dark clouds hang above the hilltop, but the night-time covering of snow has added a luminous sheen to its otherwise bleak and rocky presence.

Rebecca's mind turns to Robert. She remembers that expression on the unexpected granite-like profile of his face, recalls the inflexibility of his last words of farewell. She shivers, feeling that old familiar sharp tingle in the flesh beneath her skin.

Calmness drops from the sky. Quietness drapes like a sombre cloak across the day. Cave Hill fades away while the shipyard's great yellow gantries of Samson and Goliath have melted beneath a blizzard of snowflakes.

Rebecca moves as if to take a step, then pauses. The day breathes; its breath seeps through the cloth of her coat, stealing its way through the layers of her woollen cardigan; it creeps, touching her skin and penetrating it, until beneath it seems to embalm her flesh. Her dark-coated figure becomes grey, then a mere shadow, then invisible as she disappears into the blinding whiteness of the blowing snow.